Alaska Hearts

Best Romance Novel Collection
Complete 4 Books Box Set

SCAN FOR GIFT

Harmony Noble

TrueLoveWriters

ISBN 978-1-963074-30-7 & ISBN 978-1-963074-31-4

Story creation, cover, and illustrations by Melody Noble & Harmony Curtis

Contents

**Thank you for choosing this book
by Harmony Noble. We hope the story
brought you as much joy reading it
as we had in creating it!**

We'd love to hear from you! Feel free to reach out via email at True LoveWriters@gmail.com, and don't forget to follow us on Instagram, Facebook, TikTok at @truelovewriters for the latest updates and behind-the-scenes fun.

Get access to exclusive offers, bonus content, new release updates, and recommendations for more great reads. Sign up for our e-newsletter at HarmonyNoble.com.

Unthaw My Heart

Harmony Noble

SCAN FOR GIFT

TrueLoveWriters

**Thank you for choosing this book
by Harmony Noble. We hope the story
brought you as much joy reading it
as we had in creating it!**

We'd love to hear from you! Feel free to reach out via email at True LoveWriters@gmail.com, and don't forget to follow us on Instagram, Facebook, TikTok at @truelovewriters for the latest updates and be-hind-the-scenes fun.

Get access to exclusive offers, bonus content, new release updates, and recommendations for more great reads. Sign up for our e-newsletter at HarmonyNoble.com.

This book is dedicated to the **incredible strength** and **beauty** of trans and queer individuals who understand **love knows no bounds**, to those who have faced adversity with **unwavering courage**, and to those who continue to **champion love** in all forms.

You are not just accepted—*You are cherished, celebrated, and loved. Your presence and your love enriches the world, and this story is a small tribute to your resilience and the power of love.*

YOU ARE WORTHY, ALWAYS AND FOREVER.

Unthaw My Heart

Harmony Noble

SCAN FOR GIFT

TrueLoveWriters

Prologue: Makayla Jackson

One Year Ago, Christmas Eve in Anchorage, Alaska

Despite the festive gold decorations and soft Christmas carols piped in, the fluorescent lights harshly illuminated the worried families and exhausted staff in the hospital cafeteria. The clatter of trays and loud floor polisher drown out the sound of my heart pounding with trepidation.

Bryant, my coworker, and boyfriend, stands before me. His voice—smooth as velvet but laced with male confidence—carries across the cafeteria. The calculated words command not just mine but everyone's attention.

His blue eyes sparkle with charm as he towers over me and announces, as if on a mountain and not in the sleepy cafeteria, "*Doctor* Makayla, *my love*, I can no longer keep this secret locked away within me. Will you do me the honor of becoming my wife? Will you marry me and make me the happiest man in the world?"

God, give me strength! I must be dreaming because Bryant and I have only dated for a few months, and honestly, this is unexpected.

In an instant, Bryant is kneeling, the master orchestrator of a grand performance, and he produces a box from his pocket, opening and revealing my mother's diamond ring.

"What?" I brush my greasy hair from my face, blinking hard. *Did he talk to my parents, and they consented, giving him the ring to propose? I guess it makes sense. My mom loves him, as he attends Mass with us* at St Mary's Catholic Church, and his parents also attended St Mary's school. Plus, she wants grandchildren like *yesterday*.

The atmosphere is charged with expectation as eyes move from Bryant to the ring and me. The crowd holds its breath, waiting for my response.

This cannot be real! Perhaps I fell asleep during my night shift, and I'm dreaming. The only reasonable explanation is that my head rests on a keyboard at the Emergency Room nurses' station.

But I see my new friend Jessica, who's orienting me to the Emergency Department. Marianne, my mom's childhood friend, the hospital administrator who hired me, is waiting, along with the other staff, watching me, the *new* doctor. The spectacle of their friend, a handsome man, proposing to a tired doctor in front of everyone on Christmas Eve is *too cheesy* to be in my dreams.

I'm awake, and everyone is waiting for my response.

The question fills the air, suffocating me. My heart races, and for a fleeting moment, I think of running.

Jessica smiles and nudges me.

Who wouldn't want to marry the popular and respected Respiratory Therapist, Bryant?

I glimpse my reflection in the napkin holder—my brown eyes red and puffy from the long shift. Despite the vice squeezing my chest, I put on my doctor's confident smile.

He hands me a tissue, thinking I'm overwhelmed and these are happy tears. Then he pulls me closer, his grip firm, and says, "Looks like a *YES*. We're engaged, and you're all invited to the wedding!"

The crowd claps, their eyes filled with envy and admiration, believing this is the pinnacle of a fairy tale romance - a handsome man proposing to a beautiful woman in an unlikely place.

My thoughts whirl, and my heart is in my throat. *Say No!*

He kisses me lightly, his lips branding me, marking his territory, as everyone claps and begins congratulating him. The people in the cafeteria titter and giggle with excitement.

I didn't say yes!

I reach toward him, and he takes the offered hand, slipping on my family ring. My mouth is too dry to talk, and my eyes dart around the room. "Bryant, this. . . caught me off guard. . .," I say.

He leans closer. "Mak Attack, you are perfect for me: ravishing, a doctor, rich, and Catholic. And I'm perfect for you. We'll be the hospital's power couple. You won't disappoint me, our friends, and your family." He winks at me and smiles broadly at the crowd.

I hate the nickname Mak Attack!

I'm exhausted from my shift, and I *do like* Bryant. Obviously, I've considered marriage, or I wouldn't be dating him. I've spent the bulk of my twenties training and schooling to land my dream job, working as an Emergency Room Psychiatrist. My next goal is to have a big family. And an engagement is *just dating* with the promise of marriage, after all.

I want this, right?

"Amazing, Dr. Mak," Nurse Jessica says, pulling me away from Bryant for a hug. "You're on fire. Snagging this ER job and now snagging the most eligible bachelor. What's your secret?"

Prologue: Pauline Jacobs

ONE YEAR AGO, CHRISTMAS EVE IN SYRIA'S US ARMY CAMP

A blaring siren shatters the night's stillness, slicing through the fabric of darkness like a jagged blade. I wake with adrenaline coursing through my veins, a surge of raw fear. My surroundings are disorienting for a heartbeat—scratchy wool, dusty air, and the heavy humidity crushing me.

It's the desert—the unforgiving, fucking desert, where the Army posted me.

A heavy foreboding settles in the pit of my stomach, a dreadful hunch. My fingers tremble, lacing my combat boots. The familiar ritual usually grounds me, but it intensifies my jumpiness today.

My gut tells me *something's wrong.* I rush into the heart of the bustling machine shop; the tang of grease and the chorus of clattering tools embrace me like old friends. *There's nothing wrong–my gut lied.*

Officer Curtis spots me. "Hey, Jacobs! Coming in early?"

My gaze dances across the faces of my comrades, each one working and ignoring the near-constant sirens. Amidst the clinking tools and jokes, these men are my family in this unforgiving place—a family forged by shared work and an unspoken understanding. I finally found a place where I fit. I am not *a woman, a lesbian, a gearhead,* or *a small-town freak.* I'm a soldier.

I nod at Curtis and the mundane scene of my platoon working on engines with the hum of holiday music from the radio. "Had a gut feeling something was up. But it's probably Johnson fuckin' around with my tools—"

Then, in the blink of an eye, an explosion shatters the shop, sending shockwaves and metal crashing upon us. The once-familiar garage transforms into a nightmare of twisted metal and agonizing cries. Smoke and debris blur my vision, a suffocating haze amplifying the pain shooting through my body as I lie on the floor. A thousand needles prick my skin, and my vision turns black, telling me to close my eyes and surrender.

Chapter 1

Mak

SNOW CHAINS REQUIRED.

My attention snaps from the mesmerizing white landscape to the road sign illuminated by my Jeep's headlights.

The powdery snow flits lazily across my windshield, a whirling dance, as my tires carve a deep path through the snow-covered road. On Christmas Eve, the daylight is fading early at four in the afternoon. The tranquil, remote Caribou Hills is silent and frosty.

Buzz. Buzz. Buzz.

I glance at my phone in my cup holder, trying to get my attention with the glowing, vibrating ringing. It's another call from Bryant, my ex-fiancé, trying to convince me not to go to the cabin alone. But as soon as my eyes dart back to the road, they widen, my muscles tense, and my hands squeeze the steering wheel as I crest an icy slope. The tires lose their grip, floating over the road, and my knuckles turn white, clenching the steering wheel that no longer controls my Jeep.

"No! No! Not now!" I cry futilely. My stomach moves to my throat, suffocating me, and my left hand reflexively moves to cover the Saint Michael's medallion at my throat.

My car is in an icy, downhill freefall, and I can't stop it as I careen down the steep slope. My breathing shallow, I yank the steering wheel following the direction of the slide, praying for traction. Miraculously, the tires catch before I enter the deep ditch, allowing me to wrestle back control from the icy road.

I mutter a prayer of thanks, but the tires skate again, not responding to my direction. I desperately try to steer back onto the road, but the laws of physics are working against me. In a cruel twist of fate, the Jeep gains speed, skating faster down the hill as if it's building up momentum for a triple axel instead of slowing for the corner.

"Oh God!"

In sheer panic, my foot slams down the brake pedal, my final attempt to regain control and stop the slide. Instead, the Jeep gives me a bone-jarring jolt, veering off the road and the snowy ditch, unable to stop its speed as it *whooshes* and *thumps,* making me squeeze my eyes shut.

Being unable to stop my Jeep from throwing me into the surrounding dark woods is worse than nicking an artery during surgery—at least an artery can be clamped and repaired. I'm powerless to the disorderly elements, and I'm without my hospital team to help.

Thump.

My breath hitches as the Jeep suddenly stops, jerking my body forward. I open my eyes to the blurry snow and darkness outside my windshield. My hands remain locked on the wheel as adrenaline shoots through me like an electric shock—my heart pounds. My lungs ache for air. My hands are clenched and shaking from my close call.

The adrenaline hits my brain, allowing me to process the situation and shift into my emergency room autopilot.

Gingerly peeling my fingers from the steering wheel, one by one, I check that each of my digits is functional. I'm uninjured but can't stay in the Jeep, as no one will see me this far off the road. I look at my phone- *no signal* and my gaze drifts upward, landing on the road thirty feet away. My stomach churns as my brain processes the harsh reality. Between the deep snow and the distance uphill, there's no way my Jeep is getting back to the road.

And who knows when anyone else will be driving down this remote road. I don't have any snow gear, food, or water because I dropped everything off at the cabin days ago for my annual Christmas Eve holiday. This is my first year without my parents, and I plan to enjoy a quiet, cozy holiday—just me with a sweet romance novel and hot chocolate in front of the fire.

My cabin isn't too far, and the snow is increasing. I must leave immediately before whiteout conditions hit, or navigating there will be impossible.

I'm hiking through the snow to the cabin.

I change the gear into park, and the engine's low hum is the only sound in the eerie stillness. Shaking, I turn off the Jeep, cutting off the engine noise.

"Dear Lord, give me strength," I whisper, tucking my holiday hat over my head and zipping up my woefully thin jacket.

Opening the door, the wind and icy snow slap my face, and I tug the Santa hat further down as my boots crunch against the unforgiving ice, a bleak soundtrack to the frozen challenge of walking back to the road and then to my cabin.

Teeth chattering, I trudge onward, a lone figure walking in the biting cold. Every breath creates an icy halo around me. Trying to stay calm, I wrap my arms around my shivering body, attempting to preserve my heat. My fingers are frozen sausages, aching with the cold, and only the garish Santa cap shields me from the biting wind.

I berate myself for this unlucky situation. *Why? Why didn't I take the time to ensure I had my winter chains in my Jeep?*

The thought of an Alaskan Emergency Room doctor freezing to death on Christmas Eve in a blizzard is absurd—*Impossible!* And someone discovering me on Christmas, frozen solid in my cheesy Santa hat, makes me want to throw the hat into the woods. But I like my ears, and frostbite is no joke.

My plan was to be nestled warm in my cabin for the holiday, far from the chaos of work and the fresh wounds of my recent breakup with Bryant. Instead, I'm slogging through knee-deep snow, battling an unexpected Alaskan blizzard.

"Time to check for a signal," I mutter aloud. The sound of my voice solidifies my resolve as I trudge onward.

And there *it* is, the last message from Bryant lighting up my phone screen. *Call me if you need anything. I'll come out there and join you, Mak Attack.*

The words hang in the air, my mind playing them on a loop, and I yell at the useless *phone*, *him*, *the blizzard*. "I'm *stranded*. No one can find me! Bryant, I wouldn't call you *if* I had cell reception. *I DON'T LOVE YOU!*"

The snow muffles the words as it obscures the moon and starlight. My cheeks flush with embarrassment as I replay the disappointment clouding Bryant's face when I ended our engagement weeks ago and his desperate attempts to convince me that "love grows from friendship" and I needed to "give *us* more time."

However, the truth is, *my heart is telling me Bryant isn't the one.* Freezing to death is karma's way of punishing me for shattering a man's heart who did nothing wrong but love the wrong woman.

With each freezing step into the wind, I'm kicking myself for my poor clothing choice. Jeans were an unfortunate decision, and my feet should be warm in wool socks, not my thin cotton work socks. The Alaskan winter is unforgiving and doesn't care about my cold feet and misery.

Adding to my regrets, I didn't check that my snow chains were in the Jeep when I rushed out of the house. And confounding my misfortune, I didn't stop at the Ninilchik gas station to put on the chains before going off-road. If I had, I would have realized I didn't have them and bought another pair to put on the Jeep. The gas station attendant might even have warned me about the weather, and I wouldn't be in this predicament.

No one but Bryant, hours away in Anchorage, even knows I'm out here.

I clap my hands together to get the blood flowing.

Why did I bolt without snow gear and chains? I'm Alaskan AND a doctor—I should know better!

In any other place, calling Roadside Assistance would be a no-brainer. But here, miles from civilization, with no cell service and zero chance of a tow truck locating me. I'm an idiot for not using snow chains and my stupid clothing choice.

Still, I bite my dry bottom lip and tightly smile to maintain my optimism. *At least I'm able to walk rather than being crushed inside my crashed Jeep.* In Alaska, danger lurks in every pristine snowdrift, as I know from working in Emergency Medicine.

I'm alive, walking, and I will make it to my cabin.

The wind howls around me, cutting through my clothing.

Why didn't I pack my snow gear? Why didn't I bring a thermos of hot chocolate?

My thoughts spiral negatively, but the thoughts distract me from an even bleaker possibility—succumbing to hypothermia and dying alone in this relentless snowstorm.

And why don't I love my handsome fiancé, Bryant? That's the million-dollar question I ask myself too many times and can't seem to answer.

He cares about me and wants me to spend the holidays with him, not at the cabin. And if I'd have shown him any kindness and asked before rushing out of the house, he would've put the snow chains on the Jeep.

The scene, hours old, plays out in my mind. Coming home from work, I planned to shower and dress, then head to my parents' cabin. But Bryant was home, lingering, trying to talk me out of going, to instead stay home with him and make a new holiday tradition.

I don't need a new tradition! Also, I'm not marrying him, so he will *not* be part of my upcoming holiday traditions.

He hasn't moved out, and he's not accepting the break-up well despite me bluntly sharing my feelings with him.

We haven't officially announced our breakup to our coworkers. So, on top of being exhausted from a shift at the hospital, where all my coworkers wished me a Merry Christmas with my new fiancé, I have to find the energy to tell him, *again,* that I'm not *marrying him* and forcefully eject him from our home.

Our hospital schedules are chaotic at St Mary's Alaska Medical Center, where we work, and this cabin trip was supposed to give me some much-needed space and time to reflect. But Bryant ignored my plans.

He lit candles and baked Shepherd's Pie when I arrived home. I had hoped he'd pack his things and move out before Christmas, but he's attempting to rekindle our nonexistent love.

His voice echoes, "Mak, can't you see I'm perfect for you? We're getting married, and we work together. Your parents approved of us! You are ruining a perfect relationship. What will everyone think when you tell them you're dumping me?"

I didn't argue—I fled my house and Bryant's dinner for the cabin. I have everything I need at the Caribou Hills cabin. Moreover, *I need to be alone.*

That was my first mistake!

Why did I let his arguments bother me? Why can't I get him to accept we are no longer together, and he'd be better off with anyone but me? I cannot marry someone I don't love!

Since my parents' funeral, we haven't been happy. *Really, we weren't jolly before, either.* Their sudden death made me reevaluate my life and my happiness. Instead of clinging to Bryant for support, I found myself pushing him away, realizing that just because he is perfect on paper, attending the same church, working with me, having similar hobbies, and having my parents' approval, it didn't mean he was the right person for me.

If he's my soulmate, why am I so unhappy when we are together?

Our interactions are tense and resentful, with him trying too hard to be friendly and irritating me. It's a cycle of dating, fighting, apologizing, and dating again. We are functional at work, in the chaos of the Emergency Room. But, our relationship crumbles outside St Mary's, and we aren't even friendly roommates anymore, giving each other the silent treatment, driving separately to work, and sleeping in different rooms.

To be fair, we've *always* slept in separate rooms because of our Catholic values. And perhaps that's why Bryant is rushing our engagement. It's hard for a modern guy to wait almost a year before sex, even if he is Catholic.

"Arrrrgh!" I yell into the night.

Unable to feel my extremities, I curse my decision to run away to the cabin.

Why did I trust the Jeep would safely make this sixty-mile journey through the Alaskan wilderness? Last week the trip was easy.

There are no signs of life, no roadway markers, an endless expanse of snow-covered tundra far removed from the Alaskan highway system, and no cell towers out here. The cabin is even more remote, miles away from the dirt road.

If my rough calculations hold, I'm a mere two miles away. I *must* summon the strength to hike there.

I shut my eyes briefly, attempting to revive my frozen eyeballs, but darkness offers no respite. Despite my horrible situation, I'm not hypothermic—no confusion, hallucinations, or slurred speech.

I can make it. I WILL make it to the cabin!

At the cabin, I have my winter gear and a ready wood stove. But the looming question is, *what if I don't make it?*

My shaking body and my fast, shallow breaths urge me to hurry. *Dying is not an option!*

How can I be in this situation?

I should *be happy* in my *perfect* relationship with my new job, having a cozy holiday with my family—*not freezing to death alone in the dark tundra!*

Chapter 2

Paul

The cool concrete floor on my face brings me back to reality. I look up at the people surrounding me and murmuring around me.

"Paul, Paul." My mother breaks through the haze and people, snapping me back to the present. I remember a distant boom, but everything from then until now is a blur.

"Mom, uh." I clear my throat, attempting to regain my composure. "Sorry," I mumble to the crowd and get onto my feet.

The booming fireworks must have triggered me. My heart jackhammers as if the enemy is bombing my army bunker. Beads of sweat coat my brow, and I attempt to regain control over my racing heart with the slow, measured breaths I've practiced at therapy.

My mother, always understanding, steps in, diverting their attention. "Paul's okay. He just needs some air. How about some of my famous rummy eggnog, everyone?"

The crowd obediently disperses, drawn to the promise of warm eggnog. My mom's a pro at handling situations like these. She touches the pin on her lapel; those blue, pink, white, pink, and blue stripes symbolize her support and understanding. She's been with me through my struggles with defining my identity and living with PTSD.

My dad, ever the military man, engages our neighbors in cheerful conversation, a deliberate distraction from his kid's breakdown. He might not express it openly, but his silent support speaks volumes.

I close my eyes and take deep breaths, focusing on the mantra my VA therapist instilled in me. *Breathe in*—one hour at a time, one day at a time. *Breathe out*—let the tension flow away. *There's no enemy here, no threat, just war's residue.*

"Why is your daughter a guy now?"

A child's innocent curiosity pierces through my racing thoughts, and I grimace as I pull myself up.

She's only asking what everyone is thinking.

My mom kneels to the child's level and explains, "Oh, sweetie, Paul is like a superhero who's about to put on his cape to become the hero he truly is. You know how superheroes have secret identities and don't show their true selves at first? A trans man is like that. Paul's a superhero who knows deep inside that he's a boy, even though he was assigned a different gender at birth. Superheroes know, but the world doesn't always recognize them."

The child nods. "Like Wonder Woman."

My mom smiles as the pigtailed girl skips off for another sugar cookie.

I take a deep breath, my racing heart now steadying. My momentary breakdown and my mom's impromptu explanation leave a bitter taste in my mouth.

"I'll haul the sled over to the Taylor's with the propane," I grumble, with my need for solitude and an escape from the party spurring me into action. The garage calls, a haven where I can lose myself in the familiar hum of diesel engines and assist my parents in their propane fuel delivery business.

Getting away from the curious looks and ceaseless chatter is non-negotiable.

The snowmobile carries me through a blur of snow-covered trees, their forms rushing past like white streaks. Delivering propane to a customer's remote cabin miles outside Ninilchik relaxes me.

My parents gave me this job delivering fuel and fixing diesel engines in Pop's shop. They worry, fully aware of the grim statistics concerning returning soldiers and their battles with mental health, and keep me close to watch over me.

They are right to worry.

My return to civilian life here in my hometown is one hell of a challenge. Dealing with my PTSD, a relentless burden, is made worse by what my VA therapist labels as survivor's guilt. *I'm a shit show!*

Before my military service, I didn't fit the mold, even of a tomboy. Tall and gangly, I defy societal expectations, especially in small-town Alaska. Sports held no appeal for me, and I had no interest in the boys who pursued me.

Instead, I sought solace in my mechanical pursuits, tinkering with greasy engines while other girls in my class focused on fashion and dolls. When I graduated, the military became my refuge, where gender distinctions didn't matter. Skill and determination were the only yardsticks.

Glancing down at my wrist, I glimpse ink peeking from beneath my glove—a heavy black army insignia with an unmistakable wrench and rifle. My teeth work to pull the glove back, covering it while my other hand instinctively tightens into a fist over the handlebars.

In the army, I was the only woman in our diesel shop, but I was a vital cog in a well-oiled machine.

Fast forward six months, and the Army bid me an early farewell, thanks to my cursed post-concussion migraines and dizziness. Fixing tanks and Jeeps became an impossible task. The doctors labeled the malingering symptoms as PTSD, a shitty gift from my time in the warzone. Discharged and adrift back home, I attempted the four-hour drive to the Anchorage VA hospital for the prescribed treatment regimen. But even in my quiet childhood home, sleep remains elusive, and I cancel more therapy appointments than I attend, retreating, haunted by the relentless memories of men, sirens, and explosions.

My roots run deep in Ninilchik, where I grew up in a small village community. Despite being a *local,* the villagers treat me like an outsider, avoiding me and calling me the "Dyke on the Bike," as if homosexuality is contagious.

I let their words slide, busy with my mechanical hobbies. In a town with limited options, I found my niche: trucks. I'm the best diesel mechanic these folks have seen. Fortunately, fixing engines and my parents' propane deliveries don't demand much human interaction, which suits me.

My parents, bless their hearts, have a mantra: "We don't live in Alaska to be city folks. We are villagers, part of a community where everyone knows everyone. We might not have city amenities, but we have the *real small-town Alaska.*" But living remotely also means access to regular therapy and medical care is as elusive as restful sleep for me.

Yet, here I am, instead of accepting my parents' care and the VA's help, I'm taking reckless chances riding into a snowstorm, testing the thin ice on streams, and pondering a question that shouldn't cross my mind: *If I were to vanish tonight, would it cast a permanent shadow over my parents' Christmas Eve? Wouldn't it be easier not to go home?*

The howling wind and relentless snow bring to mind the Alaskan elders' tales, those who, in their ailing years, chose to wander into the wilderness, leaving behind their tribes, burdens, and worries. Theirs is an honored departure, giving more food and resources to the rest of the tribe.

A desperate thought flickers through my mind—*it'd be easier to disappear into these unforgiving landscapes, to let the cold and isolation claim me, sparing my loved ones the constant struggle of supporting my broken soul.* The idea is a shadow, but it lingers.

As I zip through the snow-covered trail, my trained eyes automatically scan the surroundings. Something strange catches my attention—a distant figure, an anomaly in the snowy landscape.

Instinctively, my training kicks in, and I tense up before reminding myself to breathe.

Stay calm.

It must be a lone moose meandering along the dark trail or a caribou seeking refuge from the cold in the shallow snow rather than the deep snow in the ditches. After all, dusk has settled, and the wildlife follows the most accessible paths navigating this tundra.

Drawing closer, it's not a moose. The figure moves, unsteady and faltering—*It's a person!*

The diminutive person is in dark pants, a lightweight jacket, and, *unbelievably,* a festive Santa hat sparkling from the headlight. The figure sways erratically, veering toward the side of the trail before collapsing. My heart clenches in my chest as I realize the gravity of the situation: *a person walking at night in a blizzard with no one around but me.*

Shit!

My instincts kick into high gear as I approach and stop next to the dark form in the snow, invisible if I didn't know where to look. I yell over the engine's roar to check if they're conscious. But there's no movement in the dark lump.

The figure stirs, their activity a strange mix of stiffness and floppiness as if their body can't decide how to function. Slowly, they manage to push themselves up and shuffle towards me.

"Hold on," I call out, my words snatched away by the relentless wind. I stride over with my long legs and lift the limp form into my arms.

"Let me help you," I repeat, but my voice disappears into the frigid night.

I carry the person to my snowmobile, my well-worked hard muscles and height easily allowing me to lift the smaller, rounder person. I settle them awkwardly on the bench seat.

It's a young woman out here alone, in the middle of nowhere, dressed in gear hardly suitable for this kind of weather. Questions swirl in my mind, demanding answers, but the priority is clear: *Get her to safety and warmth before this blizzard kicks into high gear.*

She clings to me as I assist her, wrapping both arms tightly around my frame. My cheeks flame and adrenaline surges through me because I haven't felt the arms of another person in too long to remember.

"What are you doing out here? Where's your snowmobile?" I ask, my tone clipped and to the point.

"My Jeep ... it crashed on the corner of Falls Creek. I wasn't sure if I'd make it ..." she says, thankfully opening her eyes as she sputters through her chattering teeth. Her voice wanes, tears build in her eyes, and she slumps against me out of energy.

I give her a slight shake to wake her, and she points westward, which I hope indicates her cabin is nearby. *She could be pointing to the building storm, though.*

I need to get her to shelter, and I'm already twenty miles away from Ninilichik.

Her cabin is the best option.

I make another attempt to get answers. "You're out here alone. Where's your cabin?"

She points again. "Just past the stream ... the one with the orange door."

I know the odd orange-doored cabin, although it's not on my delivery list. It's not far from here.

Good! It must have a wood stove and, hopefully, people there to help.

They better have dry wood and hot coffee at her cabin. With this raging storm, there'll be power outages, and we'd be lucky if there's a phone line intact with the wind gusts attacking and knocking down the creaking trees surrounding us.

"I'll take you to your cabin and get you warmed up. Then we can figure out what to do about your Jeep," I outline. My military-sharp mind formulates a plan. I know what's required to save her life, and I intend to do it.

All my army medic training comes rushing back. Losing body heat and exposure to the cold is fatal, and the quickest remedy is to share your body heat with your comrade. I envelop her within my frame, tucking her body in front while reaching around her to hold onto the snowmobile, my eyes inexplicably glistening with moisture. I settled in behind her. My arms wrap around her to provide comfort and support.

I feel her relaxing into my embrace. Her shimmering eyes lock onto mine as tears begin to flow. My instincts make me tighten my hold as I offer her warmth and support.

It's been *forever* since I've touched another person. As I sit behind her, holding her close, my body slowly softens—a tingling sensation courses through my veins, unfamiliar and electric. I've not felt a connection with another person since working alongside my platoon.

As we speed toward her cabin, I sneak glances at her, studying her soft, full features and lustrous black hair. My heart beats with a different rhythm, and I realize this is a chance to make a difference. Amid the improbable snowy wilderness, I find this beautiful Latino woman, and my unique skills are needed to save her.

The heaviness and kicking in my chest are unexpected and unfamiliar feelings. Amid my plans to lose myself *alone* in this storm, I found a connection—*a purpose*.

The snowmobile hums beneath us as we navigate this *damn* relentless storm, each twist and turn to bring us closer to her cabin.

As the cabin comes into view, its orange door a beacon against the white backdrop, a wave of relief washes over me.

We've made it!

The tension in her body eases, and she leans further into me, her relief palpable at arriving at the cabin.

I guide the snowmobile to a gentle stop before the cabin, the engine's growl subsiding into a hushed silence. As I help my frozen passenger off the seat, her eyes are closed, and her body is unmoving.

My nerves fire, and my breathing increases. I look around. The cabin is dark and uninhabited. There's no help here or for miles.

I need to work faster!

Chapter 3

Mak

My heart races, a wild drumbeat against the backdrop of the blizzard's fury, each snowflake emphasizing my desperate situation. However, God has an odd sense of humor, and as I'm contemplating a future as an Alaskan popsicle, a rescuer on a snowmobile appears from the icy darkness of the storm.

Thank God! Someone is here!

I squint through the blinding snow. My rescuer is a genuine Christmas Eve miracle. Tears fill my eyes, and I put my hand on my neck, covering my medallion. *God answered my prayers in the nick of time.*

I pause and swallow. *My rescuer better not be a hypothermic hallucination!*

I hear his shouting.

He's real!

I numbly follow his lead, unable to talk or move. He places me in front to hold the handlebars as he wraps my frozen body with his sturdy frame, and an immediate rush of warmth flushes me. My relief floods me as I lean my icy body back into the stranger's sturdy frame. My eyes brim with a wordless thanks as we ride.

His unexpected, strong, extra-tight embrace on the snowmobile brings me more warmth.

I'm saved from this freezing nightmare and dropped into a dramatic rescue movie. Our connection is fiery hot, and even as my teeth chatter,

I imagine this as a sweet Hallmark movie and not the popular brooding, anti-romance novels my friend Jessica reads at work.

As his arms envelop me, I'm powerless with the strength in them and his protectiveness. It's more than cold, making me tremble. There's something about this stranger who's come to my rescue, sending shivers down my spine and making me fantasize about romances.

The montage plays out in my numb mind with us reaching the cabin, having a playful snowball fight, rolling in the snow together, and then laughing over a cup of hot chocolate to the swelling of a soft, romantic ballad strumming. The scene's end would be me leaning into the handsome rescuer and our lips meeting sweetly, cozy in front of the wood fire.

I'm shielded from the biting wind inside his muscular frame as we race through the snow-covered trails to my cabin, and he revives my spirit and confidence.

I'm safe!

The snowmobile's growl harmonizes with the noise of my heart roaring in my ears. With each bump, twist, and jolt, I cling to him, my lifebuoy in the raging sea. My rescuer's attentiveness and protective presence draw me closer—his warmth seeping into my very bones, melting away the numbness.

Amidst my gratitude and borderline hypothermia, my mind clears. Despite the catastrophe and my near-death, one truth is undeniable—I'm ready to let go of Bryant and our toxic relationship *for good*.

God put me in this situation for a reason, and this realization and rescue are the reasons. I whisper a prayer of thanks for the rescue and the rescuer.

This unexpected connection with a stranger and the rush to survive heightens my emotions and feelings in the remote wilderness.

The stranger's arms tighten around my weak body, grounding me in reality. It's odd how, as my body weakens, my mind awakens, as if it is rallying to live.

Mak—Stay Awake! Please, God, don't let me die this close to being rescued!

As we navigate the wintry wilderness, my hypothermic state blurs with the warming tingle from my rescuer's embrace. I'm not merely holding on to the snowmobile—I'm clutching my new determination to break free from the grip of my broken engagement and the sadness of my first holiday without my parents.

God, I promise I will begin living the life I deserve—the one you've granted me with the gifts you've given me! I silently promise, feeling liberated, my mind clear, and the tension dissipating from me into the dark, swirling cold behind us.

I'm alive, and I won't waste this opportunity!

My grip weakens with this revelation, and my fingers slide off the handlebars.

Sensing my drifting consciousness, my rescuer pats me gently to keep me focused on the situation and awake. He holds me tighter, whispering unidentifiable but comforting words the wind snatches from me.

When I can't hold on or stay awake any longer, my cabin appears through the white walls around us.

Summoning every ounce of strength, I lift my arm, pointing. My body shakes with coldness and relief.

"Thank God!" I utter aloud.

He sees my gesture and expertly maneuvers us to the front.

I close my eyes and let my head fall back as we stop at the cabin. I want to untangle myself from his grasp and rush inside to warm up. However, my stiff, cold limbs refuse to cooperate, and moving is impossible.

My labored breathing and chattering teeth break the snowy silence. I try to release my grip on the handlebars, but my frozen fingers barely respond, leaving me hunched over the snow mobile's handlebars. I panic. My mind assesses my current physical state. *I might be closer to hypothermia than I thought!*

Sensing my struggle, he bends down, assisting me in removing my hands from the grips, finger by finger. He lifts and pivots my legs to sit on the side of the snowmobile. Then he helps me stand by holding me at the waist and hoists me up like I move my immobile patients in the hospital.

His small actions reveal his strength and experience. *Does he work in healthcare? A Physical Therapist, perhaps?*

It fits. He is taller than me but slimmer and maneuvers and lifts me with a practiced ease.

My mind scrambles to piece together a coherent question, but my attention remains focused on the orange door and my critical need to reach it. The questions I long to ask are lost in the urgency of my need for warmth, shelter, and the comforting embrace of a heated room beyond the inviting door.

Stumbling towards the cabin, he supports me with his steady arms. He's not much taller than me, though he's strong and quick. My feet trip us, and he bends down and pulls me into his arms to carry me the rest of the way to the door.

My numb fingers fumble, pulling the keys in my pocket.

Why did I lock the door in wintertime? There's not a soul in sight for miles around this remote cabin.

Miraculously, I retrieve them. With sheer willpower, I unlock the door, as I can't feel my fingers, and my hazy vision leads my fingers to grasp the correct key, put it into the lock, and then turn it.

With the cabin's protection from the howling wind washing over us, he supports me as I stumble inside. My body is still waging a frosty rebellion to my commands.

His unwavering grip reassures me, and I crumple my face into his shoulder as he carries me to the center of the one-room cabin, where a couch awaits. The air fills with his scent of vanilla and the masculine scent of machine oil. His aroma awakens my senses, and I note the warmth of his breath on my neck.

It sends butterflies fluttering around my stomach and ending in a location lower in my abdomen.

My remote family cabin is a cozy, rustic retreat deep in the Alaskan wilderness. It's a wooden A-frame structure with a steep, snow-covered roof, allowing snow to slide off during heavy storms easily. The cabin is surrounded by tall pine trees, creating a picturesque, secluded setting. Inside, it's furnished with warm, comfortable furniture and a wood-burning stove that keeps the space toasty during the long, cold Alaskan winters. The windows offer panoramic views of the snow-covered landscape, and there's a well-stocked kitchen and bookshelf. This cabin is my place of solace and holds cherished family memories.

He carries me, rescuing me and delivering me to the cozy in a winter cabin. This scene is from a romantic holiday special starring my foxy rescuer and me. *Two strangers brought together by a twist of fate on Christmas Eve, stranded inside a cozy cabin, near death, while a blizzard rages outside . . .*

I shake my head. *Mak, wake up!*

Gently, he places me on the couch, then turns to close the door before expertly tending to the woodstove.

With each passing second, my body regains sensation, and my mind sharpens.

Thanks to his quick actions of warming me on the ride and getting me to shelter, I'll survive. My doctor's brain takes over, assessing the hypothermic patient—*me*. Sensation returns to all my limbs, and sharp daggers of pain shoot through my toes and fingers.

Pain is a welcome sensation—*More*, it's a sign my body is functioning. *I'm going to be okay.*

He ignites the fire in the woodstove, and the dancing orange light washes over the room, dispelling the darkness masking his face. His features are sharp but soft in a ruggedly handsome way with high cheekbones, intense brown eyes with long lashes, glowing, rosy cheeks, and a long, lean neck.

Holy Mother of all Rescuing Saints!

I move my hand to my medallion, reminding myself I just thanked and promised to follow God's plan minutes ago. And God rescued me from the storm and brought me together with this striking, strong person for a reason.

Before me stands a stunning *woman*!

Her features are balanced and captivating without makeup and handsome. The revelation leaves me frozen in awe, an unexpected twist sending a shiver down my spine. I rub my eyes in disbelief.

My rescuer moves with graceful precision, each action purposeful as she approaches the hooks and bench at the front door, shedding layers of snow gear. She removes her helmet and hat.

A gasp escapes my lips as she lifts it away, and her beautiful brown, tousled hair springs out.

Is this real? Am I imagining the woman of my dreams saving me?

I narrow my eyes, my chest tightening. *Perhaps I am hypothermic, lying in the snowy ditch, dying.*

I sigh. I'm satisfied with this ending if this is my dying hallucination.

I don't love Bryant because Bryant isn't the man in my romantic fantasies. My fantasies are of *women* and a fearless woman, *precisely* like my rescuer.

I smile, *God knows my truth*, and close my heavy eyelids.

I've died!

Chapter 4

Mak

My shaking body wakes me.

How long was I asleep?

Uncontrolled shivers race through me on the couch, and I clutch the blanket for warmth.

The grumbles of my rescuer's curses catch my attention, and I strain to hear her husky voice. The wind stole her soothing words earlier, and hearing her fierceness captivates me.

Her voice isn't the melodic, tender voice I expect from my protector in the blizzard—her voice is pragmatic, Alaskan, direct, and no-nonsense.

Who is she, and why was she out on Christmas Eve in this storm?

My rescuer checks her phone, frustration etched on her face. She reaches for the old-fashioned landline on the counter. "No service and no damn dial tone. This storm knocked everything out. Not that anyone could reach us out here anyway."

Her simple statement underscores our situation's gravity. This cabin is our only refuge from the raging storm outside the window, and I'm teetering on the brink of hypothermia. We're screwed if I don't warm up quickly.

"Are you okay? Are you injured? Can you feel your hands and feet?" Her voice softens as she fires questions at me.

I gaze back at her. The gratitude swelling within me at her saving me outweighs my discomfort. I choke and cough, saying, "I don't know." My voice sounds weak, even to my ears.

Moving to the wood stove, she stokes the fire, casting a warm glow across the room. Then, she tends to the propane heater, deftly adjusting the valve and lighting it with a match.

"Do you have any more wool blankets?" she asks.

"Yes," I reply, nodding towards the chest in the cabin's corner.

She retrieves the blankets from the chest and settles closely beside me, her eyes lock with mine. She's hot, confident, and dangerously attractive, flexing her large hands and pushing her fingers through her short brown curls.

"There." She gently presses the blankets around me, and my heart flutters. Unbeknownst to me, tears are on my cheeks, and she wipes them away with a tissue.

A few years older than me and taller. It's more than her height, making me smaller. I study her sharp features, illuminated by the soft flicker of the firelight.

"Better?" she asks, her intense brown gaze melting mine as she kneels before me. She dabs my cheeks gently with a tissue, her closeness stealing my breath.

I nod in response, as my mouth doesn't feel functional enough to ask her questions, and she turns back to tending the fire.

She begins, "I s'pose I ought to give you a proper introduction. My name's Pauline, but call me Paul. I'm trans, so I use the pronouns he and him." He glances at me, gauging my reaction.

"I'm Mak." Those few words are all I can say before my jaw jitters and a round of shivers goes through me.

"I was out on my propane delivery route—my work—when I spotted you. Army's my background. I'm wired to deal with any scenario, especially survival."

I stay quiet. My frozen neurons aren't firing fast enough for a reply. Luckily, he's not waiting for one and continues.

"Honestly, I wasn't plannin' on heading home. I'm a fuckin' mess and useless outside the military. I'm a drag on my folks," he shrugs. His gaze shifts back to me, and he absently rubs the back of his neck, a grimace crossing his face as if revealing too much.

He stands abruptly, moves to the entry, and sheds his remaining heavy boots and Carhart work overalls, revealing his lean and athletic physique. My gaze lingers on him, and my heart races. His strength and beauty captivate me, and though I see despondent patients in the Emergency Room, I cannot fathom why he'd consider such a desperate act.

The only thing that comes out of my mouth is a raspy "Thank you for helping me."

Paul's eyes meet mine, and there's a brief pause before he speaks, his words measured and direct. "I served in the military, deployed overseas to a war zone. I've seen things. Things *no one* should ever have to see. It changed me in ways I can't describe. I thought I could leave it all behind when I got home, but the memories haunt me."

My heart aches for the pain he's endured. "PTSD," I whisper, understanding the weight of those four letters. *I've treated patients with it, but coming face-to-face and being rescued by someone with PTSD is unexpected.*

Paul nods, his eyes holding mine. "I'll keep talking. *You* stay awake."

I realize he's being vulnerable to keep me engaged and listening. *It's working*—I want to know more about him. "Deal," I say.

He continues, sharing his inner struggles and reasons for seeking solitude in the wilderness. "It's a daily battle, trying to make sense of it all. I needed to escape the world, the expectations, the judgmental stares, my parents' disappointment, and my own perceived shortcomings. I had to get away. But *you*," he adds with a crooked smile and a light chuckle, "you ruined my plan."

I offer a reassuring nod and cock my head listening.

"I couldn't leave you out there to freeze. And here we are, against all odds, alive," he reflects.

I reach out and gently touch his arm, offering a wordless gesture of support. "I'm glad you found me," I say, "And thank you for warming me up and talking to me. You're braver and stronger than you realize."

Paul presses his lips together, turning to the fire. "Not strong enough. I couldn't save my platoon, stay in the army, or even watch fireworks tonight without freaking the fuck out."

The fire crackles, casting dancing shadows on the walls, and the storm outside rages on.

He sits by me on the futon, and my heart thumps with newfound sensations. His chest is broad and flat, which added to my assumption that he was a man during our snowy journey. His physique, one of someone accustomed to manual labor, defied conventional expectations.

I've never experienced an attraction like this, as my demanding medical studies limited my dating experience. The odd and exhilarating feelings are fizzing and popping inside me, creating a frenzy to discover more.

With my tummy fluttering and cheeks flushing, I examine his bare arms and strong shoulders. His heavy black tattoos represent his uniqueness, and the scars narrate his past. I yearn to hear the stories behind each one, to understand who he truly is, and *know* him.

I yearn to trace his contours with my finger and explore the heat building within me. Yet, my warming body steals my heat and causes me to hold my breath. My thoughts are foggy, and forming a coherent question is daunting with my unusual, electrifying attraction.

Thankfully, he maintains his gentle banter, a soft melody to calm me. He gracefully moves about as he speaks, starting the kettle and adding logs to the crackling fire.

I consider sharing with him a piece of my own journey, the darkness that consumed me after my parents' passing, the sense of isolation and loss. I want him to know that there's room for change, even when it feels like despair will never fade. For me, the healing process began here, in my parents' cabin, accepting they were gone and deciding I must live for myself, carrying their love.

I twist my mother's engagement ring that Bryant had once slipped onto my finger. It's different being alone, as I always had my parents and Bryant. Without my family, I don't have the connection and big holiday plans with a meal, presents, and festivities I'd had in years past. But being at the cabin with Paul, my holiday sadness is lighter.

Could it be God who brought this person into my life to offer a connection to the world?

He leans closer, his voice quieting as he notices my eyelids drooping and my body struggling to stay awake. "What else do you need?"

You! But the words don't escape my lips. I'm utterly drained from the emotions of my crash, my near death, the surprising rescue by my dream partner, and my gratitude for being alive with him at my cabin.

Instead, I manage a weak "Thank you. I'm okay now." I give a smile to alleviate the concern etched around his eyes.

"You're still cold," he says, touching my cheek. "I've got to defrost you." He pokes the fire and tucks the blanket closer to my body. "The kettle is on for tea to thaw you out."

"Please don't leave," I say, moving to hold his hand, desperate to connect with him and afraid he will be gone forever if he leaves my side. I can't shake the feeling this is a hallucination, and I'm dying. *I don't want to be alone.*

He sits close, holding my hand in his large, warm hand. As the heat floods the small cabin, my shivers gradually subside, and my hands and feet throb and tingle. I gasped at the sensation of the heat penetrating.

He says, "I'll hold you to warm you up faster. Is that okay?"

I give a slight nod. My mouth is suddenly dry, and a deep desire awakens within me, the longing to be touched and held by him. My devious mind remakes the Hallmark movie to include a foot rub and tea.

Paul doesn't hesitate, enfolding us both in the woolen blankets, recreating the snug embrace we shared on the ride here. His long arms wrap around me, dispelling the numbness and replacing it with a comforting warmth.

Involuntarily, I inch closer, savoring Paul, my eyes closing as I breathe deeply and surrender into the embrace.

"Thank you for sharing your story," I say, looking up into Paul's firm, intense eyes.

Paul's brown eyes blink hard. "I wanted you to understand . . . with losing my platoon, my hometown not understandin' me, and my parents' burden . . . that's why I was out tonight, and if you don't live, then I'll probably head right back out that door."

"Sorry. I'm going to live. I can't let my rescuer go back out into the blizzard," I say and snuggle further into Paul, wiggling my arms from my sides to wrap around him, embracing him tightly back.

"Umph," he says, a warm breath ruffling my hair. "You're beautiful," he whispers.

I lean back to look into his soft eyes, and his lips part slightly, with his tongue darting out to wet them.

"You are beautiful, too," I say. The words escape before I can second-guess myself. Doubt crosses my mind: *did I choose the right word? Could it be perceived as an insult to this rugged Alaskan transgender man?*

The screeching kettle shatters the fragile, passionate atmosphere. He stands abruptly and, with brisk efficiency, rummages through cupboards for mugs, honey, and tea bags. "You warmin' up?"

Should I say, 'No,' so he returns to the couch and holds me again?

"I think so ... but ... I still feel frozen," I reply, looking at his inked, solid arms pouring the kettle.

Paul returns, setting the tea on the table beside me. "The hot tea will warm you up."

I move and successfully take a drink, my body finally complying with my brain and not too shaky. Paul isn't sitting as closely, so I move the blankets and scoot alongside him. "I'm still feeling a bit cold," I say with a smile, then I bite my lip and look up at him, batting my lashes.

He smiles and shakes his head. "I'll keep you close, *just* to raise your body temp. You keep drinkin' tea," he orders, his words carrying an authoritative tone, one I'm familiar with from scolding my patients in the emergency department.

I nod, pressing my lips together as I move closer to his open arms and welcoming embrace.

Lifting the blankets, Paul nestles me in a warm, secure embrace, enveloping me. Warmth courses through me as my body awakens, rekindling more than my cold skin. He ignites the internal flame of my dormant passion.

I'm uncertain if it's the crackling fire's warmth or the electric connection between us, but butterflies flutter, and my skin flushes. I've never wanted to be naked with another person as much as I do in this moment, and desire coursing through my veins.

With Bryant, I never felt anything like this. The passion and the need to be near him were absent. And this new passion of fluttering wings explodes from my core, pushing my blood to pound in my ears, and I'm barely able to stop shaking with excitement.

"You are still cold," he says, holding me tighter as I wiggle.

In the cozy, one-room cabin, its log walls adorned with hand-sewn quilts, our attraction burns brighter than the flickering fire. Paul's arms embrace me, his firm, solid body pressing against my softer, more petite frame, the stark contrast intensifying our magnetic connection.

His touch against my dark skin sends shivers of desire coursing through me. I nestle into him on the plush red knitted blanket beneath us, the soft cushions of the couch cradling our entangled bodies. The intimate atmosphere created by the gentle glow and our closeness heightens the urgency of my desire.

Is it the brush with death or the irresistible allure of my rescuer that ignites this fiery passion within me? I'm not sure, but I no longer wish to resist it.

Silently, Paul remains holding me, his comforting presence unwavering. With a gentle shift, he lays and envelopes me in his arms, making me the little spoon in our embrace. His strong legs intertwine with mine, and the thick wool blankets warmly cocoon us. Our breathing synchronizes, each inhale bringing us closer as my yearning intensifies with every slow exhale pressing my body further into his.

"I'm glad you're thawing out," Paul murmurs, his touch traveling from my lower abdomen up my side, grazing my ribcage and tracing the contours of my face. Our eyes lock, and the world outside fades away. Only the two of us are inside the cabin with the blizzard surrounding us.

Unable to resist the swelling explosion within me, I turn, facing Paul's solid body, my chest pressed against his and my brown eyes looking into his soft brown eyes. Desire courses through me, no longer hidden or repressed, and I'm drawn to Paul with an overwhelming hunger.

Paul's blackened wide pupils and quickening breath mirror my passion. I lean in to taste his lips.

Our lips meet in a fiery kiss that speaks of the passion we've discovered. I want more, and I'm not inclined to slow down.

"Whoa, Mak, we need to slow down and talk," Paul says.

I ignore Paul's cautious voice, filled with reason, that's attempting to intervene. I'm beyond the point of restraint. My tongue seeks entrance to his sweet mouth, and his response is fireworks.

Our kiss deepens, our tongues dancing in a slow, sensual exploration. There's no room for my Catholic shame or guilt in this intimate space, just an overwhelming sense of connection and longing. Our bodies press against each other, every inch vibrating with energy and heat.

As the intensity builds, our gazes remain locked, and anticipation prickles my skin. The fire crackles in the background, but all I can hear is the rapid beat of our hearts.

I pause, my lips hovering over Paul's, our eyes locked in a silent agreement. Then, I nip his bottom lip playfully, a teasing smile tugging at the corners of my mouth. The heat inside me explodes, and the sensations consume me. And our lips meet again in a passionate kiss.

The raging blizzard, Bryant, my sad holiday are forgotten. In this cabin, in the warmth of my desire, I'm alive and lost in a moment I've yearned for my entire life.

"Still want to slow down, Paul," I murmur through a playful smile, stealing his bottom lip. I stick out my tongue to trace his lip lightly, and his eyes dilate from the honey-brown to a ravenous black.

Chapter 5

Paul

I close my eyes, trying to find my balance, my lip throbbing and hot from her teeth and tongue. The kiss lingers, electrifying the small cabin as desire courses through us. Mak's warmth, passion, and longing are infused in her demanding kisses. The blizzard brought us together, but our need and passionate connection are more than surviving this deadly storm.

My eyes devour her stunning, captivating features with the soft glow bathing her profile: a smoldering expression in her rich dark chocolate eyes, her naturally red pouty lips, her creamy smooth coffee skin, and a soft round jaw surrounded by thick, shiny raven hair.

As I study her, Mak traps her bottom lip under her white nipping teeth and flutters her long lashes, making me groan.

She's not playing fair, and I don't want to take advantage of the woman I just rescued!

The urgency to warm her freezing body is fading, but there's another dangerous urge to take her in my arms and consume every part of her.

Mak's hands move to my chest, and I feel the warmth radiating from her, even with the layers separating us.

The small but pesky detail remains—a tight binder wrapped around my chest. As I lay against her, I'm acutely aware of this constriction, the fabric barrier separating us. My chest binder is a part of my identity, like the grease under my nails, and I wear it outside my home.

Not tonight! I want to show her everything and reveal myself to her.

She moves her hand over mine, tugging at the soft binder's seam. With hesitant fingers, her eyes meet mine as she slowly unravels the binding tightly holding me. With the binder off, she pulls the tight tank top over my head and shifts to kiss the imprinted lines around my ribs. And her lips move to kiss the scars scattered across my body.

Her kisses make my skin flush, my heart beats even harder, and a moan escapes my lips at her touch. I run my fingers through her dark hair, relishing the softness and silkiness of each strand.

"Paul," Mak says breathless from our kisses, her voice trembling and her eyes soft, "I want you."

Her words spark an unexpected tenderness in hearing her words' want, acceptance, and desire and the fiery hunger in her eyes. Mak's hands find their way beneath my shirt, our remaining clothing becoming a barrier, and I shiver at her touch.

My fingers trail down her back, and warmth flows from my racing heart through my fingertips as they graze her rich, soft, coffee-colored skin. Her heartbeat is steady and reassuring as she quivers under me amid the frigid storm raging through the windows. I trace the curves of her cool body, and her wet clothing sticks to my fingers.

Damn, I made a mistake! I left her in her snow-drenched attire, sapping away her heat.

I kick myself for the rookie mistake. I pull back slightly, looking into her eyes. "Mak, I should remove your wet clothes."

"Yes," she says without hesitation, reaching for the seam of her shirt.

My rough hands trace a path down her body, memorizing every luscious curve and perfect contour, leaving my fingertips tingling in her wake. Her skin is warm and soft—so soft my fingers feel like sandpaper in comparison. It's a stark contrast—the ruggedness of my battle-worn hands against the delicate lines of her body. Her smooth skin rests softly against the hard scars etched onto my torso.

My calloused hands chafe against her delicate skin as I quickly, but gently, remove her damp shirt. As I pull the cloth from her curvy body, my army medical training forces me to check for hidden injuries.

Her fingers move to her pink bra and unfasten the clasp to free herself. She looks at me, her eyebrows raised, and I smile back.

My fingers graze over the engagement ring on her finger, and I carefully adjust the medallion hanging from her neck, ensuring it doesn't catch on her pink bra as I assist her out of her shirt.

Questions whirl in my mind. *Is she unavailable? Where's her partner? Does she really want to be with me, or is this post-rescue horniness?*

I shake my head. *Stay focused! Don't get distracted by those curves.*

I want to ask about the ring, but as I catch my breath, I see the desire mirroring in her eyes. Instead, I ask, "Mak, are you sure?"

She nods, runs her finger lightly over my bottom lip, and looks deeply into my eyes. "I've never been more sure of anything in my life."

The fire crackles in the background, casting a warm, intimate radiance over us. The blizzard's relentless howling winds are replaced by the sweet sounds of our sighs and moans, the crackling fire a passionate soundtrack to our desires.

The small cabin fills with the sounds of our needs, passion, and the whispers of love. Mak makes me forget the world outside, the blizzard, the past, and my pain.

I exhale deeply, a weight released, and enjoy the harmony in this unexpected intimacy.

I'm not going back out into the storm.

Chapter 6

Paul

A jolt of cold pierces my body, startling me from sleep. My eyes flicker open, disoriented. *Where am I? And why does it feel like I'm holding an ice block?*

Peeking beneath the blanket, I find the source of this icy intrusion—*Mak's frozen feet* nestled against my leg. I suppress a yelp when a toe twitches, sending a cold shard through me.

Steady now. You've faced war—do not react. It's only a cold toe! I remind myself not to wake her with a sudden movement or shout.

I adjust the blanket, allowing the firelight to reveal her feet further, ensuring they're not frostbitten.

Nope, they're pink—surprisingly cute, albeit cold, for this very hot woman, and the pink painted toenails make me want to kiss her sweet frozen toesies.

The pink makes me smile as I remember her pink panties and bra, which I now think are *entirely appropriate* Alaska winter gear.

As she stirs and snuggles closer, her icy feet move to a new home on my warm calves.

Unbelievable! But it's hard to be mad at such a lovely woman. Suppressing another yelp, I remind myself she *was hypothermic* not too long ago. *And keeping her warm is my mission for the night.*

I tighten the blanket around us, creating a barrier between her frozen toes' icy attacks and my warm legs. I settle into our spooning embrace, and an unfamiliar, comfortable intimacy warms me.

The sensation of her against me goes beyond physical heat as it melts the icy walls around my heart. I never expected to be comforted in the arms of an unknown woman, yet *here I am,* drawn into this unexpected connection with *her.*

However, lingering questions rather than nightmares prevent sleep from claiming me. *Why is she wearing an engagement ring? Who is she?*

"Why are you here on Christmas, not with your fiance?"

She cracks open her eyes and softly answers, "Umm? What did you ask, Paul?"

"Why aren't you spending Christmas with your family?" I ask, amending my question.

"I don't have family anymore. My parents are gone and being here reminds me of past holidays with them."

I nod.

"I guess we are both stuck with the ghosts of Christmas Past," she says and nestles closer, her feet trying to bypass the blanket.

Her words resonate, and I have spent too much time with my ghosts. Holding and talking with her last night makes me want to try living again. An involuntary smile tugs at my lips, and she meets my gaze, returning the smile.

"I'm happy," I respond.

"The perks of rescuing women," she says. She sighs and wiggles further into my warm frame as I wrap my arms around her.

"Actually," I murmur, my voice filled with tenderness. "Thank *you* for giving me . . ." Words fail me.

Her hand grazes my cheek, and her eyes crease with her deep affection. She moves closer, her body pressing against mine, her lips tantalizingly close. "A reason to live?" she finishes for me.

"Yeah," I say. "I said last night. You might not remember."

She turns, pushes the blanket barrier away, and presses her body against mine. "I remember."

Our bodies remain entwined, facing each other, our warm breath mingling in the cabin's stillness. The crackling fire casts playful shadows on the walls, setting the scene. Our vulnerability binds us in our raw embrace, and she nestles her head on my chest.

As her breathing steadies, a sense of unease creeps in, tightening my gut, and my warm feelings dissipate with the fading firelight. Despite my asking about her family, she's not mentioned her engagement ring and relationship status.

I don't want to ask directly and shatter our new connection, but I *must* know. *Is this real? Does she care about me? Can we have a future together?*

In the midst of my internal struggle, she stirs from her sleeping state, her arm instinctively curling around my shoulder, pulling me closer. Her warmth soothes the raw edges of my uncertainty. Her breath caresses my neck, and I breathe her scent and warmth.

I focus on her, not letting my mind wander into darker territory. Our fingers meet, and I relish the softness of her touch, the genuine tenderness. I allow myself to savor the comfort of her body against mine, the rhythm of her breathing, and the gentle brush of her lips on my shoulder.

Our connection is *real, tangible, and undeniable. This* is what matters.

With a determined exhale, I close my eyes and slow my chest to synchronize my breathing. My heart beats faster even as my breath slows. As my VA counselor taught me, I let my breath out and slowly let another in, holding it and releasing it.

I *will* not let my mind wander along its usual dark paths.

Tomorrow, I'll ask her about the ring and be open to whatever truth she tells me. My arm tightens around my cold little spoon as sleep claims me.

Tomorrow!

Chapter 7

Mak

The first rays of sunlight gently coax me awake, their golden tendrils weaving warm ribbons throughout the cabin. Carefully, I extract myself from the comfort of the bed, not wanting to disturb Paul. He lies peacefully sleeping, a serene but tough figure.

I sigh and quietly ensure the woolen blanket is snugly wrapped around his enticing body, a silent gesture to protect him as he protected me last night.

Stepping gingerly across the creaking wooden floor, I make my way to the wood stove. Its radiant warmth brings back fond memories of our passionate night, and I tend to the embers, nurturing the flames that ignited our desire.

My gaze drifts across the room to Paul. I contemplate the queer feelings swirling within me—lust, need, and an overwhelming sense of comfort in his embrace. I have a foreign, physical craving that defies all logic and reason.

Was it the brush with death that compelled me to acknowledge my long-hidden desire?

My fingers trace the St Michael medallion around my neck, a gift from Marianne, my biggest cheerleader since my mom's passing. It's a reminder of God's protection over me and the Catholic values instilled in me from a young age.

During his enlistment, my father wore a similar medallion of Saint George, which protected him during the war. He was a devout man of few words, and he rarely discussed the trauma he endured. His hidden pain and the unshakeable shadow of his past fueled my desire to become a Psychiatrist and help people confront their inner demons.

Last night's events were *most definitely not* within the Catholic teachings or my upbringing. A flush burns through me, and I move my hand quickly from the medallion, my mom's ring tangling in the chain.

The ring reminds me of the upcoming task of getting Bryant out of my life. Last night reinforced my decision: I'm not getting back with Bryant. But he hasn't moved out or moved on because I haven't made it public yet. I can't bear to disappoint Marianne and my coworkers.

What would Marianne and the St Mary's staff think about my unorthodox relationship?

The thought alone is enough to make me queasy. No doubt coming out could cost me my job. St. Mary's Hospital is deeply rooted in Catholic teachings, guided by bishops, and bound by policies that align with the Church's doctrine. They won't perform life-saving pregnancy terminations or prescribe birth control to unwed women.

I look away from Paul and into the crackling flames. The thought of losing my job and the ensuing rumors churns the acid in my stomach.

I move to rid myself of the stress by tidying. As I move about the room, gathering discarded clothing, my fingers brush against something hard in the inner pocket of Paul's jacket. Curiosity gets the better of me, and I reach inside, retrieving a familiar item—an Epi-Pen.

My stealthy snooping fails when the EpiPen tumbles to the ground with a clatter echoing loudly in the cabin.

Oh, no!

Chapter 8

Paul

My eyes snap open, and my body tenses at the sharp nearby sound. My heart races, my head pounding, and the scent of ash instantly overtakes me. *Fuckin' PTSD!* I can't shift gears with my body yelling at me to fight or take cover.

Mak quickly moves, placing a calming hand on my shoulder, which helps ground me to the cabin and her. My heartbeat slows.

"Paul, it's okay. You're safe," she reassures me. "Take a deep breath with me, in ... and out." She takes a slow breath, and I follow her lead.

She continues her gentle guidance, helping to alleviate the panic gripping me. Gradually, my racing heart slows, and the pounding in my head subsides. The smell of ash fades into the background until I only smell the wood fire and Mak's sweet scent.

Calmer, I meet Mak's wide, golden-brown eyes tentatively locking onto mine, and I remind myself *I'm still alive in a remote cabin with the gorgeous woman I rescued last night.*

"Merry Christmas," I manage with a small smile. Despite the startled wake-up, there's a pleasant hum in my body. And I haven't had restorative sleep in weeks.

Mak's tousled long hair is fanned across her shoulders as she bites her plump lower lip. *An attractive bedmate might have contributed to my good night's rest.*

"Merry Christmas," she replies, her voice quiet as she moves away to finish gathering my scattered belongings and hangs my jacket by the door.

Does she regret last night?

"What's the epi-pen for?" she asks.

I furrow my brows, wondering at the change of conversation and coolness in the air between us.

"I should have said–I'm a doctor. I work in the Emergency Department with mental wellness. It's automatic, asking invasive health questions," she continues, with a hint of playfulness.

My heart skips a beat at her smile. Her revelation of being a doctor surprises me, but in hindsight, *it makes sense*. She's caring and certainly knows her way around a body. Her professional-like listening skills and compassion should have given away her job.

"I'm deathly allergic to lavender, and ginger, and there's a few other random things I'm mildly allergic to. My worst allergy is from Benadryl, of all things. So I keep an EpiPen with me," I explain.

Mak is like a truth serum. I can't lie to her piercing, kind eyes. Besides, seeing her in a tight tank top stretching dangerously over her curves, outlining her nipples, steals my breath away. *I'd tell her anything!*

"Really?" She turns to face me, her brow raised. Her deep cleavage and the light tracing her body steal the air from the room, and my heart pumps in overdrive.

Damn!

I glance away. The snow outside has stopped. Then I add, "My parents don't have allergies. I'm just unlucky. I had to keep an allergy journal to determine what soaps, chemicals, and foods triggered me."

"Your allergist is very patient to help you figure it out," she replies and returns to sit with me on the futon.

"My mom did it all. She's amazing!"

She places her hand over mine, and her eyes sparkle. "I wouldn't want you to have an emergency in the middle of nowhere." She laughs and moves the blankets to snuggle against me.

My cheeks flame at her jest. Her soft contours fit into my hard angles, and I wrap my arms around her, *my little spoon.* A lingering longing relaxes me, but the harsh morning wake-up leaves me with a bittersweet ache.

How could a stunning doctor be interested in a filthy, messed-up mechanic?

She sits up. "I'll whip up some toast or something."

I smile and nod. With my emotions brewing, I decided to break my vow. *I am not asking about the ring.* I want to enjoy being with her before reality sets in.

She squeezes my hand and interlaces her fingers with mine. Then she brings my hand up to her mouth to lightly kiss it as she gets up.

Her soft lips on my hand make me freeze.

Say something, soldier! Don't be creepy!

"Err ...," I clear my suddenly dry throat. "I could eat."

She heads to the kitchen, starting the kettle.

"I have an idea for a rural veterans' support group. Village patients can't attend in-person sessions and my dad, a veteran himself, found peace staying out here in Caribou Hills. People shouldn't have to leave the peaceful countryside to go into the busy city for care."

I frown, shaking my head, more startled at the conversation change than seeing her pink underwear over her voluptuous butt.

Damn! "You want me in therapy?"

I move quickly to put on my binder and an oversized sweatshirt, not wanting to reveal any more of myself to *the doctor.*

Does she see me as a broken soldier or her lover?

"No. . .I mean, yes, but when *you are ready.* I was thinking aloud. Sorry, I need to turn off my professional brain. You're my friend, and I want you to be happy. Let me make you breakfast, okay?"

I look away, avoiding her gaze and hiding my hurt as I realize our passionate encounter was her way of comforting me and more of a one-night stand than an invitation to a relationship. I'm just *her friend*.

Mak moves further away, giving me some privacy while she keeps herself busy. She says, "Actually, I'll make you my famous breakfast sandwich and coffee, *stat*."

"You had me at coffee," I respond weakly, but I must get out of this cabin and away from her.

She grins, oblivious to the mood change. "It's a toasted bacon, banana, peanut butter, and honey sandwich on sourdough bread. An *Elvis specialty*, you'll love it!"

I have already found something I love, and it's not food.

She continues talking while working in the kitchen."I expected to be alone. I only have comfort food here. But, if I was dying or on death row, this is the meal I'd pick."

I nod, folding the blankets and trying not to stare at her shapely butt.

"What would you request as your last meal?" she asks, toasting sourdough bread in a frying pan next to the thick, peppered bacon. The savory scent fills the small space, and my stomach rumbles louder, betraying me.

I might as well eat and be friendly. "I'd pick an overnight, slow-cooked pulled pork with Frito pie and sweet tea," I respond.

She laughs, and her chest jiggles.

My heart flutters more. She's not mentioning anything about our future or the wedding ring. I look out the window. "Are you ready to head out soon?"

"Sure. I have to work this evening," she says, pouring coffee and plating the sandwiches, then setting them on the table by the futon.

I sit and take a big bite. "Mmmm."

"Good, right?"

I nod and polish off the sandwich and coffee in record time.

"I'll drop you at the gas station and Jim'll get you set up with a tow or ride to Anchorage."

She nods and takes our plates as I get up, throwing on my snow gear.

I wish she'd asked me to drive her or say *anything* to indicate she wants to be more than a friend or a doctor referring me to therapy.

She stays silent, tidying the cabin.

"I need to get back and let my parents know I'm okay," I add. I open my phone and quickly send a message. My parents were probably worried sick as I didn't check in with them last night.

"Hey, Paul." She looks at me with her deep brown eyes. "If I didn't say it, thank you for rescuing me." She pulls me into a long, tender embrace.

I accept the embrace and hold her close for a few seconds. Trying not to enjoy it or imagine it means anything more than it does.

"I need to warm up the snowmobile. I'll see you out there," I say, excusing myself and exiting abruptly.

If I don't leave her now, I'll never leave. And she clearly doesn't have room for me in her life. I'm a headcase to her. *Broken!*

Chapter 9

Mak

"Mak! Doctor Makayla Jackson, I need you here. Now!" Nurse Jessica's voice slices through the tranquility of the Emergency Department, jolting me from my daydream. I slam my computer closed, hiding the tabs opened on the browser: St Mary's employee's morality clause—*Employees must follow the Catholic teachings*— PTSD counselors in Ninilchik—*There's none*—and checking Paul's social media—*He has no accounts.*

My daydream of seeing Paul again is ruined by the harsh reality of work pulling me back into the present, where I'm a respected doctor in a bustling *Catholic* hospital.

I wasn't the rational choice for the position. Still, my mom's friend recommended me, and "I fit in with the St Mary's culture," according to the hospital hiring committee, which refers to me being a St. Mary's Catholic Church parish member.

My magical night with Paul replays in my mind like a catchy jingle on an endless loop throughout my day. Falling for someone like Paul doesn't fit this hospital's old-fashioned culture. He's not a rational choice—but my heart doesn't care what's sensible and that the relationship could cost me my job.

Worse than that is the guilt of using work to escape Paul and the discussion of our intimacy. I ran away without even getting his number or saying a proper goodbye. I retreated into the safety of the known, my doctor persona instead of acknowledging our connection and exploring the possibility of a future together.

I frown, walking through the sterile, white hallway, following the sound of nurse Jessica's voice. I weave through the department, where Christmas decorations adorn the walls, and the gentle strains of holiday tunes emanate from speakers. Amidst the medical apparatus and the constant beep of monitors, the nurses' station glimmers with stockings and garlands, a festive gesture for staff and visitors.

Jessica grabs and nudges me playfully, "You were bringing me a pen." She raises her eyebrows, and I sigh, handing her my pen. *I forgot.*

"I *swear*, if I didn't know you, I'd say you were twitter-pated," she teases, widening her blue eyes and waiting for my response.

I respond with a sheepish smile, attempting to suppress my thoughts. "No, I'm tired of doing *both* our work while you dance around to Christmas carols," I quip, smiling.

"Really? I saw your butt swaying along, too, Beyonce." She raises a perfectly arched eyebrow and pouts her glossy red lips at me.

I shake my head and grin. Whatever, Shakira!"

Working the same shift as my friend is a blessing, but focusing on working while she teases me and tries to figure out why my head is in the clouds is challenging.

Jess's infectious mood spreads, prompting a grin wider. I glance around cautiously, ensuring our conversation is private, before confessing, "I'm contemplating my future and someone special."

I chose my words carefully as I can't reveal my broken engagement before talking with Bryant or the new relationship consuming my thoughts. Jessica's open-minded, but what Paul and I share isn't conventional or expected from *me*. I've *never* indulged in a one-night stand *with a person like Paul, except in my secret fantasies.*

Jess leans in, giving my butt an affectionate pinch, her tone playful. "That's obvious. You're practically oozing sexual energy, girl."

"Stop!" I protest, my eyes darting around for eavesdroppers. We may be a Catholic hospital, but the gossip mill thrives, spreading faster than a glitter bomb.

She chuckles. "Yeah, right. You aren't a nun. You've had your fair share of workplace romances. Where *is* McDreamy? Did you get stuck in the supply closet with him while fetching me a pen?" She winks and nudges me.

"You know I don't discuss my personal life at work. Let's talk after shift." I shouldn't have hinted at my mood. This is not the place to talk about it or drop a truth bomb on her.

"Ooof. Try next week. I'm working doubles to cover."

I nod. Next week, allows me to sort out my feelings and talk with Bryant. By then, I will be public with our break-up, and he better be out of the house!

"Earth to Dr. Mak. You're daydreaming about Dr. McDreamy, aren't you?"

Her teasing is good fun, but I'm distracted and can't tell her the truth even though my glowing skin and constant smile hint at my secret.

Jess is my closest friend, yet I haven't told her the truth about my relationship—or the *lack thereof*—with our coworker, Bryant. She did *introduce us,* and I hate to burst her bubble on being a fantastic matchmaker. It's part of what initiated our friendship.

"You look more in love than ever. Seriously, Mak!"

I look around, ensuring there's no one to overhear us. *I can share a little. I need to tell someone!*

"I've had a few relationships before, but I've found it—the sweet, Hallmark romance we always joke about, you-know, the as-seen-on-TV passionate instant love."

Her eyes light up. "Ahh! It's a real Christmas miracle! You're lucky, Mak. You're starting your fabulous career, embarking on life with a *serious hottie*, and you look absolutely radiant. Love suits you!"

I bite my lip from correcting her assumption that I'm referring to Bryant. The nurses adore him. I want to confess about Paul and the lack of passion with Bryant, but I can't.

I nod and reply softly, mindful of the nearby secretary, "Thanks, Jessica. I appreciate you. I'm taking you on a coffee date next week."

Beneath the surface, I'm grappling with a more daunting dilemma of redefining my sexual identity and *when I will see Paul again.*

Also, what will happen if I reveal my non-traditional feelings and new relationship?

I'm already the newest doctor on staff, a minority as a female and Latino staff, and adding another label, especially one referring to my unusual sexuality, doesn't make me their ideal diversity hire– it makes me a sinner in the eyes of this Catholic establishment. I can envision my coworkers' sidelong glances, the rumors, and disdain.

Is being fired worth being honest and trying a relationship with Paul?

I love my job and the people I help. I touch the medallion from Marianne that reminds me of my father. My dad and mom were proud that I was a doctor working at St. Mary's. This *was* my dream—*our dream*—before I met Paul.

Chapter 10

Mak

"Hey, Mak, we need to talk." Jessica's voice slices through my concentration like a scalpel, making me jump a little. I quickly click, saving my notes on my bereaved patient's chart.

"Jess, what's up?"

She looks at her feet, then says, "There's some gossip in the Respiratory Department. People are saying your wedding is off."

Oh no!

I inhale quickly. "What? Who's spreading this rumor?"

Is it a coincidence the rumors have started from Bryant's department? Maybe he's finally accepting our break-up and telling people.

"Is it true?" She looks directly into my eyes.

The chaos of the Emergency Department is forgotten as I stand and motion for her to follow me to a quieter corner of the busy nursing station.

"Jess," I begin and bite my lip. I say in a lower tone, "Yes, it's true. Bryant and I aren't getting married."

She turns to me and touches my hand briefly. "What?"

I take a deep breath, my heart racing. "Bryant and I ... I broke off our engagement."

"What happened? You two are *perfect* together." Her rapid questions run together.

I'm unsure how much to reveal, but I *must* confide in someone, especially if the rumor mill is churning. *How am I going to contain or control this?*

I bite my lower lip, holding back the waves of emotion crashing over me as my heart pounds. "It wasn't right, Jess. We were pretending. I didn't love him, and *he* doesn't love me."

Her eyes widen, and she gasps. "Mak, are you serious?"

"There's more. The reason Bryant and I aren't getting married is—" I sigh, thinking of how to explain my feelings for Paul. "It's complicated."

She leans forward and touches my hand. "Complicated? Like how? Cheating? Pregnancy?"

I pause at her rapid-fire questions. "I'm not sure if I should say anything. I need to talk to Bryant."

Her hand moves to mine, and her eyes lock onto me. She says, "Mak, you know you can trust me. Whatever it is, I'm *your* friend."

"I know, Jess, and I appreciate you. But it's hard to explain and I need to talk with Bryant first. I think he's feeling jilted and doesn't want to give up on our relationship, even though it's been stagnant for a while. I need to have that conversation with him, and it's going to be tough. He's a great guy, but I have feelings for someone else. And this is about more than canceling the wedding. It might affect my job."

Her hand springs to her throat, and she scrunches her nose. "Whoa! Your job? What do you mean?"

I inhale deeply, steadying myself. Saying it aloud would make it real. But my friend deserves to know, and *I can't hold this back any longer.*

"There's something I haven't told you," I begin in a whisper. "In Caribou Hills, I didn't have snow tires and slid off the road and got stuck in my Jeep in a blizzard. And I thought I was going to freeze to death. It was terrifying, but it also made me evaluate my life."

My friend leans in, her expression softening. "And you came to work? I had no idea. Are you okay?"

I nod, and despite the seriousness, I smile softly, recalling the events of the last twenty-four hours. "Yes, I'm okay *now*. But here's the thing: as I was hypothermic and losing hope, praying, a miracle happened." I touch my pendant.

Her eyes widen, and she asks, "What kind of miracle?"

She must be surprised if she's not asking her usual five questions at once.

I take a breath. My voice trembles as I explain, "I was saved by a stranger who was also in a desperate situation. God threw us together, and it was a surreal situation. It's hard to describe." I shrug.

She touches my hand again and wordlessly waits for me to share more.

I grab her hand, and my heart flutters. "It was love at first sight like God answered my prayers. I was rescued, but there was more, a deep, instant connection between us."

I pause and shiver from the excitement coursing through me as I say, "It was everything I dreamed of when meeting my soulmate. Those romance novels we read and romcoms we watch together–it was just like that."

Her gasp fills the room, and her eyes widen more. "Mak, that's ... That's incredible! What about Bryant? Who is this new guy?"

Before I can answer, her brow furrows, and she says, "If you're not engaged to Bryant anymore, are you guys still living together? You know you are already pushing it, dating a coworker and then living together not married. The only reason the hospital board has ignored it is your relationship with Marianne."

I bite my lip and nod. "I know, Jess. That's the problem. Bryant was going to move out, and we were going to have a friendly, public breakup *after* the holidays."

She nods and holds my hands tight.

"Now, with this rumor, I have no clue what to do. I haven't talked to Bryant since my trip. I was reviewing the hospital's morality clause and I think I could lose my job."

She places a reassuring hand on my shoulder. "Mak, you've got to do what's right for you. You're a brilliant doctor, and there's no way the hospital will fire you," she says with conviction.

Then she adds, "The only person they've fired on the morality clause was a guy who turned out to be gay, so you have no worries. And the board is supposably trying to reflect the community by moving to be more inclusive."

I sigh and bite my lip. How do I tell her my soulmate is an amazing trans man? Would she still be my friend and stand by me if she knew?

My mind races with the situation's complexities—I need to talk to Bryant and make a plan, stat. The overhead speaker blares before I can ruminate further.

"Emergency Room 14. Code Blue. Code Blue. ER 14."

Chapter 11

Paul

My dad eases into the well-worn chair beside me and hands me the wrench for the truck without me even needing to ask. Taking the tool, I want to open up to him about my recent encounter and new feelings.

Pop and I share an unspoken connection, but lately, with my dark mood, we are distant. I want to bridge our gap but struggle to articulate my feelings.

"Pop," I begin, my words slow, "I'm doing some serious thinking. I can't help but feel like I'm missing something in my life, something—deeper." I shrug, with my pathetic attempt at explaining my emptiness and describing the recent fullness I felt with meeting Mak. My hand tucks her left-behind Santa hat deeper inside my cargo pants pocket.

Just touching it makes my heart thump, and I lick my lips.

His gaze meets mine. He nods and gives a knowing look that suggests he's attuned to the thoughts weighing on my mind. "Go on, Paul. I'm all ears."

I draw a deep breath, attempting to gather my thoughts into coherent words. "It's not that I'm unhappy here with you and Mom, per se. It's this shitty, aimlessness, like I'm stationary while traffic moves around me." I shrug. "I can't explain right, but I have this feeling I should be dead, not the one alive. But that's not it. There's something more."

I pause and don't say anymore. My words are flat.

Pop nods, his eyes crinkle in understanding, and he places his hand on my shoulder. "I get it, son. Life's path can be winding. We are *proud of you,* and it takes time to come home from the war."

I lean back in my chair, the weight of my contemplation heavy. "Yeah. I'm doing some soul-searching, trying to figure out what's missin'. Maybe it's time I connect– you know? With something or someone. A bigger purpose."

His smile is easy, and he squeezes my shoulder. "Paul, let me show you something." He reaches into his pocket and retrieves a weathered medal.

Something from his military days?

"This belonged to a dear friend of mine. He was a better man than me, but he's not here and *I am*. Friends and connecting is important. He helped me through rough patches and reminded me to focus on the good– you and your mom." He smiles and looks down at the piece of metal. "I strive to be the friend and man he saw me as."

He hands it to me.

I take the small medallion on the chain, and it's a dog tag but an image of a Saint imprinted into the metal. My finger traces the well-worn etching.

"Saint George. He's yours, to remind you, that *you are enough*. You survived, like me, and you deserve happiness," Pop's voice carries the weight of memory.

I swipe my teary eyes at his revelation. My dad avoids talking about his past, but I know this trinket must mean more to him than his displayed Medal of Honor since he carries it close.

"Thanks, Pop."

"Caribou Hills is a special place, and I moved here for the community and the wilderness. I was a mess when I came back to your mom after the war. I'd take off into the tundra, like you, trying to outrun my demons. Then I ran into an old friend who understood. We leaned on each other for support, for a connection. We ran in different circles, but I knew if I needed him, he had my six."

I wrap my hand around it and feel the significance, not in its physical weight but the meaning it holds to my Pop.

"What are you sayin'?"

He leans closer, his eyes searching. "Paul, sometimes the connection we seek isn't what we expect. Have the courage to let go of the past and step into the future with whoever has your back. You aren't alone."

"Pop, I can't take this."

"Yes, you can. And remember, me and your mom always have your back. You'll meet friends along the way. You're not alone, and you deserve to be alive," he says, putting his mitts over my fisted hand.

I absorb his words, recognizing the medal as the cherished symbol it is. Dad found this knowledge from his friend. Now, he's passing the wisdom to me—a bridge between generations, a link within my fisted hand.

My fingers rub the medal, and a peculiar sense of peace washes over me as the metal warms in my hand. "Pop, I'll cherish it. Thanks."

He nods and lets go of my hand.

I add, "I've met someone special who I connected with. It terrifies me."

He pats my shoulder, his eyes reflecting warmth. "I know. Good. I have no doubt you'll find your way. Remember, you're not alone."

He smiles, adding, "Maybe you'll even have a wonderful kid, like I did, someday."

"Ugh! Pops, don't ruin it!" I smile and cuff his shoulder.

As we sit there, my uncertainties are lighter, and a newfound connection fills me. I slip the medal into my pocket.

"Your mom's taking the ham out of the oven," he interrupts, suddenly looking at the door and remembering why he came out to the garage.

My mom will be hollering at us soon, no doubt.

I slide my tools out from under the truck and wipe my hands on my coveralls. "I was about to take a break, Pop. Perfect timing."

"How's Bob's truck coming along?" my dad asks, leaning over the truck as I put away the tools.

"It'll be purring like a damn beast once I'm done," I reply, giving the truck a solid pat.

"I've heard folks talking about hiring you for the municipality fleet. You're the go-to diesel mechanic in Ninilchik. I'm proud of you. Now, let's go eat," he says, patting my back and flashing me a brief smile.

"Thanks, Pops. Talking with you and working here is good."

"I know you had your sights set on leaving this small town," he says, "but it grows on you, right?"

Growing up, I couldn't wait to escape. I didn't have friends and didn't relate to the girls in my class who were engrossed in boys and fashion— I had a rough time growing up, but we don't discuss it much. Our conversations lean toward trucks, hunting, and guy topics I enjoy.

I nod.

He continues, "It's not so bad here. And I appreciate having you around to do the deliveries. Everyone in town likes having a diesel mechanic. You could do well staying."

"True," I say, pausing.

Mom must have put him up to trying to get me to stay, and I don't want to get her hopes up. There's no place, aside from the army, I've ever felt comfortable. I'm not gonna promise to stay, but at the same time, there's nowhere else for me.

My thoughts drift to Mak, her soft body curled warm against mine. She makes me want to stay, to have a home to share with her. The warm, comfy feeling of waking up next to her is more home-like than any location on a map. I could get used to that feeling.

I frown, sorting my tools. *Home with her is impossible.* This town's only good things are my parents and this garage.

My mom enters the shop from the house.

"I overheard you guys chatting. How about a break for early Christmas Dinner? You know most people take the day off, right?" she jokes.

"The work's gonna be waitin', either way," my pop and I say in unison.

We laugh, and my mom smiles wide, wiping her hands on her apron.

"Paul, that's the first time I've heard you laugh in a while. It sounds good." Her eyes shine, and she smiles at me.

I turn away, hiding the blush on my cheeks as I think about the reason I'm in good spirits–*Mak*.

My pop adds, "We can eat."

My mom's stern gaze fixes on me, her response blunt. "And Paul, you need to put some meat on those bones. I've got pecan pie *and* apple pie with ice cream ready."

I chuckle, raising my hands. "Alright, alright. I surrender. I'll eat."

"Can you even recall the last decent meal you had?" my pop quips, poking fun at me.

Without missing a beat, I reply, "An Elvis sandwich this mornin'."

My mom's eyebrows raise, and she asks, "What in the world is that?"

I shrug. "It's a mishmash of crispy bacon, peanut butter, bananas, and a drizzle of honey on sourdough bread," I explain, a grin tugging at the sides of my mouth.

My dad's eyes opened wide in surprise. "All together—in a sandwich?"

"Trust me. I'll make you one. You'll love it." Knowing his love for anything involving bacon, this will become his favorite sandwich. *Maybe his last meal request.*

"I'm pleased to hear that *you* want to cook," my mom ribs me, "I'll eat anything you make." My mom's warm smile lights up her features.

"You do seem different—happier—since returning from your blizzard rescue this morning."

I gave my parents the abbreviated version of the story.

My dad nods in agreement, and I hide a smile once again. I'm getting used to laughing and grinning again.

My mom puts her hands in her apron. "Not to suggest you were unhappy before or you needed to change. We're your parents, and we only want the best for you."

"I know," I grumble, giving my mom a nudge with a clean part of my arm.

My mom looks down at my black hands. "Paul, you're a greasy mess!"

"I'll wash while you're settin' the table." I stride to the sink and reach for the industrial cleaner. "Gimme a sec. I'll be right out."

"Table's set. I'm waiting for you," my mom calls.

"Roger that. I'm on the way," I reply, saluting her before turning on the water.

"I forgot. I got you guys new shop supplies. I'll grab out the towels for your workbench." She goes to the cupboard.

My mom's the best. If smiling makes her happier, then I'll smile more. I *could* call my therapist and restart sessions. For Mom, I'll make time for the weekly phone call, and I have a feeling if I run into Mak again, she'll be happy to hear. She may track me down. Ninilchik is a tiny village, after all, and she was thinkin' to get me into that new rural PTSD group.

I wouldn't mind talking to her again. I smile. *I might need to track her down first.* I could always ask Jim where he had her Jeep towed to.

My parents are trying their best to help me, givin' me support and being there. My mom has gone above and beyond, feeding me, housing me, getting me back to work, doing laundry, and becoming my cheerleader. Even my pop transformed his garage to accommodate a diesel shop in it for me. Clearing away years of clutter and organizing the shop was no easy task. But PTSD requires therapy, and I'm ready to start workin' on it.

As the foamy soap lathers in my hands, a sharp burning sensation jolts through my skin, sending shockwaves of pain through my body. I yelp. Acid is searing my hands, and the burning is moving to my chest.

Thump.

The soap bottle falls into the sink.

My heart races and a wave of dizziness washes over me, disorienting me and making me rock back on my heels.

Am I having a flashback? A heart attack?

"Paul, you alright?" My pop's concerned voice pierces the haze as he hurries toward me.

I try opening my mouth to assure him everything's okay, but my throat is closed, and only a strained wheeze escapes.

The realization hits me like a freight train—*I'm having an allergic reaction.* To make matters worse, I know where my EpiPen is—*my jacket on my bedroom floor.* Nowhere nearby.

Dammit!

I struggle to stay on my feet, gripping the sink's edge. The world around me blurs as my vision fades to black.

I hear my pop's urgent instructions for my mom to call for an ambulance.

My mom barks orders at Dad to check my pockets for the EpiPen while telling 9-1-1 the situation.

I focus on my dad's voice, speaking a steady mantra. "It's alright. It's alright. It's alright." A reassuring chant and my focal point.

My arms are numb, and I release the sink, collapsing to the floor. My vision is only a tiny tunnel of black narrowing until *nothing.*

The last sound I register is the loud *thwack* of my head bouncing on the concrete floor.

Lucky for me, I've got a skull as thick as a bunker door, is my last thought.

Chapter 12

Mak

Room fourteen is alarming. I rush, ready to calm an escalating patient. The ER's chaos surrounds me – a storm of medical expertise, compassion, and urgency. Amid this, Respiratory Therapist Bryant stands out, a familiar figure in the whirlwind.

"Nice to see you, Bryant," Dr. Anderson says, the ER doctor in charge. His welcoming words skip past me to acknowledge the other male in the room, Bryant.

To be fair, Bryant is an essential and experienced Code Team member, navigating the room's frenetic energy effortlessly and assessing as he pulls out the respiratory supplies. As the Code Team arrives, they flash smiles and nod greetings to him. He's charismatic, and his smile is inviting, even during an emergency. His casual confidence eases the room's heavy atmosphere.

I bite my lip. *If only I had a sliver of love—of desire—for this modern-day Don Juan.* His confidence, easy smile, and intelligence *should* be a perfect match for me.

Watching him work, a complicated tangle of emotions surges within me – a mix of exasperation and longing. His magnetic personality draws others, but I'm more hypnotized by the smooth moves of his hands administering treatments and swiftly moving the patient into position.

"Extra towel," he says.

I hand him a rolled towel to place under the patient's head to hold the position, keeping the airway open. Working alongside him, I predict his moves, making it look like we are a flawless team– the perfect couple– working smoothly side-by-side.

He winks at me and tucks the towel under the patient's neck.

I look away and glance around for the family to comfort, but there are only the patient and staff members in the room.

Does he know about the rumor circulating? How will I get him alone to discuss my new feelings and kibosh our relationship once and for all?

Dr. Anderson nods, approving the tenuous airway placement by Bryant, and looks over to the oxygen monitor.

No. He must not have heard the rumor, or he'd have told me, and he wouldn't be winking at me. Bryant may look like a playboy, but he's honest, making me feel horrible about what I must do today.

I must kick him out and tell him, unlike our previous breakups where we argue and then get back together– *this time is for real!*

I catch a nursing student slowly moving her eyes from his wavy brown hair to his thick biceps and then to his tight butt. At least the nurses' with their sticky eyes and sly smiles, will be excited to hear he is back on the market.

Why can't he move on to find an adoring woman charmed by his humor and Henry Cavill-like handsomeness?

Strangely, the idea of him with this nursing student or anyone else doesn't bother me or make me jealous. It would make this break-up easier, and he deserves passionate love–the kind of love I've discovered.

I blush and join the team, focusing entirely on stabilizing the seizing patient, who seems to have settled. Bryant's expertise and the teams' early interventions have stabilized the patient without any more danger.

I take a breath, and we high-five each other, dispersing as the patient wakes up and all his vital signs are stable.

"Thanks, guys," the nurse, along with the nursing student, says as we leave the room to return to our regular duties.

I need to finish my charting.

"Hey, Mak Attack. I thought you'd call me yesterday. The least you could do is wish me Merry Christmas," Bryant says, catching me in the hallway.

I should have called him, but he should also stop treating our relationship like it's a real relationship.

Turning to face him, our coworkers buzz around us, and I can't say what I need to in this too-public hallway. Instead, I look down the hallway and cross my arms.

The other nurses unwittingly block my path with the code cart and trap me in the hallway with him. Seeing Bryant at work is unavoidable, though, and I need to talk to him when we don't have an audience.

"I was busy," I reply curtly, maneuvering around the cart.

I'll remain professional until we can talk. There's no need to add any validity to the current rumor until we decide how to announce our breakup and cancel our wedding.

He smiles warmly and hands me a mini candy cane from his pocket.

Damn him! Why can't he be an asshole then I'd feel better about our breakup?

"It goes both ways. You could've called me." But I bite my lip, remembering *he did call me,* and I didn't return any of the messages.

I'm the jerk, and he's the good guy.

He shrugs good-naturedly and hands out candy to the passing nurses, who are more enthusiastic than me to receive his attention.

"You're the best, Bry," a nurse purrs at him with a flutter of lashes as she pockets the candy.

I'm terrible at faking or lying, and with an adoring audience around, the pressure is on me to keep my interactions with him normal until we talk. I look at the clock. Only a few more hours, then my shift is done, and I can discuss the whole situation with him and home so we can make a game plan that might save my job and not make me look like such a jerk for canceling the wedding.

Ignoring the nurse's flirting, Bryant follows me. His demeanor shifts, and he leans in, his words loaded with familiarity, and whispers, "Hey, you know I've been thinking about us."

He hands another candy cane to the nursing student, who has no reason to hang out in the hallway. He winks at her and then grabs my hand to stop my escape.

Meeting his gaze cautiously, I respond firmly and shake my hand out of his grip. I'm tired of this recurring conversation.

"Bryant, we've been through this. We're better off apart, and you can literally have any nurse here. You promised you'd move out over the holidays and we would talk to HR together and announce our breakup."

His smile fades at my calm response. And his eyes flash, the warmth replaced by a sudden intensity. "You aren't giving me a chance, Mak. We've been together too long to break up suddenly. At least give me another shot. I am going to be on the mortgage, and you were just starting to combine our accounts, so I can take care of all our financial stuff, while you take care of the household and our kids."

Kids! Am I hallucinating?

I give a shake and look into his eyes. *I wish I felt as committed to him and our future as he feels about me.* It's Christmas, and he's ending a long-term relationship which is difficult. He's probably a little blue and lonely this holiday.

He's right. *I should have called him.*

"No," I say, firmer this time. I won't give in to his attempts to rekindle our relationship or let him believe we have a future.

I quickly scan the hall, silently praying for Jessica to rescue me, but I only see other staff milling about.

No luck.

"You tell patients to be open-minded in trying new therapies." His words hang in the air.

Guilt creeps into my heart, making me want to give in to him. I know prolonging our relationship and breakup isn't good for us. But he's really hurt, and everyone deserves a second chance.

I shake my head. We've rehashed this conversation too many times for me to do it one more time.

He leans closer, his eyes searching. "Mak Attack , remember all the good times we've had. The plans we made. The life we have together. You can't just throw all of it away."

I sigh and rub my forehead. "Bryant, the past is the past. We've *both* changed, and it's time to move on."

His voice softens, and he reaches for my hand, but I stuff it into my lab coat's pocket.

"I love you, Mak. I have since I first saw you and Jess introduced us. Give me one more chance, for old times' sake. *Please.*"

I meet his gaze, my eyes unwavering. "Bryant, love isn't enough. We need more than history to make this work. I'm not happy and you aren't happy. It's time we *both* find happiness elsewhere."

He opens his mouth to protest, but I don't give him a chance to continue. I turn away, determined to end this no-win conversation.

We still share a house and a workplace. *I must maintain civility.* I agreed to let him be the one to announce the breakup after he moved out and to stay on friendly terms with him since we must work together. But I'm unsure what he will do when he finds out I met someone else.

"You'll never find a guy who's willing to be in a relationship with all your baggage. Plus, I could have any woman I want. Do you see the way the nurses' look at me? You're making a big mistake," he mutters in a low tone, keeping our conversation discreet.

His spiteful words, intended to make me apologize, have the opposite effect.

I smile. "Bryant, you're right. But then you're always right, aren't you?" My agreement disarms him.

He smiles triumphantly, done arguing with me, and extends his hand for me to take it as if it only took him mansplaining the situation to make me want to stay with him.

I lean forward to whisper, "You're right. I won't find another *guy* like you because I don't *want to be with you*. I'm in love with someone else." I slide off my mom's ring and put it in my pocket. I don't want him to misconstrue that I'm wearing the ring because of him and not to honor my mother.

I'm done with trying to save my job, make him look good, and pretend to be someone I'm not. I can't do it, and it's not fair to Bryant!

His hand clenches into a fist, and his face contorts with the rage of a man scorned, *which he is.*

"Mak, I'll tell HR that I'm unwilling to work with you and you'll get fired. I'll tell everyone you're a cheating *slut* and make sure you can't move to another department," he spews, his words stinging like a slap. "You'll give me another chance *or else*. I haven't wasted a year of my life *for nothing*."

Before I react, the intercom diverts our attention.

"CODE BLUE ER 4. CODE BLUE ER 4!"

His intensity wavers, replaced by the profession in him. It's as if nothing happened, and he conveniently forgets the threat to me as he pivots to room four. His intense, threatening demeanor dissolves, replaced by the confidence he effortlessly wears. In the blink of an eye, he's an ER team member, focused on the task.

I move with the flow of our coworkers, their attention fixed on the impending crisis, unaware of the tense undercurrent.

Chapter 13

Mak

I settle into my chair to complete the final round of charting for the day. Exhausted and drained, I chart on my patient, who is close to alcohol poisoning because of her holiday family stress. The radio crackles with the EMTs calling from the helicopter, jolting me out of my weariness. An emergency patient is coming to us.

I multitask, trying to type up my notes double-quick and wishing I could get a coffee, but I don't have time to pee anyway.

I should've known better than to work on Christmas—*It's a full moon! Codes are being called every few minutes. I'm fighting with Bryant!*

In the background, the EMT's brief report crackles over the radio to prepare us for the emergency transfer en route.

"Ninilchik... a twenty-five-year-old woman, in respiratory distress ... possible anaphylactic reaction ... eighteen-gauge IV placement ... unknown history ..."

My heart flutters with anxiety, and my thoughts suddenly drift to Paul—probably because Paul is dominating my thoughts all shift. *He's twenty-five-ish from Ninilchik.* I shake the idea from my head, trying to finish charting, and ignore the radio.

It's a coincidence. I bite my bottom lip and taste salt.

What if this is Paul?

Ninilchik is full of people—I'm sure my one-night stand isn't the patient being rushed here. Even with a full moon, this is too far-fetched. My overthinking and nerves are getting the best of me.

My stomach clenches, and my hand covers the medallion at my throat. *God, tell me I'm wrong, and give me strength if I'm not.*

Even if it is Paul—an improbable *scenario*–an anaphylactic reaction is easily fixed. I can handle seeing him, and there's no shame as it wasn't some lewd, illicit affair. *I'm a single adult, after all.*

Love isn't bound by gender expectations nowadays, right? The hospital doesn't need to know, and they are *supposedly* becoming *more progressive.*

I must be tired or hungry. Or tired *and* hungry because why does my brain jump to *worst-case scenarios*?

Also, *two people in a blizzard, alone in the wilderness– a hook-up would've happened to anyone in that situation, according to every romance story ever written.*

The picture of Jesus hanging by the clock *judges me* and disagrees.

Oh God, please, please don't let this be Paul!

The backdoor slams open, and I shut the chart to greet the patient as the EMTs push into the ER. Machines and people surround the gurney, but I notice a Santa hat with green glitter tucked into the pile of belongings at the foot of the bed.

My hat! Paul!

My heart lurches in my chest, and I gasp. My professionalism unravels. Tears unwittingly pool in my eyes, and I clutch my Saint Michael, whispering a prayer for protection as my eyes water.

Paul is buried in blankets, an oxygen mask covering his face, and tubes and wires weaving around him. He looks vulnerable yet captivating, an embodiment of raw strength, the inked arms with ropy muscles and the pale fragility intersecting. The machines dwarf his powerful frame, but there's no doubt—this strong person who rescued me in the blizzard last night and carried me to safety in those IV-laced arms.

My professional demeanor crumbles, and I cannot stop my emotional response. Instinct takes over as I rush to Paul's side. Instead of taking the chart or helping to push the gurney, I reach my trembling hand to touch him.

I want to assure this is real and reassure him that I'm here and he's okay.

A tender murmur is on my lips as he grimaces and tenses with the EMTs, bumping him through the doorway. I ache to wrap Paul in my arms and transfer my strength to his fragile body.

Reality stops me, and I stop moving, making me stand awkwardly in the hallway. I can't embrace Paul in a room full of my colleagues and the prying eyes of my ex. Besides, Paul might not even have the same feelings for me. *It was one crazy night.*

My heart pounds, an increasing drumbeat thundering in my ears as I stand torn between professionalism and the tumultuous emotions surging inside me. I've got to keep it together and remain composed. But that's easier said than done.

Rather than comfort him, I open the emergency room five's door, my fingers trembling slightly as I pull the curtains aside, revealing the sterile interior of the trauma room.

Jessica is taking charge of the room with the monitors set up and ready to transfer the patient to the bed. Her eyes flick toward me with an unspoken question.

"Do you know her?" she inquires, her eyebrows raised as the EMTs heave Paul onto our bed.

I lock eyes with her and bite my lip. Words fail, and I chew inside my cheeks, unable to articulate the emotions threatening to spill out.

A nod from Jessica tells me she notices my tears, and she moves the patient's belongings to the table, pulling out my hat to sit on top of the pile. She looks at me, her eyes widen as she understands and is putting together the pieces from my odd admission of falling in love, the Bryant rumor, and Paul appearing in our Emergency Department from Ninilchik with my hat.

Her eyes hold unasked questions— *What is going on?*—but there's no time for answers right now.

Paul's difficult breathing fills the room, a whistling, high-pitched inhalation jolting us into action.

My feet are encased in cement, rooting me to the ground as I watch, helpless.

He's groggy, his skin an alarming shade of blue, and each of his desperate gasps are a knife wounding my heart. I hold my throat and do the only thing I can think of—*pray.*

"We need to intubate her ASAP. We're losing her airway," Jessica says, cutting through the chaos.

Brant pushes me aside. "Move, Mak," he says, irritated, as he moves equipment beside Paul, the situation's urgency prompting him to action.

I want to stay by his side and offer comfort, but simultaneously, I realize *I need to leave*—immediately.

"Mak, is she a full code? Any medical history?" Jess's questions pierce through my fog, demanding answers.

Bryant looks at Jessica, spots the Santa hat, and then looks at me, his eyes narrowing.

A breath escapes my lips, and I force myself to respond, my voice steady despite my heart hammering. "Full code. Give him everything," I reply.

"Let's get the airway secure," Dr. Anderson orders.

In a swift and fluid motion, the emergency technician swiftly peels away Paul's shirt, exposing the chest binder splayed open beneath him. At the same time, the relentless glare of the hospital lights illuminates this intimate intrusion. A gasp escapes my lips as I witness his private, vulnerable form violated in this sterile environment. Tracing down his arms, the scars I kissed intertwine with his military tattoos, hinting at his traumatic past.

Paul, breathe!

"He's an army veteran, dealing with PTSD, but otherwise in good health," I say, recalling snippets of our conversation last night.

"He?" Bryant scoffs as he positions Paul's oxygen mask.

"Do we have another respiratory therapist for this patient?" I hear Jessica whisper to a nurse. The nurse leaves, hopefully calling in another RT to replace Bryant.

"Yes, Paul is *trans* and uses the pronoun *He*. If you have a problem with that, you should get out!" I snap, pointing to the door.

Dr. Anderson looks up for a beat but says nothing, focused on his stethoscope over Paul's lungs.

The ER tech gasps, and Bryant's jaw tightens at my outburst, but the medical team continues working as if staff arguments are routine. Jessica shoots me a reassuring nod as she focuses on Paul's needs, deftly removing the binder from under him while moving the blanket to maintain his dignity and privacy.

Thank God Jessica's here!

I look away from Bryant's acidic stare, and Paul struggles to breathe. The person I spent an unforgettable night with is here. Fear, love, regret, and longing propel through me with every woosh of my heart.

As the team continues to work, I'm left standing in the doorway, torn between my professional duty of detachment and my emotions swelling. My St. Michael's medallion is cool and reassuring under my fingertips as I watch. As the team continues, I'm paralyzed in the threshold, caught between my obligation of detachment and the surging tides of my fervent sentiments. The medallion against my skin grants a resolute chill that steadies me as I pray, watching the scene.

"Do you know his allergies?" the doctor asks.

Bryant's face contorts into a deep scowl as I falter, my recollection shrouded in a fog of uncertainty and my thoughts spiraling frantically.

"Umm...He carries an EpiPen and is allergic to lavender and ginger," I add, trying to remember the information Paul told me when I woke him to his EpiPen falling from his pocket.

"Medications?"

"No ... Well. Maybe," I hesitate. With my mind racing, I can't grasp the answer.

I wish I could remember more.

"Get outta the way already so we can work on her," Bryant yells from across the room at me.

He's rude but right.

I am hindering instead of aiding. As my gaze meets Jessica's, her expression changes to grave, with her lips tight and her eyes on Paul. She'll ensure Paul receives the necessary care, leaving me no choice but to retreat from the room.

Outside, I snap into action. I will notify Paul's family and update them on his condition. Also, since he's military, I'll call the Veterans Hospital and get his records *stat*.

Jessica passed by me, grabbing more intravenous fluids, an epinephrine vial, and Benadryl from the medication cart. I watch from the nurses' station, determined not to interfere or ask how Paul's doing.

She needs to focus, and I don't want to delay his care.

As she swings open the door to the trauma bay, a sinister wheezing escapes from Paul's unconscious form. The urgency intensifies as they struggle to secure his airway, with every passing moment becoming more critical.

My hand instinctively reaches for my throat, feeling the weight of impending doom. If the wheezing and swelling persist, Paul will be in trouble soon! A whirlwind of thoughts swirls through my mind as I desperately search for the fragments of knowledge teasing me.

God, what am I forgetting?

"Get me another vial of Benadryl!" Dr Anderson shouts, and I blindly grab the vial from the nursing station cart and follow the shouts back into Paul's room.

As I hand the medication to Dr. Anderson, Bryant's voice pulls me from my coursing thoughts.

"So you know her, huh?"

He's adeptly pulling out the nebulizer and breathing medications to administer to Paul.

"I do, and as I said earlier, *Paul's a him, not a her,*" I reply simply, my emotions boiling beneath the surface.

"How?" His inquiry is a loaded question, and I note his hands in fists and his searing gaze.

"None of your business," I snap back, irritation making my voice louder.

His attention should be fully on Paul's breathing, not on me.

Our gazes lock in a silent but deafening argument. If my coworkers doubted the break-up rumor, there's no question of its truth seeing us now. Bryant's jaw is tight, and his eyes are hard with hurt and anger.

"What do you think, Doctor? Does the army tranny need to be tubed to breathe?" he asks, looking directly at me and not Dr Anderson.

"His name is Paul!" I say in a rush, and Jessica grabs my suddenly raised-fisted hand.

Bryant snatches the chest binder forcefully from the table, launching it toward me with a fiery fury. "Get out and find a different boyfriend to cheat on!"

I manage to catch the binder mid-air, clutching it tightly against my quivering body, desperate to quell the anger coursing through me.

Dr. Anderson steps to the head of the bed between Bryant and me. "Let's watch Paul," he says, using his preferred gender, "seems to be improving with the breathing treatment. Keep the intubation breathing kit at the bedside."

Jessica nods, and the requested new Respiratory Therapist appears.

"Gina, take over for Bryant. *He's on break.*" Jessica meets my eyes and releases my hand to dismiss me, too.

Bryant steps back, handing the breathing nebulizer machine to Gina.

I flash a quick smile, my fingers gripping the binder tightly and then setting it down. Jess's nod tells me she's in control and will protect Paul.

As Bryant inches closer to me while making his departure, there is an unnerving proximity that sends shivers down my spine.

His eyebrows raise as he growls with an air of astonishment. "Paul? Really? That's a unique name for a lady," he remarks, his tone dripping with incredulity.

Suppressing my mounting irritation, I respond with a forced smile that barely conceals my simmering fury. "Unique? Paul is the perfect name for him," I retort sharply, the words laced with venomous defiance and unwavering resolve.

He says, "So *Paul's* the cock blocker, huh? I expected a burly Alaskan man. Guess I misread you."

"Completely," I agree, glaring back. My cheeks are red, and my hands form fists again.

I focus back on Paul's monitor from the hallway and am relieved to see the numbers improving.

"A woman. Really? You're no lesbo," he mutters.

I tilt my head and ignore Bryant and the stares from our coworkers. *The rumor mill is going to be churning tonight!*

"We can laugh this off at home. Why don't you let me show you what being with a man is like? Then you'll stop this nonsense," he says in a lower tone, forgetting the audience.

In the tense moment, Jessica's eyes darted to me, overhearing his growls. She scans us to see if I need backup.

I mouth, *I'm okay.* I'll explain this messy situation to Jess after she stabilizes Paul and we are off-shift.

For now, her unwavering attention is on Paul and his dwindling oxygen levels. She may be my friend, but she is a nurse first and will do anything to protect her patient, including kicking Bryant and me out of the room.

I save her the worry and move to the nurses' station with Bryant trailing me.

"It's not what you think—" I say, but it *kinda is.* Then I take a breath and look at him squarely. "I told you we are done, and it's nothing to do with you. *I love Paul, and I don't love you.*"

As my words hang heavy between us, I watch anger and hurt flash across his eyes. His usually confident gaze falters, replaced by a fiery intensity. His pupils narrow, sharpening into daggers, his brows furrowing as he contains his seething anger.

He smiles, remembering the audience, and talks to me and the onlooking staff at the nurses' station. "Do tell, Mak Attack. Even better, show us the pictures," he laughs, his eyes daggers.

"Stop, Bryant," I hiss. "We have a patient to take care of."

Before he presses any further, Jessica calls out, "Did we get the chart from the VA?"

I take a deep breath and turn away from his cutting gaze to check the fax machine. "I'll see."

The nurses' desk buzzes with activity as my heart races with anxiety at the dangerous situation and the scene Bryant is causing.

I pull papers from the fax, and one piece of information grabs my attention, leaping off the page: *Benadryl allergy.*

In the cabin, amidst our intimate conversations, Paul divulged all his secrets, including this one. This crucial detail slipped through the cracks of my memory and now thunders in my mind.

Panic courses through my veins as I sprint back to Paul's room. The sound of his labored breaths is worse and amplified by the confining mask and his silent, unconscious form.

"Benadryl!" I exclaim urgently, the word tumbling out of my mouth. "Paul is allergic to Benadryl."

Without hesitation, Jessica clamps the IV Benadryl drip shut and exchanges it for a saline bag to flush it out of the system, moving with practiced precision.

The doctor nods. "Good catch, Doctor Jackson. He was starting to decompensate again, heading back into respiratory distress."

Thank God for small miracles. I touch St. Michael and look at Paul's monitor, showing his heart and breathing slowing to a regular rate.

"Excellent work, everyone," the doctor's voice rings out, a proclamation signifying the end of the emergency.

We can stand down.

As Paul rests, his breathing steady and no longer in distress, I take a deep breath and glance out the window. The moon bathes the snow-covered city in a gentle, ethereal glow. I look back to Paul.

Another snowy night with an emergency, and this time, I saved you!

As emotions engulf me, an overwhelming surge of relief swells, threatening to burst through my calm exterior. Tears cascade down my cheeks, acting as a release valve for the immense weight of tension that I've been carrying since Paul came into the ER. With bated breath, the medical team silently retreats from the room, leaving behind a flickering monitor and Jessica attentively watching Paul.

Jess nods and brushes by me, gently touching my arm as she leaves the bedside since Paul is stable and resting.

I break my gaze from Paul.

"Good job, Mak. You stay here and I'll let you know if you're needed. You only have an hour left on your shift anyways and I think Paul would appreciate you here."

I numbly nod and take the seat by Paul.

She shuts the curtains behind herself, leaving us alone.

With the calmer atmosphere, Paul stirs, his eyes fluttering open. My eyes meet his, and his sleepy eyes reflect recognition and warmth. He hasn't forgotten our unspoken connection from last night.

Paul's fingers twitch, and his hand reaches out for mine.

I grasp his hand, and he smiles, drifting back to sleep with the steady beat of the monitors and my hand warming his.

"Merry Christmas, Paul," I whisper, kissing his hand.

Chapter 14

Mak

"Paul," my voice trembles as I clasp his hand, "There's something I need to confess. Something I've realized but I didn't tell you."

We are alone as the morning sun dances upon the frost-kissed windowpane, casting icy sparkles throughout the room. My Christmas night shift ended hours ago, but I remained at Paul's bedside, unable to leave. As I watch Paul in this hospital room, our fleeting connection has grown into an unexpectedly intimate bond.

God keeps bringing us together for a reason.

The soft, rhythmic beeping of the heart monitor and Paul's breaths are within normal ranges. Reason tells me his survival is assured, but my heart refuses to accept such certainties. I can't bear to leave Paul's side if there's a chance he could go into respiratory distress and need me to rescue him again.

Bryant and my coworkers have an inkling of my innermost feelings, yet there's one person to whom I concealed the depths of my emotions. The thought of baring my heart to Paul fills me with unease as if by saying aloud, I will ruin our connection. Deep down, I know I should've told my truth at the cabin. Yet I ignored it and said nothing when I had the chance.

With my feelings haunting me ever since waking up with Paul on Christmas Eve, I don't plan to ignore it this time. *What if something had happened to Paul and he didn't wake up?*

I'm telling Paul and everyone else, too.

Paul's chest rises and falls with the steady rhythm of slumber, a reassuring movement. I gather strength from him, knowing he's here with me. Even if he doesn't hear me, I need to tell him.

I start, "I knew I was different, and conventional relationships never quite fit." I continue, my words heavy with the weight of memories. "I had my life planned out, as a doctor, then a big wedding, thinking I knew my path. But God's will or *fate*, if you'd rather call it that, has a funny way of surprising me."

Inhaling deeply, I feel my heart pounding as I struggle to tell Paul. "I've fallen in love with you, Paul," I confess in a whisper. "And you're not at all part of my plan."

Tears blur my vision as I explain my truth, which I can no longer deny, even if it costs me my job.

"I never imagined I could feel this way for someone. Loving you is so natural and easy," I say, trembling. "I finally understand why I couldn't fall in love with Bryant and why I couldn't initiate a physical relationship with him. He wasn't the right person."

Paul stirs in their sleep, a soft murmur escaping his lips, urging me to continue telling him my secrets, similar to how he whispered his secrets to me. I grasp Paul's hands, and a smile plays on his lips.

"I ended the engagement before I met you but without properly explaining the reasons to him. And he couldn't move on because I didn't even understand why I didn't–*couldn't*– love him. *Not until I met you*," I stroke Paul's cheek lightly.

"Bryant," I whisper, my grip on Paul's hand tightening, "my ex-fiancé, didn't truly love me. He loved the idea of being engaged to a doctor, and of having me as a status symbol on his arm. And he wasn't a terrible person. There's this pressure from my parents, then my coworkers, and after my parents died, I didn't want to change everything they were so proud of me for. I've been lying to my friends and coworkers—And *lying to myself about who I am*."

Tears stream down my cheeks as I bare my soul, each word a cathartic release.

"It didn't *feel* like such a terrible lie, only a *little* lie. And I was going to tell everyone the truth after Bryant moved out. Then I met *you*," I say, pausing to look at Paul's relaxed and radiant face. "You helped me discover real love and passion and *who I am*. Now my little lie feels like a *huge* deception that spilled out, and I can't keep hiding it."

Paul sleeps peacefully.

I continue, "I trapped myself in this false relationship and false narrative. I didn't fully understand that I didn't love Bryant. Working in a Catholic hospital and having traditional parents, I didn't consider a different path. The truth is, *I did know*, deep in my heart, and you gave me the strength to confront it."

I take another deep breath and place my hand on my medallion to gather strength from the St Michael medallion, like the one my father wore.

A lightness washes over me, and I hold Paul's hand. "When you arrived by EMT, and I saw you on the gurney, I realized I made a mistake. I needed to tell you how I feel, what you mean to me. I should have told you yesterday at the cabin."

"You fill my heart and love me for who I am. I have to tell you," I confess, my heart beating faster as I speak aloud, "I love you, Paul. That's it. *I love you*."

The truth is out, and I'm free of my secret. *I only hope Paul feels the same.*

A throat clearing surprises me, and Jessica is standing in the doorway. Her eyes are unblinking, but she's smiling.

I wipe my moist eyes and offer a shrug. "I'm sorry, Jess. I guess I'm not exactly who you thought I was."

Her radiant smile reaches her eyes, and her eyes twinkle at me. "You're a wonderful doctor and friend, which is exactly who I know you are. I don't care who your partner is and I didn't want to wear an ugly bridesmaid dress anyways. I want you to be *you* and happy."

Our eyes meet, understanding passing between us, and her friendship makes me smile warmly back to her.

She tilts her head toward the door and then closes it—the mood shifts. "Bryant was up at HR this morning, looking very smug, and I don't like it," she confides in a low voice as she clasps her hands together.

I frown. I thought–*hoped*– Bryant went home to pack and move out once and for all.

"Whatever happens, me and the rest of the staff have your back, Mak. You deserve to be here as much as any other doctor or respiratory therapist. This hospital's Catholic old-fashioned morality clauses are ridiculous."

Chapter 15

Paul

My eyelids blink open reluctantly, and the sterile scent of antiseptic, white walls, and the rhythmic beeping of monitors greet me. A flickering fluorescent light overhead amplifies the throbbing, jagged pain in my head. I squeeze them shut again.

Hospital.

I'm in the damn hospital, waking up just like after my army platoon's attack. A painful lightning bolt hits from my temple to the base of my skull.

My thoughts are foggy, but my brain recalibrates to the present as the throbbing subsides. *I'm not in the army.*

The accident at the shop, my parents, the Emergency Room, and Mak's voice, the whole ordeal floods into my head in broken bits and pieces. I move my hands to my head, expecting to feel a dent, like a car's busted fender after hitting a snowbank. There's a bandage, but it's intact despite the throbbing.

Clearer thoughts filter back into my consciousness. *Mak.*

Mak was here. She held my hand and whispered in my ear. She was at my bedside.

I force my eyes to stay open, shifting my gaze to the side of my bed. Sitting in the chair next to me isn't Mak. Instead, a stranger stares quietly, intensely at me.

My heart rate ratchets up, and I clench my fists ready.

He doesn't react and sits unmoving, studying me with an unsettling gaze. I'm his prey through the sniper's scope, and his calm, explosive stare denotes danger.

What is he planning? Who is he?

Lightning strikes my temple again, and I grimace, which makes him stand.

He's young, fit, with no visible weapons, wearing blue scrubs and a nametag pinned to his pocket.

"Bryant," I croak out with a gravelly voice.

He doesn't respond and maintains his unsettling stare, sizing me up from the dominant attack position above me. *He's hostile as hell.*

I fist my hand around the heavy call light to pack more of a punch.

Breaking eye contact with me, he lifts his chin at a vase of pink carnations sitting by the window.

I squint, keeping him within my sight as I try to make sense of the man and flowers in my room. *He didn't bring the flowers, and I didn't buy them.* Plus, I have no friends, and my parents would've got me a burger, not flowers.

The thought of my parents makes me break eye contact with the enemy, scanning the room again. My heart pounds louder than my head. My mind races, and it clicks.

Pretty, pink, casual flowers—*Mak.*

"Those are Mak Attack's favorite, too," he says, biting each word.

Suddenly, the pieces click into place, and the gears in my brain turn. *Mak must've left them here while I was sleeping—a token since she had to work, or she wasn't ready to out herself with me at work.*

I'm trying to remember anything she whispered, but only her warm presence remains. My banged-up brain missed the exact words or where she said she was going.

I lick my dry lips and manage a weak hacking cough before grunting, "You doin' a test or something?"

"Your breathing's fine, thanks to me." His tone remains cool, eerily flat.

I narrow my eyes, his arrogant posturing grating on my nerves. I've stayed in hospitals long enough to know it's *a team*, not one person that takes care of a patient. If anyone is to thank, my heart tells me it's Mak.

"Yeah," I mutter, my headache pounding as my heart rate slows, making speaking difficult, but I am ready for the fight.

His smirk falters, an icy stare replacing it. "Don't get any ideas, *Pauline.* Mak's mine and marrying me. She's *not gay.*"

He spits out the last part, and I unclench my fist, releasing the call light. He won't fight me–he's a chained dog, barking. This must be who gave her that ring.

"Her parents would turn over in their graves at *you.* They raised her to be a good Catholic girl, for God's sake! She doesn't know what she wants and needs someone to take care of her."

His words reek of possessiveness, and anger surges through me instead of fear.

Does this guy think he can claim Mak? Like hell he can! She's a grown-ass woman, not anyone's property, and I won't let this jerk stomp her down.

I lift my chin, my intensity meeting his gaze. With clipped words, I say, "Mak's choices are hers. She's more than capable of picking *who* she wants to be with."

His eyes spark, and his lips curl into a sardonic smile. He towers over my bed, relishing his position. "Right. *Doctor* Mak makes great life choices: driving into a winter storm without snow tires or chains. She was asking for me to spend the holiday with her. She wanted me to chase her and save her. That's not a capable, intelligent woman, is it? She wants *a man to* take care of her."

My fists clenched, my patience wearing thin at his impotent conversation. *I need sleep.* "What's your problem?"

He moves in further, his breath attacking. "My problem? You shouldn't have been out there. I had everything under control. I would've saved her, and you almost got her killed."

His words ignite my fuse, amplifying the painful throbbing. *Who does this guy think he is?* Mak doesn't need this asshat stalking her.

"Mak can handle herself. You can leave," I growl at him, my pain adding a fierceness to my words.

"Oh, really? Are *you* going to save her? You're a real *lesbo in shining armor*, I see," he sneers.

Narrowing my eyes and pushing through the throbbing pain, I say, "You don't know a damn thing about *either* of us."

Tension fills the room, and I wait for the explosion. My heart rate ratchets upwards. I glance around, half-expecting my platoon at my back, a show of force. But it's the two of us, no witnesses.

He should be afraid. I'm in control and won't *allow* this asshat to belittle Mak and threaten me.

"*Miss Pauline*," he taunts, saying my unused legal name, "You are really messing up my plans." His tone drips with arrogance. He steps from my bedside, backs down, and pokes around my room.

I keep my eyes glued on him and the door, wrapping my hand around the call light, ready for his approach.

"Leave Mak alone. Her parents died, and she's emotional and confused. She's nothing like you and she's my fiancé."

He pummels my chest binder at me like a grenade, and I flinch.

I leave it on my bed, my focus remaining on him as I wait, prepared.

"Or else," I challenge. I'm in no condition to fight, my lungs burning, my head splitting, but I'm a trained soldier. My body is tense with the threat of this inflated man-child.

Newsflash: he couldn't win a fight against me even if I had no arms.

I wait for his response, wondering how much trouble I'll get into for punching a hospital employee. It probably won't be much, but I don't want to add stress to Mak's plate.

He leans back, his demeanor shifting from threatening to amusement. "Oh, you don't know, *do you*? About *her* and *me*?"

A foreboding tightens in my chest. "What?"

His eyes narrow as he puffs his chest out, smugly saying, "She came back and begged me to stay with her. She wants a big wedding and to have my children. We *live* together, and she's not leaving me. She's Catholic, if anyone finds out about you then she loses everything. She's not destroying her career and her life for *a freak*."

His words hit me like a sledgehammer, a cocktail of disbelief and betrayal coursing through my veins. My head aches, struggling to process.

Mak and he are living together?

My muddled brain can't sort fact from fiction. Bryant is handsome, and if Mak has to pick between a doctor and a fucked-up army vet, I'm not sure she'd pick me, especially if her career is involved.

Whispers of last night's conversation start resurfacing, and I'm sure she told me she cared for me. *Didn't she, or did I imagine it?*

The lightning in my head vies with the anger exploding in my gut. Bryant's words pound in the harsh truth of Mak's decision, and the lightning in my head adds to my defeat. His smug demeanor fuels my need to fight, though.

"You're a lying piece of shit," I spit, my voice cracking. I knew my dream–*Mak*—was too good to be true.

He leans in, his eyes reflecting the twisted satisfaction of winning. "Am I? Think about it, *Paulinah*. Do you honestly believe she'd choose a broken lesbo soldier over *me*?"

"You're a lying shit," I repeat, my voice more potent this time, despite the throbbing in my head. I will not let Bryant break me.

"Mak and I share something special. Something she never had with you."

Bryant's face contorts with a blend of anger and frustration. Clearly, he didn't expect me to stand up to him and his threats.

"Did you sleep with her?" His face turns bright red, and he faces me with his fists.

I stare him down without acknowledging anything but the deadly force I will use.

"You don't know her," he snaps. "She needs stability, her job here, not some wild, meaningless fling with a mentally unstable soldier."

"She might not pick me," I say, "But she's not going to pick an *asshole, like you*!"

His face darkens, his eyes narrow, locking onto mine, and the room crackles with the anger between us.

"You have no idea what I went through with her. How much *she* owes me," he hisses. "I put in the time and dealt with her backward *good Catholic girl beliefs of saving herself for her husband—Me!*"

My fingers clenched into fists beneath the hospital sheets. "Mak's capable of making her own choice. And if she chose you –*unlikely*–I'll respect that. But trying to force her and sayin' *she owes you*—that's not love, bro."

My door swings open, and a nurse comes to an abrupt halt, seeing us. She looks behind herself and at me as if she's entered the wrong room. Then she steps forward.

"Is everything alright here?" Her gaze shifts to Bryant. "What are you doing, Bryant?"

He straightens up, irritation coloring his tone. "Hey, Jessica. We're just having a conversation."

"You can't *be* here. Another respiratory therapist is assigned to him." She moves closer and points to the door for emphasis.

Instead of moving, he takes a menacing step closer to me, his body rigid.

As she takes another step forward, Jessica's demeanor indicates she can handle a threat and a fight if needed. "Bryant, I *understand* the situation. *Get. Out. Now.*"

He flushes. "You don't know anything!"

She moves closer and maneuvers between Bryant and me. Her tone remains stern, addressing him. "I understand you're a weasel trying to start a fight with someone in a hospital bed and trying to get my friend fired. And now, you want to manipulate her into marrying you. You're pathetic, and I'm sorry I ever introduced her to you. I'm calling a *Code Strong* if you aren't gone in one second."

She moves her hand over the sizable red code button on the wall, and he retreats, huffing.

"Jess, I'm the one who was dumped so don't treat me like the asshole!"

She grabs his arm and practically shoves him from the room. "Good decision. You don't want to lose your job today."

My eyes widen, and I stay wordless at Jessica's actions. *She's Mak's friend.*

Her added information makes the pieces fit. If Jessica knows he's manipulating Mak, then Mak knows.

I hope to God Mak isn't planning on marrying him!

"Where's Mak? Is she going to lose her job?" I ask, my gaze fixed on Mak's friend and my brain spinning as my heartbeat lowers.

"Mak's alright, and you're fine too. She stayed with you all night and went to the lounge to shower for her shift," she assures me.

She looks at the door and clears her throat. "I'm sorry. I wouldn't have left if I knew he was coming in to bother you."

I shrug. At least I figured out why she wore a wedding band, and I've met Mak's fiancé—*ex-fiancé.* "No prob."

"You have visitors, and I can't keep them out any longer." She goes to the door and waves.

My parents enter, and I wonder, *how much of our conversation did they overhear?*

My pop grins, "I'm glad to see you are well enough to give the staff hell."

My mom looks at me and asks, "Did you punch that guy? He looked like he was punched."

"Nah, just makin' friends. You know me," I say, relieved to see them.

The nurse interrupts, "Dr. Anderson mentioned you'll be discharged this afternoon, and your parents can drive you home." She nods and steps back, allowing my parents to surround me.

"Thanks," I mutter.

I wonder if I'll get the chance to see Mak before I leave.

Chapter 16

Mak

The St. Mary's Alaska Emergency Department lies quiet compared to the bustle of yesterday's shift. My fingers curl around my third cup of coffee, its warmth seeping into my palms. I appreciate the caffeine jolt for my sleepy brain and the warm cup on this frosty day.

"Have you talked to Paul yet?" Jessica asks. It's the same question she's asked every hour *as if* I could forget.

"I will. He's sleeping and I'm waiting for *the right time,*" I say.

She gives me a you-can't-fool-me look and then asks, "What about Bryant?"

She's relentless. I want to forget about my personal drama and focus on work. Too much is happening too quickly. I'm getting whiplash and need a moment to breathe.

She raises an eyebrow and asks, "Did you happen to see what was in the back of Bryant's truck?"

I pause at the change of topic, taking a sip. *Snow?*

"Jess, I'm done with him. I'm packing and moving *today,* even if it means giving him the house. I can't live under the same roof as him."

"Good." She nods. "You can stay with me. But I wanted to say he's got snow chains in his truck. I'm sure he's going to apologize and give them to you. He cares. Don't get me wrong, he's a transphobic jerk, but he's also Catholic." She shrugs, "You've been together a long time. You could give him one last chance. I mean, are you sure about Paul?"

I contemplated her words, my thoughts swirling like the snow outside the unit's windows. Before I answer her, footsteps approach, making me glance up.

Bryant, with a smirk, strolls past the desk. He must have overheard Jess.

Why did he volunteer to work a double and stay here with me? To win me back or to keep me away from Paul?

The truth hits me with a slap, making me gasp.

He didn't have time to buy me snow chains. Those are my missing chains—he used my spare keys and *removed my Jeep's winter chains before I left to go to the cabin. He sabotaged me!*

"Hey, Mak Attack. I'm really sorry about what I said to Pauline—"

I shoot up from my chair, the force causing it to crash to the floor. *Pauline? Really!*

Jess stands too, uncertain of the situation but standing at my side as my backup.

"How could you?" I direct my anger at him, and he raises his hands, stopping and looking at the growing audience.

I don't give him a chance to respond.

"You hate that Paul rescued me," I say, trembling, "Because you orchestrated the situation to leave me stranded in a blizzard. You took my chains! You tried to kill me!" My words are loud and fill the quiet unit.

"I would've come if you called. It's your fault. Why didn't you call and ask for help like a normal human being? Why would you choose a cabin in the woods for Christmas Eve, anyways? You should've chosen me and been home with me!" He matches my volume, his hands on his hips.

A heavy silence hangs in the air, and the nurses turn to me, waiting to see how I'll respond.

"We aren't together. You aren't my fiancé and you aren't my hero," I continue, "You could've killed me. Did you even think about that?"

The room is charged, and Bryant's face is an angry shade of crimson. "Spare me the sob story, Mak," he says. "You need someone to take care of you and hold your hand, or you make idiotic choices like driving in a blizzard or hooking up with *a freak* to make me jealous."

Jessica steps forward, her hand protectively on my arm, while the ER doctor moves to stand on the other side of me.

"Yes, I didn't choose you. I chose a freak because I'm different too—something you'd realize if you took the time to get to know me instead of using me as your arm candy," I retorted, my hand moving to my neck.

Bryant opens his mouth to respond, but I stop him.

"Paul isn't a freak," I say, my hands moving to my hips and stepping forward. "He is a hero who selflessly served our country and saved my life without hesitation. I'm tired of your toxic attitude and your twisted narrative. I should have stood up to you and told you the truth. I don't love you, and I couldn't because I'm queer! I love Paul."

The room holds its collective breath as the words echo. These words haven't been uttered in this hospital, let alone by a staff member, *ever*. The room's tension is as tight as Bryant's fist.

His eyes narrow. "You're blinded by your emotions and delusions, Mak," he spits out, his words hard. "You have a weakness for broken people, and I'm the best person in your life. You're going to regret this. You'll be sorry."

"I already am." I meet his eyes without flinching, taking a confident step forward. "We're done, and we've been done for a long time. I choose Paul because he is an amazing person who's lived through hell and deserves happiness. I won't stand by while you belittle him or me."

Bryant hisses, "You man-hating bitch. You need—"

"That's enough, Bryant," Jessica's voice cuts through the room like a scalpel. "Mak deserves respect. You aren't the person I thought you were. And being with you seems like it would've been hell. You are sabotaging Mak's career and her happiness. She doesn't need you!"

His face turns purple, and the veins in his forehead throb dangerously. With no one standing by him, he's outnumbered and outmatched at the nursing station.

Jessica holds my hand, and I keep my ground. *I can't believe I was going to marry him.*

"Is there a problem here?" Marianne approaches, flanked by the hospital's CEO and CFO. Her presence and voice command our attention.

Bryant's face pales, but he quickly attempts to regain his composure, brushing invisible lint from his scrubs. "No problem at all—a small personal disagreement."

She turns to me. "Doctor, would you care to share your opinion?"

I exhale, and with Jessica and the staff at my side, I explain, "A patient and I have a prior relationship. He's an incredible army veteran who's overcome the loss of his entire platoon. Bryant, my *ex*-fiance, is angry, jealous and causing a scene. He's been disrespectful to me and the patient. It's inappropriate, and I won't tolerate it."

The nods from Jessica and the rest of the staff serve as a powerful confirmation of their unwavering support for me in this difficult position and defending my queerness and Paul's differences.

The management team exchanged glances before addressing Bryant. Marianne asks, "And what about you, Bryant? Do you have anything to add?"

He shifts uncomfortably, his smile faltering. "It's a misunderstanding. No harm intended."

The atmosphere shifts, and silence envelops the nursing station.

"It's more than a misunderstanding when you lodge a complaint detailing Doctor Makayla's private, personal life to everyone at the hospital. And you shared a patient's personal information with the entire management team. Complaining to Human Resources about a doctor breaching the hospital's rules insinuates you are intending harm. And emailing every management member was a big mistake."

My heart pounds in my chest as I fix my gaze on Marianne, feeling a lump forming in my throat. The air has been sucked out of the room, leaving me drowning in my anxiety. The weight of her words hangs heavily in the air, threatening to shatter everything I've worked so hard for.

Marianne, my Catholic godmother, holds a place of utmost respect. Her unwavering faith and moral compass have helped me to become who I am today. *How can I face her disappointment? How can I bear the thought of being ostracized by someone whose love and acceptance mean the world to me?*

I stare at Marianne, my mouth dry. Jess told me Bryant was complaining, but I cannot believe he did this. He told them *everything*.

"Bryant, we don't fire people based on their sexual orientation or for past relationships with patients," Marianne states firmly.

Jessica glares at Bryant, and I shake my head in disbelief. *Was he hoping to get me fired? Or was he being spiteful for being rejected?*

Marianne continues, "We do, however, take privacy and workplace harassment seriously. Our staff must be professional and compassionate to *each other and our patients.*"

Bryant nods begrudgingly, his jaw still clenched.

Marianne turns to me. "Doctor, I'm sorry you've been dealing with this situation. And Mak, on a personal note, I am here for you and like your coworkers, I stand by you."

Bryant starts, "Seems a little unfair–"

She cuts him off and continues, "Considering your commitment to respectful and compassionate care, we are establishing a hospital committee to promote inclusivity and equality. We'd like to offer you the position of leading this committee."

My surprise must be visible since Jess nudges me. *Instead of being fired, the hospital is promoting me!*

The doctor beside me shakes my hand, and the nurses congratulate me.

"I'm honored and very surprised. Thank you," I respond sincerely.

Marianne nods and turns her attention back to Bryant. "I didn't expect to walk into this, but since we are here. . ." She looks to the other hospital management staff and continues, "Bryant, your actions directly violated our privacy laws and hospital policy. We are terminating your employment, effective immediately."

"You can't fire me!"

Marianne meets his stare. "Patient confidentiality is non-negotiable. And creating a hostile work environment is an automatic termination. Human Resources is expecting you," she says, dismissing him.

With that, Bryant storms away, leaving behind the crowded nursing station and me, a smile on my lips.

Marianne nods to me, and the management team disappears, leaving the nurses' station to return to normal activity.

Co-workers congratulate me on my new position, and I realize I'm more popular than I thought.

"Hey, I'll still see you for dinner tomorrow, right?" Marianne asks.

"Yes, of course," I say and hug her tightly.

She whispers, "You know your mom is proud of you no matter what. She always loved you and I love you, too, Sweetie."

A tear rolls down my cheek, and I nod, not trusting my voice. I'm becoming quite the emotional Psychiatrist.

Also, I'm relieved by not worrying about losing my job, Marianne, and hiding my feelings for Paul. I exhale with a wave of relief washing over me. *Finally, I can explore my new feelings, be myself, and embrace whatever the future holds.*

In that moment of liberation, I see an older couple standing by the door. As if on cue, Paul stands behind them, his gaze fixed on me and eyes wide.

Jessica spots them simultaneously and quickly says, "Sorry folks, I'm getting those discharge papers."

She turns to me and bites her lip, then mouths, *Oh. My. Gawd. I'm so sorry!*

I don't need to be an expert lip reader to understand her since I feel precisely the same way.

How much did they hear?

Chapter 17

Paul

Preparing to leave the hospital, flanked by my parents, with my pop still apologizing for not catching me when I fell, my attention is diverted not by the gusting Alaskan winter outside but by her - *Mak*.

She's standing at the nurses' station, her voice a melody of confidence and assertiveness, tugging at my heartstrings. The scene unfolds like a movie's dramatic climax: the underdog confronts the bully and wins.

I'm stunned witnessing her raw honesty, which makes me want to hug her and give Bryant the knuckle sandwich he deserves. She's brave and unflinching, making my turmoil pale in comparison.

My mom, holding the carnations, looks at my dad with a smile. My pop puts his hand on my shoulder and squeezes as we stand there, a silent trio, while Mak admits to loving me and confronts the man who was once her partner.

My parents remain quiet, and my mom's gaze shifts to me. "Looks like you've got a cheerleader, huh? Better not let this chance slip away."

"Get her number this time," my dad quips, propelling me forward.

Thanks, Pops! The movement makes Mak and my nurse turn, flushing when they spot us.

Jessica approaches, fidgeting and apologizing.

Mak rushes over, and her approach breaks the tense silence after the dramatic scene.

A nervous smile tugs at my lips, and I nod to Mak as she approaches us.

"I'm sorry about that. I'm Mak. It's lovely to meet you," she says, holding her hand to greet my parents.

My mom nods and takes her hand. "Sandy and Ben. We are Paul's parents. We heard all about you, and it's lovely to meet you, too."

My mom's hand doesn't let go of Mak's, and she says, "Doctor Mak, we can't thank you enough for what you've done. We haven't seen Paul this happy in a long time." She pauses and looks at my dad.

"We could have done without the emergency bringing us here, but it's worth it to meet you in person." My dad grins and nods.

"You are a true blessing to our family, and we're grateful," my mom continues, gushing.

"Hey, glad to see you," I say to Mak, biting my lip at my parent's over-the-top greeting.

Mak's flush creeps down her cheeks to color her neck as she looks at me. She turns to my mom. "Thank you for your kind words. It's an honor to help Paul and meet you." Mak moves her other hand to extract her hand from my mom.

Instead, Mak's hands circle my mom's hands, and she squeezes them, adding, "I am so sorry if you witnessed that inappropriate scene. Paul is an incredible person, and he deserves respect."

My mom looks at Mak sideways and holds her hands, squeezing back. "I wanted to extend our condolences for your parents. I saw they passed, and they were lovely people. I'm so sorry," my mom adds.

My dad nods.

I fill the uncomfortable silence by pulling Mak's Santa hat from my pocket, which dislodges the Saint George medallion, and it clatters on the hospital ER tiles.

"That medallion was from your father. He was my special friend, and I miss our long talks. We served together." my dad says to Mak as I bend to pick up the medallion.

Mak's eyes widen, and her plump lips part, a blend of surprise and disbelief in her eyes. Her hand touches the St. Michael medallion on her throat, under her scrubs.

My parents knew Mak's parents! My dad's war buddy is Mak's dad. What?

"I went to the cabin hoping to find his medallion. I remember it pressed against my cheek when he hugged me tight when I was younger. It was such a part of him and comfort to him and me." Her eyes glaze with a nostalgic, faraway stare, and tears collect in the corners.

My dad says, looking at me, "I gave it to Paul."

I stand, holding the silver chain and medallion. My mom gives me a nod, and I turn to Mak and reach out to hand her the chain.

The tears spill, and she bites her bottom lip, taking the medallion from my hand and holding it to her chest. Then her face softens, and a smile forms when she looks at my dad and then at me.

"Paul, can I really have this?"

Her whispered question is heartbreaking. "*Of course.* It's your father's. It's yours."

"I replaced the chain," my dad says.

I move my hand over hers and then place the necklace over her head so it lays against her chest and her heart.

Mak turns to me and puts her hand back over her St Michael's and St. George's medallions. She removes a chain, holds it in her hand, and looks at me.

I'm uncertain, but I nod as she reaches around my neck to secure the chain around my throat. The weight feels familiar, and I realize she's given me back her dad's medallion and kept hers. The weight is similar to wearing my dog tags again. I smile a thanks to her.

Then, with her gleaming, wet eyes, she explains, "I think Saint George can bring you peace, and my dad would've liked you to have it." Her warm breath tickles my ear and warms my insides.

I take a steadying breath, summoning courage. "Mak, I'd like to ask you for your phone number and a proper date."

Before Mak can answer, Jessica holds her hand, stopping the conversation. "No! Sorry to interrupt, but I need you to sign the discharge paperwork, Paul. We can't have a hospital committee head dating a patient. Let's make you *legally* available."

Mak laughs, and her laughter breaks the seriousness that enveloped us, making a cascade of chuckles escape me.

My mom nudges me, and my pop winks.

"Paperwork first," she says and steps back for Jessica to hand me the forms.

I chuckle as I swiftly sign the papers, and my hand shakes as I give the clipboard back to Jessica.

"Are they proper now?" my mom asks.

"Mom-" I start.

"Has Paul ever been proper?" my dad asks.

I smile at Mak and shake my head. "So, about the date ..."

"Yes. Let me give you my number so you don't have to have an emergency to see me," Mak says, her grin infectious and my parents laughing at her joke.

Spontaneous and unexpected applause erupts from the Emergency Department staff, catching me off guard, and my cheeks heat with embarrassment. *We are parent-approved and staff-approved.*

She graciously bows to the applause and jokes, "I'll sign autographs in the breakroom later. Now, go back to work and stop gossiping!"

As the applause subsides, I look at her, and the spark between us warms me. She is gorgeous, even in scrubs.

"I'm looking forward to your call and our date, Paul," she says, pressing her wet lips together, and her warm brown eyes melt me.

"Me too."

My parents laugh. "We all are!" They embrace Mak warmly, and I see tears in my dad's eyes.

"I should have caught Paul so he didn't hit his head," he says again.

"His head is hard, and he needed the excuse to see me," she responds and winks at me.

"How about we go out and warm up the car?" My mom nudges my dad, and they wave as they head into the snowy parking lot.

Without my parents and the hospital staff scattering, Mak and I stand together.

"You know," she whispers with a playful smile, "I still have bacon, bananas, and sourdough bread at the cabin."

I laugh, my heart light and free. "Elvis sandwich date?"

She grabs my hand. "A stupendous idea! I love it but *after* our date. I don't want to rush you into the commitment of bacon mixed with fruit too soon."

"But you already have," I laugh and hug her.

She melts into me. "I know. I've ruined you!" she whispers, her warm breath on my neck. "Um, and I still get to enjoy feeling the St. Christopher charm." She presses her soft breasts further onto me, our tender embrace intensifying as her warmth fills me.

"I'm on to you, Dr. Mak," I say with a smile, untangling from her arms before this embrace ruins me further.

"I'll let you walk the patient out," Jessica calls out, breaking us up, and shoos Mak and me to the door and out into the cold.

Jessica really missed her calling as a waitress—she interrupts at the *worst possible moments.*

Alaska isn't too unbearably cold when we step outside into the wind and snow. I have her warm hand in mine as we walk, fingers intertwined into the biting weather. The familiar sensation of Mak's touch makes my heart race in anticipation, the same feeling I had at our first touch.

There's an unthawing of the last icy layers around my heart.

Did I rescue her, or did she save me?

Epilogue: Mak

"It's here." I turn to Paul, handing him the envelope.

Paul brushes his hands on his flour-dusted apron from making biscuits and gravy for breakfast, his Alaska specialty with reindeer sausage. Since we moved to the cabin last year, his cooking skills have improved. My days are filled with remote hospital board work, online counseling, and organizing outdoor hikes with my patients for PTSD therapy.

"Thanks!" he says, taking the envelope from my hand.

We sit in front of the fire, and he slowly opens the envelope while I hold my breath. The paper emerges, and he unfolds it with a plastic card falling out. He picks up the card, and his eyes fill with emotion, then hands it to me.

It's *Paul Jacob's* new Alaska driver's license with his updated picture.

I whoop with joy. "It's official—I'm marrying Paul next year!" I give him a big hug, and we laugh together.

Apart from relocating my practice to the Caribou Hills and Paul moving into the cabin with me, the most significant change in our lives has been getting engaged and Paul's determination to be legally recognized as a man before our wedding. He's always known he's Paul, but his battle with depression had hindered him from taking this step. This license is the final confirmation, the acknowledgment of the man I love.

Seventeen months have passed since that fateful Christmas Eve winter when our paths converged. Our love blossomed like the wildflowers adorning the hills. We've grown closer, our hearts joining in the beautiful Caribou Hills.

Paul's resilience and strength warm my heart. He's confronted his demons and found solace in the camaraderie of fellow veterans during the therapeutic forest bathing hikes I manage for the group.

His determination inspires us all, a testament to the strength of the human spirit. Even though he prefers solitude and nature, he still joins me at hospital social functions and the local Caribou Hills Cabin Hoppers parties.

My work has evolved. I continue to run hospital committees, but I've set up my psychology practice from the comfort of our cabin. In the wilds of the Caribou Hills, I've found a unique way to help veterans on their path to healing.

I organize therapy hikes in the summer, and in the winter, we snowshoe. I invite the veterans to immerse themselves in the wilderness, as it played a significant role in my journey to self-acceptance and finding peace.

Surrounded by the tranquility of nature, the tundra becomes a safe space for them to share their stories and confront their trauma. The healing power of the tundra, the moose, and the blisters they get from carrying a rucksack is astounding. I'm honored to guide them on their path to recovery.

Paul hikes with us, and our love deepens with each passing day. Our cabin, once a refuge for our hearts, is now filled with the memories of a love that thrives despite adversity.

As we stand on our cabin's porch, gazing at the vast expanse of the Caribou Hills, gratitude fills my heart. My prayers are filled with gratitude for the love God brought me during a deadly blizzard, for Paul's strength on his healing journey, and for the breathtaking Alaskan wilderness.

Paul turns to me, his eyes shining with love and a hint of mischief. "You know, Mak, I'm so lucky to have you in my life."

I grin, my heart overflowing with love. "And I can't imagine my life without you, Paul. You've warmed my cold feet on the worst winter nights."

Paul laughs. "Is that going to be in your wedding vows? Why won't you wear wool socks? Why must you test our love every night?"

I laugh. "I can't sleep in socks, silly. Besides, you are the one who likes to sleep without any layers between us."

Paul shakes his head and pulls me close. Our lips meet in a tender kiss, sealing our love amidst the beauty of Alaska. The winds whisper their blessings as the Caribou Hills bear witness to our ever-evolving love story.

If you loved Mak & Paul's sapphic adventure, then you'll love Baby and Poppy in *Wilderness Rescue: Winning Love.*
CHECK IT OUT HERE.

Discover the books in the *Wilderness Rescue* series.
CHECK IT OUT HERE.
Keep reading to enjoy the next book.

Wilderness Rescue: Winning Love
Chapter 1:

Win·ning

Dictionary - Definitions from Oxford Languages

/ˈwiniNG/

Adjective

1. gaining, resulting in, or relating to victory in a contest or competition. *a winning streak*

   ○ Similar: victorious, successful, conquering, triumphant, unbeaten, first, top

2. attractive; endearing. *a winning smile*

   ○ Similar: engaging, persuasive, charming, appealing, sweet, cute, pretty, attractive, lovely, captivating, enchanting, adorbs

/ˈwiniNG/

Noun

1. money won, especially by gambling. *He went to collect his winnings.*

   ○ Similar: prize(s), money, gains, spoils, booty

Shplop!

My cold, wet bra falls on my face from the makeshift clothing line stretched across the narrow room, and my bunk jumps under me in an off-kilter way.

What in the unbuttered sourdough muffin is going on?!

Groggy and disorientated, my eyes open to darkness, the room tilting and water rushing in. I flail in the dark, panic surging through my veins as I roll, scrambling out of my bunk, and open the hatch into the dark hallway.

Chaos erupts as people rush past, shouting and shoving into the tiny space. My heart pounds, and my mind races as I fight against the crowd in the narrow hallway, trying to get up onto the ship's deck.

It's the Titanic! I'm in a death trap. I will drown stuck inside or die freezing in the arctic waters!

I must escape! My mind relives the movie scene with people falling off the rails into the gray, icy water—*OMG, why do I always default to the worst-case scenario?*

I see her, my Leonardo DiCaprio. She's a whirlwind of color and energy amidst the chaos–*Poppy*. My mind slows to take in the scene of Poppy wearing her comfy, brightly colored workout gear and hiking boots. Her caramel, sun-kissed skin, shiny black hair, and athletic physique make it impossible to mistake her for another crew member. Like me, she's an Alaskan indigenous woman. And she is also my secret summer crush.

"Come on, *Baby!*" Poppy calls out, her voice calm amid the panic. She grabs my hand and pulls me to the emergency exit.

I grasp her, my lifeline, as I stumble along to safety.

"It's Bailey," I whisper breathlessly and tighten my grip, securing my connection to her hand. Unlike Leo's character, dramatically releasing Kate, *I'm not letting go!*

Weeks ago, I got the courage to introduce myself to her, the most gorgeous crew member at the ship's Bon Voyage Mixer. I'm shy and barely talk to other crew members, and no one knew my name to introduce us, so I bravely approached her and introduced myself. But with the loud music, she misheard me and has called me "Baby" ever since.

I meant to correct her, but how she says *Baby* melts my heart, like drinking a hot dark mocha on a cold winter night. Since I never corrected her, and she's socially assertive, she *helpfully* introduced me to the rest of the crew. For weeks, I've been answering to the name *Baby*.

I'm changing my name. That's the obvious, least-embarrassing solution.

Poppy doesn't hear me. She kicks her hiking boot into a cabin door, whooping when it opens with a loud pop. Her vibrant brown eyes sparkle with determination, and her free-spirited laugh is out of place in this dire situation but entirely predictable for her. She propels people to the upper deck.

"Keep moving, Hector!" She shouts back to the dishwasher, whom I've never talked to before, let alone learned his name.

I bite my bottom lip—Correcting my name doesn't matter. Plus, I don't want to slow her—*us*—down, even though I'd like to go back and get my shoes and my phone. We reach the upper deck hatch together as icy water surges into the hallway, and I gasp as the cold water hits my bare legs.

Crack, a sharp noise hangs in the air as Poppy kicks another hatch open. Then, I am weightless for seconds when we plunge off the rails into the frigid waters of Kachemak Bay.

The shock of the cold water steals my breath. I cling to Poppy, who effortlessly treads water and keeps us afloat. Easy for her—she's a triathlete. I know because I'm stalking—I mean, *following*—her on social media, and sometimes I *accidentally* bump into her when she's working out on deck.

Together—*mostly her pulling us through the water*—we fight against the Arctic current, swimming toward the nearby rocky shoreline.

Thank God it's only two hundred meters away! As I tread the frigid water, a shiver races down my spine, back up my spine, and into my skull, causing my teeth to chatter incessantly. The icy ocean seeps through my pajamas and goosebumps my skin, numbing my feet and moving up my legs. My muscles tense in response to the biting cold, and tiny pins and needles dance through my body.

Is it possible to die of hypothermia while swimming to the nearby beach?

I'm still clinging to her with my death grip, and my toes probably have fallen off my feet since I no longer feel them.

I glance at the impressive Grewingk Glacier. We dropped our cruise guest off yesterday, and it's invisible in the dim morning. The tourists marveled at seeing the "real Alaska" and are tucked cozily at the Driftwood Lodge, where we were supposed to pick them up tonight in this bay overlooking Seldovia. The village of Seldovia is cast in a warm golden glow, nestled in the mountains and bordered by glaciers and the icy water I'm swimming in. The picturesque village's beauty starkly contrasts with the mess unfolding in the bay as the crew yells and the ship sinks.

My feet touch the rocks under the water, I gasp for breath, and I stumble with Poppy going the last five meters. *Perhaps I was overreacting a little, comparing this to the Titanic.*

As we reach the rocky shore, Poppy grins at me. "Baby, we made it, and the sun's coming up. Let's count this as our daily workout!" Then she laughs in pure relief, and I respond with a wordless smile.

I'm not dead! And Poppy holds me up as we crawl onto the rocky beach. If she releases me, my rubber legs will *for sure* give out. I also missed another opportunity to correct her.

It's actually Bailey—my enchanting mermaid—but you can call me Babycakes.

I'll tell her the first part when it's not an emergency. The second part, I'm keeping to myself!

As we stand here shivering and soaked, I'm in my sleepwear: a tank top and shorts. She's wearing her soaked heavy layers, a swimsuit, t-shirt, jeans, and hiking boots that didn't seem to slow her down during our swim.

Instead of being out of breath, she's exhilarated, and I can't deny the fluttering in my chest when she looks at me with her endless brown eyes and long raven hair fanned over her chest. Her vibrant spirit radiates warmth and strength despite our current situation.

She stops laughing to help pull up our other crew, crawling up the beach to join us.

"Look, it's the Titanic," a crew member points.

The colossal cruise ship, once a symbol of luxury and Arctic exploration, is listing at a dangerous angle. It defies logic, its form tilting as if the laws of physics are contorting under the weight of the calamity. I expect it to roll, but the ship dips and bobs before sinking into the bay like a killer whale, appearing and disappearing silently.

"That's... our belongings and our home!" My voice is calm, and the others' hysterical laughing evaporates. "How are we supposed to get paid?" Then I realize how selfish I sound and look at my feet, embarrassed. Of course, we lost our belongings, summer employment, and income, but we are alive and on the beach.

Poppy doesn't say anything about my comments. She meets my eyes, and her eyes mirror my disbelief. "Our summer jobs... They're gone, for sure. And there's no way we are getting our stuff.

"Reality punches me in the stomach, and I lean over dry heaving. *Thankfully, my stomach is pre-breakfast empty.* All my dreams of making enough money to fund my grad school tuition vanished just like our ship.

"We can't just stand here." Her voice refocuses me, and she helps me stand up from my failed vomiting. "We need to help. There are still people in the water. They could freeze before help comes."

As much as I admire her courage, swimming to the sinking ship is absurd. We are lucky not to be dead of hypothermia. "Poppy, no! You can't swim back out there. It's too dangerous."

Her eyes look at where the ship disappeared, and she looks through me and says, "I have to do something. I'm a strong swimmer. I can help."

"Are you out of your mind?" I say, my words cracking with panic. *If she swims out there, she's not returning*.

"You'll freeze out there, and what can you do even if you reach people? We need to find someone with a radio to call for help."

Another person, not a crew member, on the beach overhears and says, "There's no signal here. There's never a cell reception in Seldovia. We don't have any towers."

Panic churns in my stomach as the truth hits me—we're stranded, cut off from the world, unable to reach out for help, and stuck on this beach among strangers with only the wet, cold clothing on our backs.

Polly puts her arm around me, and we look back to the water.

"Damn it!" I shake my head.

Poppy isn't alone in wondering what to do now. I notice the movement of locals coming onto the beach to see the activity in the bay.

A person wraps a heavy blanket around my shoulders, and before I can say thank you, the person moves on to hand a blanket to the next shivering crew member.

"Walk up there, and the volunteer firefighters can help you." A man points up the sloped beach, directing everyone to walk up the hill to town for help.

I don't want to swim out to our coworkers, but walking away feels like selfishly abandoning the crew stuck in the water and swimming to shore. We can only stand on the beach and shout for them to keep swimming.

Poppy grins, and her face lights up, pointing to the fishing boats chugging their way to rescue people. "See, Baby, the whole village is comin' to the rescue! Alaskans are always ready to lend a hand!"

I exhale and rub my hands together for warmth. My shoulders slump, and I bite my lip, kicking at a rock. "What are we supposed to do, then? Just stand here?"

"Don't worry. We'll figure it out!" Poppy puts her arm back over my shoulder, and we huddle on the beach watching.

What should we do about our situation?

Seldovia is an isolated little community that is not connected to the mainland except by boat. I can't drive, fly, or take a train home. I can't leave by a boat ferry with the bay and docks blocked. Worse, I have no money, phone, or family, and my parents don't expect to hear from me for weeks. They won't even realize I need help.

At least I don't need to reason with her not to dive back into the frigid water.

A sudden burst of commotion breaks through the gloom. A distant roar of engines grows steadily louder. A Coast Guard vessel emerges on the horizon, slicing through the bay.

I say, trembling slightly, "Thank goodness, the Coast Guard's here!"

A ripple of excitement courses through the crowd as the vessel draws closer. It's a majestic sight. Her hand finds mine, and we squeeze each other's fingers.

My hands are warm in hers and wrapped in the wool blanket.

The Coast Guard crew springs into action, deploying their rescue boats and reaching the shipwreck survivors still clinging to debris in the frigid water. Their efficiency and determination are astonishing.

We watch in awe as they pull our drenched crew members to safety. It's a moment of triumph and allows us to relax. Thank goodness Poppy won't be diving back into the ocean again.

She must have read my thoughts. "You know the water isn't that cold here. I take a thirty-minute swim in it on my training days."

"But you swim knowing a warm shower and coffee await you. Also, you're amazing," I say. "The rest of us aren't mermaids. We're more like sloths."

She shrugs her agreement, and we watch as the Coast Guard safely rescues the last crew member. A collective sigh washes over the beach, and we share smiles and high-fives. *We may have lost everything, but we've survived.*

Poppy and I smile, moving our fingers to lace together. The warmth of the blankets and coats chase away the beach's chilly winds. The wind doesn't seem too bad, and the cheering around us almost makes me forget that my toes are numb and we're stranded.

Oh. My. God. We are stranded here with no place to stay and no money!

A bystander's grim assessment reaches my ears, "Somebody must've messed up big time with those repairs. That ship went down fast.

"There's a grumbling agreement and relief that we didn't have any guests on board, and there doesn't appear to be any crew missing. The boat's emergency was unexpected, but we followed our training, and everyone made it out.

It's too bad the navigation crew and Captain are on the Coast Guard vessel–I'd like to give them a piece of my mind. *Who sinks a ship in calm waters near a dock?*

The weight of the situation bears down on me, suffocating my happiness at being so close to my crush and being alive.

Another voice jests, "Well, folks, this is Alaska's way of ending the tourist season. Go get coffee at the Visitor's Center or Fire Station. It's on the house!"

"Frank, the coffee is free there, and no one is going to charge them, anyways," a woman, who is probably Frank's wife, says, poking him.

A reluctant chuckle escapes my lips at the absurdity. The irony of the joke hits home—tourists are nowhere in sight, and our summer is over with our summer employment sinking along with the ship.

The other wet crew members wander up the hill into town with the helpful villagers. Poppy and I, still in a state of disbelief, stay behind and sit huddled together near the rocky shoreline, watching the sun rising and the bay filling with boats and strange equipment. The aftermath of the shipwreck leaves an air of uncertainty hanging over us, and sitting together in silence is comforting.

A figure stumbles towards us as if on cue, his uneven gait revealing his inebriated state. The smell of alcohol wafts from him, fouling the salt-laden breeze. He holds his breakfast beer loosely, the contents sloshing as he nears.

"Hey there, ladiesss," he slurs, his gaze shifting between us.

Poppy's arm tenses under my hand, her discomfort palpable. Linking my arm with hers, I send her a reassuring glance. We are together here."Hey," I reply cautiously. My voice's hesitancy matches the unsettling feeling in my gut.

The man's gaze lingers on Poppy, his eyes tracing her wet form in a way that makes my skin crawl. "You two are far from home, aren't ya?" he muses.

Her grip on my arm tightens, her instincts aligning with my own. "We're here for work," she replies.

He chuckles. "Work, huh? Well, the bay's gonna be closed until the Coast Guard's finnish, and I've got a boat. I'll take yous back to Homer, no skin off my nose, any."

His proposition and leering casts an ominous shadow over the already scary situation. The hairs on my neck prickle as I exchange a glance with Poppy.

Poppy stands. "No thanks."

"We're okay," I add, my voice steady and my gut churning.

The man steps closer. "Come on now, sweethearts," he slurs. "You don't need to be alone. I can help yous out."

My grip on her arm tightens, and I dust the sand off my legs, leaving. With a forced smile, I nod toward the village. "We appreciate the offer, but we'll stick around here for a while. Enjoy your walk."

As we step away from his lingering gaze, the unease and the cold make me shiver. Poppy and I quickly walk opposite him, away from town and the almost empty beach. His threatening interaction ruins our excitement of being alive, and I'm tense and cold on a deserted beach.

My breath hitches, and my heart clenches, making me taste acid.

We're trapped in the wilderness—a place without rules, where danger lurks.

I link arms with Poppy, and she confidently walks, slowly navigating the unfamiliar wilderness with me since I'm barefoot with numb toes.

As we walk away, the ocean drowns out any sound of the man.

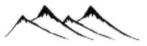

Chapter 2: Poppy's Winning Scheme

Strolling on the rugged shore, we're quiet, lost in our thoughts as the sun rises.

Baby's anxious vibe is weighing her down–even I feel it. She's frowning at the rocky ground instead of savoring the pink and orange reflecting across the ocean. She chews on her lips, hiding her quirky smile.

I *must* lift her spirits. After all, optimism is my specialty, and choosing hope makes every situation bearable. *We are alive, on a beach with a beautiful sunrise—things could be much worse!*

"Poppy, what are we going to do?" Baby asks as we roam on the rugged shore, the morning stretching to afternoon.

I nudge her playfully. "Don't worry, Baby. Everything's gonna work out. Worrying won't change or help us. The sun is out, we have each other, and we'll figure it out."

My reassuring words are to lift her spirits and *mine*. We *are* in a sticky situation, stranded in this picturesque but unfamiliar part of Alaska. Without money or our phones, it's a little different than a usual hiccup when I travel.

The unknown and traveling to new places don't bother me because I'm training to be an elite triathlete. I travel all over to enter competitions, and I'm always in a strange place with no friends or family. Having the ship sink and being stranded is unexpected, and my competitive mind races to figure out how to win.

If only this were a test of strength or endurance, I know I'd be fine. I swim miles in the Arctic Ocean, trail run over mountains, and bike from Alaska to Canada, but our situation is vastly more complicated.

We need somewhere to sleep tonight and something to eat, then a way back home. *I won't even think about our lost jobs and our paychecks.*

"We could ask the locals for help," Baby suggests, her gaze flickering toward a small group of fishermen.

"The locals—like the guy offering us a ride?"

Baby bends down to pick a flat stone and skims it across the water. 1-2-3 skips. "Was it just me, or did he seem a little. . . creepy?"

I chuckle.

"Oh yeah–definitely a *Creeper*. I doubt he even has a boat."

She looks out over the peaceful water. "But what about our summer work? Do you think we are even going to get paid for the summer cruise season now?"

I pick up the perfect flat round stone, toss it, and it skips eight times. Smiling, I pat her back. "We'll figure it out. Maybe we can find odd jobs around town or something. And hey, worst-case scenario, we could always work the *slime line* at the salmon cannery."

She wrinkles her nose at the thought of standing all day, cleaning the guts out of fish. The slime line is the lowest of the low of jobs in Alaska.

"I can't believe you'd even suggest that."

I wink and give her a grin. "Desperate times, my friend. But who knows, maybe we'll get lucky and stumble upon a pile of gold nuggets."

As if the gods heard my unasked prayer, there's a commotion ahead around the bend in the next little bay. A flurry of activity, cameras, and people scurrying around the beach grab our attention.

A surge of curiosity motivates me, and I gently grasp her arm, encouraging her to move closer. Destiny is providing, and I *refuse* to disregard an opportunity placed directly in our path.

"What in the world is happening over there?" Baby asks.

"Let's check it out," I say.

Amidst the whirlwind of activity, no one notices us wandering among the group despite our damp, odd appearance. We blend into the chaotic mix of people too engrossed in their own world to pay us any mind. Half of them are busy admiring their reflections on their phones, applying beauty products, while the others are pre-occupied with their high-tech equipment. It's as if we are invisible in this sea of trendy, technology-obsessed individuals.

Dressed in jeans and shrouded in a weathered blanket, I wander into the fashionably dressed crowd.

I wish I could stealthily acquire one of their shiny, brand-new puffer jackets and a sturdy pair of boots for Baby. She needs the extra warmth, and this touristy bunch wouldn't notice the absence of their photo props, the bright, name-brand cold-weather gear. Likely, they'll never wear it again after their obligatory vacation selfies for social media attention.

"I *must* get a selfie with a penguin," a blonde with two-inch manicured nails whines to another blondie, who responds by ignoring her and holding her phone up, trying to get unavailable cell reception.

Penguins are in Antarctica, not Alaska. This group's tour guide needs to educate these tourists seriously.

"When is the Director's ferry dropping him?" a young guy in the group, hunched over cameras, yells to another who is just as young but holding a clipboard, denoting his authority.

Mr. Clipboard, a Californian-cool guy with shades on despite the sun barely peeking through the clouds, scans the horizon and checks his watch. "He should be here any minute, guys. Let's shoot some nice opening shots and background shots. Go ahead and get started.

"The guys exchange uncertain glances and shoulder shrugs as they set up to film the bay.

This group is clueless about the chaos just past their rocky beach; to be fair, they don't have a direct view of the bay around the corner. Even so, if one of them glanced further than the extent of their camera frames, they'd notice the boats rushing into the bay.

"Did you hear that guy?" Baby says, pointing to a huddle of men with expensive equipment filming the panoramic view of the ocean, mountains, and rocky beach.

"I was distracted by the women looking for penguins." I point to the group of stunningly beautiful women shivering, their sun-kissed blonde hair blown by the wind. They huddle together, forming a circle of golden-haired figures with rosy cheeks clad in stylish, albeit impractical, high-end fashion attire. Their designer parkas, heeled boots, and cashmere scarves do little to ward off the breeze.

Baby giggles with me. She says, "I overheard a snippet of conversation. They are filming and it's their first day."

Well, that explains the commotion and the odd assortment of people.

"It's got to be a reality show. But why out here on a remote beach?" I ask aloud.

She shrugs, and we notice a makeshift camp in the woods, complete with cameras, lights, and chairs lined up, like a movie set for some glamorous camping scene.

The film crew left a big rack of tourist winter gear: overly warm skiing puffer jackets, fleece layers, useless Ugg boots, and hats announcing brand names.

It looks like the wardrobe crew left some goodies for us. I'm sure they wouldn't miss a few items.

Who are these filming tourists? I glance at the white-skinned, blonde-haired bunch, shivering in the warm weather.

An Alaskan visit from the Housewives of California? American Idol tryouts in a unique location?

"Should we ask them what they're doing? They look like they need Alaskan guides," she adds thoughtfully.

"We definitely know the area better than them. I spy the breakfast spread. Let's check that out first." I hook Baby's arm, and we meander from the two groups to tables and RVs in the woods behind the beach.

I can't shake the feeling this is an opportunity as we venture closer. Our stomachs rumble, and we enjoy the abandoned table spread with muffins, fruit, and coffee. *I doubt most of these blondies even eat carbs.*

I snag a muffin and pass one to Baby. "Well, look at us, scavengers in the wild. At least we won't starve."

She takes a bite of the blueberry muffin. "Desperate times call for desperate measures," she says, more determined than anxious.

Baby's cute when she gets motivated! I nudge her and give her a wink.

As we nibble on our impromptu meal and sneak on some fleece ski vests, I unfold a paper, reading:

!!!FOR THE DIRECTOR'S EYES ONLY!!!
  The Smoking Hot, Arctic Bachelor
Description: Get ready for the ultimate Alaskan adventure as ten fear-less, beautiful bachelorettes battle it out to win the heart of our very own Arctic bachelor, BURLY! Join us as we take you on a wild ride through the untamed wilderness, where love, passion, and survival skills are put to the test. With Alaskan challenges and steamy, pas-sionate romance, this is one ruggedly unique dating show.
Bachelorette Challenges:
1. "Iceberg Surfing": Contestants must ride icebergs in frigid waters

while attempting to stay balanced. The last one standing wins. Bikinis or formal dresses are preferred for Bachelorettes.

2. *"Polar Plunge Date": Bachelorettes go on a date in sub-zero temperatures, dressed in skimpy bathing suits, and must take a dip in an ice-cold Arctic ocean to win time with the Bachelor.*

3. *"Snow Sculpting Showdown": Contestants create intricate snow sculptures using only their hands and essential tools. The most creative sculpture wins.*

4. *"Salmon Wrestling": Bachelorettes will fish, catching and wrestling live salmon with their bare hands in a freezing river alongside grizzly bears fishing.*

5. *"Blizzard Blindfold Challenge": Contestants are blindfolded and dropped during a snowstorm. They must find their way back to camp without any assistance.*

6. *"Extreme Northern Lights Dance": Bachelorettes compete in a dance-off under the Northern Lights, where they incorporate their best Arctic dance moves into their sexy routines.*

7. *"Eskimo Fashion Show": Contestants have to create stylish outfits from materials found in the Arctic, such as wild seal fur and icicles, and then strut their stuff on an icy runway.*

8. *"Avalanche Escape": Bachelorettes are placed in a simulated avalanche scenario and must work together to escape before the "snow" engulfs them.*

9. *"Arctic Cooking Challenge": Contestants must cook a gourmet meal using only ingredients they can scavenge from the wilderness: aprons and chef hats per Costume Designer.*

These challenges will test the Bachelorettes' beauty, commitment, and adaptability while providing plenty of entertaining, authentic Alaskan moments for the viewers. Adapt challenges to the environment and materials available—winner (s) to be chosen by the Director or Arctic Bachelor, Burly.

Timeline:

*Two weeks of heart-pounding Arctic challenges, romantic rendezvous,
and unexpected twists. Who will withstand the elements and capture
the heart of our Northern Arctic Bachelor?*
Winner Payout:
*Our lucky lady will win the chance at true love with our Arctic Wilder-
ness Bachelor and walk away with the generous cash prize of $50,000!
(Winner TBA by the Director)!!!EMPHASIZE: THE INTENSE
DRAMA, SULTRY ROMANCE, AND UNEXPECTED VIC-
TOR!!!*

"Are they *for real*?" she asks, looking over my shoulder. "This is ridiculous!"

I shake my head, trying to talk over my bubbling laugh. "Did you read the *challenges* list? It's like they think Alaska is a big winter wonderland, all year!"

She rolls her eyes and laughs. "Seriously, *iceberg surfing* and *snow sculpting* in the middle of summer? They clearly did no research before coming here."

I can't stop laughing, and she quiets me by pulling the blanket over our heads before we draw attention.

"And don't even get me started on the *Polar Plunge Date*. We just swam in the bay, it's not something I see any of those women doing for fun!" she adds.

I look at the woefully unprepared contestants. Seriously, I can't imagine any of those stylish models fishing, hiking, and *definitely not iceberg surfing!*

I would watch a show that teaches them to ice fish and build a makeshift shelter. It would be hilarious!

"Yep, those poor ladies have no clue what they've gotten into. It's too bad because I could win this against them."

She raises an eyebrow. "You're not seriously considering entering and winning an Arctic reality show, are you?"

I pause. *I wasn't—until she mentioned it.* "Oh, I am. And *we* are entering! We'll use our Alaskan knowledge and teamwork to outshine these other bachelorettes. Plus, it's $50,000! That's a fortune, more than winning first place at an international triathlon. You need this money for grad school and I need it to start my triathlete career. We'll split it."

"You're crazy, Poppy."

I look at her and lift my eyebrow, giving her my most conspiring look with a grin.

She laughs and then looks at the huddle of princesses. Shrugging, she says, "I guess, I can't end summer without my grad school money—I'm in!"

I smile and clap. "Yes! Let's show them what *real* Alaskan women are made of."

We have a plan. Winning this gameshow is *way more* money than we would've made working on the cruise ship.

She smiles, scrunching her nose.

I grab the papers off the table, scribble her name under "contestant," and hand it to her. "That's the spirit! Now, let's fill out these applications and join our competitors."

Before we iron out our plan, the clipboard manager waves at us. "You two, over here!"

We look at each other and nod, walking over to him. He's tired, and a name tag identifies him as Conner, the "Producer."

Conner's eyes flick between us, his gaze lingering on Baby for a moment longer. "You ladies are here for the show, right?"

"Of course!" I say, giving him my dazzling smile.

He smiles back. "Great! I knew you two were our local contestants. Finish your forms so we can head to camp. We are starting without the Director and Host, but at least we have all ten contestants."

I whisper to Baby, "It's time for *full Alaskan mode*, okay?"

Entertaining tourists on the cruise sometimes means stretching the truth about being Alaskan, like how we live in igloos and travel by dog sled. The crew jokes that this is *full Alaskan mode*. Tourists love it, and we get great tips when we tell them about our fictitious wild Alaskan lives.

She nods and flips through the application, which looks more like a dating application than a work form. I scribble, filling in the blanks with my weight and hobbies. I wink at Baby. "Guess who's an iceberg yoga instructor among the whales on Glacier Bay?"

With a giggle and her quirky smile back, she responds, "Really? I took you for an Arctic canoe guide who dreams of settling down on an Alaskan homestead making rose hip jam for your twenty children."

Our laughter catches the attention of Conner. "Glad to hear laughing. The other contestants are complaining about the cold weather."

He's distracted by an Alaskan beaver fur hat on a crew member. "Can we get that hat in faux fur? Fur is so 2000—No fur on the set!"

As we hurriedly finish filling out the sheets, I glance at the women gathering in camp. They're striking, each one more attractive than the last. The realization hits me—we're about to compete against some seriously stunning women.

I look at my filthy clothes. *I hope this Alaskan guy is looking for more than a blonde with boobs.*

Baby's motivated and snatches my sheet, handing it to Conner so we can join the others in front of the yurts.

Walking away, I overhear Conner talking to a crew member. "Every dating reality show needs an ugly girl and an underdog– you know, for the viewers to root for."

Baby hears, too. She frowns and turns to me. "Am I the ugly one or the underdog?"

"Neither! It doesn't matter what he thinks, remember. We'll charm the Alaskan guy, Burly, and the Director to win."

She nods and smiles, her lips free from biting them with worry.

I'm happy her anxiety is gone, and she's back to her bubbly self. She's shy, but underneath, I see the effervescent, intelligent person she is.

I look around at the shivering, unhappy, beauty-pageant women.

"Baby, you're going to be the winner!"

Continue reading Baby's heartwarming story in *Wilderness Rescue:* *Winning Love.*
CHECK IT OUT HERE.
Join us to discover your next favorite story at <u>www.Harmon yNoble.com</u> & sign up to receive the e-newsletter for exclusive news and giveaways.
CHECK IT OUT HERE.

Coming Next

WILDERNESS RESCUE: WINNING LOVE

Lights, camera, complication: Two coworkers team up to face off in Alaska's ultimate reality dating show, but when the game is love, who's really keeping score?

Get ready to be swept away by a sizzling romance with coworkers, Poppy, a free-spirited situational-sexual athlete, and Baby, a no-nonsense grad student, as they join a high-stakes Alaska reality dating show. With a bold plan of winning at all costs, leading both contestants to a heart-pounding competition where love becomes the ultimate prize!

Poppy and Baby find themselves stranded in isolated Seldovia, Alaska, with no work, shelter, or money when their cruise boat jobs sink. Desperate, they stumble upon an absurd reality show: "The Smoking-Hot, Arctic Bachelor." With Alaskan savvy and their new-found partnership, they hatch a plan to win the hefty cash prize and the heart of the hunky Arctic Bachelor.

As Poppy and Baby navigate the reality show's challenges, their alliance blossoms into something more. When faced with the choice between love and the prize, they deviate from the script, turning the romantic game show into an unforgettable spectacle of true love.

Author's Note: Join the adventure in the sapphic romance series, Wilderness Rescue.

Experience the forced proximity, small-town love story Baby and Poppy in *Wilderness Rescue: Winning Love.*

CHECK IT OUT HERE.

Discover your next favorite story at www.HarmonyNoble.com.

OTHER TITLES BY HARMONY NOBLE
For the most up-to-date list visit Harmony's website at
www.HarmonyNoble.com.

Aurora's Wilderness Love:

Hot Girl Summer Love

Wilderness Rescue Sapphic Romance Series:

Crashing Into Love
Unthaw My Heart
Winning Love
Stormy Hearts
Scoring Love
Flooded Hearts
Healing Hearts
Tides of Love
Iditarod Love

Coffeehouse Romance Series:

Love, Joy & Lattes (Joy's Story)
Test Driving a Millionaire (Tara's Story)
Shattering Crystal a Bully Romance (Crystal's Story)
Choosing Love, Namaste (Meaghan's Story)
The Wrong Bride for Christmas (Monica's Story)

Coffeehouse Romance Short Stories:

Joy's 4th of July Holidate
Tara's Valentine Holidate
Crystal's Easter Holidate
Meaghan's New Year Holidate
Monica's Halloween Holidate
My Accidental Christmas Fiancé
Joy's Coffeehouse Romance

UNLOCK YOUR GIFT

Happy Reading & EMBRACE TRUE LOVE!

Snag the latest swoon-worthy reads and stay tuned for upcoming stories at www.HarmonyNoble.com.

mak's
ELVIS Sandwich

 2 servings    20 minutes

*Experience the King of Flavors with Our
Elvis-Inspired Sandwich: Peanut Butter,
Honey, Banana, & Bacon –
a Rock 'n' Roll Delight for Your Mouth!*

INGREDIENTS

- 4 MEDIUM SLICES OF SOURDOUGH **BREAD**
- 4-6 SLICES OF **AMERICAN BACON**
- 4 TBSP **PEANUT BUTTER**
- 2 **BANANAS**, SLICED INTO SMALL CHUNKS
- HONEY DRIZZLE

DIRECTIONS

1. Add bacon to a large non-stick pan & cook over medium heat until crispy. Remove bacon, leaving the fat in the pan.
2. Lightly butter one side of each slice of bread. Flip them over so they're butter-side-down. Spread peanut butter over all four slices, then top two of them with banana then bacon. Drizzle honey over the bananas . Put sandwiches together with butter facing outside.
3. Place sandwiches in pan. Fry each sides over medium heat until golden, peanut butter may start oozing.
4. Cut in halves & serve up this sweet, savory, gooey delight.
5. Enjoy!

About Author – Harmony Noble

Meet the unstoppable twins from the rugged wilds of Alaska—Harmony & Melody, the duo of "Author Harmony Noble." Fueled by endless lattes, their character-driven stories brim with authenticity, humor, and heart—featuring Alaskan grit, journeys of self-discovery, and swoon-worthy happily-ever-afters.

When they're not crafting adventure romances, the twins can be found hiking trails with breathtaking views, enjoying charming coffee shops, or exploring new cultures and destinations worldwide.

**Join the e-newsletter for exclusive content and giveaways at
website: https://harmonynoble.com**
Email: TrueLoveWriters@gmail.com
Instagram/Facebook/TikTok: @truelovewriters

Flooded Hearts

Harmony Noble

SCAN FOR GIFT

TrueLoveWriters

**Thank you for choosing this book
by Harmony Noble. We hope the story
brought you as much joy reading it
as we had in creating it!**

We'd love to hear from you! Feel free to reach out via email at True LoveWriters@gmail.com, and don't forget to follow us on <u>Instagram</u>, <u>Facebook</u>, <u>TikTok</u> at @truelovewriters for the latest updates and behind-the-scenes fun.

Get access to exclusive offers, bonus content, new release updates, and recommendations for more great reads. Sign up for our e-newsletter at HarmonyNoble.com.

To the Ex-Husbands, who probably won't open this,

Ah, the unsung heroes of my past.
Gratitude is in order—
for the lessons that were taught,
and taught,
and taught,
and retaught!
May the four of you have romance
with bedmates who meet your requirements
of toasty tootsies.
After all, warm feet are the real key
to everlasting love, right?

From the woman with perpetually chilly feet and a warm heart always
willing to fall in love.

Flooded Hearts

Harmony Noble

SCAN FOR GIFT

TrueLoveWriters

Chapter 1

Lucy

My phone's blaring emergency alert shatters my few hours of relaxation during the serene Alaskan morning.

I'm jolted from the depths of much-needed sleep, reaching and fumbling for the ear-splitting source of my wake-up. Groping, I flail to find my annoying phone. I misjudge and bang my hand into the solid cherry wood nightstand. The contents on top of it, a lamp and my noisy phone, clatter to the floor with a sharp pain radiating from my hand, fully waking me up.

Damn! I reach for the glowing device on the floor and hit buttons until it silences.

"Ugh," I groan. There's no chance of returning to sleep, and my hand needs an ice pack. Rubbing my eyes, I think *I can't afford a clumsy injury on the most important week of my career.*

Then, shifting in bed, I notice a warm, foreign presence beside me.

Double Damn!

I wrack my brain, desperately trying to piece together the events of last night, my memory foggy. *What happened in the culinary mayhem of my dinner service? Who is this mysterious, unmoving lump I'm sharing a bed with?*

I rub my eyes harder, and a memory resurfaces of my horrible ex, the queen of gaslighting.

Annoyingly, my ex, Vivian, called me. Despite wanting to block and ignore her, I reluctantly picked up because I had *to* for work. She's my old employer, and I must maintain contact with her professionally since she owns and operates high-end restaurants in Anchorage.

Between boasting about her questionable culinary prowess and insinuating that she's the Gordon Ramsay of our generation, she dropped the bomb—the Michelin Star Reviewer is in Anchorage. The reviewer will be traveling around Alaska and visiting small-town restaurants. She promised to call me with more details.

I bite my frown and smile, thinking about an upcoming review because I am more than ready for the visit. Finally, my sweet, sweet validation is coming–*I'm an outstanding, talented chef, and I will prove it!*

I hold my tongue with her backhanded compliments and outright insults for the rest of her phone call. *I need her precious insider information, and I can't risk severing the connection with her until after my vindication.*

Vivian's the top dog, owning the fanciest restaurant in Anchorage. She can't become my enemy because her opinions are respected everywhere *except among the chefs who know her.* Clawing her way to the top, she's stolen all her innovative ideas and awards from the hard work and sweat of others. If a chef, such as myself, steals any of her spotlight, she fires them instead of admitting their contributions or giving them any compliments–*even if they're her girlfriend.*

After the call, she offered me my old job back at half the salary. I politely thanked her for giving me the update and the offer. But she continued, forcing me to listen to the laundry list of my faults to *help* me improve my chances of getting a good review. She told me how bad my pairing ability was, that I needed "to practice using spices," and that I needed to work under her to "perfect my culinary skills."

I thanked her for the suggestions through clenched teeth, hung up, and needed a stiff drink. But last night's liquid comfort came with the side of unexpected company.

The sleeping woman stirs, and a low mumble escapes her lips. The recovery from my ex's insults included more than drowning my anger in a fine wine. *Did my one-night stand help me feel better, or was it just done to show Vivian that I didn't need her?*

With a shake of my head and a deep breath, I clear my thoughts. I must prepare the restaurant and my menu for the upcoming Michelin review. I look at the lump–*I also need to eliminate the aftermath of my drunken rendezvous.*

I straighten my bedside table and flick on the lamp, trying to remember the girl's name.

"Barbara, wake up!" I bark, shaking her shoulder. The bed sheet falls away from the soft curves of her glowing ivory skin. I'm starting to remember something about her being a hot firefighter, which explains the flaming snake tattoo curving up her delicate rib cage.

The gorgeous firefighter groans, her sleepy green eyes blinking at me. Disheveled waves of amber hair fall around her sleepy face in a cute cascade. If I were in the mood for cuteness, *which I am not*, I'd kiss her awake and do a morning workout in bed.

"I'll wait for my breakfast in bed," she giggles, turning to cocoon in the blankets and wiggling her butt at me.

I sigh and rip the blankets off. My annoyance echoes, and I ask her, "Why are you still here?" Realizing I sound aggressive and rude, I add, "Sorry, I don't have time for this. I need to get ready for work." I wave my hand, signaling her to leave.

She flips over with a pout and a flirty sparkle in her eyes. "You know my name is *Brenda*," she huffs, unamused by my morning grumpiness and using the wrong name.

Barbara–Brenda–It was a pretty close guess.

She sits up to reveal a nearly perfect, toned body. She pauses to stretch and, infuriatingly, takes her sweet time to get out of bed.

"Your food is excellent, but you need to work on remembering names, *Chef Lucy*."

I shake my head—*hook-ups don't have names*. Pulling on my jeans and tank top from the neatly folded pile on my dresser, I retort, "And you need to work on not overstaying your welcome. I have the lodge to manage."

She stands unabashedly naked, fluttering her lashes, pulling her hair back, and pushing out her perky breasts. "You liked me well enough last night. Don't be a grump!"

I roll my eyes at Brenda, my patience wearing thin. "And you enjoyed it, too. *Please* get dressed and get out. I have a restaurant to open and a menu to check." I rub my eyes and put my hands on my hips, waiting for her to move.

She gives up on being flirty and collects her scattered clothing, slinking to the bathroom. *She better not be getting in the shower.*

"Why are you being so rude? I thought you'd be fine with me staying the night. We're both single, and you invited me to your room. I'm new here, remember. I thought we could hang out," she whines as she slams the door.

I grumble to the closed door, "Hurry up. I don't date, and I don't have time to hang out. I'm not looking for a girlfriend."

She probably can't hear me, which is good since I sound like a jerk. I recall her complimenting the dinner I served last night, then we hung out until after closing time of my lodge's restaurant.

We drank too much wine. Brenda complained about working in nowhere Alaska, while I lamented about the missed chance of getting a Michelin star last year when the reviewer came on an off day. Instead of my usual excellent fare, they got a cold, poorly seasoned risotto. *Not this time*, I vow–I've worked too hard, and my business needs this star.

I'm proving to Vivian that I'm worthy of a Michelin star. She was an idiot for firing me. When she said I was the best chef she'd ever met, that she couldn't run the restaurant without me, and promised me the head chef job at her fancy downtown restaurant, Poseidon's Last Restaurant. *I believed her.*

But she was stringing me along, paying me poorly, stealing my recipes, and she traded me in for the next hot thing, an Asian fusion male chef. She's *not bi-sexual,* she's narcissistic-sexual. Whoever she can use and abuse to get to the top, she does.

Turning my back to the bathroom, I pull open the blackout curtains blocking the Alaska summer's twenty-four hours of daylight. The sunlight immediately blinds me, taking over the room.

Shit! I've got to hustle, check out the dinner menu, and start my workday.

The sun is playing tricks on me, making it seem like noon instead of early morning hours. Not that I mind–I'll take the extra light over the gloomy, dark winter month, any day.

Brenda turns on the shower. I snatch my phone and storm out onto the deck overlooking the Kenai River that winds through the small town of Cooper Landing, giving my guests a million-dollar view of the river, the eagles' nests, and the snowy mountains. I bought this restaurant and lodge for the perfect vacation get-away, remote wilderness location, and the gorgeous newly remodeled restaurant. It's a hidden gem, a better kitchen than the posh Poseidon's Last Restaurant, but so far outside of Anchorage, no investors noticed it.

"What?" I rub my eyes.

However, the odd rushing muddy water catches my eye. The Alaska landscape is a raging beast—the usually sparkling blue river flowing through the valley is a brown-gushing ocean. The peaceful canoeing and kayaking river is thundering below, devouring fishing cabins along the river's edge.

My jaw tightens as the gravity of the situation settles in–*what the actual fuck?*

Then I remember the blaring alarm that woke me. My senses are immediately on high alert. I pull out my phone, fumbling and squinting at the screen broadcasting an emergency flood alert in *Cooper Landing*.

What? An emergency in our little town of less than two hundred residents? I have never even seen a real Emergency Alert on my phone—it's always an annoying *test*. I didn't give the alarm a second thought.

Now, however, the flooding is morphing our beautiful fishing river into a dangerous, threatening expanse of water, destroying the banks of the Kenai River. The lodge is safe on high ground, but all those cabins are in danger. I've seen people swimming and fishing off their decks in the morning.

God, I hope they got the alert, too.

"Brenda, grab your stuff. Get out!" I shout with an unmistakable urgency, moving and pulling on my trusty jean jacket, snatching my keys, and hastily tying my hair into a messy knot.

She appears beside me, fully dressed. Her firefighter instincts must have kicked in when she heard me shout. Wide-eyed, she looks outside. "I've got to get to the fire station. Do you know if they have a boat or jet skis?"

Jet skis? She must think we're in California, not backwoods Alaska. "The fire station has the Alaska State Trooper river boat for lake rescues. I've seen it. It's close to the boat launch on the south side of the bridge." Waving her to follow, I stride ahead.

"Good," she says, no longer flirty.

"I will drop you off at the fire station. I must warn anyone who didn't wake up that their houses are flooding." My heart races, and my brain slows everything down, like when there's a busy night at the restaurant. I focus on the task at hand, checking on those cabins by the river.

I look out the panoramic windows and see the magnitude of the situation–I hope the bridge over the river is still standing. I've never seen or heard of the river overflowing like this. If anyone is still in their cabins, they don't have much time.

I rush to my Jeep, and Brenda follows. We navigate the narrow gravel roads of Cooper Landing, the water rising ominously as we follow the river to the valley. Rain starts pelting down, and I know that the rain isn't helping the roaring river. I grip the wheel, my focus unwavering. I'm accustomed to the high-stress kitchen environment, and my emotions have never slowed me down. The situation fuels my determination, and I step on the gas.

"Lucy, slow down!" Brenda yells, gripping the dash to avoid bouncing into the window.

"Seriously? We don't have time to slow down. There's one road in and out of this place. You should understand better than anyone what that means. It's still early. People might be sleeping. Lives are at stake," I snap, glancing at her.

She swallows with her eyes saucers, looking at the river rising almost to the road. "I've only been a firefighter for seven weeks. I took this Alaska assignment for the pay. *I don't know anything about flooding*!" Her words spill out, directed at the window as if she's embarrassed to look at me.

"Hey! I've never been in a flood, either. Let's get to the station and see what the Fire Chief says."

Cutting through the roads of Cooper Landing, I don't see a soul.

Maybe everyone *woke* up with the Emergency Alert and already went to higher ground. I brought the Jeep to a screeching stop next to the fire station parking lot, my heart beating harder at seeing the water licking the road.

I had better get back to the lodge before there's no road to drive back on.

My passenger is frozen.

"Barbara, get out and help. It's your job, right?" I instruct, pointing to a group of firefighters huddled outside the station.

She unfreezes and shakes her head. "Brenda!" she corrects while slamming my door. She stomps away without a thank you.

Good riddance. I don't need drama in my life.

I look up the mountain towards the Cooper Landing Lodge, sighing with relief when I can see the lodge nestled in the forest *high* above the water line. I start the drive back, navigating the mud-slick, winding roads along the river and to the lodge.

At least it's early spring, so there are few tourists or locals in town. Cooper Landing isn't busy until summer. I suspect most people aren't at their vacation cabins, and it's not fishing or hunting season for the Alaskan cabin hoppers.

According to the report playing over the radio, the rain is slowing, but the waters are rising due to early mountain snowmelt and the unusually warm winter. My Jeep rumbles along the waterlogged streets. Passing the dark cabins surrounded by the encroaching floodwaters, my conscience makes me slow down and ensure that no one's out here despite my desire to rush back to my lodge.

The cabins are dark, so there is no need to stop. I will knock on any doors with cars outside their cabin to ensure they get the flood warning to go to higher ground.

I pause and take notice of a big truck in the muddy driveway of the last cabin on the road. The property is sloped, with sheds and a gravel parking pad at the top, protected from flooding. It'll be a shame if they lose their cabin, but worse if they lose their life. I screech to a stop, close to the river as it's almost on the road, and I avoid chickens roaming outside, agitated by the flood.

I hop out of my Jeep, tripping over a chicken to knock on the door. The dumb animals are flapping in the muddy water. I try waving my arms to shoo the distressed birds away from the growing river alongside the house. One chicken is teetering dangerously close to the rushing water, about to be swept away. I snatch it up and knock again, urgently with the chicken flapping mud under my jean jacket.

Stupid chicken!

I glance at the dark home and see muddy boots by the door. I intensify my pounding and try the locked door. "Hey! Is anyone home?"

There's no answer. I consider wading through the muddy water to knock on a side window. Anyone here would have surely heard the alert and left.

I knock one more time and look at the chicken in my arms.

"Did your farmer leave you? Do you want to become a nice chicken stock for dinner?" I ask, the rising floodwaters wetting the tops of my boots.

I turn with the chicken. *Whoever was here is long gone.*

"Are you stealing Puddin?"

I turn towards the voice and catch my breath as I see a naked figure in the dark doorway, leaving me in an awkward state of stunned and speechless. Today's theme is waking up naked women–*beautiful* naked women.

The mocha-skinned, heavily tattooed, raven-haired woman is the second naked woman I've encountered today. This is an unusual occurrence, even for a Casanova like me.

The door swings open, revealing the stranger basking in the morning light. Without asking a question or putting on a robe, she barks, "Well, don't just stand there. Help me catch the rest of these chickens!"

My initial shock transforms into action as I follow her lead. She slips on her boots and passes me to catch the chickens in the yard.

I move quickly with the rising waters and scattering chickens. I throw Puddin' through my open window, safe inside my Jeep. And I join the naked chicken herder to grab the rest of the birds.

"There was a flood alert," I explain lamely, handing her my jean jacket.

She gives me a confused look, shrugging. "My phone is dead." She looks down and laughs, realizing she's naked. "I guess I could take a second to put on clothes, huh." She pauses and throws the chickens inside the Jeep. Taking a second, she leans in her open doorway to pull on a Metallica T-shirt and slips into a pair of Carhartt coveralls.

I chased the last chicken and caught it, pretending not to stare at her voluptuous, solid curves. "Sorry to surprise you. I was checking the cabins on the way to the lodge." I am talking too much, which isn't like me at all, to fill the silence she left.

The chickens cluck in distress, the water inching higher, and the urgency of the rising flood forces me to finish corralling the chickens. With no time for formalities, I quickly helped her get the rest of the panicked birds into my now mud-spattered Jeep.

"We need to get them to higher ground. The river is rising too fast," I state, shivering in my tank top.

She nods but returns to the flooding cabin and gives me the sign to wait as she rushes inside. She must be saving photos or her computer, but she emerges with only my jacket.

"Thanks for helping, Lucy," she says, extending her hand.

I shake it, wondering how she knows me and how I have no memory of my gorgeous, tattooed Inuit neighbor.

The water and screeching chickens override my questions and any awkwardness as we get inside the Jeep with the muddy, flapping chickens. I start to drive, but she grabs my arm.

"Give me a moment," she says, "I should set those guys free, give 'em a fighting chance if the river gets that high. Pigs are smart. They'll go to higher ground." She opens what looks like a shed but is a pig's pen.

The fatten hogs rush out, and my mouth waters, imagining the bacon I could make from organic, local pigs. Even in an emergency, my brain is working on the dinner menu. I wish I had a bigger truck to take the pigs with us.

I shake my head and glance at the rising river as she returns to the Jeep.

"Ready," she says simply with a nod.

Her calmness and the absurdity of two women sharing a Jeep with a dozen muddy chickens make me laugh.

She looks at me with a raised brow, her large brown eyes edged with green, and her lips in a natural grin. "You better get a move on, Lucy. If the water rises too much, we'll never get over the bridge to your lodge."

How is the naked, sleeping farmer the sensible one in this situation? I shake my head and drive.

Chapter 2

Deb

I climb back in the Jeep, soaked from the rain, collecting wet chickens and the rising river. My heart pounds, and I close my eyes for a long blink to let it slow down as I chill out. *What will be, will be, and I can't stand in the way of nature.* I only want to help my pigs to survive.

A chicken flies into my lap. *Puddin missed me.* I chuckle as Lucy shakes her head, laughing at the chicken and the situation.

I smile, thinking of the surprise in her eyes when I appear naked. You'd think she didn't have the same body parts as me. I suppose these high-strung city folk are made from a different earth than us villagers.

I take the emergency in stride. I am a farmer and an Alaskan, so avalanches, grizzly bears walking up to me, and snow in June, I'm basically acclimated for any emergency, even the naked flooding type.

Rain is pouring, the river is rising, and I didn't have much to do today anyway but sit at home and wish I could go back in time. I miss being married and waking up to my warm partner in bed.

I swallow and refocus. Instead, I was woken by a cold stranger, talking about eating Puddin, and looking rather scared despite her bravery in checking on all the cabins. Life in Cooper Landing, Alaska, sure has a way of keeping me on my toes.

"Is there anyone else here we need to save?" Lucy shoots me a quizzical look, studying me the way a person looks at a stranger they are trying to decipher.

It dawns on me just then—*Lucy, the devil's club stuck in my heel*—doesn't know who I am, which is absurd.

There are only a handful of people who live year-round in Cooper Landing. Plus, she saw me three days ago in our town's little convenient store, Tundra Tits Trading Post. It's the social hub and the only grocery store.

Sal gave it the quirky name because she sells homemade beaver fur bras, and the odd name is nothing compared to Skinny Dick's Halfway Inn a few towns over.

"I mean, anyone aside from your feathered friends?" Lucy continues, snapping me back into the cold, wet reality of sharing a truck with the rude city transplant and my clucking friends.

I smile and lift Puddin. "Do I need anyone else? I have these girls that keep me busy."

At least as an outsider, she doesn't know me or my popular wife, Willow. I *really* don't want to answer questions about her, as she left me. Willow leaving would be some juicy gossip in our small town.

Willow's coming back soon. There wasn't a fight or any reason for her to leave me or to file for divorce. She loves this cabin and the little community we grew up in. I'm taking care of everything until she realizes her mistake, misses me, and returns home to snuggle in bed with her favorite person.

"Nah, just us. My wife is out of town. But hey, thanks for the rescue and lift," I add.

"Lucky her," she responds, looking at me. She is white-knuckling the wheel and chewing her lips.

As we navigate the flooded streets, my mind swirls like a rising river. I break the tension by saying, "I'm Deb. I manage the Alaska Subsistence Food Co-op, you know." Although she never contributes to or pays to get the monthly Co-op box of salmon, eggs, meats, berries, and produce.

Lucy nods, giving me a polite, tight smile, but I can tell she's drawing a blank on me and the business. It's as if I am invisible to her, along with this entire community around her fancy business, the Copper Landing Lodge.

"Nice to meet you, Deb. Thank you for introducing me to your chickens. I've never thought I needed hand-to-hand combat training until now," she says with a wry smile and tensely moves away from my hand as I attempt to pat her shoulder.

She doesn't like touch, noted. These are cold city folks. Why even bother moving to a small community if you're not friendly and don't want to meet your neighbors?

"They're a hoot," I quip, scratching Puddin's feathery head. "But, you know, we met at Sal's, the store. You bought out all the fruit last week and didn't leave any for the rest of us. I had to scramble to deliver Co-op blueberries and salmonberries to everyone because of it."

"Umph," she says, scrunching her nose with no apology or recognition of me or her selfish action. She squints, thinking hard, but shakes her head again. "Oh, yes, the store–Tundra...errr...Trading Post," she says, avoiding saying the word tits, which makes me laugh at her avoidance of the name. "I'm there quite a bit, getting supplies for the lodge. It's a busy life running a business."

I roll my eyes at her lame excuse. Lucy's fancy Cooper Landing Lodge, which she bought last year, only caters to tourists with expensive rooms and more expensive cuisine. All of us locals end up with empty store shelves because she hoards the essentials. Eggs, butter, veggies–gone in a blink. Her greed results in community members waiting a week for the next grocery delivery after she decimates the shelves.

"It'd be nice if you were more considerate to the community you live in and at least offered local specials. We'd like to eat out, too, and there's no other restaurant in Cooper Landing," I suggest, not hiding my irritation well. I'm not the type to pull punches. I tell her how it is —*she should be friendly* and more considerate.

Then I blush when I realize she just woke me up and saved Puddin and me from floating away in the flooding river.

Lucy glances at me, catching the edge in my voice. "I'll keep that in mind."

We drive on in an awkward silence, interrupted only by the occasional clucking protest from Puddin and the rest of the flock. The tension inside the Jeep is thicker than the Alaskan morning fog, and she's still white-knuckling the drive.

I change the subject, hoping to thaw the icy atmosphere and relax her so she doesn't have a heart attack driving us up the hill to the lodge.

"So, what brought you to Cooper Landing, Lucy?"

Lucy chuckles nervously, glancing at me as if testing the waters. "I run a lodge and restaurant here. It was a great opportunity and location."

"Unless it floods," I chuckle, shaking my head and looking out the window at the fast-moving muddy river. "French food, though. Is that something you trained for?"

Lucy shrugs, seeming genuinely surprised I asked, and smiles, her hands relaxing to a pinkish. "I finished my culinary training in Europe, and I enjoy cooking with butter and heavy cream. I try to offer something special to tourists. Cooper Landing is an untapped market, you know?"

I don't know. I run a small farm and egg/meat delivery service. My business is enough to pay property taxes and groceries if there's anything on the shelves to buy.

"It's special, for sure. But we're a small town. Not everyone can afford five-star meals. You ever think about making regular Alaskan food, like a moose stew, BBQing some salmon, or good ol' pizza?"

She chews her lips and nods, an uneasy flicker in her eyes. I wonder if I'm pushing too much of my unsolicited advice. However, she should be told if she hasn't figured it out that, the locals would love to be able to grab a moose chili or caribou burger at the lodge. They have comfy seating and the best views. The Jeep trudges through the flooded streets, and I've never had someone so different from me than Lucy. Lucy and I are polar opposites, oil and water–even with my laidback, forgiving nature. Lucy's indifference and big city vibe rubs me the wrong way.

Approaching the bridge, it's intact, and we cross to higher ground, the Cooper Landing Lodge. We stop, staring at the surging brown torrent filled with trees and debris. I look down at my cabin, covered by the river, with only the top of the roof now visible.

"Cheesus Christ," I mumble despite knowing what it looks like. Seeing the larger view of the river, wiping out the cabin and my land, is astonishing.

"What was that?" Lucy says, flexing her fingers and checking the rest of the route to the lodge.

I shake my head and sigh. "That's nature for you," I say, shrugging and turning to Lucy. At least the pigs, chickens and I are safe. Maybe I can salvage something from the cabin when the water recedes.

"Oh, no," she says, pointing, and I turn as I hear the cracking noise of my once beautiful cabin ripping off the thick wooden posts of the foundation into the river. The walls, the furniture, and other large pieces break off and scatter in the muddy waters.

My calm demeanor disappears. A desperate sob tears through my lips, the agony of my pain as I witness the cabin–my memories, my history, and everything I hold dear–disappearing before my eyes.

Willow and I poured our love into crafting this home after our marriage, and the debris of our shared past floated in the river. With the cabin gone, the last tangible link to our life together is severed, leaving Willow with no reason to return.

"I've lost everything!" I declare, the biting cold intensifying the tremors coursing through me as I bear witness to the destruction of my entire existence.

I gaze again at the empty area where my beautiful cabin stood an hour ago.

Lucy tries to smile and stiffly takes my arm, leading me back to her Jeep. "You are alive, and you still have Puddin," she says, pushing the chicken off her seat.

"I didn't expect this. My cabin was all I had left," I echo hollowly, staring at the space where my home once stood.

"You will stay at the lodge with me," Lucy states, an ounce of warmth in her voice. "It's on higher ground. You can regroup there and figure out the next steps."

I nod and give her a weak, but grateful smile. "Thanks for helping me, wakin' me up, and stoppin' to make sure I got outta the flood. My hogs and chickens owe you their lives. I owe you my life, too."

She chews her lip uncomfortably and says, "I'm truly sorry about your home."

We get back in the Jeep with the chickens and drive the rest of the way to the lodge in silence.

She smiles at me and the chickens. "No problem, Deb. It's a small town. We'll figure it out." She winks at me, adding, "Tell your wife I said *hello* when you call her. She's lucky to be out of town. Maybe I'll meet her when she comes to get you."

I absentmindedly pull my phone out of my overalls, look down at it, and, again, remember that the battery is dead. I don't move to make the call. I smile at her and say, changing the subject, "I'm gonna let the chickens roam free when we get to the lodge. Are they gonna scare your guests?"

She shakes her head and holds her arm up to somehow avoid Puddin's flapping muddy wings. "Maybe I'll put them in the hot tub or whip them up some French cuisine. They might enjoy a little luxury," she says, and I laugh even though I can't read her face to tell if she's joking.

Chapter 3

Lucy

My Jeep's engine purrs as we navigate the winding roads in Cooper Landing, the Alaskan wilderness stretching around us in an awe-inspiring yet unforgiving embrace. Deb sits beside me, her gaze fixed on the passing scenery. It's a peculiar silence between us, the hum of the car and the occasional noise from chickens filling the void.

Suddenly, Deb breaks the silence, her voice carrying an unusual tone of urgency. "Lucy, mind if I use your phone? Mine's dead. I need to make a call."

I hand her my cell phone, and she dials a number. The phone automatically connects to the speakerphone in the Jeep, and I can't deactivate it without hanging up.

"Sorry," I say, waving at the speaker.

"My home is destroyed, and you saw me naked. I can handle you hearing my call," Deb says with a dismissive wave.

I expect her to call her wife to update her and have the usual chit-chat or perhaps a discussion about dinner plans. The words that spill from the person answering are from a State Farm agent.

"Hello, this is Deborah. I'm calling to report the loss of my home in the flood," Deb says to them, her voice tight with emotion.

Is she calling her insurance agent before calling her wife?

I shoot a glance at her. My curiosity is now in overdrive. Deb's eyes cloud with emotion I can't quite place–shock, devastation, or maybe a determined look? My fingers tighten on the steering wheel as I focus on the road and try not to appear to be following the conversation.

The insurance agent's voice crackles through the car speakers.

"Certainly, Deborah. I need to clarify, though. Are you reporting the loss of the Anchorage home or the Cooper Landing home?"

Deb looks down at her phone with a wrinkled brow and tightens her hand into a fist. She stammers, "Wait, what? Anchorage home? Willow bought a home in Anchorage?"

The agent remains mercifully silent as I realize not only am I attracted to beautiful naked women today but also to women who have serious drama. It sounds like her wife bought a house in the city without telling her. I am unsure how to act as I am her witness to this tragic situation that is unfolding. I continue to stare hard ahead and say nothing.

She pauses and responds, "I am talking about our cabin in Cooper Landing. There's a flooding."

Another heavy pause follows, and as the agent takes the details, I can practically feel the weight of Deb's tension and anger at her wife. I involuntarily clench the steering wheel tighter as she asks for the address for the Anchorage home and types it into her phone. It's like witnessing one of those reality television shows where Dr. Phil reveals a man's second family, except her life is unraveling in real time next to m e.

The insurance agent continues, "I have records for both properties. For the Cooper Landing home, we'll proceed accordingly. I have been contacted by other property owners. I do have the incident details, and we're waiting to see if it's declared a state emergency or just a local emergency. However, your Anchorage property is fine, right? You don't get rental assistance if your other property is available to use during a disaster event."

Deb's voice trembles as she grapples with the question: "Yes. Is the Anchorage home under my name, too? My partner, Willow, never said anything about it. Our main home is in Cooper Landing. I thought... I thought she was waiting to buy a home because she was coming back."

The hurt of this revelation of a secret property in Anchorage is a big red flag. Deb's wife is building a life somewhere without Deb, and this laidback farmer is grappling with an unexpected turn of events.

I'm in uncharted territory with Deb, but I do have a plethora of experiences with poor choices in partners. I unpeel my fingers from their grip on the steering wheel and attempt to offer her comfort by holding her fisted hand. She's a stranger, but she is a neighbor who lost her house and, apparently, her wife. It must be hard to have your entire life crumble in an instant.

Deb lowers the phone, her gaze fixed on the landscape passing by. She sees nothing and opens her fist to grasp my hand. I can see the storm of emotions brewing within her, and I, in my awkward way, attempt to help.

"Hey, it's going to be alright," I say, my voice surprisingly soft. "We'll figure this out together at the lodge. Maybe your wife has an explanation for everything." I shrug as those are the only words of encouragement I can offer her.

Deb glances at me, her eyes reflecting gratitude and sorrow. Our differences fade into the background, and I squeeze her hand, knowing love is dangerous. It's best to learn to avoid getting serious because people only hurt you. I'm only sorry she must learn the lesson in the middle of this disaster.

She looks at me and smiles. "Thank you. There's an explanation for this. Willow loves me. Thanks for letting me stay at the lodge while I figure this out. At least I have a place to move to in Anchorage."

I nod but internally cringe at her optimistic assumption that her partner would invite her to an undisclosed home.

Chapter 4

Deb

I took my time unloading my chickens, finding a nice dry area under an elevated deck away from the lodge building to create a nest for them. Lucy directed me to look in the kitchen for some old milk crates and anything else I needed to give my feathered friends a nice new home until I could move them back onto my property.

After settling them, *I need to return Lucy's car keys.*

I stroll towards the lodge. The makeshift sign that is being put up catches my attention: "Emergency Planning Headquarters." It's unreal, like being in a movie, not my sleepy Alaskan town. Cooper Landing has seen its fair share of calamities, but nothing major and nothing that required a headquarters location. I shake my head at the drama and wish this was a crazy dream and I didn't just become homeless.

Quickening my pace, scanning the area in front of the lodge. Fire trucks, cars, and random people huddle near the lodge. As I approach, I glimpse Lucy confidently barking orders to the emergency personnel.

Figures, she's definitely the bossy, city-type.

"Lucy!" I holler, finally catching up to her as she directs the traffic of first responders. "Did you approve of this makeshift HQ at your fancy lodge?" She doesn't seem like a community-minded person to me.

She lifts her chin, her icy blue eyes briefly flickering over me. "Where else is the high ground? Everyone's welcome here, even if I don't serve old-fashioned *burgers and pizz*a."

I blush. I said too much and offended her earlier. I chuckle, saying, "You and your posh lodge. Even in the middle of an emergency, you're probably planning an elaborate dinner tonight. Don't you dare add *my chicken* to the menu!"

She raises an eyebrow, giving me a sly grin. "I have some chicken in the kitchen already. I do have some recipes that work well for this larger crowd, and someone's got to bring a touch of class to this Alaskan wilderness. Otherwise, it would be all wild game meat of bears and moose, with no style whatsoever."

I roll my eyes. I bet she would love tender moose steak if she would give it a chance and salmonberry cobbler. I may be annoyed at her lack of sourcing her food locally, but deep down, I can't help but admire the way she manages and organizes things. Lucy is a city girl, but she's got this calm confidence that's contagious. As I enter the lodge with her, my eyes wander over the place. I've never really been inside the lodge.

Cooper Landing Lodge stands tall and proud, a log-built Alaskan beauty that Lucy somehow manages to infuse with an air of sophistication that feels almost too much for our small town of Cooper Landing. The exterior, adorned with intricate woodwork, gives off that traditional Alaskan vibe, but it's a different story when you step inside.

The lobby showcases modern elegance, with sleek furniture and subtle lighting that creates a warm ambiance. Lucy's restaurant, Le Boisé Bistro, as the golden-lettered entrance announces, harmonizes with the elegant lodge's vibe. Despite the disaster outside, the interior is orderly and sophisticated.

"So, what do you think?" Lucy glances at me with pride.

I look around, trying to find words to describe it. "Well, I ain't seen anything like this around here. I stepped into a different world."

Lucy nods with a sparkle in her eyes. "That's the idea. I want people to experience something unique when they come here. Wilderness outside and elegance inside—the best of both worlds. Cooper Landing Lodge is not a run-of-the-mill Alaskan lodge."

"Yeah," I commented, giving her a sidelong glance.

She chuckles. "It's my baby—a little piece of sophistication in the middle of nowhere. Keeps things interesting."

I smile at her audacity. Lucy's lodge is a far cry from my humble cabin, tucked away from the world. The contrast between her polished establishment and the rugged Alaskan cabin I woke up in is more than I can list. But, oddly enough, I secretly love it, even if it's not what I'd call *Alaskan* or a *cozy lodge*.

My stomach tightens with a wave of nausea, and the heavy sense of loss creeps in about my wonderful cabin that is now destroyed. I guess I'm homeless now, and even though I didn't have anything of large value in the cabin, I still lost everything. My eyes water and I swallow as I navigate through the lodge.

Lucy seamlessly directs people, telling a red-headed stunner named "Barbara," who frowns as Lucy talks to her, to assign rooms and cabins to everyone. She then orders the kitchen staff to set up a banquet. She is calm and direct, never missing a beat. Her composure is more impressive than the very impressive lodge or the crowd of firemen helping with the emergency. It's clear she thrives in high-stress situations.

"You know, Lucy, you might be an outsider, but you sure know how to run this place," I remark with genuine admiration.

She smiles, her eyes meeting mine. "Deb, you can't judge a book by its cover. I might be all about perfection and fancy French cuisine, but I know how to handle the real crises, too."

I raise an eyebrow. "Perfection? Fancy French cuisine? You're aiming high for rural Alaska, aren't you?"

"Hey, someone's bringing class to this town. Plus, people love it. Even if *they pretend not to*," she says to me and winks.

I do like it. I can't deny it. There's more to Lucy and her lodge than meets the eye. And as much as I hate to admit it, maybe adding some sophistication to Cooper Landing isn't a bad idea after all. I bet Willow will love this place.

I follow Lucy to the restaurant on the side of the lodge. Lucy points a spatula at me, her eyes narrowing in a serious chef's way. "Deb, put on an apron. You are going to help me cook for everyone. You seem to have some meal idea, and we've got a small crowd to feed."

I catch the apron she tosses at me and raise an eyebrow. "Sure, Lucy, but what about Barbara? Can't she help you?" I feel a few sparks there. I imagine Lucy and Barbara are hot items.

Lucy waves a dismissive hand. "Barbara couldn't handle the kitchen and she's assigning people to rooms. Let's go, Sous Chef."

I chuckle and, with a nod, join Lucy in her expansive, sparkling-clean restaurant kitchen.

The usual kitchen staff is nowhere to be found, and Lucy takes charge, kicking out a fireman rummaging through her freezer looking for snacks. Her kitchen, her rules. "I don't usually improvise or cook for a crowd, but I'll make an exception. I'm blaming any problems on you, though. I can't take a hit before my Michelin star reviewer visits in a few days."

"I wondered why you assigned me to cook. You needed a scapegoat, huh?" I laugh. Judging by her kitchen and attention to detail, I bet she won't have any complaints about her lunch.

"You know, Lucy, for someone who's outta her depth, you look pretty calm," I tease, rolling up my sleeves.

She shoots me a look that could make a grizzly drop a stolen salmon. "Deb, this is my kitchen, my kingdom. Everything has its place, and every meal has a recipe. Today, we are going without the recipes and will probably run out of soup spoons. People will be eating today's special with whatever utensils and food we scrounge up."

I nodded, happy to help and finally be able to eat something at the lodge. "Alright, chef, what are we cookin'?"

She hands me a knife. "You wanted a stew. You're making beef stew. Something hearty and use whatever's in the walk-in cooler. They're probably tired, hungry, and worried. A familiar home-cooked stew is a welcome addition to today's menu."

I grin. "Beef stew it is! Simple, it'll warm their souls. Have you got any secret ingredients? Caribou meat, ground moose meat, I'd even settle for deer at this point?"

She smirks as she pulls out ingredients for sandwiches. "If I told you, they wouldn't be secret anymore. Just chop veggies for your stew, and don't ruin the meat."

I get to work chopping veggies as Lucy moves around the kitchen with a grace that suggests she's danced this dance many times before. She might be used to her fancy French menu and her team of cooks, but today, it's just the two of us. She's already made a dozen sandwiches and is starting on another soup herself, a seafood bisque.

As the stew simmers, I catch her eye. "Are you trying to make lunch classy with that French soup?"

Not stopping cooking, she says, "I did go to culinary school in France—trained by the best."

I chuckle, "France? Is that by Kodiak? So, you're not just a chef. You're a *fancy* chef."

She chuckles and comes behind me, tasting my stew. Her eyes widen in surprise, and she says, "Deb, this is... this is incredible."

I raise my eyebrow, putting on my best nonchalant face. "You mean *damn good*. It turns out us Alaskans know a thing or two about comfort foods, like stew."

She laughs and continues dancing around the kitchen, giving plates, fruit, coffee, and such for the servers to bring out. I hear a happy hum behind the doors in the dining room.

We continue working side by side, the banter flowing. I enjoy cooking alongside her, tasting the dishes, and she adds flourishes of spices. Lucy's tough, but she knows her way around the kitchen.

After a while, Lucy looked at me, a glint in her eyes. "Almost ready?"

I chuckle, a warmth spreading through me. "Well, Lucy, I might not cook fancy French cuisine, but this is a mean stew."

She laughs, the sound blending with the sizzling and chopping. As we finished cooking, Lucy opened up about her culinary journey, her hard work moving from sous chef to head chef in Anchorage, and the challenges she faced in the competitive world of working in top-tier restaurants.

"So, Lucy, you've got your Michelin-star plan. That's a pretty high standard for Cooper Landing. What got you into all this?" I ask, curious.

She glances at me, her eyes misting. "I love cooking and I wanted to have an extraordinary, special place. Something hidden and memorable in Cooper Landing."

I nod, "You're doing a hell of a job. This meal will be a Michelin-star winner."

She chuckles, "Maybe I should add it to the menu, my Alaskan-inspired beef stew."

I wink at her. "Make it bear or caribou stew, then you're talkin' Alaskan. Give those French dishes a run for their money."

She gives me a spoon of her seafood bisque to try. I'm blown away. It's a flavor explosion in my mouth and the best soup I've ever had. "Lucy, this is incredible. You've got some serious skills."

"Turns out French cuisine isn't just about escargot and lamb, Deb. We know how to make a damn good soup, too," she says with a smile.

I chuckle. "Alright, Chef Lucy. You've earned my respect. I'll give you a five-star review."

I glance at Lucy, stirring the bisque with intense focus. "You know, you're pretty good at this."

She glances up at me and rolls her eyes. "Deb, tell me about Cooper Landing. I actually don't get out of the kitchen much to explore."

I lean against the counter, happy to talk about our home, "Cooper Landing is a tight-knit community. We look out for each other. You'll meet all sorts here–fishermen, hunters, artists, and folks who've been here for generations."

Lucy listened intently, her eyes focused on me. "Sounds like a different world than the hustle and bustle of Anchorage."

"It is," I reply, "We may not have fancy restaurants and expensive shops, but we've got something special. The land, the people, the traditions—it's a very special way of life."

Barbara pokes her auburn head in the kitchen and bats her eyelashes at Lucy. "I'm ravenous. Do you have anything *special* for me?" she asks, overhearing the end of my conversation.

"Yes, Barbara. Take out this bisque. The waiter can show you where to place it," she throws potholders at Barbara's open mouth.

She frowns, "It's Brenda." She stomped away with the soup.

"Looks like she was upset about you calling her by the wrong name. But she seems to be mad about something else," I tease. "Are you in a relationship?"

"I have no time for dating. I have the occasional fling. But I don't think I'm going to find an available partner in the backwoods of Alaska," she says seriously.

"True. You just missed getting a hunting tag for the elusive, lesbian hunting season," I joke.

She pauses to turn off the stew and scoop it into a serving dish. Looking at me, she asks, "What about your wife? There seems to be some miscommunication there. When is she coming back?"

"That's the question of the hour," I say, taking a moment to figure out how to answer. The truth is heavy on my tongue, but I don't lie. "I'm the opposite of you, in that, I've only had one love and I married her."

"You're the real lesbian—bringing a U-Haul on the first date," she teases.

I swallow. "Well, you see," I begin, a slight quiver in my voice. "Willow and I, we're divorced. But I know she's comin' back. We have plans. It's just–our cabin, the one we built together, it's gone." My voice trails off, and tears sting my eyes.

Lucy pauses, then places a comforting hand on my shoulder, giving me a compassionate look. "Deb, I'm so sorry. That must be tough."

I lean into her hand, and she hugs me as I blink away the tears. I've never talked to anyone about Willow because it's just me and the animals at home. "Thanks. That cabin was more than just wood and nails. It was our dream and where our marriage started. Now it's gone."

Lucy squeezes me in and steps away to grab a napkin to hand me for my eyes. "You know, Deb, there's still plenty for Willow to come back to. You are wonderful. Plus, you can rebuild the cabin."

I managed a small smile, "Thanks, Lucy."

She steps back, and I take advantage of her kind mood, asking, "Can I ask for a favor?"

She chuckles. "What do you need Deb?"

I grin. "I've got the co-op's meat and berries in a freezer in a shed we passed on my land. Can I store some stuff here, so it doesn't spoil? I can at least get locals their salmon and blueberry orders when the river goes down?"

She nods. "Why not? We're a community, right? I have room in my backup freezer that's close to the back door. Anything that doesn't fit in that one you can put in the commercial freezer."

"Thanks, Lucy. I owe you. I'll give you some local produce or moose meat in return. We do a monthly box, and it seems like you cook a bit and may like the challenge of using different ingredients."

She winks. "Deal."

Leading me to the back, she shows me a smaller hidden freezer. "This is where I'm hiding my Michelin-star menu items so I'm ready. Fois gras, duck confit, the whole shebang. I'm not letting another year go by without getting my star," she says with fierce determination.

She leans in close to me and whispers, "I keep the expensive wine in this cabinet." She points to a small cabinet near a sink hidden by the commercial freezer. She indicated that there was room in the small freezer for me to use.

"Oh lala. Putting my rose hips and moose meat with your foie gras is an honor. Merci," I tease with a fake accent.

With the freezer sorted, we return to the kitchen to serve the waiting community. The lodge transforms into a warm and lively place as we set up the table family-style. The volunteers and a handful of community members gather, faces lit and already buzzing with appreciation for the food and coffee.

Lucy raises her water glass, a twinkle in her eye. "To new beginnings and unexpected collaborations."

I clink my glass against hers, the sound echoing in the silence. "To you, Lucy. You saved my life, the food is delish, and you're a gracious host. Thank you!"

Cheers erupt, filling the lodge with a festive atmosphere. Lucy and I shared a glance, and in that moment, I realize that despite our differences, we're alike in working together to create this yummy food. We share the sense of belonging, warmth, and community that is the spirit of Cooper Landing. This is our town, and Lucy is experiencing it without leaving her kitchen.

Chapter 5

Lucy

The dining room hums with the cheerful chatter of satisfied diners during lunch. Neighbors and volunteer firefighters, who are guests at the lodge, talk and celebrate the news that the flood waters are receding. We have the perfect view from the restaurant of the river, and we wait for it to recede while eating.

My dining room buzzes with pleasant conversations, laughter, and the clinking of cutlery against plates. The atmosphere is vibrant, warm, and filled with the scent of the delicious meal Deb and I prepared. The Red Cross announces that the governor is declaring this an emergency, which makes filing insurance claims and getting state funds easier. Hence, everyone is happier despite the ruined cabins and flooding disaster.

I'm enjoying the food and meeting people in the community. Gliding through the room, I let my eyes sweep over the contented guests. When I opened the restaurant, I assumed locals would come to eat there.

But Deb was right. The menu is a little steep for the average person, and maybe my upscale French restaurant is off-putting to them. Now that they enjoy my food, everyone welcomes me, and I'm meeting community members.

With the community forced into my lodge and restaurant, locals genuinely enjoy the lodge, and the festive mood in the room is contagious as the emergency fades. I avoid the table Brenda is seated at and wonder if she's recovering from me absentmindedly calling her the wrong name. Also, I refuse to flirt with her or give her the idea that I want a repeat of last night.

I greet a few familiar faces and receive compliments on the seafood bisque. When someone compliments me on the beef stew, I say, "That's Deb. She's my current sous chef."

Pointing through the crowd, I notice Deb stands on the outskirts, avoiding social interaction. Her subdued energy strikes me as odd, considering her buoyant demeanor and jokes in the kitchen with me. Could it be that she's not comfortable in social settings?

A pang of guilt washes over me as I watch her step back and shift away from the approaching firefighters. Realizing she might need a break from the crowd, I decided to rescue her again.

I make my way toward her, determined to make her comfortable. I weave through the tables and smile at guests along the way. When I reach her, I notice a subtle tenseness in her posture, and her eyes flicker around the room.

I gently place a hand on her shoulder, offering a reassuring smile. "Hey, Deb," I whisper, "Everything okay?" I notice that touching her is becoming unusually normal and unusually comfortable.

Her brown eyes meet mine, and I see a flash of surprise in her eyes, as though she hadn't expected anyone to notice her hiding. "Hey, Lucy," she replies, her tone tentative. Yep, it's all good. I'm just enjoying the food."

I nod, though something's amiss. "You seemed a little...distracted," I venture, choosing my words carefully. "Is everything *really* okay?"

She hesitates before sighing softly. "Honestly, Lucy, I've been better," she admits. "It's just...been a tough winter, you know? I've kinda been avoiding socializing, especially with Willow gone. I've been hiding in bed mostly."

But before Deb can continue, our conversation is interrupted by the approach of Fire Chief Jimbo, his boisterous voice cutting through the ambient noise of the dining room.

"Deb! There you are," he exclaims, his tone jovial as he claps her on the back. "I was hoping to catch you. Is Willow back in town? I had the pleasure of visiting the new place in Anchorage. It's super swanky, and that Persian cat—I'm still finding hair on my jacket." He laughs.

I feel Deb tense beside me, her discomfort palpable as she fidgets nervously. It's clear she's not told anyone of her divorce, and she's not prepared to field questions about Willow. I silently curse myself for unwittingly putting her in this position.

"Actually, Chief," I interjected smoothly to diffuse the situation, "I was just asking Deb to give me a hand with dessert."

"I'm full of the delicious stew!" He holds his stomach. "I don't know if I'll have room for dessert, but I'll certainly try." With a smile. His voice shifts, and he says in a softer tone, "I was downriver and saw your cabin taken. I am so sorry."

"Thanks. Fortunately, my animals and work sheds were spared. Lucy came to the rescue," she smiles at me.

I smile back, my cheeks suddenly flaming as I recall saving her and seeing her naked. That image is branded onto my brain, like the tattoos on her body–memorable and permanent. Will I ever forget her, standing naked in the doorway, then chasing chickens in only boots and her birthday suit? She was not shy then. Thinking of her long legs and dark hair takes my breath away.

"Well, Lucy, I might need you on my volunteer firehouse roster. If not to knock on cabin doors, then for this amazing stew."

I point to Deb. "Deb cooked stew. It's delicious."

"I guess I'm signing you up, then, Deb." He pats her back, "I better coordinate with the Red Cross. They are planning on setting up tents and emergency shelters, but no one's going to leave this place for a tent."

"I hope not. I'd be offended," I say with a smile as he walks away.

We lock eyes and she returns a grateful look, and I smile back, finding myself holding her hand. *When did I take her hand?* And why does it feel so nice, fitting perfectly inside of mine? I have a surge of protectiveness for her.

She's obviously going through stuff with being recently divorced and not ready to discuss Willow with others. She's lost everything on top of that. I want to hug her, but I hold myself back.

She grips my hand and says, "When Willow, my wife, divorced me over the winter, it was a shock, and it was easier to pretend it didn't happen. I've been holed up, trying to figure things out. I haven't mentioned it to anyone because if I say something, it makes it more real, and I'll have to answer questions. Willow suddenly left and sent papers in the mail. But I know that she will get tired of city life. She'll be back, and we can start over."

I have a surge of empathy and a desire to comfort her. I can't imagine being completely abandoned in a relationship that you thought was good. Then, the person leaves you and makes you question everything. Then my mind flashes to Vivian–*maybe I can imagine it, and that's why I am so empathetic.*

"I'm so sorry. The only long-term relationship I've been in was a long time ago, and I've not missed them at all. I've only done better without a partner." Then I realized how dismissive the last part sounded.

"Sorry," I say, biting my inner cheeks, "I didn't mean to brush off your relationship issues. If you need to talk, I'm here."

"Thanks, Lucy," she says, a warmth in her eyes. "I appreciate that."

"We can really go back and make some dessert," I add. "I could whip up a mousse or tart with a vanilla glaze."

She chuckles, "What, only fancy desserts, no cookies or ice cream?"

I smile and say, "I only know how to do *fancy*, as you say."

As we continue our playful mingling, I notice the vibe lightens. The crowd continues to chat and eat, not ready to leave the social atmosphere.

However, I overhear Barbara—*or rather, Brenda*—loudly correcting someone.

"My name is not Barbara," she growls. She glares at me, meeting my surprised eyes, and I sense trouble brewing from the angry redhead. She suddenly rises from her seat to address the table, her words loud.

She starts to talk but is cut off by someone shouting, "Yes, Barb, give a toast!"

And another fireman shouts, "Toast! Toast!"

Her face turns red, and the table of firefighters becomes silent, waiting for the social butterfly's toast.

She picks up her glass with a mischievous smile, saying, "To a great group of firefighters and Lucy, the gracious hostess who goes above and beyond for her guests." She lifts her glass and lifts her eyebrows as she glares at me. "Lucy has many *talents*, but remembering names is not one of them."

My cheeks burn with embarrassment as Brenda's words hang in the air. I bite my inner cheeks and wonder if anyone else catches the sarcasm in her playful voice. I should really try to remember her name and be friendlier. It's not her fault I'm kind of a womanizer.

I raise my glass and drink as I look around the room. I wonder if anyone can tell that we slept together. The room falls into an awkward hush, and all eyes are on me, waiting for my response.

"Thank you, Brenda," I hold up my glass and say her name in a clear, loud voice to emphasize that I do remember her name.

Jimbo leans in as we clink glasses and whispers in my ear, "I'm catching the vibe here. You're not off the hook. You can't seduce the summer recruits when I have a hard enough time keeping the firehouse staffed. If I lose any of my new recruits, you're taking their spot."

So much for keeping my brief relationship a secret. I lift my glass and drink.

Chapter 6

Deb

Beep... beep... beep...

The kitchen at Lucy's lodge is a mystery. I'm busy putting away my frozen berries, halibut cheeks, and smoked meats collected from a trip to my shed courtesy of Jimbo. And as I'm stuffing everything into Lucy's fancy freezer, out of nowhere, a beeping starts. It's not from the freezer or anything I've touched. And I see no lights flashing in the kitchen or problems.

Beep... beep... beep...

The sound bouncing off the steel appliances and tile continues to alarm me. I can't seem to locate the source.

I'm no expert in fancy kitchen gadgets, but that sound doesn't sit right with me. I check the fire alarms and look at the stoves–nothing. The pesky beep is driving me crazy. Checking under pots, behind jars, and even inside the oven, I feel it's a treasure hunt, with my search turning empty.

"Where are ya, little alarm?"

Just when I'm about to give up and let the beep win, I see electronics behind the pantry and move jars to see if the noise could be there. However, the beep isn't coming from the box, blocking a discreetly hidden, small camera mounted on the wall.

Why is there a camera hidden in the kitchen?

I bump the shelf, pulling my hand back, and a jar of anchovies jumps at me—the lid pops off and drenches me in smelly oil.

Beep... beep... beep...

"Oh, for the love of—"

I better find Lucy. This beep isn't stopping and could be trouble. We've had enough emergencies today. I'm not going to let something go unnoticed in the bistro kitchen.

Reeking of anchovy oil, I trekked out of the kitchen. After doing my Co-op chores and searching the kitchen, I look disheveled and smell worse than I look. Of course, I ran smack into Barbara—I mean, *Brenda*.

She holds her nose and scowls at me.

"Hey there, Deb. Did I miss a salmon wrestling competition?" She looks at me, amused.

I shoot her a growly look that says don't mess with me. "Nah. Just lookin' for Lucy. Heard an alarm in the kitchen and thought I better tell her."

Brenda's eyes do this fluttery thing, and she gives me a sly grin. She's quite the flirt and is always underfoot, but at least she's friendly and helpful. Lucy could do worse if she's looking for a partner, which she denies—*but aren't we all looking or waiting for love?*

"Lucy's in room 69 if you need her. And if you two need *more* company tonight, you can always call me. I'm in room 20. She knows." She tilts her head and winks a green, amused eye at me.

I open my mouth and taste fish.

Yuck! I don't usually get flustered because I've never had a reason to—*I don't get hit on.* And today, covered in fish oil and completely sweaty from unloading stuff, Brenda's hitting on me–hard.

Firefighters are a weird bunch.

"Sure. But I'm more concerned 'bout the alarm," I say with a shake of my head.

She giggles as if I'm tickling her. *Is she drunk?*

"Sure thing, Deb. Pro tip: Don't let Lucy forget your name!"

With Brenda's parting wink, I make my way down the hallway to Lucy's room. I don't know much about city folks and people from the lower forty-eight, a term for the tourists in the other states, but Brenda's an odd duck.

I count up the numbers to 69 and reached the thick wooden door.

I knock softly, hoping Lucy's in there. It's late, and I don't want to wake anyone. But this might be an emergency, and she may need to do somethin' with the alarming kitchen.

"Lucy! Open up. It's Deb. Got an emergency in the kitchen," I yell through the door.

I stand, waiting, with the oily fish smell making my eyes water, which is saying a lot since I've worked in fish canneries growing up. After processing millions of fish in the summer and raising pigs, nothing bothers me.

If the knock doesn't wake her, the anchovy oil stench will. *I hope she's not asleep already.*

The door creaks open with the next harder knock. It wasn't properly shut, and before I call out a second time, I hear the door open at the end of the hall. Sal from the trading post is emerging, talking loudly with another person.

My heart sinks, and the impending doom of the upcoming conversation makes me search for a place to hide. She will ask about how Willow is doing and where she is. I've avoided being cornered by her until now. Sal's a lovely person but always on the lookout for hot gossip.

I pushed quickly inside the door in a desperate bid to escape. Lucy's door swings wide open with no resistance, and I stumble in. I shut it quickly without giving Sal a second glance. Sighing, I lock the door behind me, escaping the imminent interrogation behind me. *I'm safe.*

As I turn around to announce myself, my eyes widen, and my voice catches in my throat. Lucy, standing in all her dripping post-shower glory, is utterly naked, wide-eyed, and speechless.

"Oh, sweet Cheesus," I mutter and put my hands over my eyes, turning around as fast as possible. The door has already shut behind me.

The initial embarrassment freezes me, and I redden in shame. My blush spreads from my cheeks to my toes.

Lucy bursts into infectious laughter. I chuckle along. Despite the mortifying circumstances of walking in on her, she's laughing.

"Did you say 'Cheesus' instead of Jesus?"

"People say that all the time," I say, straightening my spine from behind my hands.

"Well, okay. If you say so," she says, grabbing her towel.

I whisper, "Sorry!"

"The gods have evened out our odds since I saw you chasing chickens in your birthday suit this morning. Here's my birthday suit," she says.

"I wasn't naked. I had boots on earlier," I corrected her, then added, "Sorry, Lucy. I didn't mean to barge in on you. I just wanted to dodge Sal and her questions about Willow. She's well-meaning, but also, she's the biggest gossip in town."

"I see," Lucy says as I stare at the door.

I shrug, still hiding my eyes, and say, "The next thing I know, I see a full moon...err... Monty? However, you'd say it... a Lucy birthday suit."

With amusement in her voice, Lucy says, "No harm done. If you can keep your eyes averted, I'll get a robe on."

"Sure," I squeak. I hear a rustling, and she says, "I'm decent."

"I'm so sorry, Lucy," I turn and start, but she waves off my apology.

"We are both adults here. We might as well embrace the chaos that is taking over our lives. You, especially, have a lot of it going on," she says, tilting her head and studying me. "And I get it. Sometimes, you need a breather from people. With everyone staying at the lodge, it's hard to hide."

I nod. "Thanks, Lucy. It seems like I say that to you a lot."

"You do. It's not a problem," she laughs, and her demeanor shifts, becoming more serious. "Hey, Deb, you can hide in my room anytime."

I meet her gaze, realizing that a friendship is developing between us in the awkwardness—and that it's tough not to move my eyes down to the center of her loosely-tied silk robe. "The reason I came to see you is a kitchen emergency."

Lucy sits up straighter while wrapping and tying the robe tighter. I keep my eyes above her pointed nipples. She looks at me impatiently, waiting for me to continue.

"Ummm. I was loading my food into the freezer and heard it. It's a beeping coming from somewhere in the kitchen. I walked around, but I couldn't find it. I thought I better let you know." I stop talking, and my nervousness at seeing her naked is making me chattier than usual. I pause to lick my lips.

"Good. You got your stuff, alright, and there was enough room?"

I nod. "I put a frozen box of rose hips in the bigger commercial freezer too. I guess I had more than I thought."

"What kind of beep was it?" She tilts her head. "Like a, beeeeeppppP... beeeeeppppP... beeeeeppppP, or Beep, Beep, Beep." She mimics the different beeping noises.

"The second one," I say with a grin at her diagnostic work.

"That's the signal that the dishwasher is done," she states, laughing. "Sorry to laugh. I had the same reaction when they first installed the dishwasher. Because of the tile, it echoes through the kitchen and is super, annoyingly loud." She cracks another smile and adds, "But efficient."

"The dishes are done then," I say. I smile and shake my head at the non-emergency, my cheeks cool down as I step back.

"Hold on. Why are you a mess? What's that smell?" She looks at the front of my shirt.

I forgot about the attacking anchovy incident. I look down at the oily shirt stuck to my chest. The placement directly over my breasts is unfortunate. "A jar of anchovies spilled on me while I searched for the beep." However, I don't want her to think I broke something, so I add, "It didn't break. The lid just popped off when I moved it. I stuck it in the cooler for you and got a little messy."

Why am I so nervous around Lucy? It must be her boss-like presence or her busy, don't-waste-my-time demeanor that makes me chatty.

"Good. I'd hate to deny anyone their Caesar salad tomorrow," she says with a wink.

"Do you want to shower here? I've got the lodge's best high-pressure showerhead," she offers.

"Okay," I say, thinking of Sal in the hall and more than ready to remove these smelly clothes.

"Hey, I guess we're friends now. You've seen all of me, and I've seen all of you. I think that makes us either BFFs or lovers," she says with a broad smile, turning to dig clothes out of her closet.

"Is that a question?" I ask, and she answers me by handing me a set of fresh clothes.

"Here, I thought you might need these. It's just comfy sweats but keep them. You can't live in your work clothes. You'll need something before you go shopping. *Especially* if you're avoiding Sal."

"Great," I say, realizing she is completely right because Sal's store is the only place to buy hoodies and other clothing in our area. My nose wrinkles at the fish's oily smell, and I hold the clothes out to keep them clean. Her smell lingers on them, and I'd love to smell like her. The shower beckons, so I head to the open bathroom.

"There are extra towels in there. I'll look and see which rooms are empty. You will have a place to sleep," she says with a smile.

"Thanks. I wanted to ask since Brenda didn't give me one. I half think she was purposely trying to get me to share a room. . ." I say, "But I'd love to stay here awhile if it's not an imposition."

"If you want, you can help me with the meals, and even after everyone goes. I enjoyed cooking with you, and maybe you could help me get some hearty Alaskan dishes on the menu—you know, for locals."

I smile at her kind words and the offer of adding real food to her menu. "Thanks. I'll probably need a month to rebuild a new cabin once I receive the insurance money. Until then, I'd love to stay here, and I could help."

"Thank, Cheesus!" she says with sparkling eyes.

I chuckle, "Were you just waiting to say that."

She laughs in response.

"Were you able to find all your pigs when you went back to get everything from your freezers? I mean, I have room for them in my freezers?!"

"Yes, I found them eating some carrots not too far from my place and was able to put them back in their pens. One of my neighbors is going to check on them once a day if I promise to give her ham and their smoked ears for her dogs."

Lucy wrinkles her nose. "I have never considered smoking the ears, but pickled pigs' feet are delicious. Can I buy the fat around the pancreas from you as I know it's the best for making pastry doughs?"

"Yes! You don't need to pay for it as you saved my life and their lives, so consider it yours."

"I'll be quick," I call out, walking into the bathroom.

She smiles at me and says, "Take your time. I have an endless supply of hot water."

I enter the steamy bathroom, enveloped in the lingering scent of soap and fruity shampoo. A blush warms my cheeks, realizing that

Lucy was in here just moments ago, enjoying a shower. With a smile, I peel off my odorous clothes, the hot water already streaming as I turn it on. The shower's warm cascade washes away the lingering scent of fish from my skin, and I focus on scrubbing away any thoughts of Lucy and the contours of her body with strong muscles and soft curves now hidden beneath her robe.

My thoughts wander to Willow, the last person I shared a shower with. A longing for her presence fills me, and I eagerly anticipate the day when we can once again enjoy the simple pleasure of showering together.

Chapter 7

Lucy

The Le Boisé Bistro pulses with the energy of a busy dinner. The cooking in the kitchen, along with the dinner service, provides a familiar rhythm, a soothing backdrop to me despite the busy atmosphere. With the additional emergency service personnel, insurance assessors, and government officials populating the restaurant tonight, I have more people to serve. Still, doing the family-style buffet of comfort foods is immensely easier: soups, casseroles, and desserts. My chef's duties are mainly supervising the staff and keeping drinks flowing.

I grab a bottle of white and walk through the dining room. "Some wine?" I ask Sal and the poor red-faced government official she's talking up.

"Yes. You'll put it on your tab, right?" she asks him.

I made it clear today, after seeing last night's drinking, that the food would be free, but I am charging for the alcohol.

"Sure," he says, handing me his government credit card.

As I'm refilling their glasses, my phone vibrates suddenly, interrupting my routine. I wave and move into the kitchen to answer.

Deb's urgent voice demands my attention. She's supposed to rest as we've worked the kitchen together all day. I step into the kitchen, finding a quieter corner to talk with her.

"Can you come to the lobby? I've got a surprise," she says in a rush.

"Sure. I will come straight away, Deb," I shut the phone and pass a bottle of wine to a server.

Walking into the lobby, I see Deb with a tall, thin wisp of a woman dressed in expensive slacks and a silk shirt. She is too nicely dressed for a government worker or a local.

"Lucy, Willow's here," Deb announces, a glimmer of excitement in her eyes.

"Oh!" The news hits me like an unexpected punch, stirring surprise and sadness. Willow, Deb's ex-wife and the ghost of her past is stunning, poised, and unexpected. "It is so wonderful to meet you, Willow. I have heard so much about you from Deb," I say with a warm smile, recovering from my shock.

Her response is a curt nod, eyes scanning my apron and work clothes indifferently. She has a very cold, calculated demeanor that reminds me of my ex. Plus, now that I am closer, I realize she has a similar blue eye color.

I sense Deb's eagerness to spend time with Willow and bridge the gap between their separation. The woman she loves is back, but an unspoken discord lingers beneath the surface.

Of course, at this moment, Brenda walks in with a drink and leans casually against the reception desk, chiming in, "Looks like we are going to have a party tonight! The government guys are buying, and the insurance people promise to hand out checks in the next few days. Everyone is in a party mood. You free, Lucy?"

I am annoyed with Brenda's continued flirting and efforts to create a relationship with me, but I have realized that she has a clingy personality. Right now, her distraction is a relief. "I better make sure the servers don't over-pour and the city folk are warned about how much you can drink," I say, backing up and shaking my head. I'm pouring wine tonight because the locals drank almost all my beer last night.

Deb nods, but her eyes stay glued to Willow, and a smile more expansive than I've seen before stays on her face while they talk. Her rose-colored glasses paint Willow in a loving light. I don't see her charm.

"We will be in for dinner shortly."

I give a departing wave and rush back into the dining room to assess the situation and check on how much wine we have in the back. I must leave one bottle of red and white hidden in case the Michelin reviewer arrives before next week's order.

I spent the next hour refilling glasses and clearing tables, my eyes wandering to Deb and Willow's table, which Brenda joined. She'd noticed how attractive Willow is and, in her drunken state, was ignoring Deb and shamelessly hitting on Willow. She put her hand on Willow's arm while giggling.

Brenda's approach is desperate and loud, a comical attempt to make me jealous as she tries to catch my eye and smiles at me when I pass.

Deb is oblivious, but maybe it's exhaustion. Her eyes droop, and she gazes out the window. I pass her and nudge her shoulder. She jerks and looks up at me.

"You look tired. Do you want a coffee?" I ask her, ignoring Brenda's smirk and Willow's icy stare.

"No. You're right. I'm hittin' the hay," she says, standing and looking at Willow.

"I'll finish my drink, dear," she says aloofly, moving Brenda's hand off her leg.

"Deb, I look forward to cooking brunch with you tomorrow. Maybe we can try one of your breakfast ideas: biscuits and gravy?" I asked to distract her. She didn't deserve Brenda's wrath.

She nods but turns to Willow and gives her a warm smile. She grabs her hand as I retreat into the kitchen, managing the clean-up and assessing our stock for tomorrow's menu.

Deb gives me a wave and smiles at Willow before departing.

To her credit, Willow gives Brenda an amused look and scoots her chair back. I hope Willow can see through Brenda's antics, as I am unsure how much more of this over-the-top behavior I can tolerate. And I don't want Deb to be hurt if she thinks Willow is responding to Brenda's overtures.

Despite Brenda's persistent efforts to get my attention, I remain unfazed. She is making me reconsider my policy of only having one-night stands. Not that I want a long-term relationship, but I don't like the drama of being pursued relentlessly by Brenda and having her hit on Willow.

I move to the kitchen to continue cleaning and start a pot of coffee for the last few patrons who may need a cup to return to their rooms.

"Please stop serving," I tell the staff to indicate we are closing for the night.

After an hour, I look up, and Brenda is still weaving tales to Willow. I can tell that Brenda is very intoxicated, and Willow is not. I decided to bring them their bill as they are the last customers in the dining room.

I pause, approaching when I catch a fragment of their conversation.

". .. Take all the insurance money and leave her with nothing. She has the land and her dumb business. I deserve the insurance money, too, as I lived there. I want to decorate my new house in Anchorage, and it's about time I free myself from this backwoods village."

My heart tightens, a sudden chill coursing through me. *What is Willow talking about?* My instinct is to confront her, but I force a smile and set down the bill. I try not to over-analyze the unsettling words I overheard.

"Coffees and your bar tab," I say.

Brenda glares at me, pushing her red hair behind her ears. She takes the last drink of her wine.

Willow picks up the bar tab and waves her credit card, not looking at me. Her aloof city attitude reminds me instantly of my ex. Perhaps it's her charismatic presence or her cold demeanor. My thoughts evaporate when she suddenly says with a sharp edge, "It's a shame you couldn't rescue the cabin. That's the real tragedy. It was such a rustic retreat."

I feel a surge of defensiveness toward Deb, my newfound friend who doesn't deserve her uncaring attitude. Before I can stop myself, the words escape my lips: "It was a home. And it can be rebuilt. Saving Deb was the important thing. She's special and irreplaceable."

The tension thickens, and Brenda huffs, rolling her eyes. Willow pats her mouth with a napkin, offering me a tight smile.

I nod at her, mustering a smile back. "Again, it was a pleasure meeting you, Willow."

Poor Deb, she is oblivious to even see what's coming. First, she loses her home, and now gets what she wishes for. Willow has returned. But I wish I could remove Deb's rose-colored glasses and show her what a *jerk* Willow is.

Deb deserves better.

I shake my head and wipe the table while picking up dishes at a neighboring table. I move through the dining room. Deb's my friend, and although I don't want to be the one who points out the apparent lack of love that Willow has for her, I feel that I need to tell her somehow that it's time for her to let go of her dream of their relationship rekindling.

I shake my head and remember the smile painted across Deb's face. She looked the happiest I've ever seen, and maybe I got the wrong impression of Willow. Maybe my initial impression of Willow was wrong. I acknowledge my bias due to Willow's resemblance to my ex, which has tainted my perceptions.

I choose to withhold my opinions, as I am not the right person to give relationship advice with my track record of selecting toxic partners or avoiding serious relationships for short-term physical relationships. I decided to give it more time to see their relationship when they aren't in the middle of a disaster.

Chapter 8

Lucy

"Does anyone know what this is?" Deb asks us, holding up a morel mushroom, which I identify without needing to examine it further.

"A mushroom!" Brenda yells enthusiastically. She instigated this mushroom-foraging trip. She sat beside me at lunch today and mentioned an old forest fire area she hiked through.

Deb overheard and, with excitement, told her we were all going mushroom hunting after lunch. I smiled at her enthusiasm, even as Willow shuttered at the suggestion. She must have changed her opinion, or she was worried that I had overheard her. She must be afraid I will tell Deb if she's begrudgingly hiking through the wet, cold forest with us.

Willow, dressed inappropriately for the outdoor excursion with white slacks and a massive sun hat, trails behind us on the trail. Her discomfort is palpable, and her reluctance to participate is evident as she isn't carrying a mushroom basket and looks ready to turn back at every step.

How did she live in this area for so long? She looks like more of an outsider than me, which takes a lot as I spend all my time in my restaurant and the lodge, appreciating the forest surrounding the lodge, only looking through the windows at the view.

Deb smiles at ease in the forest and is happy to share her joy of foraging with us. She says, "It is a morel mushroom. I collect these delicious guys for the co-op, and they grow in old wildfire areas. I saved this guy to show you, too."

Brenda lifts her brow and says, "Which is also a morel mushroom?"

Deb holds up a Ziplock bag containing a redder, larger morel for our examination. "This is what you don't want. It looks like a morel, which is why it's called a *False Morel*. They are toxic and see," she says, pointing to the cap, "It's more wrinkled, has a reddish color, and the stem is solid, not hollow. That's the difference, but I'll check all your mushrooms before we clean them."

The sun hangs low, casting a warm glow over the sprawling landscape above the Kenai River. A gentle breeze carries the earthy scent of pine through the air as Deb, Brenda, Willow, and I embark on gathering morel mushrooms. We amble, circling trees and filling our baskets.

As I trek through the undergrowth, I pull a morel from the mossy earth and hold the delicate fungi in my hand. I marvel at their unique shape and earthy aroma. The forest is calming, and I can't believe this is my first time hiking around the lodge. Why have I never taken a walk in the beautiful forest before?

Deb sidles up to me, a mischievous glint in her eye. "Surprised?" she asks.

I admit, "Yes, I had no clue about morel mushrooms in our backyard. This is amazing. Thank you for inviting me. I haven't been hiking or out of the lodge since moving here."

With a playful twinkle, she leans forward, and I smell her earthy sweetness, my insides tightening. I part my lips and lean forward, thinking she's about to kiss me in this romantic secluded spot.

She whispers, "I have an ulterior motive. I hope you'll accept these as your gift for letting me use your freezer." She lifts her brow, and Willow frowns at me as she watches the exchange.

I chuckle and blush at my mistake. "If you don't, I had planned to steal them," I tease. I turn, pretending to search so she can't see my blush at her closeness.

"Did we get enough? Can we go now?" Willow asks, and Deb returns to her side to get her to search for the morels. Her impatience clashes with the peaceful foraging expedition. Deb and Willow's mismatched dynamic is increasingly apparent as she complains, and Deb tries to appease her.

I caught Brenda's eye—she's the reason I'm here. I walked up to her to talk, which was my plan before I knew about the morels. Now I want to speak with her *and* get some delicious mushrooms. I'm already thinking about what I can make with these: stuffed morel mushrooms, a morel and gruyere tart, and veal with morel cream sauce— my mouth is watering at the possibilities.

"You look happy," Brenda says.

"This is actually fun," I say. "Thanks for showing us the spot."

She nods. We move to a quieter section of the forest. The crunch of leaves beneath our feet provides a natural soundtrack to our conversation. I start, "Brenda, I need to talk to you about last night."

She fiddles with her basket and nods in acknowledgment. "I get it, Lucy. I didn't think it through and drank too much. I didn't really want to cause problems."

I appreciate her apology, but I wanted to discuss something more important. "Thanks for that. I'm sorry I misled you about our night together and forgot your name."

She giggles. "I guess I wasn't as memorable as I thought." She looks at Deb, "And I'm not your type."

I chew the inside of my cheeks and debate how to ask this gently, but there's no pussyfooting around the question. "What do you think of Willow?"

She tilts her head and responds, "Very sexy and a little snobby. Why are you interested in her?"

"No, I think she's trouble for Deb, and she doesn't even realize it. She's so in love and happy she's back that she doesn't see any of the red flags. I overheard her talking to you. She is here for the insurance money and not for Deb, right?"

She frowns and picks up a mushroom before saying, "I did drink a lot and flirt with her just to get your attention. But she is definitely not in love with Deb. From her ramblings, she already signed the cabin to her in the divorce. Apparently, the only way she'd get half the insurance money is if Deb thinks she's getting back together with her."

She shrugs and looks at me, "I guess I'm pretty bad at picking women."

I smile and ask her, "Can you delay the insurance guy and try to get evidence so we can show Deb her real plan? I feel terrible that she will use her, leave, and break her heart again."

"I can do that. I like Deb too, and you guys are cute, cooking together daily." She raises a brow and asks, "Are you ready for a long-term relationship?"

I scoff and shake my head. "I care. I don't want to see her get hurt." But Brenda might be wiser than I give her credit for. I look at Deb, trying to reason with Willow to stay out for ten more minutes. She deserves a person just as wonderful as she is. Willow is not that person! The only problem is, how do I get her to realize that?

A frown creases my brow as I process, and I can't ignore the heaviness in my stomach. Deb has been dreaming about Willow coming back to her, so I'll need some damning evidence to show her that Willow isn't the person she thinks she is.

The forest is getting darker, and a chill creeps over me. I tell Brenda, "I'm going to continue talking to Deb and win her trust. Maybe I can help her see the truth." Determination fills my voice as I contemplate how I'll do that.

Deb is glowing next to Willow, and I hear her asking if she needs a sip of water, then laughing at her asking for wine.

My phone vibrates, and I see Vivian's name. I sigh. At least I know how terrible my ex is. If only I could get out of her toxic grip. My stomach clenches.

I turned on the phone and read, "Michelin Reviewer ETA dinner tomorrow. A tall, geeky, white guy will ask for dinner special & Château Margaux. You better up your game, Girl, because you're not going to impress with your usual shitty food."

My stomach heaves, and I lean over to stress vomit in the quiet forest.

Chapter 9

Deb

The kitchen at Le Boisé Bistro is filled with the scent of fresh rosemary and the low hum of appliances as I sneak through the doors. After foraging, I returned to a voicemail box full of messages asking to buy Alaskan rose hips from the co-op. On further research, there's a viral post about the health benefits of this hidden Alaskan delicacy, and suddenly, everyone wants to get their hands on rose hips. It's midnight, but I want to check the freezer to see how many rose hips I collected and cleaned before I start returning calls.

"Lucy?" I freeze, surprised to walk in on someone in the kitchen at midnight. I know she's a workaholic, but even she needs to sleep sometimes.

She turns, sniffling and wiping her hands on her apron. There's a cutting board of carrots, celery, and onion in front of her, and tears on her cheeks.

"What's going on?" I asked, approaching with concern for her. I've not seen the put-together chef crying before, and I'm unsure if I should step away to give her space or hug her to comfort her. I hate seeing her upset with worry etching her brow.

She wipes away her tears and shrugs. "I have the Michelin star reviewer coming soon, and I need to prepare. My ex sent me a text," she explains, pointing to her open phone on the counter.

I picked up the phone and read the rude warning that is from one of her contacts labeled *Ex GF Chef Vivian*. My stomach tightens reading the condescending words, and I'm angry at her for the horrible message.

"No wonder she's your ex! Your food is amazing. This is nonsense. Don't let her get to you," I say.

She gives me a small smile. I continue, "You're an amazing chef, and this place is gonna to impress that Michelin star reviewer, for sure."

She nods, and her hands move swiftly to finish chopping the vegetables. She sighs, her shoulders slumping as the weight on her chest lightens a bit. "It's just that she's always done this, you know? She undermines me and makes me question myself. She pretends she's helping me by offering me my old job and sharing information, but she's not doing it to help. I think she likes making me feel like crap."

Poor Lucy! Not one to mince words, I pull her into a comforting hug. "She's jealous, Lucy. You're amazing. Forget her."

Lucy leans into me, her body stiff, then takes a deep breath and relaxes. She wraps her arms around me, and I squeeze her in the warm embrace and kiss the top of her head. She deserves better, and I want to punch Vivian for making her so stressed out. "Forget her, really. You're great, Lucy," I whispered into her soft brown hair.

She releases me and nods, her tears dried up. "You're right," she says, calmer.

I smile, "That's the spirit. Now, how can I help!"

She looks around the kitchen. "I already have my meal prepped in the back freezer. I was just stress-slicing."

"Says the serial killer," I tease, and she cracks up at my joke, the last of her tension melting away.

Her sparkling blue eyes meet mine, and she asks, "Wait. Why are you in the kitchen at midnight?"

I quickly gave her the lowdown on the odd, rose hip trend, and I came to check my stock, prep it, and call people back to sell it tomorrow.

"Can I help you with that?" She asks, tapping her cutting board with a knife.

I smile, happy for her help. "That'd be great. Thanks. Just rinse, chop, and bag 'em. It'll be a nice profit that'll go to the contractor to start the cabin when the ground dries out."

As I pull out the rose hips, we prep them for tomorrow and chat. Her chopping and easy conversation turns her worried frown into a grin. *She really does like chopping.*

"Tell me about your tattoos." She asks casually while continuing to chop. "I know we are pretending we haven't seen each other naked, but you have interesting body art that was hard for me to ignore."

"I'll tell you about my tattoos as long as you keep chopping," I say to tempt her to continue to help me.

Lucy smiles and nods.

"You know, these tattoos," I gesture toward my arms adorned with intricate patterns and symbols, "they tell a story. A story of my Alaska roots, my people, and the beautiful land that shaped me."

Intrigued, Lucy stops chopping and moves closer, giving me her full attention. "I'd love to hear about it."

"Keep working," I bark. Then, I relent and extend my arm towards Lucy, and her fingers delicately trace the lines of the tattoos. As I speak, my voice carries a mix of pride and nostalgia. "These here," I point to the inked designs on my left arm, "represent the animals of the wild – the bear, the salmon, and the eagle. Each has its significance in our culture. The bear symbolizes strength and protection, the salmon represents abundance and life, and the eagle is about freedom and vision."

Lucy nods, absorbing the cultural richness of the imagery. "And what about that one on your right arm?"

She eyes my four-leaf clover tattoo peeking out of my shirt on my inner arm. "What's the significance of that tattoo?"

I flip my palm up to show the inside of my arm proudly, revealing my clover. "It's a lucky clover. You wanna rub it for luck?"

She laughs and hesitates, touching it softly and sending chills down my spine.

Lucy continues to trace the four-leaf clover tattoo, curiosity lighting up her eyes. "That's a unique choice. What's the story behind the clover?"

I smile. "Ah, this little guy," I say, gesturing to the tattoo. "It's not just about luck, though that's a nice bonus. It's about weaving different cultures into my life, like I do with my tattoos."

Lucy leans in, intrigued. "Weaving cultures?"

I nod. "Yeah, it's a reminder to appreciate and respect diversity. You see, I've always been drawn to incorporating elements from other cultures into my own. Just like you respect the French culture with your French cooking," I add to help her understand.

Lucy chuckles. "Touché. But how does the clover fit into that?"

My smile widens. "Well, the four-leaf clover traditionally symbolizes luck, right? But each leaf also represents something different – hope, faith, love, and luck, of course. For me, it's a reminder to embrace those virtues while respecting the unique qualities of each leaf, just like I do with people from different cultures."

Lucy nods, impressed by the symbolism. "That's a beautiful way to approach it. So, it's like a little beacon of unity on your skin."

"Exactly! In a world that can sometimes feel divided, it's my way of saying, 'Hey, let's appreciate each other's uniqueness and create something beautiful together.' Just like the diverse flavors we create in the kitchen."

Lucy smiles, appreciating the perspective. "I like that. It's not just a tattoo. It's a life philosophy."

I laugh. "You catch on quick for a city girl. So, what about you, any tattoos?"

Lucy leans back, a thoughtful expression crossing her face. "Oh, I don't have any now, but I was planning to get one to celebrate if the restaurant is awarded a Michelin star."

I laugh, "Maybe a food tattoo, as you seem devoted to the kitchen. I can inspire you by making Italian pizza with Alaskan sourdough bread and smoked salmon—a blended culture of foods. I like taking the best and making it mine."

She grins and cocks her head, "Sourdough pizza with smoked salmon? That sounds interesting. You'll have to make it for me sometime."

I chuckle. "Deal!"

Talking to Lucy and working in the kitchen feels so comfortable. I must remind myself I only met her two days ago. Working with her is fun. Maybe after this disaster, she'll need help in the kitchen, and I'll stay. I smile at her enthusiastic knife skills and wonder how she could choose such a lousy partner and boss.

Being from a small town, I know the pool of available, single, similarly-minded women is small. I was lucky to find Willow, as we grew up together, but she grew out of me and the small town. She'll get tired of the big city, miss our friendly neighbors, and return soon. Cooper Landing and the people here are extraordinary.

Lucy looks up, feeling my eyes on her, and smiles back at me.

I hope she sees how unique Cooper Landing is and stays. And I'm ashamed that I thought she was a selfish outsider. She's helped everyone with food and shelter, and she's helping me with my Alaska Subsistence Food Co-op business.

"What do you do with rose hips exactly?"

I laugh. "What don't you do? They're the sweet and tangy rose fruits after the bloom. I use them for tea, jellies, and syrups. The popular social media recipe people are calling about is for rosehip candy."

"That sounds unique. Maybe we can try some recipes together when the restaurant slows down and after this reviewer. Do you think you can share some of your Alaskan recipes with me? If they aren't a secret, that is," she asks with a question in her eyes.

"No secret. I'd be happy to," I grin, happy she's making plans with me.

The kitchen is warm with our conversation and the clinking of filling little Ziplock bags of chopped rose hips. We work side-by-side, and I'm happy to share Alaskan recipes and welcome her into our little community.

She voices my thoughts, placing her hand on my arm and leaning in to tell me, "Hey, I'm glad I met you, even under these weird circumstances. And I'm happy you're here to help me. Really, I am lucky to have the help during my stressful Michelin visit. I didn't know I needed a friend until you came along." Her eyes sparkle, and she blushes slightly as she tells me this. She turns quickly to move the cutting boards to the sink.

Our heart-to-heart talk revitalized her, and she no longer cried. Her movements are purposeful, and her eyes, once clouded, are sparkling with determination and vigor. I marvel at her hands moving with practiced ease, cleaning the equipment and wiping down the counters so they sparkle.

"Just how clean this kitchen is should earn you a star," I say.

She chuckles, appreciating my confidence. "Thank you."

Laughter echoed through the empty kitchen as we worked side by side, creating a sound of our friendship and shared enjoyment of cooking. The weight of Lucy's ex's harsh words and stress dissipates with the time we work together.

Feeling relaxed, I decided to use the moment of connection with my new friend to talk about a sensitive subject. "You know, Lucy, sometimes the best people are attracted to the worst people. But your luck is going to change; I know it," I said with a wink.

"Um, then how does that explain your relationship with Willow? You're a nice person, so what does that make her?" Her gaze meets mine, gazing steadily and making me frown with the implication.

I chuckle, saying, "I guess it's not a hard rule because Willow is charming."

She raises her brow, and I wonder if she's jealous of Willow or didn't get a chance to get to know her. She seems indifferent and quiet, but Willow is very nice when you get to know her.

I'm glad that she's still not upset by Vivian's text. "You'll find someone great who is supportive and likes to cook, too. I'm sure."

She smiles back and suddenly jumps as she's putting away the knife.

I looked, and she had cut the palm of her hand. "Are you okay?" I rushed over with a dish towel to wrap her hand in.

"Some Chef I am when I injure myself doing dishes," she says glibly and rolls her eyes.

"I distracted you." I hold the towel to her hand, and the bleeding isn't bad. But I'm afraid to let go because I don't want it to start bleeding again.

She looks at me, her eyes inches from mine. "I needed the distraction."

"Sit down, Lucy. Let me take care of this," I lead her to a stool, and she holds the towel. I go to the wall to get the first aid kit down and rummage through it, grabbing antiseptic cream, bandages, and tape.

She obeys, sitting and watching me and then holding her hand to me.

"Ready?" I ask, and she nods in response as I remove the towel.

"This may sting," I say before spraying the antiseptic on it, wrapping her hand quickly, then taping it. My chest fills with a familiar warmth, and even though her hand is taped and done, I don't want to let go. "I may not be able to make a seafood bisque, but I work on a farm. I know first aid." I smile at her.

Her eyes are filled with tears again, and she doesn't release my hand. Her gentle touch and closeness spread warmth from my hand to my core, and the air sizzles with our spark.

I face her, our eyes lock, and an unspoken energy passes between us. The kitchen's hum fades into the background, leaving only the soft murmur of our breath.

Lucy inches closer, my whole being tense, unprepared for the imminent moment. It's been ages since anyone kissed me, and the memory of such intimacy feels like a distant echo. As her lips draw near, my mind struggles to comprehend the unexpected warmth that fills me when our lips finally touch—a soft, tender connection that catches us both by surprise, leaving us suspended together, frozen by the moment of unexpected intimacy.

Stunned, I retreat, my eyes wide with astonishment. Equally taken aback, Lucy apologizes hurriedly, her gaze pleading for understanding. "I'm sorry."

I brush off the apology, ready to pretend this did not just happen. "Today has been an emotional rollercoaster. Please, let's not let this change our friendship."

The words hang in the air, a fragile bridge between us. After a brief silence, I hear Lucy chuckling, a mix of relief and amusement. "No problem. Friends kiss, no big deal." I offer a nonchalant shrug and head to the pantry, dropping the towel into the hamper.

She smiles bashfully. "I guess we got a bit carried away there."

Despite the intensity of the accidental kiss and the warmth I feel, I can't be anything but her friend. Willow is back, and there's no way I'm risking my relationship with her and ruining my new friendship with my gut feelings. I step further away from her.

"You can go take care of that hand and sleep. I'll finish cleaning up," I say, waving at the last mess.

She nods numbly and chews the inside of her lips, thinking. Then, with a small smile and a nod, she settles and walks away.

"Get some sleep. I'll see you tomorrow," I called out to her.

She turns and says appreciatively, "Thank you, Deb. You've been a lifesaver tonight."

I wave it off and chuckle. "I was just helping a friend. Now, get some sleep. I'll finish up here."

The door shuts behind her, leaving me in the empty kitchen with my swirling emotions. I compare her warmth to Willow's coldness to Lucy's easy companionship. Willow hasn't kissed me since coming home, and I realize I might be feeling something more than friendship for the charming chef.

I sigh, a subtle smile playing on my lips. Surprises fill my night, and I can't deny my growing connection with Lucy. However, I was in my cabin moping the last few months, so maybe my relationship radar is broken. Our kiss was innocent, and we are friends and circumstantial coworkers.

Chapter 10

Lucy

The morning sun bathes Cooper Landing in a soft glow, promising a new day filled with possibilities. I'm confident and happy, strolling into the kitchen. Today, I'm going to get the Michelin star I deserve. I'm ready to organize the brunch and lunch service, letting the staff and my capable friend, Deb, take care of those services so I can focus on tonight's exceptional dinner.

I run through my to-do list in my head, starting with unthawing meats, missing spices, and starting sauces, and my anticipation makes me practically float into the kitchen. I'll be wowing the Michelin Star evaluator with the irresistible flavor combinations I've spent the last year perfecting. Nothing is stopping me.

As I push open the kitchen door, excitement bubbles within me. I am eager to begin the preparations. I start by making a quick brunch /lunch menu for the staff and making a note to ask Deb if she'll add another stew or whatever dish she feels inspired to add to the meal.

When I finish, I move to the back of the kitchen to start preparing for the dinner I've been waiting to serve for almost a year. But as I reach the freezer, the door is open. What? I turn to see who is in the kitchen with me at this early hour, but there's only me.

When I step forward to check the freezer, a gut-wrenching stench hits me and overwhelms my senses. My eyes water and widen in horror at the rank smell of spoiled meat slapping me in the face.

I hear a shuffle behind me, and Deb walks in. She pauses. "Cheesus Christ!"

I don't turn as I desperately hope to find something salvageable among the rotted foods. A messy puddle of foul, thawed ingredients, spoiled meats, and wilting vegetables—a culinary disaster.

My heart sinks seeing all my curated ingredients ruined. My dream of crafting the perfect meal shatters like a dropped wine glass, destroyed by the spoiled food—all my meticulous planning, the carefully chosen ingredients—all gone instantly. The freezer looks like a crime scene. The box of once-frozen treasures of some of Deb's local foods have become grotesque, smelly, unusable mush. This is a culinary nightmare.

"What the...?" I mutter, my voice skeptical and frustrated. The mess before me must be a nightmare. That's the only explanation.

Deb steps beside me, asking, "Lucy, what happened?"

I see a bag of her rose hips, and I narrow them. I step away from her and say, "You tell me, Deb. You were the last one in the kitchen last night. Did you leave the freezer open?" My tone is sharp, my frustration finding using words as a weapon to accuse my friend of destroying my dreams.

She shakes her head, and her eyes widen in surprise at my words. "Lucy, you've gotta trust me. I'm not a kitchen perfectionist but closed the freezer up last night."

She's right. *I am a perfectionist,* and for good reason. I know that I will do the job right and things won't get screwed up when I'm in charge. The hurt in her words increases my anger. I snap back, "Trust you? Like the last time I trusted someone in the kitchen with my career? Like when Vivian sabotaged my chances at getting a good Michelin review the last time I had this opportunity?"

She looks offended, hurt dancing in her eyes. "What? Lucy, I wouldn't do somethin' like that." Her eyes tighten, and she swallows, asking, "Who would do this? Was there anyone else in the kitchen? Do you have any enemies with access to the kitchen?"

I shake my head and try to shake myself away from this nightmare.

"What about Brenda? Did you sleep with her again, since the last time?"

My heart races. *Really?* She is slut-shaming me because I am not interested in a long-term committed relationship. I snap back, "No. I'm no saint, but at least I know what my relationships are and am honest with them and myself. Willow doesn't even like you. She's only here to get some or perhaps all of your insurance money," I retort, my words laced with acid.

Her stern expression crumbles, and she's on the verge of tears, her cheeks coloring and her bottom lip quivering. She pauses and says, "I know you're raging mad, but I'm your friend. You can't be so hurtful to people you care about."

"I. Don't. Care. About. You. Get out of my kitchen!" I roar.

The tension between us peaks, the air thick with sharp words and accusations. Just as the confrontation starts to escalate, the kitchen door swings open, revealing Brenda. She casually walks in, braiding her hair and humming–stopping when she sees us. She steps back and takes in the scene with a furrowed brow, sensing the murderous atmosphere.

She holds up her hands and looks at me with her cutesy, wide eyes. "I just came in for coffee."

I shake my head, and the rage deflates, making me feel like an empty, over-stretched balloon.

"This looks serious," Brenda says, looking over my shoulder at the ruined food and Deb's red face. "What's going on?"

I deflate more, and my mouth is too dry to make words. Reality sinks in of my ruined meal, no menu, and my dream out of reach. It's all my fault this time. My dream of impressing the Michelin Star evaluator tonight and shoving Vivian's words down her throat is obliterated. The pungent smell of spoiled meat and greens replaces my dream.

Deb stays silent, but her eyes plead for understanding, and Brenda's confused gaze flits between us. The tension in the air is thick enough to cut with a knife, and I'm ready to scream or cry.

"Really, Guys. What's going on?" Her annoying but innocent inquiry breaks the frozen moment, giving us time to calm down.

I take a deep breath, trying to rein in my anger. "Someone," I stop here to glare pointedly at Deb, then continue, "left the freezer open. All my ingredients for tonight's special menu are ruined. I can't serve dinner." My voice wavers and my eyes fill with disappointment.

Deb steps forward, a defensive posture with her hands on her hips. "Lucy, I didn't leave the freezer open. You havfta trust me. I know how important today is to you."

There's the word *trust*, again. The word echoes in my mind, a reminder of my past trust and betrayal. I glance at Brenda, who is an unwitting bystander caught in the crossfire, and she's watching in fascinated horror. My accusation hangs in the air. I know this wasn't random. My freezer doesn't open easily. Deb is sabotaging me.

"Why?" I ask her. "Are you mad we kissed?"

"Whoa! You guys are finally hooking up. Nice," Brenda raises her hand to high-five Deb but puts it down when there's no response.

Deb looks hurt, and her response stings. She shakes her head. "You're pissed but don't take it out on me." Then her hurt eyes focus on me, and she says, "You have a camera. Let's see what happened."

"How do you know I have a camera?"

She waves her hand and says, "I saw it while looking for the beep. Why do you have a camera?"

My anger is too much, and I fill in the rage with despair. My shoulders slump, and I explain, "My old boss, Vivian–she was my girlfriend, too," she explains to Brenda, "made me feel crazy, losing things in the kitchen, saying I added or didn't add spice to food I knew I had done right. The kitchen was my safe space, I felt confident there, but she destroyed my confidence. When I moved away and bought this place, the first thing I did was install a camera. I wanted evidence that if anything went wrong, it wasn't me. I didn't want to get gaslighted again."

Deb looks at me, her eyes no longer hard. She says softly, "I'm sorry she did that to you. You're a great cook. Having your boss and partner undermining your every move would be terrible. I'm sorry."

She pats my back with more understanding in her eyes, but I'm still unsure if I want to trust her. I guess the only solution is to watch the tape. "Thank you. Let's see it. I have it linked to my phone. I'll rewind it so we can see." I pull out the phone, and Brenda and Deb crowd around to see who's trying to destroy me.

Brenda adds, "I believe Deb. You guys are such good friends, cooking together, laughing, and obviously in love. There's no way she would do this."

I cock my head and squint my eyes at Deb. She nods, agreeing with her sentiments, if not her exact wording.

She adds, "I promise you'll see I didn't leave the freezer open."

We hold our breath as I start the tape at one am and fast forward until there's movement on the screen. Brenda tries to slink away. But before she can, we see her appear on the screen with Willow. There's no volume, but they are laughing and drunkenly swaying.

"So I may have drank a little last night," she starts. I hold up my finger to quiet her, needing to see what happened. Deb tries to ask her a question, but I shush her, too.

After watching ten minutes of them making out in the kitchen, we are silent. Each of us is lost in our thoughts.

"Wh–"

"I–"

"Since–"

We all talk at once, then stop. I hold up my hand. "My kitchen, my rules. Brenda, explain yourself."

"You saw, all we did was kiss. I left before she opened the freezer and took the wine." Lucy's glare melts her, and she pleads, "You told me to hang out with her. I was only doing what you wanted."

I shake my head. Brenda is causing more problems as my friend than as a jilted lover, but Deb's incredulous voice interrupts my thoughts.

"Lucy, you told Brenda to break up my marriage?" She looks more angry than I could imagine her being.

"No, I–"

"I can't believe you were yelling at me about trust and accusing me when you're the snake. I thought you were my friend. I trusted you!" Tears are in Deb's eyes as she says this.

She turns to Brenda. "And you, stealing my wife. Destroying our marriage. How could you?" Deb's question hangs in the air, filled with despair instead of anger, making it worse. I hate that she found out like this, and I've hurt her when I only wanted to help my friend.

Brenda shrinks back, guilt written all over her face. "Willow said you're divorced, and she's leaving you. Plus, Lucy said never believe us . . ." Her voice trails off, and her discomfort is palpable. She fiddles with her braid, undoing the bound red hair.

Deb turns to me, her eyes searching for the truth. "Did you tell Brenda to hook up with Willow?"

My heart pounds as I try to find the right words. "No. Well, yes. Sort of. I—"

"I was your friend. I was helping you in the restaurant. How could you do this to me—break up my marriage when you know how much I want Willow back? She just came back home to me." Her eyes fill with tears, and I'm speechless.

Silence fills the kitchen, broken by the creak of the door opening. Willow walks in nonchalantly.

"Where's the coffee?"

The room tenses as Brenda shrinks and Deb opens her mouth, but nothing comes out.

I guess I'll be taking charge and talking first. "You stole wine and left the cooler open, ruining the dinner service."

Willow looks at us all and raises an eyebrow. "Okay, but where's the coffee?"

Her icy response makes Deb ask her in the saddest voice, "Willow, you didn't mean to kiss Brenda, right? And you taking the wine, leaving the door open, was all an accident. We are still good."

Willow doesn't answer and appears to be formulating a response.

Brenda shakes her head and looks down.

"We aren't married anymore, and I am allowed to date. I can be happy without you. Why can't you be happy without me?" The sharp words that slice through the kitchen shatters the fragile peace.

Deb whispers, "But you still love me and came back. . ."

"I came back because the insurance money is both of ours, we built that house together and I deserve to be a part of rebuilding it. I can help you get contractors setup and work to help you rebuild the cabin. We aren't married, but I still want to help you and I can take care of everything. The insurance company said you can just change the address to mine and ask them to issue any funds to me to handle everything."

"No." Deb says quietly, "You are a monster. I don't know you anymore and frankly, I don't want anything to do with you."

"That's not true. Everything I do is to help you." Willow pleads.

Deb cuts off Willow. "You already decided to remove me from your life when you left, and then you bought a house without even telling me? I'm allergic to cats and you got a fluffy cat. I know you never planned to come back here, and you never planned to include me in your new life. I hope I never see you again."

Willow turned on one heel and stomped out of the room.

I hold my breath waiting for the flood of tears from Deb after that scene. To my surprise Deb starts laughing.

"She doesn't realize that I have the only room key," Deb dangles the key and grins.

Brenda hugs Deb. "I'm so sorry. Really, I didn't mean for this," Brenda says helplessly, her eyes begging me to forgive her.

I pull both in for a hug because after witnessing that I need one, too. Both Brenda and Deb are shaking and crying. Our apologies to each other overlap, and the staff starts filtering in around us. I smell coffee, and we release each other, tears in our eyes.

"This is exactly the kind of threesome I was hoping for," Brenda says, and we all laugh.

Chapter 11

Deb

Something shifted within me. The gorgeous, cold woman walking away wasn't the sweet Willow I dreamed about, the one who would come home and mend our fractured relationship to live a happy marriage with me. This Willow is a stranger–a bitchy, uncaring outsider.

Maybe, just maybe, the dream I've been holding onto isn't real. The loving relationship I want to rekindle only exists in my imagination.

I am glad that I have two strong women to support me as I don't know that I would have let Willow go if not for them.

"Hey, Deb, I wanted to say I'm sorry about Willow. I didn't want you to get hurt and when I heard her talking about just taking the insurance money and running. . ." she stops and takes a deep breath. "I should have told you. I know that I made a mistake in not telling you right away, but you seemed so happy and you had just lost everything. I didn't want you to lose hope in love, too."

Brenda appears behind her. "Yeah, I'm sorry, too, for flirting with and kissing Willow. I started to make Lucy jealous of our thing, but then you and Lucy were so sweet together...working in the kitchen, our foraging, and everything. When I realized what Willow was up to, I agreed to help expose her because I like you. My spying just went too far," she says sheepishly. "I guess, I'm not a very good undercover agent."

I sigh and lean on the kitchen counter. This is heavy, but I'm not mad at Brenda or Lucy—I'm mad at myself.

"Thanks, Brenda. I don't know what to say. I didn't see it all for what it was. I've always wanted to be married, livin' on a farm in my small town. I projected that onto Willow and this make-believe makeup and future. It isn't Willow's fault, either. It sorta sucks to see that." I swallow and wipe my eyes.

Brenda nods, and Lucy says, "But we can all agree that Willow's a pretty cold bitch, right? You can do so much better."

Brenda stifles a laugh and nods.

"Yeah. I understand, and Lucy, you're right. I wouldna believe you sayin' Willow wasn't who I thought without the proof," she said with a shrug, "thanks for taking the video and telling me what I needed to hear."

Lucy sits next to me and puts her arm around me. "Love sucks. I was blinded by a bitch, too."

I laugh and add, "It happens to the nicest of us."

She squeezes me and says, "That's the truth. You've sure been through a lot the last few days, but I hope there's something good you've got, too—a friend and someone to forage with."

Brenda pipes in, not taking Lucy's hint, "Yes, Deb. I'm your friend, and we can go foraging tomorrow. I think I saw some salmonberries the other day."

I smile because I know Lucy was referring to herself, but then again, *I do love salmonberries.* My co-op stores could use berries after losing the stock in Lucy's freezer. At least I got my generator running and moved my meat to the freezer in my shed yesterday, or it'd be a huge loss for the co-op. "That sounds good. I may need a few days to recover from all this," I add.

"Great. We can go out Monday before the local's BBQ night, Lucy's planning," she says, rubbing her hands, planning and oblivious to the sparks between me and Lucy on the couch.

Lucy smiles, looks at me, lifting her brows at Brenda, and smiles broadly at me. "I'm glad you didn't get fooled by Willow." Then she wraps me in a warm, big bear hug. "We are here for you. Take all the time you need, Deb."

"Apology accepted," I tell her and look at Brenda. "I think we can add one more to our foraging date, right?"

She laughs and nods, "I assumed you'd be together now."

Lucy shakes her head at Brenda, "You sure move fast, Barbara."

She grins at her and winks. "That's what you like about me."

"I may have to wait a few days to forage as I need to plan a new menu."

I'm sure she's anxious about the restaurant and Michelin reviewer, but she doesn't mention it with my drama, and I appreciate her for it.

With everything settled, I said a silent goodbye to Willow, who left without saying goodbye to me. She didn't get any insurance money, but she still broke my heart.

Brenda says, "Hey, you aren't going to leave Lucy to do this on her own in the kitchen are you? I'm pretty sure you could help her make an amazing dinner for that reviewer."

Chapter 12

Lucy

"Welcome to Le Boisé Bistro," I say, ushering the tall single man to a seat at the chef's table. He's not an emergency management government person, a local, or a volunteer firefighter. *He can only be the Michelin reviewer.*

"Tonight, you're in for a taste of Alaskan-French fusion like never before," I smile broadly and hand him the Specials Menu and the Wine Menu. "Take your time and a server will be there to explain the Specials and take your order."

"I'll start with a glass of Château Margaux," he says dismissively, waving me off.

I seized the opportunity, and instead of telling him we didn't have that option, I introduced him to our evening's wine pairing, leaning toward the customer with a conspiratorial smile.

"Instead of the predictable Château Margaux, may I suggest something truly Alaskan? The Aurora Borealis Blush is a berry-infused wine that dances on the palate with a refreshing twist from a winery in Alaska. It captures the essence of our small community which is the theme of tonight's signature dinner service, a blending of French cooking and local ingredients."

He looks at me and asks, "Are you the chef tonight?"

"I'm Chef Lucy, the head chef and owner. I'm happy to have new guests. I'm introducing a new menu tonight. Cooper Landing recently had a flood, but I've been able to keep the restaurant open and serve free meals to the community by using local staff and local ingredients from our Alaskan Food Co-op," I explain.

"That's great, Chef. I'll have your signature menu tonight."

"Excellent, Sir. Please let me or my staff know if you need anything or have questions. Enjoy the view," I say with a wave at the beautiful Kenai River valley with the stunning mountain view.

Walking back into the kitchen, Deb asks, "Is that him?"

I nod and look over my ambitious Chef's Signature Menu for the night:

Wine: Aurora Borealis Blush

Appetizer: Pain Plat de Saumon Fumé et Têtes de Violon Grillées (Smoked Salmon, Fiddlehead Sourdough Flatbread)

Soup: Bisque de Morilles avec Crème de Champignons (morel mushroom cream soup)

Main Course: Ragoût de Légumes Copieux à l'Élan (hearty vegetable moose stew)

Dessert: Merveille de Soufflé au Chocolat, Sirop de Cynorhodon, et Baies de Saumon (Rose hip syrup chocolate cake with salmon berries)

Deb winks at me. "It'll be great, Lucy. This time you have friends to help, and we're all working together to get you a good review," Deb says with a confident smile.

I grin and nod back, determination and confidence fill me. My nerves are calm, and I have created a delicious meal. "If he doesn't like it, at least he will be eating an authentic Alaskan menu. Let's do this team."

Brenda adds, "We do have the freshest ingredients with my foraging. He's going to taste what Cooper Landing is known for. . . delicious Alaskan food made by a passionate, talented chef."

"Are you trying to win me back?" I laugh.

As we work side by side, the energy in the kitchen is a focused, happy energy. I let Deb convince me not to close the restaurant tonight with her simple question, "Whaddya got to lose?"

Instead of giving up, I'm using Deb's Co-op products and the ingredients Brenda foraged to create a Cooper Landing-inspired French meal. And with their encouragement, I crafted new recipes and made a full dinner menu.

Deb is right—*I have nothing to lose,* and everything to gain by letting go of my old menu and embracing a new adventurous menu. My idea tonight is not to focus on perfection but on originality. At least I will tickle his taste buds and make him my unique once-in-a-lifetime dishes.

I take a moment to survey the ingredients, a mishmash of Alaskan bounty, and my French staples of butter, cream, and spices. The rose hips Deb generously provided simmer down on the stovetop for a sweet and tangy syrup. Brenda is rinsing the salmon berries as I look to the sink. The moose stew has been cooking for hours, so the meat is fall-off-the-bone tender with spot-on delicious spices. I smile, ready to make a show-stopping dinner.

And I am letting my team help me and sharing the kitchen with Deb. Rather than being stressed and doing it all solo, I'm having fun in the kitchen tonight. I can't believe my passion and creativity are reigniting at the stress point in my career.

I guess the ingredients I needed were friends.

"Hey Deb. Do you have time to do something special for me?" I ask with a mischievous smile.

Deb is stirring the stew and cleaning the kitchen. "For you, I can do *extra-special*," she says with a wink and smile back.

"I just got an idea. You explained how to smoke salmon and chop it with an ulu earlier. Can you do that tableside for the chef's table and add it to the flat bread I bring out?"

I lift my brow. This recipe was inspired by her, and she has local knowledge. *Why not? I have nothing to lose.* And Deb is an amazing teacher of traditional Alaskan foods. No wonder she runs the local food co-op.

She brings her ulu, salmon, and a cutting board and winks, heading out to the dining room. I see her walk up to the table and ask if she can give a lesson in traditional Alaskan culinary techniques along with local ingredients. He must have agreed, as she effortlessly slices through the smoked salmon, showcasing the precision of the ulu and explaining the process and the salmon season in Cooper Landing.

"What's the time on the appy?" I ask my staff, and it's in my hand, ready to serve before they answer.

I approach the table and present the flatbread for the salmon Deb is preparing. The reviewer is watching with genuine interest. Deb offers him the ulu, and he is trying to cut salmon.

I spread the salmon on the bread, drizzled it with lemon and basil balsamic dressing, and then served it to him. As he took a bite of the flatbread, his expression transformed into sheer delight.

"This is extraordinary. The marriage of flavors is exceptional. I can't wait to see what you are serving for the next course."

I smile and say, "Me either. I better get back to the kitchen and whip something up for you."

He laughs and thanks me again as I hear a server offering him more wine, and he continues to enjoy his meal. Deb gives me a wink as I look back.

The evening unfolds in a whirlwind of activity as Lucy, Brenda, and I embark on the daunting task of impressing the Michelin reviewer. The kitchen buzzes with anticipation, a symphony of clinking utensils, sizzling pans, and hurried footsteps. Deb is at my side, her presence a reassuring anchor amid the chaos.

As the courses progress, each dish tells a story – from the Arctic Salad featuring foraged greens along the Kenai River to the bisque with Morel Mushrooms crowned with Salmon Bacon, capturing the essence of Cooper Landing's culinary cornerstone of Kenai River Red Salmon. The Michelin reviewer savors each bite, appreciating the narrative woven into every dish.

Then comes the moment of truth, the grand finale: the rose hip soufflé. The meal has gone without a hitch, and I present dessert with a flourish, the delicate aroma of rose hips filling the air.

His eyes widened in surprise and a pleasant revelation is evident on his face.

"Rose hips, you say? This is inspiring. I saw a rose hip trend on social media, and you've found a way to incorporate it already into your menu. Bravo."

I nod. The satisfaction of his approval washes over me, validating the risks I took and the unexpected collaboration with Deb. I thank her silently, realizing that this journey has transformed my approach to cooking and forged a bond with Deb.

As the Michelin reviewer finishes his dessert, I catch Deb's eye. There's a shared sense of accomplishment between us, an unspoken understanding that this collaboration has transcended the confines of the kitchen. It's a celebration of Alaska, of traditions, of unexpected connections.

Brenda shoos us away from the busy kitchen. "He's done, you guys have worked hard. I'll clean up with the staff. Take the night off early," she says with a wink and a smile.

Deb and I share a glance, and without a word, I lean in for a hug. I'm not a hugger but it feels right, and as she squeezes me, I shed happy tears.

"Lucy, you did it. Are you glad to be done?" she asks.

I release her and say, "It's a relief but I am excited to tinker with these dishes and try a new menu tomorrow. I can't believe I'm not stressed."

"You don't need to be. He loved it!'

I ask her, "What do you think of a rich salmonberry sauce over a poached salmon?"

"I think I'm in for a treat tomorrow," she says with a sparkle in her eyes.

And I'm so happy that with a spontaneous burst of emotion, I lean in and press a soft kiss to Deb's cheek. My kiss is equal parts gratitude for the successful evening and affection for her friendship and support.

She dips her head and flashes me a genuine smile, her eyes reflecting the warmth of our shared triumph.

Chapter 13

Lucy

Michelin Star Review: A Culinary Symphony Unveiled in Cooper Landing

A thousand flavors dance on the palate in Lucy's culinary masterpiece at Le Boisé Bistro, a foodie haven nestled in the heart of Cooper Landing. From the first bite of the Arctic Salad, a vibrant ode to local foraging, to the Bisque de Morilles with Morel Mushrooms and Salmon Bacon, each dish tells a story of Alaskan-French fusion, capturing the essence of the region's rich culinary heritage.

The pièce de résistance, a rose hip soufflé, takes center stage. It is a delightful surprise that seamlessly weaves a trending ingredient into a delight of flavors. Lucy's innovative approach and her staff's local expertise elevate the dining experience to unparalleled heights.

The former chef at Bistro le Anchorage improved after my last taste of her meals. This chef needed the freedom to make food her way with Alaskan passion and French flair. The meal is an adventure guided by Lucy's genius. The collaboration with the community, the mishmash of Alaskan bounty and French staples, and the genuine passion infused into each dish reflect a culinary journey that transcends the ordinary.

Le Boisé Bistro, under Lucy's visionary leadership, presents a culinary narrative that celebrates Cooper Landing, its traditions, and the remarkable connection between land and plate. This dining experience is not just a feast for the senses but a testament to the power of reinvention and the magic that happens when unexpected friendships flourish in the kitchen.

In the heart of Alaska, Lucy and her team have created more than a restaurant; they've crafted a culinary sanctuary where tradition meets innovation, and every bite tells a story of passion and the spice of Alaska. A Michelin star is not merely awarded; it is earned through exceptional dedication, creativity, and an unwavering commitment to the craft. Le Boisé Bistro, with Lucy at its helm, stands as a shining example of culinary brilliance in the heart of the Alaskan wilderness.

I stand at the entrance of Le Boisé Bistro, my sanctuary, and where I've found my passion for cooking and life. Smiling, I straighten the golden frame of the glowing Michelin reviewer, and next to it, the Michelin star is proudly displayed.

I'd say I was lucky, but my straight-talking partner, Deb, would correct me. *I am talented and hardworking.* Finally, I'm recognized for it. My restaurant earned a Michelin star, and Cooper Landing Lodge is now a foodie hotspot to visit outside the city for the food and the views.

It's funny that a natural disaster sparked magic in my career when I was forced to adapt and incorporate Alaskan ingredients into my meals. And this magic spilled over into my dating life, sparking a relationship with Deb. Even though I should know better, I'm dating Deb, my new Sous Chef.

Thinking of my relationships must have burned Vivian's ears because my phone suddenly buzzed. I glanced down to see a message from Vivian.

"Congratulations, Lucy. Well done! But, obviously, that reviewer had no taste. Enjoy the one star while it lasts." She added a smiley face emoji.

It was a classic Vivian move, trying to undermine my success. But her words slide off like a cake sliding from a well-greased pan. I deserve this star, and her bitter words can't change my magnificent mood.

I smirk at her attempt and laugh in delight at what I get to do next. I have been looking forward to this for over a year since she fired and broke up with me.

With the glow of victory surrounding me and a shimmy of satisfaction, I text her back a truth bomb. Vivian's restaurant didn't receive any positive notes, and I am now the "it" chef everyone wants to talk to. No thanks to Vivian, who was trying to hold me back.

"Vivian, I can taste your toxicity, and it seems the reviewer could too. I've earned my Michelin star without your manipulative games. You are a narcissistic psychopath. I've moved on. Lose this number because I'm not playing your game anymore. Goodbye!" I smile and hit the block button.

I'm ready to put the past behind me and embrace a new chapter. I glance at my wonderful dining area, and confidence courses through me. For too long, I allowed Vivian's toxic opinions to shape my culinary journey. Now, with a Michelin star, I've severed the last tie to her. The future is my creation, and I am a culinary master at adapting successful recipes with whatever Alaskan ingredients are in season.

Deb puts her hands in her apron and tilts her head. "Well, it seems like I'm your good luck charm. What'll happen to our little bistro if I leave?" Teasing me she lifts her arm to show me her four-leaf clover tattoo.

I laugh with her and reach over to softly rub my fingers on the tattoo. The laughter stops as we share the feeling of unity with this victory.

"Does that mean I have to rub it before every meal I serve?" My cheeks are starting to flush as I hold my breath hoping she will continue to work with me.

"Yes, of course." Deb smiles

The noise of the door breaks the moment of intimacy between us. Brenda appears in the kitchen as if she knows exactly the wrong time to enter a room.

"I smelled the fresh bread baking." Brenda investigates the kitchen at the ovens for the bread, and the dish that Deb and I have been working on, the simmering rosemary caribou roast.

"That looks really good."

I nod. "It does." I turn from Deb and now face Brenda, "What have you decided?"

She nods her head. "Yes. I'll take your guys' offer. I'll work with Jimbo as a volunteer firefighter, and I will manage the lodge so you can take some much-deserved time off."

"I'm not sure about taking any time off," I say, and look at the star hanging. "With the review out. We're booked solid through the summer. Except for room twenty. I knew I'd need to keep that one blocked for my newest employee, the Cooper Landing Lodge Manager."

Brenda beams at me and Deb. Her eyes are shining, and for once, Brenda's speechless.

I add, laughing, "Employees don't get drinks for free so don't get too excited."

Chapter 14

Deb

The bright summertime sun illuminates the bustling Cooper Landing Lodge's rustic yet elegant lobby in warmth, a stark difference from the quiet atmosphere of the lodge before the Michelin star reviews and travel sites discovered it two months ago. Tourists bustle around, their excitement infectious. I'm helping Brenda at the lodge check-in counter instead of working back in the kitchen. I frowned, looking at the lobby crowded and wishing I could sneak back to the kitchen. I'd make salmon chowder without having to talk or be interrupted.

Brenda hands me the check-in registry as she talks to another guest at the counter. After the Michelin review, the Cooper Landing Lodge is thriving and in high demand. Then, there was an article about us being "voted as the best lodge in Alaska" on *TripAdvisor*.

As I sort through check-ins, a voice interrupts me. "Deb, where do you want these Co-op boxes to go?"

I glance up to see a familiar face: one of my neighbors dropping off a monthly subsistence supply for the Co-op. "Is it the razor clams?" I ask, looking at the unmarked box with the styrofoam cooler inside.

"Butter clams," he says.

"Oh, Lucy's gonna love that. Don't let her see or she'll steal 'em. It goes back in the new cooler, just follow the signs. Easy-peasy," I reply, relishing that I'm balancing being a Sous Chef and running the co-op. Now that it's located at the lodge, the co-op is easy to manage. Food drop-offs, cleaning, and sorting items are quicker. With the lodge becoming a community hub after the flooding and thanks to the Monday BBQ gatherings on the patio, everyone picks up their co-op boxes here. I have more time despite having two jobs.

Lucy, my partner, is part of that equation. Somehow, having a supportive partner makes everything easier. She even adds a special touch to the co-op by creating new recipes inspired by the fresh produce and meats available in each order. Having a Michelin-star chef curating recipes means there's a Co-op waitlist, and my hobby business is turning into a surprisingly successful venture.

But then again, I look at the bustling lobby. All the recognition has attracted tourists and bloggers, having a positive spillover on all the businesses in Cooper Landing. Even Sal at Tundra Tit's Trading Post has hired two employees this summer. She's never had anyone working in her store before.

One of the new trading post employees catches my attention, a raven-haired newcomer in the lobby. I already know why she's here. I follow her lovestruck gaze to Brenda, finishing giving directions to tourists on "when the Northern Lights are scheduled next." She helped them download the Northern Lights app, showing infinitely more patience than me. She's found her calling in a hospitality job.

"You're too nice," I whisper to Brenda after he leaves.

She laughs. "You're from here. You don't appreciate the amazing sights and wilderness like outsiders do. It's easy enough to help people download an app or give out a map," she says with a sparkling smile and toss of her amber waves.

"Wait. Do you have a map to see the Northern Lights?" I laugh, "Is it just an arrow pointing up?"

"No, unless it's the elusive single-girl traveler. Then, I give them the map to my room!" She laughs, and I shake my head, annoyed, hoping that she is making a joke.

I grumble, still shaking my head, "I still can't believe your nametag, and that everyone calls you Barbara."

She eyeballs me with her green stare and says, "I guess Lucy was right about my name, after all. The name kind of grew on me." She laughs, and the raven-haired woman is drawn to her giggles like a moth to the flame.

On cue, a flirty customer asks about lodging, and Barbara, busy with tasks, is too busy to give in to her admirer's flirtatious intent.

A young woman, a lodge guest, approaches me. "I love this cozy Alaskan lodge, and the food is stellar. I have never had a chocolate mousse so melt-in-my-mouth delish before." I smile at her praise as she continues inquiring about booking a wedding for the upcoming Spring.

Barbara, leaning casually on the counter, responds to the flirtatious customer, who is now bending over to tie her hiking boots in an attempt to show off her round butt and ripe body to Barbara.

Barbara says, while finally taking the bait and noticing her curvy, ripe body, "Well, if you're looking for a place to stay, I think we could offer a new local a pretty sweet deal. How about I set you up with a weekly rate, and we could do some foraging together before you head off to the trading post?"

I chuckle at the small-town romance. Flipping through the bookings, I ask, "What dates were you lookin at?"

But I found an unexpected clash—– there's already an event booked for those dates.

Perplexed, I turned to Barbara. "Do you know anything about a wedding that is booked for the Spring? There's nothing in my events calendar, but it's written in the book." I point to the booking.

"Hmm," she muses, her brows furrowing. "Why don't you run back and ask Lucy? It's probably a mistake. I haven't heard of a Spring wedding," she says while biting back a grin, looking at her morning foraging date.

"Just a moment, please," I say to the customer, who responds with a casual nod.

The unusual booking discrepancy nags at me as I return to the bistro to find Lucy. To my surprise, the Bistro has undergone a magical transformation in the short time I've been away. White balloons adorn the room, candles flicker on every surface, and a rose-petalled runway leads to Lucy, holding a silver dessert platter covered with a dome.

Confusion clouds my expression as I glance behind me, half-expecting to see someone else entering. With its white carpet and cheering crowd, this setup resembles a surprise marriage proposal. Discomfort and bewilderment well up within me as our friends cheer and clap. My heart thunders as the communities' eyes turn to me. I make my way through the sea of white petals toward a smiling Lucy amid phones' flashings.

We've only been dating for a few months, and this grand spectacle feels like *too much, too soon.* As our friends part and create an opening for me to approach Lucy, she winks at me and gracefully gets down on one knee.

This whole scene feels rushed. We haven't even defined our relationship, let alone said we were exclusive–not that I'm dating or thinking about dating anyone else.

As the guests cheer and I reach Lucy, she winks at me and gets down on one knee, holding the elegant dessert tray before me like an offering.

Caught in a whirlwind of emotions, I feel the weight of the past, with its scars and mistakes, on me. I've barely recovered from my divorce with Willow. I just started to rediscover myself as a single woman, and now my casual girlfriend and perfect boss is proposing to me.

I can't shake the feeling of impending disaster with the sense of déjà vu from my failed relationship with Willow. The room spins, and I grapple with emotions—love, fear, and overwhelming uncertainty.

This surprise proposal fills me with a tight dread. Lucy's intentions might be pure, but the timing triggers me. I stand frozen. Rushing into a relationship is a mistake, even if I am blissfully happy with Lucy.

Chapter 15

Lucy

I stand in the middle of the decked-out dining room, my heart pounding as I realize I've made a mistake. Deb doesn't look thrilled at my romantic setup.

Nope. She looks uncomfortable and pale, beads of sweat forming on her forehead and her hands trembling.

I've made a mistake.

Her face reflects sheer panic.

She's propelled by our friends to walk through the center of the room to me. A visible tension replaces her usually calm demeanor. I can almost taste the apprehension swirling around her as she walks as if in a nightmare she can't wake from. The white decorations and flickering candles are a stage for an impending disaster, not a celebration.

But there's no turning back now, and I need to hurry this along before she faints or runs. With a deep breath to steady my nerves, I step forward on the white rose petals to meet her and kneel down with my surprise for her in my hand.

I meet her gaze and hold it with a warm smile, hoping to reassure her. There's no excitement or the surprise happiness I planned for. Instead, there's a flicker of something else, something darker.

I clear my throat, trying to push my doubt. "Deb," I begin, my voice carrying through the room, "I've been wanting to tell you just how much you mean to me. You've helped me build my dream and supported me when I needed it most. More than that, you've shown me the beauty of stepping back and letting others in, accepting help, and building a community."

With a flourish, I lift the dome from the platter, revealing the pièce de résistance—a décadent French dessert meticulously crafted with layers of delicate pastry and rich, creamy Alaskan blueberry filling. There's no ring nestled atop the dessert, no grand gesture of marriage. Instead, it's a small silver goat-shaped keyring with a key glinting in the soft candlelight.

Deb shakes her head, a smile playing on her lips. "Cheesus Christ, Lucy. You surprised me."

Hoping to pacify her nerves, I add, "This isn't a wedding proposal or engagement party. I know this isn't what you were expecting," I continue, my heart pounding. "I've been thinking a lot about us, about our future together."

I take her hand, pulling her closer until we're inches apart. "You've been my rock, Deb. You've supported me, and believed in me, even when I didn't believe in myself. And I realized that I want to build a future with you, one that's not just about me, but about us."

She laughs nervously and looks around. Then she meets my eyes, and her eyes soften.

I continue, "I came here with a career goal in mind and tunnel vision for it. You helped me slow down and enjoy our community by hiking, tasting local foods, meeting neighbors, and trying new things. You brought joy back to my cooking and my life. Thank you."

She takes a finger swipe at the dessert and licks it. "Umm. . .I can't even hear you over this yumminess."

Everyone laughs, and the tension is gone.

"If I'm not mistaken, you're the one I should be thankin'. You saved me, from the flood, and becoming a hermit, who didn't leave her cabin. You helped me move on and gave me purpose. Thank You, Lucy," she says back to me with tears of happiness in her eyes.

"So now for my proposal," I say with a smile as I propose my idea of our shared future. I pause, taking a moment to gather my thoughts. "I bought the stretch of land between your cabin and the lodge."

She cocks her head and looks at Sal. I know she's wondering how I kept this a secret in our small town.

"I want us to expand our businesses—a locally sourced farm with a variety of vegetables, goats, pigs, and chickens. And," I add with a smile, " we've been talking about making cheese and yogurt. Let's start a little dairy together."

Deb looks at me, a mix of surprise and relief crossing her face. She laughs, the tension draining from her body. "Cheese, huh?" she quips, her eyes sparkling.

Barbara, always quick to add her two cents and for the spotlight, chimes in. "Veronica here," she gestures to a raven-haired girl who steps forward, "worked for Tillamook Dairy in Oregon. She'd love to help get a little goat cheese operation running for us."

Veronica smiles shyly. "I've got some experience. I'm excited to bring a bit of cheesy goodness to Alaska."

Her nerves eased, and Deb looked at me and said, "I've got a proposal of my own."

Deb gets down on her knees, bringing us to the same level, and looks into my eyes. "Will you be my partner? Not just at the restaurant, but I want you to be a permanent part of my life as a long-term, serious relationship. Can you do that with me?"

Instead of answering, I lean in, capturing her lips in a sweet, spontaneous kiss. The dessert, forgotten in the moment, slips from my hands, clattering to the floor. Our friends collectively gasp at the beautiful dessert splattering on the floor, followed by laughter and cheers.

Barbara quickly reassures everyone, "Don't worry, folks! We have backup desserts."

The staff then unveiled a hidden dessert table adorned with an array of delectable treats, cakes, a chocolate fountain, and a tray of the pastry dessert I presented to Deb.

Deb pulls away from the kiss to look at the sweet table. She laughs with happiness glistening in her eyes, "You should've led with that!"

As the warm kiss zings through me, the air is filled with the sweet aroma of desserts, and I laugh. "Do you just want me for my sweets?"

"Absolutely!" Deb says back as we marinate in our friends' joy and the beautiful future. The smell of sugar, laughter, and the promise of a sweet ending is in the air.

If you loved Lucy & Deb's sapphic adventure, then you'll love Caitlyn & Peekaboo's skiing, winter romance in *Wilderness Rescue: Healing Hearts.*
CHECK IT OUT HERE.

Discover the books in the *Wilderness Rescue* series.
CHECK IT OUT HERE.

Keep reading to enjoy the next book.

Wilderness Rescue: Healing Hearts
Chapter 1: Caitlyn

The frigid Alaskan mountain air nips at my rosy cheeks as I carve Girdwood's sun-glistened slopes at Alyeska Ski Resort. Racing down the double black diamond Midnight Express, I grit my teeth, determined to ski through the constant pain in my left knee. With each thud of my skis turning sharply against icy moguls, my leg jolts with pain, cruelly reminding me of my unwelcome changes since the previous ski season.

I've had a whirlwind of a year since the rock-climbing mishap that claimed my left leg. But here I am, back in action and ready to embrace the great outdoors again.

With single-mindedness, I ski down the snow-covered slopes, chasing the remnants of my Alaskan adventurous spirit. The icy breath of winter bites and makes my eyes water as I gulp in the pristine air, igniting my soul—this is precisely the feeling I missed while injured and rehabilitating the last few months. Also, I missed the exhilaration of the mountains during my grueling recovery. Finally, I can enjoy the outdoors again. Consequently, I'm back downhill skiing the slopes of Alyeska, rediscovering the adventurous Alaskan spirit that defines me. With a radiant grin, I glide gracefully down the snow-covered slopes, reconnecting with the thrill-seeking essence that pulses through my veins.

The familiar and challenging Alyeska ski mountain stretches before me with the whooshing winds, daring me to slice through them on my ski edges. This mountain has been my playground since the tender age of six when I fearlessly carved my way down its icy trails while my parents called out futile warnings to rein in my speed. Despite their attempts to tame my wild spirit with ski lessons, I left a trail of defeated instructors in my snowy wake. The adrenaline rush from racing down the mountain is a familiar thrill, igniting a fiery passion in my soul for speed and the boundless freedom of the vast Alaskan wilderness.

As the sharp ache pierces through me, I struggle to catch my breath. I'm acutely aware of the immense challenge my winter wonderland has become in my current state. With each turn, my heart beats in perfect harmony with my skis slicing through the snow. Tentatively, I opt for a more deliberate pace, unsure of my legs' stability. The skis wobble beneath me, uncertain as I attempt to steady my racing pulse and slow my frantic descent.

Surveying the run, I find myself alone amidst the vast expanse of the desolate mountain. My partner, Michelle, is nowhere in sight. As I gaze up at the towering Alyeska mountain range, it beckons to be explored and conquered. Confidence surges through me as I race downhill. *Nothing stands in my way!*

With a rush of exhilaration, I zip down the treacherous black diamond slope. The wind whips past me. I forget my body is different until a sharp jolt of pain shoots through me as my prosthetic lower leg suddenly jams straight into my left knee. The searing pain snaps me back to reality—my right quadricep burns with a sudden effort to bear all my weight to keep me from falling.

Struggling to maintain balance and control, I fight against my rebellious left leg prosthetic, which is locked in a straight position, throwing me off-kilter. My right leg can't take all the weight for long, and my left ski is dangerously weaving.

Panic washes over me like a frosty avalanche. I frantically attempt to wrestle back control, every fiber of my being tensing under the weight of the crisis. Leaning further, I throw a wild punch at my frozen left knee in a desperate bid to force it into alignment. But, it remains stubbornly stuck. My prosthetic is frozen in place. I am unable to maneuver my skis or ease my breakneck speed.

In my desperation, I hoist up my left leg and vigorously shake it—a daring feat—all while maintaining my precarious balance. My left ski is useless, with the leg locked straight. Painful protests erupt from my right leg as my muscles strain and quiver against this unexpected situation. With each passing second, the cliff's edge hurtles closer. A decision must be made–turn or risk flying over the edge.

I scan the snowy landscape, hoping for Michelle's presence to help me. She skied ahead after I snapped a glamorous pic of her showcasing a designer outfit. Oblivious to my predicament, she skied ahead and is probably nestled in the warm ski lodge awaiting our lunch date.

To be fair, I didn't disclose my agony at skiing or the alien sensation of having a ski strapped to my high-tech, carbon fiber prosthetic, which made me unable to feel the snow under my skis. I regained my mobility and the ability to ski, but the mountain and my skis felt unfamiliar.

My solitary descent mirrors my current journey—a lonely trek filled with unending challenges and obstacles. The pain of my disappointment of not being able to enjoy skiing is worse than the stabbing leg pain.

I make the split-second decision. Leaning hard on my right leg, I attempt to execute a turn. My prosthetic leg bends suddenly, and instead of catching the edge of the ski to turn me and slow my descent, it pops—buckling. Then, the entire leg, with the ski, detaches from its anchor.

"Oh, for the love of ..." I mutter under my breath, watching my lucky pink wooly frog-adorned sock, which adorns my prosthetic leg, continue skiing down the slope without me.

Left stranded and off-balanced, I quickly adapt to balance on my wobbly right leg, careening toward the cliff's edge. I need to cut left without a left ski. Desperately, I fight for control, plunging my poles into the snow to slow me as I turn. At its limit, my right leg gives out, collapsing underneath me.

Tumbling uncontrollably through the pristine snowscape, I brace for the impending fall. With a jolt, I crash into a solid tree trunk instead, narrowly avoiding the perilous drop over the cliff edge.

Escaping disaster by mere inches, I lay breathless in the cold embrace of the mountain, frustration and disbelief washed over me.

"Well, this is just great," I mutter. The bitter taste of defeat lingers in my mouth as adrenaline courses through my veins.

I escaped going over the cliff to be buried, without my equipment to get back down the mountain. Acid fills my mouth, thinking of the familiar ski run trying to kill me by refusing me this one small victory of skiing and trapping me on this ledge.

It doesn't matter that I can ski this run in a blizzard, and I've skied black diamonds since I could walk. *I can't do it.* The mountain strips me of my confidence, paralyzing me with doubt and stranding me in its icy grip.

Alone and chilled to the bone, I lean against the tree that saved me from a potentially deadly fall. My spirit is bruised and my shattered expectations are worse than any pain my left stump could give me.

I hit the empty space in my snow pants, accidentally banging my left knee. Shooting pain fills my eyes with tears.

As I absentmindedly brush the snow from my hair, I think, *There's no reason to be alive if I can't even ski.* Half of my Alaskan winters are spent on the slopes, and without skiing, there's nothing for me during the harsh, dark Alaskan winters. I might as well resign myself to a life devoid of adventure, get a cat or three, and give up trying. I can't do *anything.* I'm as useless as the collection of left high-heeled shoes piled inside my closet.

Tears I usually hold back stream down my cheeks. There's no one to see or hear me. I indulge in a moment of self-pity. I'm *a useless one-legged freak.* Once upon a time, I soared past everyone on these slopes, but now, I'm stuck and buried in snow.

I was an adventurer and created the wildly popular "Tundra Trendsetter" social media platform with my Alaska wilderness partner, Michelle. We met in the Talkeetna competition for the Wilderness Woman title.

Michelle was glamorous, and I was aggressive in the contest's fishing, hunting, and wood-chucking race. Despite our efforts, the hairy, male crowd crowned a local woman as the winner. I didn't win a title that day, but I won Michelle, a fellow lesbian and adventurer.

Michelle is an outdoor model and influencer who loves traveling, which made our pair-up perfect since I love adventure, travel, and taking selfies atop every Alaskan peak. I'm independently wealthy, so there was nothing to get in the way of our fun until recently.

With no adventures in the last year, I haven't posted pictures of myself lately. She's become the *solo* Alaska Wilderness Woman taking over our brand, Tundra Trendsetter.

I'm a fucking cripple. I'm a has-been, a mere shadow of my vibrant self. My attempt to reclaim my glory and enjoy the outdoors, skiing on my childhood mountain, failed—*I'm the failure.* The mountain hasn't changed. My skis are the same—I'm the only one who's changed. I'm the obstacle in the Alaskan outdoors who no longer fits.

A cheerful voice pierces through the darkness of my spiraling thoughts.

"Hey, need some help up?"

I pause, hastily wiping away my tears and snot with the back of my glove. Turning, I face my rescuer. She's in a bright red Alyeska Ski Instructor uniform with her name, *Peekaboo*, shimmers embroidered in gold on her left pocket. Yet, instead of standing tall and authoritative, she perches gracefully on a seated ski contraption thingy, revealing a defect more significant than mine.

A frustrated laugh slips out with my tears at the ridiculousness of my situation. It's the blind leading the blind. With tears still glistening on my cheeks, I wearily exhale at the absurdity of our encounter—it's as if fate has brought her to show me that my life isn't too bad.

She moves closer with her specially designed adaptive rig. It's a skiing seat with three skis underneath, a hand steering device for the front smaller ski, and her poles tucked into the side. "Glad to see you're in good spirits. Let me give you a hand," she says, smiling.

I grumble, "I actually need a leg, *not* a hand." I gesture with my pole toward my prosthetic, skiing uninhibited down the slope.

With Peekaboo's poles securely anchored in defiance of the mountain's gravitational pull, she steals a final glimpse of my vibrant sock swooshing down the hill towards the ski lodge below. A chuckle escapes her red lips. "Just another day on the slopes," she quips nonchalantly, a hint of amusement dancing in her words.

Her infectious positivity cuts through my wallowing self-pity. I can't help but crack a smile at the sight of the solitary leg skiing the Alyeska slopes.

She moves her mirrored ski goggles back, and I note her rich, brown eyes framed by thick, dark brown braided hair and her sun-kissed complexion. Her face conveys happiness and her time spent outdoors—probably on this very mountain.

"This damn mountain is trying to kill me," I grumble halfheartedly as her sunny presence coaxes my grimace into a smile.

Her rainbow pride hat clashes with her ski uniform. With her nonchalant demeanor and playful smile my initial frustration dissipates. I reconsider my helplessness: *I'm alive and unharmed.* With the lodge not far below us, I sit up and contemplate how I will navigate down the mountain with my ski.

Leaning down, she tucks a stray black baby curl behind her ear before saying, "You look good. Can you move?"

I nod, brush off the remaining snow, and sit up. I look below, contemplating the daunting task of descending the mountain. Luckily, this is the last hill before the lodge.

"Slide over to my rig. You can hold onto the back for balance and ski down. We'll grab your adventurous prosthetic leg on the way down...It is a prosthetic, right?" Her playful yet confident gaze meets mine as she lifts her brows and quirks her lips.

"Yeah. It has a mind of its own," I reply, her presence melting away the last of my frustration, and I almost sound like I'm joking.

I appreciate her unwavering confidence in my ability, assuming I can easily manage the ski down. This assumption is a refreshing departure from the pity associated with my disabled condition. She treats me like any other skier she's encountered. Her happy, casual conversation speaks volumes, reminding me that I'm capable of overcoming obstacles—even if it involves skiing on one leg.

She waits with an annoyingly chipper smile, but I appreciate that she gives me space and doesn't offer to further help me or to call the ski patrol. I hate being treated differently, and I want to yell at people who hold doors for me and stand, giving me their seats. I don't–*but I want to!*

Shaking off my inner turmoil, I gather my resolve and push myself onto my knees. I groan, "I'm coming." Placing my ski poles in one hand, I unsnap my remaining ski. Holding it, I methodically use my elbows and knees to inch my way toward her, crawling the short distance as she watches without comment or rushing me.

"Hey, tie your stuff down with the bungee and hold on to the handles. There's a ledge to sit or kneel on," she explains.

I stow my ski and poles, balance myself, and hold the handles, ready. This isn't Peekaboo's first ski rescue.

"You all set back there?" she chirps, her tone more of a statement than a question.

"I'm set," I reply, trying to project confidence while sitting on the back of her fancy rig.

"Hey, what's your flava? Do you want an adrenaline rush or leisurely glide down?" Her gaze meets mine, a glint of mischief dancing in her eyes. She's egging me on.

I chuckle, relishing the playful challenge reflected in her intense eyes. "Let's go fast," I declare to the spirited ski instructor. The daring of her dark eyes reminds me of the thrill of my kayak just before I shoot into the river's rapids.

She reaches back to ensure my equipment is secure, and I notice her muscular arms straining against her snug jacket. Despite her physical limitations, an aura of strength and confidence enveloped her, leaving me in awe. In my realization that she rescued me, shame washes over me for my complaints when she faces far greater challenges and obviously doesn't let them stop her or give her a piss-poor attitude.

A unique connection blossoms within me as she propels us down the slope. I hold tight as she whoops, "Geronimo! Powder Rocket!"

Clutching onto the rig for dear life, I realized she wasn't exaggerating. Zooming downhill like a vibrant comet, we effortlessly overtake the solitary skiers below. The wind wildly whips my golden locks, unraveling my messy bun, but I relish the sensation of speed and freedom.

There's no way I'm letting go of her rig's handles to fix my unruly hair as we speed down the snowy slope with her laugh. We are a blur of motion against the pristine canvas of white. The whistling wind fills my ears, and the thrill of speed makes me grin.

Peekaboo defies gravity, slicing straight down the slope instead of a zigzagging path. She accelerates with impressive velocity. With the lodge looming ahead, she shows no signs of easing up, propelling us at breakneck speed.

I tense, bracing myself for an imminent collision with the wooden structure. But just before disaster strikes, she executes a flawless stop, the three blades of her rig expertly angling skillfully to halt our momentum, enveloping us in a cloud of icy powder.

I laugh with delight and nerves at the sudden deceleration, a dramatic contrast to our heart-pounding, high-speed descent. Her skill and precision are excellent, and I wonder how I've never seen her on the mountain before, considering I've spent half my life skiing Alyeska. Peekaboo's no newbie to these slopes.

"Consider yourself delivered," she quips with a twinkle in her eye, gesturing to the cozy lodge nestled at the snowy base of the mountain.

I follow her gaze—we are alongside the lodge.

"Bad leg! You were supposed to wait for me," I scold my leg and ski, resting against the lodge's log wall.

Her laughter rings out, a melody of warmth and joy echoing with a comforting and delightful charm.

I laugh with her and at my own light-hearted comment. Perhaps it's the adrenaline spike from our trip down the mountain because I've never joked about my prosthetic limb. Maybe it's Peekaboo's easy laugh sparking my unnatural gaiety.

Peekaboo's laughter fills the crisp mountain air, a blend of warmth and joy.

Seizing the moment, I introduce myself, "I'm Caitlyn." I shake her hand, then sit down to reattach my stupid leg. I add with a shrug, "Sorry. I'm new to this."

"I'm Peekaboo," she replies with a charming smile and a nod. "Hey, I've got a ski class to teach in a few minutes if you'd like to join?"

Her offer stings, offending me because she thinks I'm a newbie and need beginner ski lessons. I size up the young, attractive ski instructor. *I've been skiing longer than you've been walking.*

"No. Thank you for the help," I manage, politely declining her offer and masking my hurt feelings. My emotions are swirling with the adrenaline fading, and I'd like to walk away, but I'm still fiddling with the straps on my leg. Despite being safe and reunited with my leg, tears gather in my eyes.

Peekaboo shrugs, her easy smile never wavering. "Anytime. We all need a hand—*or leg*—sometimes." She quirks her lips, and they go back to her default, friendly smile. She tilts her head at me with a sparkle in her eyes.

I chuckle at her joke and the warmth spreading in me as I study her lips. "I'm going to sit the next few runs out and have some lunch. No need to ski every black diamond run today."

She winks and turns.

"I'll be around for a few more days. Will you be hitting the slopes tomorrow?" The question slips out instinctively, an unexpected invitation. I'm not even sure why I asked her this. I don't need lessons, and I'm *not* flirting.

"Catch me around the same time. I'm always here. We can do some runs before I start my afternoon lessons. I'm teaching the bunny hill class today." She looks over to the circular ski rope towing lift at the side of the lodge. A group of children, a few with adaptive skiing devices, are huddling, and waiting for her.

Oof, she's busy with a class waiting, and I'm slowing her down. I grimace, feeling a pang of guilt for holding her up. I rise from my seat with a sheepish expression, preparing to give her a friendly wave.

"Caitlyn, where have you been? I've been waiting forever," Michelle, my perfectly outfitted and coiffed partner, interrupts. She strolls up the epitome of outdoor elegance in her sleek white ski outfit, raven hair flowing around her. Her green eyes glow against the snow. She is stunning, and she looks precisely like a model waiting for a skiing photo shoot.

She turns to frown at Peekaboo, who presumably is the reason I'm late to our lunch date. She frowns at her, but her annoyance is probably at being hungry and worried. Plus, she planned for me to take pics of her hot chocolate and lunch in front of the lodge fireplace for her followers.

"Sorry to make you wait," I apologize, gesturing towards Peekaboo. "This is Peekaboo. Peekaboo, this is my partner, Michelle."

Michelle offers a polite nod. "Nice to meet you," she says without extending a hand, her long nails skittering across each other, the sun catching the sparkles in her polish.

"Hi, Michelle. It's lovely to meet you," Peekaboo smiles and adds, "I gotta run to teach. I'm sure I'll see you guys on the mountain." She winks at me, pushing off with her ski poles to glide down to the rope tow and her waiting, giggling class.

I let out a breath. Peekaboo didn't—*thank goodness*—elaborate on how we met. I don't want to hear Michelle tell me I need to take it easier or end our ski trip early.

"What are you doing hanging out with someone like *that*? People might think you're disabled, too," Michelle chides me as she gracefully turns to make her way into the lodge, expecting me to follow.

"You're giving the lost puppy vibe, chillin' with *that type* of person," Michelle playfully scolds, her tone laced with a mix of concern and annoyance. Without looking back, she makes her entrance into the lodge, leaving me behind.

Chapter 2: Peekaboo

As I enjoy a gummy from my pocket, the sour sweetness dances in my mouth, pulling me away from reality. The kids waiting by the ski lift wave, their energy contagious. Seeing how far they've come since timidly starting lessons yesterday is incredible. With newfound confidence and determination, they eagerly race to get on the lift first.

I had a crazy idea to use gummy worms as a confidence booster for the students, and it worked like magic. With a pack of gummies on hand, I've become the unofficial Gummy Worm Guru of the slopes. Yesterday's bunny slope slayers are ready to take on the aptly named Gummy Worm run without hesitation.

All thanks to a little sugar-coated bravery and my special brand of encouragement, these kids are skiing fearlessly.

Skiing away from the adorable skier I rescued, I can't help but shake my head at the scene that unfolded. Caitlyn was determined to conquer the slopes, her disability be darned. It was a familiar scenario—watching someone new to their disability try to defy it entirely. With her fierce determination, though, she makes it more enduring than annoying. She oozes independence, but a little ski instruction wouldn't hurt.

I want to help Caitlyn build her confidence on the slopes and introduce her to some nifty adaptive devices like my trusty seated ski slider for extra speed. Sure, she doesn't need a seated contraption. Still, a custom ski leg could work wonders for her stability and safety. Heck, even the outrigger ski poles with mini skis attached to the bottom could be a game-changer. There are plenty of adaptive ski options to allow her independence if she's open to trying them out.

Glancing back as Michelle steps into the lodge, I can't help but feel a soft spot for Caitlyn's journey. After all, I'd been in her shoes – well, ski boots – once upon a time as a new quadriplegic ten years ago. Who knows? Maybe together, we will carve out some epic adventures on these snowy mountains.

I wasn't a strong skier before my accident. But my accident forced me to enjoy, adapt, and slow down, which made me fall in love with skiing. Skiing and finding freedom on the slopes inspired me to become an instructor and help others find the same freedom and joy without letting their disability stop them.

Turning back to check on Caitlyn, I see her struggling to walk into the ski lodge. Ahead of her, her drop-dead gorgeous partner is gone, offering her no support. Her beautiful partner is an ice princess. Michelle didn't look back as she rushed inside the warm ski lodge. It starkly contrasts the camaraderie I teach to my students. Helping each other and asking for assistance makes skiing better for everyone. Skiing at the beautiful Alyeska Resort is a shared experience, not a solo endeavor.

I can see she's struggling, and I want to help. I'll have to gently ask about her mobility limitations. As I watch her alone outside the lodge,

I wonder, How long has she been dating the ice princess? Maybe I can offer moral support for her skiing and her dating situation.

I know about strained relationships from disabilities, too. Caitlyn is an extraordinary person, I can tell. I'm magnetically drawn to her as if we were meant to meet. With a sharp pang, I realize that I care about Caitlyn. Sure, I rescued her, and I could help her with skiing, but our connection is more than the chance encounter and a skiing rescue. I felt an immediate warmth in my chest of finding a kindred spirit when she set her fierce, blue eyes on me despite being covered in the cold snow.

The strength in her blue eyes caught my attention more than her blonde hair and flawless skin. I couldn't resist helping her ski down and making lighthearted jokes to lessen her frustration. However, my attraction to her wasn't just about helping her—I wanted to make her laugh. She made me feel a wave of protectiveness for her and a heady excitement, stirring up emotions inside me that are odd and hard to define.

Watching the determined Alaskan woman trudge through the snowy walkway to the lodge tugged at my heartstrings. With each step towards the lodge, she struggles but never gives up. Reluctantly, I turn back to my class, leaving Caitlyn with her ice princess. Skiing away, my heart flutters, hoping for another chance to see her unbreakable spirit on the slopes tomorrow.

My mind can't help but stay focused on Caitlyn. She's a total standout with that infectious laugh and razor-sharp wit tucked behind her grumpy facade. We share a love for speed and adrenaline, which only makes her more irresistible. Her wild blonde locks and athletic build perfectly contrast to my solid body and dark hair. She doesn't fit with the dainty-looking ice princess at all.

When Caitlyn threw back her head in laughter as we zoomed down the hill together, we got along like old friends, not new acquaintances.

The way she craves adventure and risks, just like me, is beyond captivating—it's a sign.

We met for a reason. She's an adventurous Alaskan woman stuck with a humorless, waiflike, green-eyed ice princess. She needs my help.

Guiding myself toward the ski class awaiting me, I smile at the group of enthusiastic kids greeting me with waves and cheers. The pure joy in their eyes warms my heart.

To my little ski students, I am not just their disabled instructor - I'm Peekaboo, the mastermind behind all things fun on the slopes. With jokes, gummy worms flying left and right, and expert guidance down the mountain, these kids are thriving. Moments like watching their pure joy and excitement make teaching worth it. Their innocence allows them to focus on the adventure of skiing rather than physical differences or barriers.

"Hey, Peekaboo! Ready for another epic day on the slopes?" shouts Jake, a spirited young boy with boundless energy. His wheelchair is transformed into a cool adaptive ski rig. His mom hovers to help, but he's got it.

"Absolutely, Jake! Are we going to break our speed record today?" I playfully respond, ruffling his hair.

"Definitely!" he exclaims, grinning.

"Take our pic," he tosses his phone at me before I can even respond. Kids and their socials! I snap the pic and hand his phone back.

I exchange fist bumps and high-fives with the kids. Each of our greetings fills the crisp mountain air with happiness. I love being their ski instructor and giving them the confidence and know-how to navigate this mountain. One of my favorite things is seeing them improve throughout the ski lessons and their confidence on the slopes years after teaching them.

Maybe Caitlyn needs a partner who sees beyond her disability and appreciates her?

With a quick mental shake, I usher the kids towards the tow rope, resisting the urge to steal one last glance back at the lodge.

I hope she takes me up on my offer to ski tomorrow. I want her to have a positive experience and the thrill of conquering the mountain without fear. Everyone deserves to ski and whoosh down the hill, uninhibited.

But it's more than my teacher's instincts. Her smile and wit that were waiting for me to trigger them makes me want to see her again and hear the sound of her happy yelps. My heart races, and I feel more alive.

I sigh, kicking myself for not getting her number. It's not like I could with her drop-dead gorgeous partner hovering.

Michelle had an aversion towards me, probably because I was messing up her plans. Maybe she sensed my strong connection with Caitlyn. She didn't exactly welcome me when we met.

Would she have been different if she knew I saved Caitlyn? I caught a nervous look from Caitlyn, silently signaling me not to spill the beans about our mountain skiing adventure.

My heart races as memories of Caitlyn struggling in the snow flood my mind. She was angry but adorable, cursing at her leg going down the mountain without her. Once she was safe, she lightened up, and her laugh changed the mood instantly until Michelle showed up.

As I approach the ski lift, thoughts of Caitlyn dance in my mind. I can show her how much fun skiing can be. The idea of making her laugh makes me blush – Caitlyn deserves someone who cherishes her laughter and companionship, not a pretty face who scolds her.

Before I dwell too much on everything wrong with the ice princess, my spirited class diverts my attention. Their enthusiasm is infectious as they eagerly surround me. With animated chatter, they push towards the tow lift line, creating a bubble of excitement around us.

I remind them amidst the chaos, "Remember to take turns and aim your skis where you want to go."

"Come on, Peekaboo," shouts Jake. "You don't want to miss the lift! I need a gummy worm, too."

The mention of gummy worms brings a laugh as I pat my pocket containing our secret snack stash. "Today, gummy worms await at the bottom of the Gummy Worm slope – let's conquer it together, team," I exclaim with a grin.

And just like that, surrounded by my enthusiastic students, all thoughts of Caitlyn fade away as I prepare for another exhilarating day on the slopes.

Chapter 3: Caitlyn

"If you wanna be treated like everyone else, stop chillin' with disabled peeps!"

My cheeks flush with embarrassment, and a pang of hurt stabs at my heart as Michelle lays into me for being rescued by Peekaboo. It's déjà vu from yesterday's lunch debacle. Instead of laughing with me over the absurdity of my leg skiing solo down the slope or being grateful for Peekaboo's help, she's angry about the situation. I thought she'd bounce back with an apology for ditching me and maybe even suggest hitting the slopes today.

Instead, she's hyper-focused on my "issues."

"I thought you were back to normal. Didn't therapy greenlight your skiing?" Michelle's words hit like a cold slap. Her frustration is heavy, turning our cozy winter ski vacation into a fight.

My heart races, catching every harsh syllable. This argument is a dead-end street, and I know she's not mad at me but hates all the difficulties with my prosthetic leg. She wants to get back to our normal adventures. I nod and look down at my leg, attached and secure, hidden under my pants and socks.

"You need to figure it out, you know. You can be normal if you want. We can get back to being normal again," she says, her frustration echoing in the small space, creating an extra layer of frost.

I'm angry and frustrated, too. I want to be normal. I want to race down the slopes without stressing that I'm going to lose my leg and potentially kill myself.

The cold Alaskan air outside the cabin seeps into the room despite our fireplace and Merino wool outdoor layers. The chill settles into my bones–so much for a relaxing ski week to reconnect with her.

I glance out the window, hoping the sparkling, snow-covered landscape will lighten the mood. The sky is perfectly blue. A blanket of white powder covered the mountain last night, making the slopes ideal for skiing today. Skiers navigate the slopes with grace outside the resort windows.

A flash of movement catches my eye. A young skier, effortlessly maneuvers downhill, navigating the twists and turns with one skied leg and two poles with skis on the ends. I'm surprised, and impressed by his skill. With a pang of guilt, I realize disabled skiers are a part of these slopes—I never noticed them until now.

Frowning at my oversight, I acknowledge the invisible bias that once clouded my vision. People like me, navigating the world with different tools, were overlooked until I joined their ranks. Does Michelle see them? Does she see me anymore?

The skier moves gracefully, carving arcs out of sight over the hillside. A part of me feels a connection, an unspoken camaraderie with him.

Yet, beneath the admiration, a twinge of tightness, a more complex emotion stirs. I'm not jealous, but I realize I'm holding myself back, blaming my leg instead of embracing the challenge.

Seeing the kid effortlessly navigate the slopes ignites a quiet determination within me. If he can do it, I can. I resolve to hit the slopes today, to fall and get back up until I conquer every run.

My mind flashes to the striking and cheerful ski instructor, Peekaboo, and her expertise in using the skiing-sled thingy. There are plenty of people on these slopes who are skiing and enjoying this activity with much more of a disability than losing part of their leg. Peekaboo is full of joy and inspiration, making skiing and just being easy when I am around her. It's funny that before, I would have seen her disability first. Today, I saw her on the mountain. I noticed the spunkiness and the foxy, outdoorsy energy she carried.

I bite my lip and wonder how I've skied these slopes for years without truly seeing the people sharing the hill with me. I was so focused on taking selfies, and pushing my speed that I ignored everyone else. Certainly, Alyeska has always had disabled skiers, and I'm just seeing them today.

I turn to Michelle, eager to share my newfound perspective, but her lips are pressed together. She's huffy about our fight and not ready to talk.

I change the conversation, saying, "Skiing was a good idea. I'm glad we came. We have loads of pics on these mountains...Good memories."

She looks back at me, tilting her head. Then her eyes soften, and she looks at me with a sparkle. "Absolutely! We can totally make some epic memories and snap more pics. You're almost back to your fab self, right? I know our vibe is off lately, and I'm totally sorry about that."

"Me, too," I say.

"I'm really craving how we were," she whispers, crossing her arms. "I miss our epic trips and races with all our fans cheering for us," she says and meets my eyes with a small smile.

I nod. I'm glad we are talking it out. Michelle is a huge part of my Alaskan adventurous lifestyle. We are a brand. When we film an epic hike, that's the it thing to do in Alaska. I hate that my accident drove us apart. We can't do activities, and we can't even share a bedroom, let alone a meal, without tension. This trip is about helping us to reconnect.

"Remember the thrill of slayin' those black diamonds in that ice crystal snow storm? That's the vibe I'm missing," she continues.

Is she talking about those once-in-a-lifetime sparkling online pictures earning her a new partnership with an outdoor equipment company or braving the crazy elements unfazed together?

She gestures toward me, her hand pausing mid-air as she points at my left leg. "This isn't what I had in mind when we started. But you can do everything. We can still heli-ski and ice cave climb. You're not holding us back anymore."

Us? Does she mean like us as a power lesbian couple? Or us, as an outdoor wilderness influencer brand? I feel the sting of her words, knowing she's not intending to be cruel, only voicing her feelings.

It's my fault, as I have hammered the point that I don't want to be treated differently and that I'm still the same adventurous woman she started dating a few years ago. But I'm struggling to ski regular runs, and she's thinking we are going back to our crazy daredevil Alaskan stunts. We aren't on the same page or even in the same book.

The person she loves has changed—I've changed.

I yearn for the past, for the effortless joy of skiing black diamonds. I want to be normal and not need to figure out how to make it through every situation. I'm functional, but reality is rewriting my dreams, and whether I like it or not, I'm different from last year.

I've been hitting a wall lately, maybe because I'm stuck in the past. It's time to take a cue from others with prosthetics who are rocking the slopes. I can't keep clinging to how things used to be before the accident—it's time for a new approach. Watching that fearless kid zooming down the hill, it hits me: why am I hesitating to adapt and embrace rocking the slopes? Time to shake off the old habits and carve out a new path, literally. Who knows, maybe this shift in perspective will lead to some unexpected thrills and adventures?

I'm a fighter—a winner. I like a challenge, and I'm not backing down from this one. Determination resonates within me. Maybe it's possible to ski again and to find a new normal with Michelle. I'm different, but different could be better.

I turned to Michelle, her eyes looking out at the mountainside. "I want to continue our Tundra Trendsetters brand with our Alaskan wilderness women adventures, but this is who I am now," I say, pleading for her to understand, "I'm still me."

She frowns and doesn't look at me, swallowing hard.

"I can't go back, and I need your support," I say, my voice cracking with emotion. "I need you, Michelle."

Slowly, she turned to me, her eyes guarded and distant. The distance between us felt like an insurmountable canyon. She lets the silence stretch, unwilling to accept the person I've become—the person I am. The realization hits me, punching me in my gut.

Tears spring in my eyes, and I say softly, "If you can't accept me for who I am now... maybe it's time we take different paths." With those words hanging in the air, the weight of reality settles into the space between us.

"We're fine. Don't be a drama queen," she says, rolling her eyes.

Michelle and I are on shaky ground, teetering on the edge of change in our relationship. Her silence speaks volumes, louder than any words could convey. She fails to apologize and only hears my words without listening to the meaning of what I am trying to share with her.

She looks away, lost in thought. "I can't do this right now, Caitlyn," she finally says with a heavy sigh.

I nod with a tinge of sadness, hoping she'd remember our shared adventures and good times. She used to say we were unbeatable as a team, ready to conquer any challenge that came our way. We survived white-water rafting in Alaska with a duct-taped hole in our raft. That was the kind of duo we were back then – united and strong.

"Let's hit the slopes," she says, grabbing her gear, all business.

Surprise and a hint of sadness fill the room as the door slams shut. Yet, I muster up my determination to join her on the lift.

A day of skiing side by side will reignite the bond we once had. And who knows? Maybe it will open up a chance for us to finish talking and work things out..

As she storms away, I fumble to collect my things and follow her. The simple act of putting on my snow pants is frustrating. My stubborn left foot isn't bending correctly, and it catches on the inside of the pants, making me fall headlong into the wall.

Michelle disappears with her skis, leaving me defeated. I plop down, determined not to give up. After a struggle, I wrangle the pants on the right leg and slip them over my left leg—victory!

I shake my head and groan. Every mundane task now requires extra time and patience. It's a reminder of how everything has changed for me lately. I'm not letting these darn pants or anything else get in my way.

Time to ski!

Continue reading Peekaboo and Caitlyn's heartwarming story in *Wilderness Rescue: Healing Hearts*.
CHECK IT OUT HERE.

Join us to discover your next favorite story at HarmonyNoble .com &

**Sign up to receive the e-newsletter for exclusive news and give-
aways.**
CHECK IT OUT HERE.

Coming Next

WILDERNESS RESCUE: HEALING HEARTS

Sometimes the steepest mountains lead to the sweetest collisions—a story of skiing, healing, and love.

Get ready to race down the ski slopes where two paths cross on a wild ride of love and self-discovery to navigate physical and emotional obstacles to find heartwarming love in this couple-swap, small town romance.

Caitlyn, affectionately known as Cat, whose fearless spirit conquers mountain peaks and marathons. However, a life-altering accident has left her grappling with a loss of confidence and identity.

Can she overcome her inner turmoil and grumpiness to reclaim her belief in herself and find love?

Peekaboo has an infectious zest for life and shines as a dedicated ski instructor, she inspires others with disabilities to embrace joy and adventure. Yet, behind her vibrant facade lies a heart yearning for something more—a love that ignites passion and fulfills her deepest desires.

On the pristine slopes of Alyeska, Cat and Peekaboo's paths converge, sparking an unlikely connection that defies the odds.

Torn between duty to her devoted partner and longing for fiery passion, will Peekaboo choose love?

Author's Note: Explore these thrilling LGBTQ+ adventures intertwined with sweet sapphic romances in the <u>Wilderness Rescue Series</u>.

Experience an inspirational story of love when Peekaboo and Caitlyn ski into a fast-paced romance in <u>*Wilderness Rescue: Healing Hearts.*</u>

CHECK IT OUT HERE.

Discover your next favorite story at <u>HarmonyNoble.com.</u>

OTHER TITLES BY HARMONY NOBLE
For the most up-to-date list visit Harmony's website at www.HarmonyNoble.com.

<u>Aurora's Wilderness Love:</u>

Hot Girl Summer Love

<u>Wilderness Rescue Sapphic Romance Series:</u>

Crashing Into Love
Unthaw My Heart
Winning Love
Stormy Hearts
Scoring Love
Flooded Hearts
Healing Hearts
Tides of Love
Iditarod Love

<u>Coffeehouse Romance Series:</u>

Love, Joy & Lattes (Joy's Story)
Test Driving a Millionaire (Tara's Story)
Shattering Crystal a Bully Romance (Crystal's Story)
Choosing Love, Namaste (Meaghan's Story)
The Wrong Bride for Christmas (Monica's Story)

Coffeehouse Romance Short Stories:

Joy's 4th of July Holidate
Tara's Valentine Holidate
Crystal's Easter Holidate
Meaghan's New Year Holidate
Monica's Halloween Holidate
My Accidental Christmas Fiancé
Joy's Coffeehouse Romance

UNLOCK YOUR GIFT

Happy Reading & EMBRACE TRUE LOVE!

Snag the latest swoon-worthy reads and stay tuned for upcoming stories at www.HarmonyNoble.com.

About Author – Harmony Noble

Meet the unstoppable twins from the rugged wilds of Alaska—Harmony & Melody, the duo of "Author Harmony Noble." Fueled by endless lattes, their character-driven stories brim with authenticity, humor, and heart—featuring Alaskan grit, journeys of self-discovery, and swoon-worthy happily-ever-afters.

When they're not crafting adventure romances, the twins can be found hiking trails with breathtaking views, enjoying charming coffee shops, or exploring new cultures and destinations worldwide.

Join the e-newsletter for exclusive content and giveaways at website: https://harmonynoble.com
Email: TrueLoveWriters@gmail.com
Instagram/Facebook/TikTok: @truelovewriters

Healing Hearts

Harmony Noble

SCAN FOR GIFT

TrueLoveWriters

**Thank you for choosing this book
by Harmony Noble. We hope the story
brought you as much joy reading it
as we had in creating it!**

We'd love to hear from you! Feel free to reach out via email at True LoveWriters@gmail.com, and don't forget to follow us on Instagram, Facebook, TikTok at @truelovewriters for the latest updates and behind-the-scenes fun.

Get access to exclusive offers, bonus content, new release updates, and recommendations for more great reads. Sign up for our e-newsletter at HarmonyNoble.com.

Dedicated to Mindy Michelle Smith Alderson, M&M
10/08/1978 to 3/03/2024

You beat me to the end of the race called Life.
I still pick up my phone to read our texts, or try to call you to share
good news, just waiting to hear your silly giggle. I cherish the precious
memories and will love you forever.

You Win,
after 41 years together you will now be younger than me.

Healing Hearts

Harmony Noble

SCAN FOR GIFT

TrueLoveWriters

Chapter 1

Caitlyn

The frigid Alaskan mountain air nips at my rosy cheeks as I carve Girdwood's sun-glistened slopes at Alyeska Ski Resort. Racing down the double black diamond Midnight Express, I grit my teeth, determined to ski through the constant pain in my left knee. With each thud of my skis turning sharply against icy moguls, my leg jolts with pain, cruelly reminding me of my unwelcome changes since the previous ski season.

I've had a whirlwind of a year since the rock-climbing mishap that claimed my left leg. But here I am, back in action and ready to embrace the great outdoors again. With single-mindedness, I ski down the snow-covered slopes, chasing the remnants of my Alaskan adventurous spirit. The icy breath of winter bites and makes my eyes water as I gulp in the pristine air, igniting my soul—this is precisely the feeling I missed while injured and rehabilitating the last few months. Also, I missed the exhilaration of the mountains during my grueling recovery. Finally, I can enjoy the outdoors again. Consequently, I'm back downhill skiing the slopes of Alyeska, rediscovering the adventurous Alaskan spirit that defines me. With a radiant grin, I glide gracefully down the snow-covered slopes, reconnecting with the thrill-seeking essence that pulses through my veins.

The familiar and challenging Alyeska ski mountain stretches before me with the whooshing winds, daring me to slice through them on my ski edges. This mountain has been my playground since the tender age of six when I fearlessly carved my way down its icy trails while my parents called out futile warnings to rein in my speed. Despite their attempts to tame my wild spirit with ski lessons, I left a trail of defeated instructors in my snowy wake. The adrenaline rush from racing down the mountain is a familiar thrill, igniting a fiery passion in my soul for speed and the boundless freedom of the vast Alaskan wilderness.

As the sharp ache pierces through me, I struggle to catch my breath. I'm acutely aware of the immense challenge my winter wonderland has become in my current state. With each turn, my heart beats in perfect harmony with my skis slicing through the snow. Tentatively, I opt for a more deliberate pace, unsure of my legs' stability. The skis wobble beneath me, uncertain as I attempt to steady my racing pulse and slow my frantic descent.

Surveying the run, I find myself alone amidst the vast expanse of the desolate mountain. My partner, Michelle, is nowhere in sight. As I gaze up at the towering Alyeska mountain range, it beckons to be explored and conquered. Confidence surges through me as I race downhill. *Nothing stands in my way!*

With a rush of exhilaration, I zip down the treacherous black diamond slope. The wind whips past me. I forget my body is different until a sharp jolt of pain shoots through me as my prosthetic lower leg suddenly jams straight into my left knee. The searing pain snaps me back to reality—my right quadricep burns with a sudden effort to bear all my weight to keep me from falling.

Struggling to maintain balance and control, I fight against my rebellious left leg prosthetic, which is locked in a straight position, throwing me off-kilter. My right leg can't take all the weight for long, and my left ski is dangerously weaving.

Panic washes over me like a frosty avalanche. I frantically attempt to wrestle back control, every fiber of my being tensing under the weight of the crisis. Leaning further, I throw a wild punch at my frozen left knee in a desperate bid to force it into alignment. But, it remains stubbornly stuck. My prosthetic is frozen in place. I am unable to maneuver my skis or ease my breakneck speed.

In my desperation, I hoist up my left leg and vigorously shake it—a daring feat—all while maintaining my precarious balance. My left ski is useless, with the leg locked straight. Painful protests erupt from my right leg as my muscles strain and quiver against this unexpected situation. With each passing second, the cliff's edge hurtles closer. A decision must be made–turn or risk flying over the edge.

I scan the snowy landscape, hoping for Michelle's presence to help me. She skied ahead after I snapped a glamorous pic of her showcasing a designer outfit. Oblivious to my predicament, she skied ahead and is probably nestled in the warm ski lodge awaiting our lunch date.

To be fair, I didn't disclose my agony at skiing or the alien sensation of having a ski strapped to my high-tech, carbon fiber prosthetic, which made me unable to feel the snow under my skis. I regained my mobility and the ability to ski, but the mountain and my skis felt unfamiliar.

My solitary descent mirrors my current journey—a lonely trek filled with unending challenges and obstacles. The pain of my disappointment of not being able to enjoy skiing is worse than the stabbing leg pain.

I make the split-second decision. Leaning hard on my right leg, I attempt to execute a turn. My prosthetic leg bends suddenly, and instead of catching the edge of the ski to turn me and slow my descent, it pops—buckling. Then, the entire leg, with the ski, detaches from its anchor.

"Oh, for the love of ..." I mutter under my breath, watching my lucky pink wooly frog-adorned sock, which adorns my prosthetic leg, continue skiing down the slope without me.

Left stranded and off-balanced, I quickly adapt to balance on my wobbly right leg, careening toward the cliff's edge. I need to cut left without a left ski. Desperately, I fight for control, plunging my poles into the snow to slow me as I turn. At its limit, my right leg gives out, collapsing underneath me.

Tumbling uncontrollably through the pristine snowscape, I brace for the impending fall. With a jolt, I crash into a solid tree trunk instead, narrowly avoiding the perilous drop over the cliff edge.

Escaping disaster by mere inches, I lay breathless in the cold embrace of the mountain, frustration and disbelief washed over me.

"Well, this is just great," I mutter. The bitter taste of defeat lingers in my mouth as adrenaline courses through my veins.

I escaped going over the cliff to be buried, without my equipment to get back down the mountain. Acid fills my mouth, thinking of the familiar ski run trying to kill me by refusing me this one small victory of skiing and trapping me on this ledge.

It doesn't matter that I can ski this run in a blizzard, and I've skied black diamonds since I could walk. *I can't do it.* The mountain strips me of my confidence, paralyzing me with doubt and stranding me in its icy grip.

Alone and chilled to the bone, I lean against the tree that saved me from a potentially deadly fall. My spirit is bruised and my shattered expectations are worse than any pain my left stump could give me.

I hit the empty space in my snow pants, accidentally banging my left knee. Shooting pain fills my eyes with tears.

As I absentmindedly brush the snow from my hair, I think, *There's no reason to be alive if I can't even ski.* Half of my Alaskan winters are spent on the slopes, and without skiing, there's nothing for me during the harsh, dark Alaskan winters. I might as well resign myself to a life devoid of adventure, get a cat or three, and give up trying. I can't do *anything.* I'm as useless as the collection of left high-heeled shoes piled inside my closet.

Tears I usually hold back stream down my cheeks. There's no one to see or hear me. I indulge in a moment of self-pity. I'm *a useless one-legged freak.* Once upon a time, I soared past everyone on these slopes, but now, I'm stuck and buried in snow.

I was an adventurer and created the wildly popular "Tundra Trendsetter" social media platform with my Alaska wilderness partner, Michelle. We met in the Talkeetna competition for the Wilderness Woman title.

Michelle was glamorous, and I was aggressive in the contest's fishing, hunting, and wood-chucking race. Despite our efforts, the hairy, male crowd crowned a local woman as the winner. I didn't win a title that day, but I won Michelle, a fellow lesbian and adventurer.

Michelle is an outdoor model and influencer who loves traveling, which made our pair-up perfect since I love adventure, travel, and taking selfies atop every Alaskan peak. I'm independently wealthy, so there was nothing to get in the way of our fun until recently.

With no adventures in the last year, I haven't posted pictures of myself lately. She's become the *solo* Alaska Wilderness Woman taking over our brand, Tundra Trendsetter.

I'm a fucking cripple. I'm a has-been, a mere shadow of my vibrant self. My attempt to reclaim my glory and enjoy the outdoors, skiing on my childhood mountain, failed—*I'm the failure.* The mountain hasn't changed. My skis are the same—I'm the only one who's changed. I'm the obstacle in the Alaskan outdoors who no longer fits.

A cheerful voice pierces through the darkness of my spiraling thoughts.

"Hey, need some help up?"

I pause, hastily wiping away my tears and snot with the back of my glove. Turning, I face my rescuer. She's in a bright red Alyeska Ski Instructor uniform with her name, *Peekaboo*, shimmers embroidered in gold on her left pocket. Yet, instead of standing tall and authoritative, she perches gracefully on a seated ski contraption thingy, revealing a defect more significant than mine.

A frustrated laugh slips out with my tears at the ridiculousness of my situation. It's the blind leading the blind. With tears still glistening on my cheeks, I wearily exhale at the absurdity of our encounter—it's as if fate has brought her to show me that my life isn't too bad.

She moves closer with her specially designed adaptive rig. It's a skiing seat with three skis underneath, a hand steering device for the front smaller ski, and her poles tucked into the side. "Glad to see you're in good spirits. Let me give you a hand," she says, smiling.

I grumble, "I actually need a leg, *not* a hand." I gesture with my pole toward my prosthetic, skiing uninhibited down the slope.

With Peekaboo's poles securely anchored in defiance of the mountain's gravitational pull, she steals a final glimpse of my vibrant sock swooshing down the hill towards the ski lodge below. A chuckle escapes her red lips. "Just another day on the slopes," she quips nonchalantly, a hint of amusement dancing in her words.

Her infectious positivity cuts through my wallowing self-pity. I can't help but crack a smile at the sight of the solitary leg skiing the Alyeska slopes.

She moves her mirrored ski goggles back, and I note her rich, brown eyes framed by thick, dark brown braided hair and her sun-kissed complexion. Her face conveys happiness and her time spent outdoors—probably on this very mountain.

"This damn mountain is trying to kill me," I grumble halfheartedly as her sunny presence coaxes my grimace into a smile.

Her rainbow pride hat clashes with her ski uniform. With her nonchalant demeanor and playful smile my initial frustration dissipates. I reconsider my helplessness: *I'm alive and unharmed.* With the lodge not far below us, I sit up and contemplate how I will navigate down the mountain with my ski.

Leaning down, she tucks a stray black baby curl behind her ear before saying, "You look good. Can you move?"

I nod, brush off the remaining snow, and sit up. I look below, contemplating the daunting task of descending the mountain. Luckily, this is the last hill before the lodge.

"Slide over to my rig. You can hold onto the back for balance and ski down. We'll grab your adventurous prosthetic leg on the way down...It is a prosthetic, right?" Her playful yet confident gaze meets mine as she lifts her brows and quirks her lips.

"Yeah. It has a mind of its own," I reply, her presence melting away the last of my frustration, and I almost sound like I'm joking.

I appreciate her unwavering confidence in my ability, assuming I can easily manage the ski down. This assumption is a refreshing departure from the pity associated with my disabled condition. She treats me like any other skier she's encountered. Her happy, casual conversation speaks volumes, reminding me that I'm capable of overcoming obstacles—even if it involves skiing on one leg.

She waits with an annoyingly chipper smile, but I appreciate that she gives me space and doesn't offer to further help me or to call the ski patrol. I hate being treated differently, and I want to yell at people who hold doors for me and stand, giving me their seats. I don't–*but I want to!*

Shaking off my inner turmoil, I gather my resolve and push myself onto my knees. I groan, "I'm coming." Placing my ski poles in one hand, I unsnap my remaining ski. Holding it, I methodically use my elbows and knees to inch my way toward her, crawling the short distance as she watches without comment or rushing me.

"Hey, tie your stuff down with the bungee and hold on to the handles. There's a ledge to sit or kneel on," she explains.

I stow my ski and poles, balance myself, and hold the handles, ready. This isn't Peekaboo's first ski rescue.

"You all set back there?" she chirps, her tone more of a statement than a question.

"I'm set," I reply, trying to project confidence while sitting on the back of her fancy rig.

"Hey, what's your flava? Do you want an adrenaline rush or leisurely glide down?" Her gaze meets mine, a glint of mischief dancing in her eyes. She's egging me on.

I chuckle, relishing the playful challenge reflected in her intense eyes. "Let's go fast," I declare to the spirited ski instructor. The daring of her dark eyes reminds me of the thrill of my kayak just before I shoot into the river's rapids.

She reaches back to ensure my equipment is secure, and I notice her muscular arms straining against her snug jacket. Despite her physical limitations, an aura of strength and confidence enveloped her, leaving me in awe. In my realization that she rescued me, shame washes over me for my complaints when she faces far greater challenges and obviously doesn't let them stop her or give her a piss-poor attitude.

A unique connection blossoms within me as she propels us down the slope. I hold tight as she whoops, "Geronimo! Powder Rocket!"

Clutching onto the rig for dear life, I realized she wasn't exaggerating. Zooming downhill like a vibrant comet, we effortlessly overtake the solitary skiers below. The wind wildly whips my golden locks, unraveling my messy bun, but I relish the sensation of speed and freedom.

There's no way I'm letting go of her rig's handles to fix my unruly hair as we speed down the snowy slope with her laugh. We are a blur of motion against the pristine canvas of white. The whistling wind fills my ears, and the thrill of speed makes me grin.

Peekaboo defies gravity, slicing straight down the slope instead of a zigzagging path. She accelerates with impressive velocity. With the lodge looming ahead, she shows no signs of easing up, propelling us at breakneck speed.

I tense, bracing myself for an imminent collision with the wooden structure. But just before disaster strikes, she executes a flawless stop, the three blades of her rig expertly angling skillfully to halt our momentum, enveloping us in a cloud of icy powder.

I laugh with delight and nerves at the sudden deceleration, a dramatic contrast to our heart-pounding, high-speed descent. Her skill and precision are excellent, and I wonder how I've never seen her on the mountain before, considering I've spent half my life skiing Alyeska. Peekaboo's no newbie to these slopes.

"Consider yourself delivered," she quips with a twinkle in her eye, gesturing to the cozy lodge nestled at the snowy base of the mountain.

I follow her gaze—we are alongside the lodge.

"Bad leg! You were supposed to wait for me," I scold my leg and ski, resting against the lodge's log wall.

Her laughter rings out, a melody of warmth and joy echoing with a comforting and delightful charm.

I laugh with her and at my own light-hearted comment. Perhaps it's the adrenaline spike from our trip down the mountain because I've never joked about my prosthetic limb. Maybe it's Peekaboo's easy laugh sparking my unnatural gaiety.

Peekaboo's laughter fills the crisp mountain air, a blend of warmth and joy.

Seizing the moment, I introduce myself, "I'm Caitlyn." I shake her hand, then sit down to reattach my stupid leg. I add with a shrug, "Sorry. I'm new to this."

"I'm Peekaboo," she replies with a charming smile and a nod. "Hey, I've got a ski class to teach in a few minutes if you'd like to join?"

Her offer stings, offending me because she thinks I'm a newbie and need beginner ski lessons. I size up the young, attractive ski instructor. *I've been skiing longer than you've been walking.*

"No. Thank you for the help," I manage, politely declining her offer and masking my hurt feelings. My emotions are swirling with the adrenaline fading, and I'd like to walk away, but I'm still fiddling with the straps on my leg. Despite being safe and reunited with my leg, tears gather in my eyes.

Peekaboo shrugs, her easy smile never wavering. "Anytime. We all need a hand—*or leg*—sometimes." She quirks her lips, and they go back to her default, friendly smile. She tilts her head at me with a sparkle in her eyes.

I chuckle at her joke and the warmth spreading in me as I study her lips. "I'm going to sit the next few runs out and have some lunch. No need to ski every black diamond run today."

She winks and turns.

"I'll be around for a few more days. Will you be hitting the slopes tomorrow?" The question slips out instinctively, an unexpected invitation. I'm not even sure why I asked her this. I don't need lessons, and I'm *not* flirting.

"Catch me around the same time. I'm always here. We can do some runs before I start my afternoon lessons. I'm teaching the bunny hill class today." She looks over to the circular ski rope towing lift at the side of the lodge. A group of children, a few with adaptive skiing devices, are huddling, and waiting for her.

Oof, she's busy with a class waiting, and I'm slowing her down. I grimace, feeling a pang of guilt for holding her up. I rise from my seat with a sheepish expression, preparing to give her a friendly wave.

"Caitlyn, where have you been? I've been waiting forever," Michelle, my perfectly outfitted and coiffed partner, interrupts. She strolls up the epitome of outdoor elegance in her sleek white ski outfit, raven hair flowing around her. Her green eyes glow against the snow. She is stunning, and she looks precisely like a model waiting for a skiing photo shoot.

She turns to frown at Peekaboo, who presumably is the reason I'm late to our lunch date. She frowns at her, but her annoyance is probably at being hungry and worried. Plus, she planned for me to take pics of her hot chocolate and lunch in front of the lodge fireplace for her followers.

"Sorry to make you wait," I apologize, gesturing towards Peekaboo. "This is Peekaboo. Peekaboo, this is my partner, Michelle."

Michelle offers a polite nod. "Nice to meet you," she says without extending a hand, her long nails skittering across each other, the sun catching the sparkles in her polish.

"Hi, Michelle. It's lovely to meet you," Peekaboo smiles and adds, "I gotta run to teach. I'm sure I'll see you guys on the mountain." She winks at me, pushing off with her ski poles to glide down to the rope tow and her waiting, giggling class.

I let out a breath. Peekaboo didn't—*thank goodness*—elaborate on how we met. I don't want to hear Michelle tell me I need to take it easier or end our ski trip early.

"What are you doing hanging out with someone like *that*? People might think you're disabled, too," Michelle chides me as she gracefully turns to make her way into the lodge, expecting me to follow.

"You're giving the lost puppy vibe, chillin' with *that type* of person," Michelle playfully scolds, her tone laced with a mix of concern and annoyance. Without looking back, she makes her entrance into the lodge, leaving me behind.

Chapter 2

Peekaboo

As I enjoy a gummy from my pocket, the sour sweetness dances in my mouth, pulling me away from reality. The kids waiting by the ski lift wave, their energy contagious. Seeing how far they've come since timidly starting lessons yesterday is incredible. With newfound confidence and determination, they eagerly race to get on the lift first.

I had a crazy idea to use gummy worms as a confidence booster for the students, and it worked like magic. With a pack of gummies on hand, I've become the unofficial Gummy Worm Guru of the slopes. Yesterday's bunny slope slayers are ready to take on the aptly named Gummy Worm run without hesitation.

All thanks to a little sugar-coated bravery and my special brand of encouragement, these kids are skiing fearlessly.

Skiing away from the adorable skier I rescued, I can't help but shake my head at the scene that unfolded. Caitlyn was determined to conquer the slopes, her disability *be darned*. It was a familiar scenario—watching someone new to their disability try to defy it entirely. With her fierce determination, though, she makes it more enduring than annoying. She oozes independence, but a little ski instruction wouldn't hurt.

I want to help Caitlyn build her confidence on the slopes and introduce her to some nifty adaptive devices like my trusty seated ski slider for extra speed. Sure, she doesn't need a seated contraption. Still, a custom ski leg could work wonders for her stability and safety. Heck, even the outrigger ski poles with mini skis attached to the bottom could be a game-changer. There are plenty of adaptive ski options to allow her independence if she's open to trying them out.

Glancing back as Michelle steps into the lodge, I can't help but feel a soft spot for Caitlyn's journey. After all, I'd been in her shoes – well, ski boots – once upon a time as a new quadriplegic ten years ago. *Who knows?* Maybe together, we will carve out some epic adventures on these snowy mountains.

I wasn't a strong skier before my accident. But my accident forced me to enjoy, adapt, and slow down, which made me fall in love with skiing. Skiing and finding freedom on the slopes inspired me to become an instructor and help others find the same freedom and joy without letting their disability stop them.

Turning back to check on Caitlyn, I see her struggling to walk into the ski lodge. Ahead of her, her drop-dead gorgeous partner is gone, offering her no support. Her beautiful partner is an *ice princess*. Michelle didn't look back as she rushed inside the warm ski lodge. It starkly contrasts the camaraderie I teach to my students. Helping each other and asking for assistance makes skiing better for everyone. Skiing at the beautiful Alyeska Resort is a shared experience, not a solo endeavor.

I can see she's struggling, and I want to help. I'll have to gently ask about her mobility limitations. As I watch her alone outside the lodge, I wonder, *How long has she been dating the ice princess?* Maybe I can offer moral support for her skiing *and* her dating situation.

I know about strained relationships from disabilities, too. Caitlyn is an extraordinary person, I can tell. I'm magnetically drawn to her as if we were meant to meet. With a sharp pang, I realize that I care about Caitlyn. Sure, I rescued her, and I could help her with skiing, but our connection is more than the chance encounter and a skiing rescue. I felt an immediate warmth in my chest of finding a kindred spirit when she set her fierce, blue eyes on me despite being covered in the cold sno w.

The strength in her blue eyes caught my attention more than her blonde hair and flawless skin. I couldn't resist helping her ski down and making lighthearted jokes to lessen her frustration. However, my attraction to her wasn't just about helping her—I wanted to make her laugh. She made me feel a wave of protectiveness for her and a heady excitement, stirring up emotions inside me that are odd and hard to define.

Watching the determined Alaskan woman trudge through the snowy walkway to the lodge tugged at my heartstrings. With each step towards the lodge, she struggles but never gives up. Reluctantly, I turn back to my class, leaving Caitlyn with her ice princess. Skiing away, my heart flutters, hoping for another chance to see her unbreakable spirit on the slopes tomorrow.

My mind can't help but stay focused on Caitlyn. She's a total standout with that infectious laugh and razor-sharp wit tucked behind her grumpy facade. We share a love for speed and adrenaline, which only makes her more irresistible. Her wild blonde locks and athletic build perfectly contrast to my solid body and dark hair. She doesn't fit with the dainty-looking ice princess *at all*.

When Caitlyn threw back her head in laughter as we zoomed down the hill together, we got along like old friends, not new acquaintances. The way she craves adventure and risks, just like me, is beyond captivating–it's a sign.

We met for a reason. She's an adventurous Alaskan woman stuck with a humorless, waiflike, green-eyed ice princess. *She needs my help.*

Guiding myself toward the ski class awaiting me, I smile at the group of enthusiastic kids greeting me with waves and cheers. The pure joy in their eyes warms my heart.

To my little ski students, I am not just their disabled instructor - I'm Peekaboo, the mastermind behind all things fun on the slopes.

With jokes, gummy worms flying left and right, and expert guidance down the mountain, these kids are thriving. Moments like watching their pure joy and excitement make teaching worth it. Their innocence allows them to focus on the adventure of skiing rather than physical differences or barriers.

"Hey, Peekaboo! Ready for another epic day on the slopes?" shouts Jake, a spirited young boy with boundless energy. His wheelchair is transformed into a cool adaptive ski rig. His mom hovers to help, but he's got it.

"Absolutely, Jake! Are we going to break our speed record today?" I playfully respond, ruffling his hair.

"Definitely!" he exclaims, grinning.

"Take our pic," he tosses his phone at me before I can even respond. *Kids and their socials*! I snap the pic and hand his phone back.

I exchange fist bumps and high-fives with the kids. Each of our greetings fills the crisp mountain air with happiness. I love being their ski instructor and giving them the confidence and know-how to navigate this mountain. One of my favorite things is seeing them improve throughout the ski lessons and their confidence on the slopes years after teaching them.

Maybe Caitlyn needs a partner who sees beyond her disability and appreciates her?

With a quick mental shake, I usher the kids towards the tow rope, resisting the urge to steal one last glance back at the lodge.

I hope she takes me up on my offer to ski tomorrow. I want her to have a positive experience and the thrill of conquering the mountain without fear. Everyone deserves to ski and whoosh down the hill, uninhibited.

But it's more than my teacher's instincts. Her smile and wit that were waiting for me to trigger them makes me want to see her again and hear the sound of her happy yelps. My heart races, and I feel more alive.

I sigh, kicking myself for not getting her number. It's not like I could with her drop-dead gorgeous partner hovering.

Michelle had an aversion towards me, probably because I was messing up her plans. Maybe she sensed my strong connection with Caitlyn. She didn't exactly welcome me when we met.

Would she have been different if she knew I saved Caitlyn? I caught a nervous look from Caitlyn, silently signaling me not to spill the beans about our mountain skiing adventure.

My heart races as memories of Caitlyn struggling in the snow flood my mind. She was angry but adorable, cursing at her leg going down the mountain without her. Once she was safe, she lightened up, and her laugh changed the mood instantly *until Michelle showed up.*

As I approach the ski lift, thoughts of Caitlyn dance in my mind. I can show her how much fun skiing can be. The idea of making her laugh makes me blush – Caitlyn *deserves* someone who cherishes her laughter and companionship, not a pretty face who scolds her.

Before I dwell too much on everything wrong with the ice princess, my spirited class diverts my attention. Their enthusiasm is infectious as they eagerly surround me. With animated chatter, they push towards the tow lift line, creating a bubble of excitement around us.

I remind them amidst the chaos, "Remember to take turns and aim your skis where you want to go."

"Come on, Peekaboo," shouts Jake. "You don't want to miss the lift! I need a gummy worm, too."

The mention of gummy worms brings a laugh as I pat my pocket containing our secret snack stash. "Today, gummy worms await at the bottom of the Gummy Worm slope – let's conquer it together, team," I exclaim with a grin.

And just like that, surrounded by my enthusiastic students, all thoughts of Caitlyn fade away as I prepare for another exhilarating day on the slopes.

Chapter 3

Caitlyn

"If you wanna be treated like everyone else, stop chillin' with disabled peeps!"

My cheeks flush with embarrassment, and a pang of hurt stabs at my heart as Michelle lays into me for being rescued by Peekaboo. It's déjà vu from yesterday's lunch debacle. Instead of laughing with me over the absurdity of my leg skiing solo down the slope or being grateful for Peekaboo's help, she's angry about the situation. I thought she'd bounce back with an apology for ditching me and maybe even suggest hitting the slopes today.

Instead, she's hyper-focused on my "issues."

"I thought you were back to normal. Didn't therapy greenlight your skiing?" Michelle's words hit like a cold slap. Her frustration is heavy, turning our cozy winter ski vacation into a fight.

My heart races, catching every harsh syllable. This argument is a dead-end street, and I know she's not mad at me but hates all the difficulties with my prosthetic leg. She wants to get back to our normal adventures. I nod and look down at my leg, attached and secure, hidden under my pants and socks.

"You need to figure it out, you know. You can be normal if *you* want. *We* can get back to being normal again," she says, her frustration echoing in the small space, creating an extra layer of frost.

I'm angry and frustrated, too. I want to be normal. I want to race down the slopes without stressing that I'm going to lose my leg and potentially kill myself.

The cold Alaskan air outside the cabin seeps into the room despite our fireplace and Merino wool outdoor layers. The chill settles into my bones–*so much for a relaxing ski week to reconnect with her.*

I glance out the window, hoping the sparkling, snow-covered landscape will lighten the mood. The sky is perfectly blue. A blanket of white powder covered the mountain last night, making the slopes ideal for skiing today. Skiers navigate the slopes with grace outside the resort windows.

A flash of movement catches my eye. A young skier, effortlessly maneuvers downhill, navigating the twists and turns with one skied leg and two poles with skis on the ends. I'm surprised, and impressed by his skill. With a pang of guilt, I realize disabled skiers are a part of these slopes—I never noticed them until now.

Frowning at my oversight, I acknowledge the invisible bias that once clouded my vision. People like me, navigating the world with different tools, were overlooked until I joined their ranks. *Does Michelle see them? Does she see me anymore?*

The skier moves gracefully, carving arcs out of sight over the hillside. A part of me feels a connection, an unspoken camaraderie with him.

Yet, beneath the admiration, a twinge of tightness, a more complex emotion stirs. I'm not jealous, but I realize I'm holding myself back, blaming my leg instead of embracing the challenge.

Seeing the kid effortlessly navigate the slopes ignites a quiet determination within me. If he can do it, I can. I resolve to hit the slopes today, to fall and get back up until I conquer every run.

My mind flashes to the striking and cheerful ski instructor, Peekaboo, and her expertise in using the skiing-sled thingy. There are plenty of people on these slopes who are skiing and enjoying this activity with much more of a disability than losing part of their leg. Peekaboo is full of joy and inspiration, making skiing and just *being* easy when I am around her. It's funny that before, I would have seen her disability first. Today, I saw *her* on the mountain. I noticed the spunkiness and the foxy, outdoorsy energy she carried.

I bite my lip and wonder how I've skied these slopes for years without truly seeing the people sharing the hill with me. I was so focused on taking selfies, and pushing my speed that I ignored everyone else. Certainly, Alyeska has always had disabled skiers, and I'm just seeing them today.

I turn to Michelle, eager to share my newfound perspective, but her lips are pressed together. She's huffy about our fight and not ready to talk.

I change the conversation, saying, "Skiing was a good idea. I'm glad we came. We have loads of pics on these mountains...Good memories."

She looks back at me, tilting her head. Then her eyes soften, and she looks at me with a sparkle. "Absolutely! We can totally make some epic memories and snap more pics. You're almost back to your fab self, right? I know our vibe is off lately, and I'm totally sorry about that."

"Me, too," I say.

"I'm really craving how we were," she whispers, crossing her arms. "I miss our epic trips and races with all our fans cheering for us," she says and meets my eyes with a small smile.

I nod. I'm glad we are talking it out. Michelle is a huge part of my Alaskan adventurous lifestyle. We are *a brand*. When we film an epic hike, that's the *it thing to do* in Alaska. I hate that my accident drove us apart. We can't do activities, and we can't even share a bedroom, let alone a meal, without tension. This trip is about helping us to reconnect.

"Remember the thrill of slayin' those black diamonds in that ice crystal snow storm? That's the vibe I'm missing," she continues.

Is she talking about those once-in-a-lifetime sparkling online pictures earning her a new partnership with an outdoor equipment company or braving the crazy elements unfazed together?

She gestures toward me, her hand pausing mid-air as she points at my left leg. "This isn't what I had in mind when we started. But you can do everything. We can still heli-ski and ice cave climb. You're not holding us back anymore."

Us? Does she mean like us as a power lesbian couple? Or us, as an outdoor wilderness influencer brand? I feel the sting of her words, knowing she's not intending to be cruel, only voicing her feelings.

It's my fault, as I have hammered the point that I don't want to be treated differently and that I'm still the same adventurous woman she started dating a few years ago. But I'm struggling to ski regular runs, and she's thinking we are going back to our crazy daredevil Alaskan stunts. We aren't on the same page or even in the same book.

The person she loves has changed—*I've changed*.

I yearn for the past, for the effortless joy of skiing black diamonds. I want to be normal and not need to figure out how to make it through every situation. I'm functional, but reality is rewriting my dreams, and whether I like it or not, I'm different from last year.

I've been hitting a wall lately, maybe because I'm stuck in the past. It's time to take a cue from others with prosthetics who are rocking the slopes. I can't keep clinging to how things used to be before the accident—it's time for a new approach. Watching that fearless kid zooming down the hill, it hits me: *why am I hesitating to adapt and embrace rocking the slopes?* Time to shake off the old habits and carve out a new path, literally. Who knows, maybe this shift in perspective will lead to some unexpected thrills and adventures?

I'm a fighter—*a winner*. I like a challenge, and I'm not backing down from this one. Determination resonates within me. Maybe it's possible to ski again and to find a new normal with Michelle. I'm different, but different could be better.

I turned to Michelle, her eyes looking out at the mountainside. "I want to continue our Tundra Trendsetters brand with our Alaskan wilderness women adventures, but this is who I am now," I say, pleading for her to understand, "I'm still me."

She frowns and doesn't look at me, swallowing hard.

"I can't go back, and I need your support," I say, my voice cracking with emotion. "I need you, Michelle."

Slowly, she turned to me, her eyes guarded and distant. The distance between us felt like an insurmountable canyon. She lets the silence stretch, unwilling to accept the person I've become—the person I am. The realization hits me, punching me in my gut.

Tears spring in my eyes, and I say softly, "If you can't accept me for who I am now... maybe it's time we take different paths." With those words hanging in the air, the weight of reality settles into the space between us.

"We're fine. Don't be a drama queen," she says, rolling her eyes.

Michelle and I are on shaky ground, teetering on the edge of change in our relationship. Her silence speaks volumes, louder than any words could convey. She fails to apologize and only hears my words without listening to the meaning of what I am trying to share with her.

She looks away, lost in thought. "I can't do this right now, Caitlyn," she finally says with a heavy sigh.

I nod with a tinge of sadness, hoping she'd remember our shared adventures and good times. She used to say we were unbeatable as a team, ready to conquer any challenge that came our way. We survived white-water rafting in Alaska with a duct-taped hole in our raft. That was the kind of duo we were back then – united and strong.

"Let's hit the slopes," she says, grabbing her gear, all business.

Surprise and a hint of sadness fill the room as the door slams shut. Yet, I muster up my determination to join her on the lift.

A day of skiing side by side will reignite the bond we once had. *And who knows?* Maybe it will open up a chance for us to finish talking and work things out..

As she storms away, I fumble to collect my things and follow her. The simple act of putting on my snow pants is frustrating. My stubborn left foot isn't bending correctly, and it catches on the inside of the pants, making me fall headlong into the wall.

Michelle disappears with her skis, leaving me defeated. I plop down, determined not to give up. After a struggle, I wrangle the pants on the right leg and slip them over my left leg—*victory!*

I shake my head and groan. Every mundane task now requires extra time and patience. It's a reminder of how everything has changed for me lately. I'm not letting these darn pants or anything else get in my way.

Time to ski!

Chapter 4

Caitlyn

Despite annoyingly having to re-learn balancing on the uneven slopes and skiing, I'm happy. Resting on my ski poles, cheeks wind-kissed and eyes sparkling with anticipation, I gaze out at the sun-kissed snow below. A radiant golden glow bathes the landscape, coaxing a grin from my lips. I let out a whoop, echoing through the vast white. But immediately, I regret it, wincing at my newly cracked lip from this dry air.

Ugh! *Mental note: never forget Carmex again.*

I'll have to apply thick cream to my lips and wind-blown cheeks when I get back or suffer a hideous rash. And now that I'm posting pictures again, a wind rash isn't on-brand. I pull my fuzzy baklava and hat tighter to cover my face.

"Awooooo!" Peekaboo barks out a wild and accurate Alaska coyote howl.

Her playful imitation of an Alaska coyote's call elicited surprised laughter from me, which blended with her infectious giggles. Our shared amusement echoes through the snowy expanse as we share a bond of playfulness.

As we stand at the top of the mountain, the crisp air filling our lungs, Peekaboo flashes me an encouraging grin. "Alright, Cat, let's get the party started," she says, her enthusiasm infectious.

This morning at the ski lift, I missed catching Michelle, but stumbled upon Peekaboo. Her face lit up with joy as she greeted me with a smile and challenged me to a race down the mountain. Enthralled by her sparkling eyes and mischievous smile, I couldn't resist accepting the dare—a little competition never hurt anyone.

With Peekaboo beside me, I launched myself downhill, focusing on her expert guidance and syncing my movements with hers. She gently coached me on adjusting my stance and technique, helping me find stability on my prosthetic leg while mastering the outrigger poles for balance. Initially, I felt awkward and worried I would crash, but each twist and turn brought a surge of confidence. Encouraging words from Peekaboo propelled me forward as I slice through the snow with newfound freedom and happiness.

As we glide down the mountain together, the worries about falling or crashing fade away, replaced by exhilaration and accomplishment. With Peekaboo's help, skiing is fun again.

When we stop at the next run, I grin at Peekaboo, and say with gratitude, "Thanks for believing in me. I couldn't have done it without you."

Two hours later, we race down the hill, and I'm grinning. As I chase her, I forget to worry about my leg. My thoughts are on the rush of cold air against my face and trying to pass her. My ski's edges grip the mountain confidently. The icy swishing of my skis is as familiar as the ski lodge's bread bowl chili. A newfound trust in my abilities replaces yesterday's fear. I know the mountain, and Peekaboo's instruction helped me regain my rhythm.

She leads me to the black diamond runs, skipping the bunny hills. She chases me as I fly through the slope's twists and turns, marveling at its ease.

"You've got this, Caitlyn! Lean into the turn. Trust your skis!"

I heed her advice, leaning into the turn and carving through the slope. I'm liberated and skiing without the weight of my worries. It's just me, the mountain, and my skis slicing into the snow.

"Yessss! Slope Siren! Slayyy!"

I laugh at Peekbaoo's weird shouts. I look back–me, my skis, the mountain, *and Peekaboo*.

We quickly bonded as ski companions, effortlessly syncing our movements on the snow-covered slopes. There's a magnetic connection, like kindred spirits united by a shared love for skiing and challenging ourselves.

I marvel at her natural ability to both instruct and allow independence. Her presence fills me with confidence, replacing my hesitation. I stop at the point where the slope naturally levels out and pull up my goggles as she stops. "You need a break, *Howling Teacher*," I tease.

She pulls up her goggles, gives me a devilish grin, and howls again on the isolated mountainside, laughing at the echo. "Life is pretty good. Right?" she asks.

I pause—overthinking her statement.

Is life really good?

"It could be worse," she adds with a mischievous eyebrow wriggle.

I shake my head but smile. "Life could also *be better*."

She swings her pole at me.

I duck, nearly getting thwacked by a laughing, innocent-looking ski instructor. I reply, "I guess skiing is fun with a crazy ski buddy."

"You bet it is, Snow Kitten!"

I laugh, "I think I at least earned the title of Snow Cat, or did I hear you calling me Snow Siren?!"

"Hey, let's capture this moment!" she says, nodding to my pocket.

As I retrieve my phone from my pocket, uncertainty washes over me. It's been a while since I captured a moment, and the thought makes me cringe. *Should I have put on makeup today? Is the sun casting unflattering shadows? Will my leg ruin the shot?* Shaking off these doubts, I scold myself for overthinking—*it's only a picture*.

Suddenly, Peekaboo grabs my phone and her eyes lock onto the screensaver image of Michelle and me triumphantly crossing the finish line at Mount Marathon last summer.

"Hey, Mount Marathon – a race I have yet to do. You guys look amazing!" she exclaims, drawing my attention to our beaming faces frozen in time. I offer an awkward smile as memories of that day flood back—my last picture with both legs.

I smile awkwardly. "Yeah, we live in Seward, so it's an annual run up the mountain, for us," I say casually, but the picture leaves a sour taste, reminding me of when I was whole and "normal." Little did I know that the next day, an unfortunate accident would leave me with my leg trapped under a rock after a harrowing fall from the treacherous Turnagain Arm bluffs.

Peekaboo senses my moment of uncertainty and gently places her hand on mine. She glances at the picture closer. Michelle was dazzling in her running gear. I was sweaty but happy beside her with our finisher medals around our necks. "You look really happy. Are you going to do it again this year?"

The question catches me off guard because I hadn't even considered it. "Maybe," I reply tentatively. "I suppose after beating you down Alyeska, I should continue my winning streak. Let's snap a picture before I win!" I tease, trying to appear confident.

Peekaboo smiles and adds, winking, "You actually look pretty stunning and triumphant on the top of this mountain."

"Don't flatter me; I'm focused on winning this race," I say with a blush, her kindness piercing through the shadows of my past.

She takes the phone and says, "Smile, like you mean it. Smile like you are the queen of this mountain!"

I laugh at her, "Alaskan Wilderness Queen!"

She snaps the pic, laughing.

As the sun bathes us in its warm glow, I take charge of the camera phone and position us for a perfect shot with the sun bathing us to look like angels in the pristine glowing white backdrop.

I snap the selfie, capturing my pink cheeks and her devilish grin. My smile is genuine, and I look radiant. The sunny, untouched mountain behind us makes the picture perfect.

For not taking pics in months, I look good–*I haven't lost it.* My leg looks like a leg, but using the outriggers, it's obvious I have a disability. I click on the enhanced lighting and decide not to edit out the poles. I proudly post it to the Tundra Trendsetter site with the caption, "Slaying the Slopes."

Grateful for living in such an awe-inspiring place, I take a deep breath of crisp mountain air and release it in a frosty cloud before adjusting my goggles and gripping my poles tightly. I smile, thinking I'm lucky to live in such a magical place.

Feeling invigorated and ready to conquer the slopes once more, I set off down the mountain with determination. As we carve zigzag patterns across its snowy expanse, nature welcomes us to paint across the hillside with our skis.

She beats me down to the bottom of the run. Resting at the next vantage point, she waits, and I stop beside her. We gaze at Sleeping Lady, an easily identifiable mountain peak shaped like a reclining woman.

Turning towards me with a mischievous sparkle, she leans in and whispers, "Have you ever heard the tale of Sleeping Lady?"

I survey the rugged landscape around us, shaking my head nonchalantly. "Nope, not familiar with it," I reply with a shrug.

With an air of enchantment, she begins to recount the legend, her hands gesturing animatedly as if painting a vivid picture before us. "Long ago," Peekaboo starts in hushed tones, "there lived a Gentle Giant people. Their love for the land, and their harmony with nature was unparalleled. Among them, a young couple, Susitna and Nekatla, fell in love. Their love was so profound that it lit up the sky with dancing lights. Their people celebrated and admired them for the devotion they shared."

As she narrates the story, I listen, my eyes flickering to the beautiful mountain but also to her deep brown eyes, her rounded cheeks, and lush lips. Peekaboo is an amazing skiing companion, an engaging storyteller, and a beautiful woman in her outdoorsy way, with brown braided hair, no make-up, and a lean body. She lights up as she tells the folklore in a way that resonates with respect for the mountains. Her voice and the tale of love, sacrifice, and the passage of time bring tears to my eyes.

"As fate would have it," she continues, "a stranger came bearing ominous news of a warlike tribe to the North. Fearful for their future, the Giant People decided to send their men to negotiate for peace."

Listening to the enchanting tale, I'm captivated by the beauty and depth of her rich mahogany eyes. Her face lights up, and she takes me along, building the excitement and questions as she talks.

My thoughts intertwine with the narrative. The lovers' separation feels similar to my unexpected changes. Their promise to wait for each other makes me gaze over the inlet and mountains as they did in the story, and I ache for them and their sudden separation.

"With Nekatla gone and no news of the returning Giant Men, Susitna waited, her hope waning with each passing day," she narrates.

As I stand here, watching and waiting for a ghost of the past to resurface, a bone-chilling cold creeps into my very core. The longing for a future that will never come, a dream long dead, has transformed her into an unyielding statue. My gaze drifts to the figure of the Sleeping Lady, frozen in eternal rest, and suddenly, I comprehend why she remained and turned to stone.

Peekaboo's voice is somber as she recounts Nekatla's heartbreaking fate. "Days turned into years, and Susitna continued to sleep, dreaming of Nekatla's return," she says.

My heart tightens, realizing the parallel between Susitna's eternal slumber and my stagnation, waiting for something unattainable. Peekaboo's voice fades, leaving the mountains to echo the silence. I gaze at Sleeping Lady with a newfound reverence. The legend touches me in a way I hadn't anticipated. Perhaps it's being on the mountainside or the start of my old fearlessness trickling in during skiing, I contemplate the inevitability of change.

I look again at the mountain, an image of someone being frozen in time unwilling to shift and lean into the change. The snowy, rocky mountain, Sleeping Lady, leaves me with a profound realization that the story, in its essence, isn't just about waiting for a long-lost lover. It's about the danger of not moving forward, of becoming a cold, lonely monument to the past. I see Sleeping Lady with a new respect, understanding her pain. *I will not become stone—I will live,* I promise myself.

Peekaboo, my ski instructor on this snowy escapade, has improved my skiing skills and ignited a flame of inspiration within me. Listening to the story makes me like the storyteller more. Her eyes sparkle with passion, and her words are soft and heavy, with the tale transcending time and place. In this shared silence, I realize I'm ready to embrace my present.

In this shared moment of quiet contemplation, I feel an awakening within myself—a readiness to seize the present with unwavering determination. With adrenaline coursing through my veins and my heart beating with resolve, I turn to Peekaboo with renewed purpose. "Thank you for sharing the legend," I whisper softly, feeling gratitude and hope mingle on my lips as I struggle to find the right words to convey my appreciation for the hope she's given me.

She gives me a gentle, knowing smile before handing me a tube of Carmex. I apply a thin layer to my lips, enjoying touching an object to my lips that has touched her lips. I glide the balm across my lips, savoring the sensation of something that has touched her delicate mouth, which is on mine. I smack my lips together. And our quiet moment stretches, the snow-covered landscape absorbing our unspoken thoughts.

In that serene moment, surrounded by the tranquil, snow-covered landscape, an unspoken warmth envelops me. Without fanfare or proclamations, a surge of energy propels me forward. Captivated by her tender gaze, I am drawn irresistibly closer to her. Our breath mingles in the cold air as our lips meet in a gentle, heartfelt kiss.

The intimate connection sends a rush of warmth through me, causing a shiver to dance down my spine. Though fleeting, her soft lips on mine ignite a fiery passion within my chest, reigniting desires long dormant. In that brief touch lies the promise of endless possibilities, signaling newfound joy in her and the world surrounding us.

As I lean back, a rush of air escapes my lungs, and the cold takes its place, leaving me breathless. The fiery warmth spreading through my chest doesn't allow the coldness inside.

Peekaboo's lips curve into a gentle smile, her honey-sweet eyes shimmer, locking onto mine in an intense gaze. My mind races with a mix of panic and excitement as I struggle to regain control of my thoughts and speech. The sun-kissed mountain before us glistens in the light, mirroring the tenderness melting in my heart for her.

Oh Shit! What is happening? Panic and exhilaration coarse through my veins as I focus my thoughts to form words into sentences and fully formed thoughts to tell her.

"That was unexpected and nice," she muses softly, breaking the spell and gazing towards the mountain. "We both have partners and happy relationships."

A mischievous glint flickers in her eyes as she challenges me to respond, but I'm left speechless. I'm still reeling from the kiss, and my heart is trying to escape my chest.

The confusion and exhilaration slow down enough so I can stammer, "Sorry, it was the rush of adrenaline from our skiing." Tasting the lingering sweetness of her lips on mine, I added with a nervous chuckle, "Consider that my friendly token of gratitude for helping me get my skiing legs back."

Anticipation hangs in the air as I licked my lips, awaiting her reaction. *Does she feel the same magnetic pull between us?*

Her laughter breaks through the crisp mountain air, sending shivers down my spine and heat to my core.

"Sure thing, friend! Come on. Last one to the lodge buys lunch!" she shouts, pushing off, and zooming downhill.

Left standing there, my mind is a tangle of emotions—confusion tied with desire. My heart drums wildly as I yearn for another taste of her. Ignited by a newfound courage, I propel myself forward in pursuit of her captivating figure disappearing over the snowy horizon.

Chapter 5

Peekaboo

"Meow," comes from under our table as we sit down after our exhausting morning of finishing every black diamond run at Alyeska.

Surrounded by cozy wooden tables and lounging skiers, the ski lodge radiates heat from the central fireplace, a welcome contrast to the snowy weather outside. Caitlyn and I settle into a quiet corner table with our steaming mugs of hot chocolate and menus on the table by our discarded wet gloves. The scent of chili and fries wafts through the air, mingling with the laughter and chatter of fellow skiers.

"My God!" Caitlyn exclaims as the lodge cat, Lucky, leaps onto her warm lap.

Unable to contain my amusement, I chuckle softly before quipping, "Lucky certainly has good taste." I give her a lighthearted wink as we share lunch at the bustling ski lodge.

She looks at the cat's hazy blind eyes, the stump of a tail, and ragged white fur, unsure if she should pet or push away the rabid-looking animal.

I try not to giggle when she tentatively pats her head like a dog. Lucky accepts the attention, and settles into her lap.

"I'm not sure *Lucky* fits her. She looks unlucky to me." She grumbles with a smile. She doesn't budge the contented cat from her lap despite her skepticism.

"I think she's *purrrrfect*," I interject playfully, waggling my eyebrows as I adjust my arm braces beside me on the chair. Caitlyn was surprised when I stood from my ski sled and walked into the lodge using my braces.

A burst of laughter escaped me at her surprised expression before I joked, "I'm not really disabled at all. I wanted to give you a chance at winning our ski race."

She fires back with a teasing smile, "You really go all out to give your students confidence." She held the door and followed me into the lodge for lunch.

I find most people write me off as a cripple when they see me with my seated ski device or using a wheelchair, assuming my limitations and labeling me based on appearance alone. Yet, the reality is that a huge range of people use assistive devices with varying abilities and unique stories. Thus, I'm happy to defy labels and challenge the stereotype of who I am as a woman who uses assistive devices in my daily life and skiing.

I've been disabled long enough to ignore the stares and not get annoyed by ignorance. If someone met me at a bar or home, they might not even recognize that I'm unique as I only use my arm braces when walking for a long time. But I cannot go downhill skiing with them, so I use an assistive ski sled to enjoy it.

Reframing the image of what it means to be a quadriplegic, particularly for my students and friends, holds deep significance for me. Through personal experiences, I've learned to overlook the stares and remain unfazed by others' ignorance. A casual encounter at a movie theater or my cabin might not unveil my uniqueness since I don't use my visible assistive devices there. But skiing, and after a long day, there's no way I'm staying upright without the aid of my devices.

Lucky suddenly revs up her loud engine, purring to welcome the affection. The vibrations elicit a bigger grin from Caitlyn. "She's *pawsitively* happy in my lap," Caitlyn quips, and we laugh as her motor roars louder. Lucky kneads her legs in a paw massage.

"Hey, Lucky has decided, you're a cat person," I declare.

"No. Nope. Never. I will not be a spinster, alone in my cabin with three cats," Caitlyn protests with mock seriousness. She shakes her head adamantly. There's an undeniable warmth in her gaze as she grins at the mangy furball warming her lap.

"You just described my life," I deadpan back.

Caitlyn shoots me a quizzical look, raises her brow, and then relents when I meet her gaze. She shrubs and adds, "Sorry. A spinster isn't too bad."

"No, I'm teasing. I *only* have two cats at my cabin." I wink and bite back my laugh.

"Well, if it's *only two,* that's *completely* different," she says, raising her mug. "To two furry mice catchers."

We clink our sweet, whipped cream hot chocolates.

Caitlyn takes a gulp, then licks the whipped cream off her lips, making my heart skip at the sight of her agile pink tongue. On the mountain peak, I reprimanded her after our lovely and much-wanted kiss. I wanted to return the enchanting kiss, but guilt outweighed my flash of desire, making me stop her. But sitting across from her, joking, her tongue transfixes my attention.

I chuckle nervously and drink my hot chocolate, trying not to lick my lips when I set the mug down. I *must* stop flirting and *stop* sending her any mixed messages. Caitlyn is wonderful and super-attractive with a captivating wit, but I'm *not* looking to date her. I'm her instructor and friend.

No more flirting, I tell myself. Even as I think that, my eyes linger on Lucky, who is lucky to be warming her lap and being gently petted by her. I stop myself from commenting on her furry pussy. Instead, I look at Lucky, who purrs with my attention and dares me to say a pussy pun.

"So you walk, huh?" she prompts, examining my metal poles with the plastic holders that fit around my forearms to give me extra stability.

"Since I was one," I say. I set the menu down and tell her seriously, "I dove into a lake in high school and broke my neck. Incomplete C8 quad is the official diagnosis. Unofficially, I can do most things, but my legs and hands are weak. I use the arm braces, the ski device, and a wheelchair occasionally."

Caitlyn nods and sets my arm braces back against the chair.

I lean forward and whisper, "Don't tell anyone I can walk or they'll take away my handicap card, and I *really* like my front row parking."

As we share this moment of candor and connection over our truths, an unspoken bond is forming and strengthening with dense fibers from something more than our surface-level flirtation. I feel like I can trust her, and I instinctively place my hand on her arm.

She puts her hand over mine and squeezes it to show her support. "I thought...with your skiing thing..." she starts, then stops, unsure how to appropriately ask what's going on with my legs.

"That I'm an invalid, confined to a wheelchair," I finished for her. "My legs are not what they used to be, but they work. I use assistive devices to stand and do long periods of weight-bearing activities, like skiing, without problems."

"That's good. You know about my peg leg," Caitlyn says nonchalantly, revealing her physical challenge with a casual joke.

I nod and move my hand, which is itching to stroke her arm. "I'm pretty lucky," I say. And I pet Lucky in her lap, my hand dangerously touching her stomach with each stroke. My belly swarms with hot butterflies. "I didn't make a full recovery from my neck injury, but I live a full life. And I love teaching people to ski. The rig actually makes it easier for me to teach and rescue cute skiers." I laugh and give her a playful wink.

She returns my laugh, adding, "Sorry for asking."

"Caitlyn, don't apologize for asking me about me. I want people to understand and I'd rather they ask than avoid it," I respond.

She nods with acceptance and understanding. When she moves her hand to pet Lucky, our fingers touch, and we leave them together on Lucky. In the cozy lodge, we share our vulnerabilities over laughter and stories, and I'm starting to feel more than friendly emotions. She fully sees me, down to my soul.

I move my hand. "My disability is no secret—not like it can be." I laugh and shake my arm braces at her. "Hey, tell me about your hardware. Are you really a cyborg?"

She smiles and sips her hot chocolate. Caitlyn's eyes soften as she recounts the harrowing tale of her rock climbing mishap from last year. She explains the story through fragments of information provided by her rescuer and her own painful memories.

I reach over and hold her hand to show her my support and care. I wouldn't wish that accident on anyone. Despite her denial of doing anything special—she's very brave to have stayed awake through the pain until someone found her.

"They had to bring in a special construction crane to move the boulder off my leg so I could be flown to the hospital. Apparently, it was a freak accident. I was climbing in the wrong place at the wrong time," she explains mechanically as if to detach herself from being in the story.

I pause, absorbing the silence, with the weight of her words lingering. Lucky meows at her, pawing her affection and support.

As she gently strokes the fluffy fur on Lucky's belly, a wistful smile plays on her lips. The weight of misfortune hangs heavy in the air like a dark cloud casting a shadow over her thoughts. Caitlyn reflects, "I felt cursed. Really, I'm lucky that I got knocked down onto the highway or no one would've found me. Then I had to choose, either lose my life or my leg." She pauses with misty eyes and a faraway look. "Sometimes I wish that Michelle wasn't at the hospital. I might've chosen differently," She says while slowly running her fingers through Lucky's fur.

"I never talk this much. Sorry," she says, shaking her head and shrugging, her blush spreading across her milky white skin.

I listen, absorbing the raw honesty in her words without saying anything. I glimpse into her vulnerability, a side of her that makes my heart ache with understanding. She's still working through her recovery and figuring out who she is and how to function with her new prosthetic. But I've seen her determination. She's driven and unafraid. Despite the challenges she faces in her recovery journey and adjusting to life with a prosthetic limb, there's an undeniable strength in her spirit. I know she'll come to terms with her accident and losing her leg—it's just rocky right now.

"People always say it could be worse," she explains, "but it could've been *a lot better* too. They should've been able to save my leg. I'm healthy and an active person. Losing a leg is more of a loss to me than someone else." She frowns and then looks at me with an apology as if she shouldn't complain about her situation to someone who's broken her neck.

Her voice holds a bitterness for what could have been, a silent plea for understanding. She looks at me with sorrow and empathy. I realize that our journeys may differ, but our struggles are parallel with trying to find joy and live in a harsh environment filled with unempathetic, able-bodied people. I recognize the bitterness and grief that her statement holds, it's a grieving of the lost life that she had envisioned for herself, a life that she planned but was ripped from her. It's a profound grief of loss that is dismissed by statements of 'it could have been worse' or 'you're lucky to have survived.'

I hold up my hands and smile. "No need to qualify your feelings. It's your situation and how you feel. That's your truth," I say before she can say anything more. "No person, no disability, and no recovery is the same. You feel and do what you need to. What I know is, you were amazing on the mountain today. You skied everything without a hitch."

"I was amazing!" she grins like a schoolgirl, adding, "Also, I kicked your butt on the last run!"

"Only because you're a *heartless monster*. You didn't stop to give that kid his lost pole," I say, playfully hitting her on the shoulder and laughing.

"I knew you'd grab it for him," she says with a smile. Then adds, "It totally gave me a chance to win the race to the lodge."

"Cheater!" I say with a laugh as someone catches my eye approaching the table.

"Hiya, Caitlyn! Oh, and..." Michelle chirps, with a casual rudeness to her sudden appearance and greeting. She looks at me, raising a perfectly groomed black brow.

"Peekaboo," I fill in for her, getting up as she sits in the new awkward silence. "I'll go order us chili and fries if you're good with that," I tell Caitlyn as her smile disappears with Michelle's arrival.

Caitlyn nods. She looks guiltily, down at Lucky in her lap.

"Hey Michelle, do you want me to grab you some grub?" I ask, being polite but hoping she'll leave.

Instead of shaking her head or giving me her food order, the ice princess frowns at Lucky. She tilts her head, and I expect her to comment on Lucky. Instead, she says in a frosty voice, "You can walk?"

Her words carry an unexpected weight, almost accusatory in nature. I fight to remain friendly to her.

Caitlyn quickly jumps to defend me, asserting, "Just because she uses assistive devices doesn't mean she can't walk." She shoots me an apologetic glance as I pivot towards the counter with my arm braces to go to place our order.

Brushing off Michelle's sharp comment, I wonder what she'll say about the new ski outrigger device that I gave Caitlyn. Michelle seems very close-minded and intolerant of people with disabilities, or at least me.

I look back, and Caitlyn is watching me while Michelle takes selfies. Her blue eyes meet mine, and she mouths, "Sorry," as I walk to the counter to order, shaking my head at Michelle's rude comment. I'm taking Michelle's non-response as a *no* to food.

Just as Caitlyn and I are exploring our feelings over lunch, Michelle swoops in and disrupts our budding relationship. It dawns on me that befriending someone with such a high-maintenance, rude partner isn't the wisest choice. I'd think small-town lesbians would band together—we've already got enough intolerance against us.

I did see the victorious screenshot of them at the rugged Mount Marathon race. I know they've been together since before Caitlyn's accident, and she's kinder when they are alone. *I hope so, for Caitlyn's sake.*

However, Michelle's character radiates negativity amidst the vibrant energy of our natural rapport. She's a regular rain cloud, casting a shadow over everything, and Caitlyn could use some sunshine.

An evil idea percolates in my mind as I contemplate a little accident with my bowl of chili spilling all over her. That could make her leave. After all, who can blame me for being clumsy with my appalling, questionable disability?

With a giggle at my scheming, I quickly ordered food and returned to find Michelle still at our table. I set my braces down and settled into the silent table. Even Lucky abandoned ship with Michelle's gloomy disposition.

"Who came up with the name *Peekaboo?* Is that, like, your *real* name?" Michelle starts, attempting to have a conversation with her backhanded insults.

Or maybe it's not an insult, but the way she says it is cutting. I've already decided not to like her since Caitlyn deserves a better, more supportive partner who is as wonderful as her. Michelle doesn't fit the bill.

"Peekaboo is what you get when your mom's a hippy and wants you to become an ICU nurse," I responded.

Michelle frowns, and Caitlyn laughs. With a grin, she explains my name to Michelle, "I get it. Peekaboo, ICU."

I laugh at her picking up on the old joke, although it's *not* a joke. I planned to become a nurse when I graduated high school and got a full-ride scholarship. But my post-graduation celebration at the lake, fueled by too much beer and the diving accident, ended that dream. It also opened up another life for me as a ski instructor. This isn't worse than my high school dream of becoming a nurse—it's simply a different path with the same result. I still work with and help people every day.

"How did you and Caitlyn meet?" I ask politely, looking at Caitlyn's clear blue eyes to size up their relationship. When will the chili arrive to execute my plan to *accidentally* spill over Michelle's white ski pants?

Michelle's tanned mocha skin glows unnaturally against the white, fur-lined ski outfit. Does she have to be glowingly gorgeous and Caitlyn's partner? At least she's a bitch. I won the personality contest against her.

Instead of jumping up from a surprise chili accident, Michelle suddenly springs up with excitement, gleefully exclaiming, "Em!"

I turn to see that Emily, my life-long partner, stands before us and laughs, "Em & M is back in the house!"

My bewildered gaze meets Caitlyn's as we gape uncomprehendingly at our partners, watching in confusion.

The air crackles with an unusual energy as they engage in a peculiar greeting ritual, mirroring each other. Their bizarre greeting is a mix of fist bumps, chest shimmies, and nose touches and ends with hip bumps. It's like watching a two-person flash mob. Passersby stop to stare, intrigued by the spectacle. As they finish their greeting, laughter bubbles with their secret girl friendship.

Caitlyn and I could only exchange bewildered looks at our partners, who share a secret world unknown to us. *What is our significant other's mysterious bond?* It feels like a scene ripped from a whimsical rom-com or a foreboding episode of Black Mirror.

"What a welcome surprise," Emily says, moving my braces to sit at the table without further explanation of the over-the-top greeting. "I didn't expect to encounter a *famous* Alaskan fashion influencer today."

"Yo Em, ditch the formality and let's chat like uni roomies," Michelle gushes, with a flutter of her lashes. She catches our confused stares and hastily adds, "Dr. Collins, this is my partner Caitlyn."

Caitlyn warmly receives Emily's grin and handshake warmly before Emily's attention turns to me. Her expression is one of playful inquiry. "Did you escort her down the exhilarating slopes of Alyeska's Midnight Gummy Trail?" she asks, her tone professional and casual, inherent in her profession and opposite of Michelle's greeting.

Caitlyn responds cautiously, "Erm, she did. The Midnight Express, it's called."

Emily smiles and says, "I don't ski but those mountains all have funny sounding names."

"They do," Michelle giggles.

"Sooo, is M&M your former roller derby, rock band name?" I ask them, their obvious connection still unclear.

"Em & M," Emily interjects with a chuckle, correcting me, "Michelle was my freshman roommate at UAA until she abandoned ship to chase fame at the prestigious Art Institute of Seattle."

Caitlyn throws up her hands, looking at Michelle in disbelief, and exclaims, "You went to university?"

"At least I'm not the only one surprised," I say, pushing the fries and chili to the middle to share as the server sets them down with extra silverware and napkins. *Thank god for Alaskan-sized portions* because we can share this with an entire army platoon. Magnanimously, I decided to not help the chili into Michelle's lap.

"Pardon, I'm going to get ketchup and mayo. Should I get anything else? Cat, do you need a drink?" Emily asks politely as we dive into the food.

Caitlyn lifts her brows at her new nickname but doesn't correct her. "Sure."

"Caitlyn," Michelle chirps, ignoring the food, because girls like her avoid carbs.

"Cat's fine. I'm a cat person," Caitlyn responds, swiping her fry in the chili before devouring it.

Michelle shakes her head. "Wait, you hate cats."

"Oh no, a mixed partnership! I know you adore puss," Emily leans in, sounding uncharacteristically like a frat guy to Michelle, then laughing and adding, "Pussy cats! We have three."

"Do you like cats?" Cat stops mid-fry chili dip to ask Michelle.

Michelle shrugs in response and winks at Emily with a sparkle in her eye.

Emily spilling Michelle's embarrassing secrets would be entertaining if I wasn't blushing. I realize that I said we had *two* kitties when Caitlyn pointed asked me moments before.

I hastily corrected Emily by stating, "We *only have two cats.* The third is a feral stray we feed." Caitlyn, or Cat, shakes her head at me and the situation, presumably.

"From the bartender." A guy interrupts, setting down two pitchers of beer.

Michelle titters, "Ah, thanks." And blows a kiss to the young male bartender, who lifts his chin at her. "Does he want my scribbles?" she says as she pulls a pen from her pocket, signing the Tundra Temptress IPA coaster without waiting.

Tundra Temptress is Emily's favorite beer–the *only* beer my partner drinks. I connect the dots, seeing the coaster adorned with Michelle's red bikini body as the pinup 50's girl beer logo.

I guess Michelle doesn't just look like a model—*she is a model.*

"Wait, is this your *nerdy roommate* from pre-med?" I ask Emily.

Michelle burst out laughing. "No cap! I wore glasses and a night guard."

"And the hair turban. Don't forget," Emily adds, and they laugh as Caitlyn and I give up trying to understand their inside jokes.

Caitlyn–*now Cat*–says, tilting her head at me and pointing to the coaster, "It was her first big modeling gig and we get alotta free beer from it."

We lift our pints to her and drink. Our table's energy picks up with the free beer and some funny college stories. Even Michelle is nicer as we finish the lunch. At the end of the day, we are all Alaskan outdoorsy lesbians, which means we share people we know and places we love to hang out.

If I weren't somewhat confused by our partners' friendship and Michelle interrupting my soul connection with Cat, I'd enjoy this comradery. We would make the perfect friend group. Now that the ice princess has unthawed, this is pleasant.

Maybe we can all be friends, and Michelle will grow on me like a hairy mole.

I look at her, applying black mascara—*in public, without a mirror!* She fluffs her raven locks and snaps a selfie.

Nope! There's no chance I'm friending the ice princess!

As this thought crosses my mind, Emily asks, "Do you two want to join us for dinner tomorrow? I have work at the hospital, but I'm off at seven. I can bake some halibut. Michelle already knows, I make a mean Caesar salad."

Michelle smiles and enthusiastically agrees, "Of course. We'll BYOB." She lifts her beer with an adorable giggle.

Ugh! Before I can make an excuse, Emily says, "Great! I'll text you the details." Emily takes Michelle's phone, and they exchange numbers quickly.

I look at Cat, who is equally surprised by the dinner invitation.

Michelle stands. "Come on, Caitlyn–Cat," she says and meows, which dissolves Emily and her into a fit of laughter.

I open my mouth, and Cat looks at me, asking, "Are we trapped in a Black Mirror episode?" She voices my exact thoughts.

"As long as there isn't a weird farewell dance..." I lift my brows, and Cat smirks.

"I booked us hydrotherapy at the hot and cold baths spa," Michelle says with a wave and takes hold of Cat's arm.

"If I'd known I was bumping into you, I'd have booked more spots," she says, looking forlorn at Emily.

"It's fine," I say with a wave.

Emily laughs, saying, "We've been to the Alyeska Nordic Spa. You'll love it and Cat probably needs it after Peekaboo's lessons."

After my lunch with Caitlyn, I have more questions than answers. I shake my head with confusion as they leave.

Chapter 6

Caitlyn/Cat

Cats, cats galore! I try to ignore their persistent presence while I nestle on the comfortable couch at Peekaboo and Emily's snug cabin. A black and white short-haired cat leaps onto my lap. With graceful agility, she climbs, circling around my shoulders before settling herself awkwardly behind my head, her soft body draped across me like a scarf.

I glance up, my eyes drawn to the enormous poster of my partner adorning the wall of the cabin–the infamous Tundra Temptress Model. My partner, Michelle, is immortalized in a beer label, poster-sized and framed picture on their wall.

"Cat, you *are* a cat person!" Peekaboo's laughter fills the room, her eyes sparkling in the warm glow from the wood stove.

I can't help but smile at the cozy atmosphere and the soothing warmth of the cat against my side. Perhaps I should consider getting a feline companion when I return home to Seward. After all, my hectic travel schedule no longer prevents me from having a pet.

"I'm only warm human furniture to her," I reply, returning Peekaboo's smile. The clang of dishes from the kitchen, where Emily and Michelle are cooking, draws my attention. The cat lifts her head, her whiskers tickling my neck and eliciting an involuntary chuckle from me.

"Hey, Biting Llama has good taste. She'd never lay on just any lap," Peekaboo teases.

"Biting... what? Should I be wearing a protective helmet, or perhaps there's a cone we can put around her neck?" I quip. I pull my blonde waves from the messy bun, adjusting my hair to shield my ears from the feline's potential nibbles.

"She's harmless now. But as a kitten, watch out!" Peekaboo chuckles.

Another furball, a fluffy white Siamese with striking blue eyes, saunters into the room. She assesses us with a regal air before settling in front of the hearth. Licking her paws, she gazes at me, challenging me to look away first. I grin and stare back, captivated by her intense stare.

These cats certainly have personalities as large as the mountains in the Alaskan wilderness.

As dinner preparations commenced in the kitchen, Emily ushered us out with good-natured insistence, urging us to relax. At the same time she ordered Michelle to tackle the cooking with her. The cats provide entertainment as they dart between rooms, weaving around our legs and demanding attention.

Oddly enough, the four of us hit it off immediately, sharing jokes and anecdotes as if we were old friends. The cabin resonates with laughter, the crackling warmth of the fireplace, and the mouth-watering aroma of home-cooked food. With a calm and professional demeanor befitting her background as a doctor, Emily effortlessly manages the kitchen like a seasoned pro. Despite her casual attire of jeans and a button-up shirt, her confidence and poise shine through as she attends to the tasks at hand. Her ability to effortlessly balance multiple tasks reminds me of her surgical precision in the operating room, managing every detail with ease.

"Wine, cheese?" Emily pops out to serve us before we'd even started talking.

I tease Emily, "Do you regret your assignment already? Didn't you remember from your university days, Michelle doesn't cook?"

Emily looks at me sideways. "I recall Michelle enjoying baking. She made bread and cookies almost every day. Her baking skills helped me gain the freshman fifteen!"

Michelle laughs, "Don't you dare blame that on me! We both had our round baby faces and thick thighs back then."

Emily ushers Michelle back to the kitchen, calling back to Peekaboo and I, "Em & M is going to surprise you."

I look at Peekaboo and say, "I've learned more about Michelle in two days with you guys than the last two years with her. Bread?" I shake my head and say, "Crazy."

She laughs, and another fuzzball joins us on the couch.

I raise my brows at Peekaboo, studying the fuzzball's rhinestone collar. "Geraldine Anne?"

"Don't let the name fool you. She's the naughty one," Peekaboo laughs, nudging the stretched-out kitty to lie in front of the fire.

Michelle appears, bringing us a plate of hummus. And I rather enjoy her domesticated side. I wink at her, noting the role reversal of her in an apron. Emily was right—she does seem quite at home in the kitchen.

"Thanks," I say, setting the plate on the coffee table and asking, "Why didn't you tell me you bake bread?"

She lifts her chin and proclaims, "I swore off carbs to get fit. I like my abs too much to bake."

In the flickering firelight, I banter and jest with Peekaboo as Michelle and Emily fill the kitchen with their laughter. The meal preparation is either going very well or exceptionally poor, gauging by their laughter. The cabin is extra cozy, with the fireplace crackling and the cats meowing for a taste of halibut providing a pleasant soundtrack. It's been a long time since I've felt this relaxed and at ease socializing.

Maybe it's the wine, but being here, in a cozy cabin with friends, *feels right.*

Despite the darkening sky, snowy weather, and chill outside, the cabin's easy atmosphere is comforting. I find myself forgetting all about the harsh winter weather as Peekaboo and I settle into a comfortable silence, accompanied by our feline companions, Biting Llama and Geraldine Anne.

A furry ragdoll tabby prances in.

"And this is Vlad the Impaler—he's the outdoor stray we feed," Peekaboo introduces as he adds his furry welcome to the crowd. "He hasn't impaled anything yet, but his namesake didn't start impaling until he was thirty, so there's still plenty of time for this naughty cat to show his true colors."

Vlad approaches and rubs his body against my legs. "I've never considered a career in impaling. What do you think Vlad—would I be a good impaler?" I pat his purring body, "it's okay to be a naughty cat." I hear a snicker from Peekaboo and blush when I realize that she was thinking of me when I made that innocent comment.

Michelle emerges with Emily, making me worry that dinner is going quite badly. Glancing out the window, I notice the snow picking up. If we need to order pizza for delivery, we should do so ASAP.

"Caitlyn, you've never considered *a career* before. You really have changed!" Michelle teases and my cheeks burn as I'm hoping the conversation doesn't continue.

Thankfully Emily interrupts, saving me.

"He's a real feral one, right?" Emily says, petting Vlad as he weaves around her calves. Her melodic laughter fills the room, causing me to grin.

Peekaboo covers her face with her hand to stifle her laughter. "Okay, guys, I admit it. He's not a stray—I'm a crazy cat lady!"

"A crazy person never thinks they are crazy, dear," Emily remarks with an authoritative tone. She leans down to kiss the top of her head.

"You are purr-fect and I love that you rescue pussy-cats while I rescue humans." She says before returning to the kitchen, with Michelle trailing behind.

"Should we worry about those two?" I ask Peekaboo.

"Wait, Am I one of the Pussy-cats that you rescued?" I joke.

"Cat, should they worry about us?" she quips back, a playful sparkle in her eye as she licks her lips in a subconscious, sexy gesture.

I laugh and shake my head. "No, I mean about dinner. I've never seen Michelle cook—do you have Pizza Hut on speed dial?"

Peekaboo blushes, scrunching her nose at her mistake. "Oh, ha! No worries, Emily's got everything under control. Dinner will be amazing."

Subtle tension from our earlier kiss and my misplaced romantic feelings flood me as I realize she's thinking about our kiss, too. I shake my head at my earlier impulsiveness, but she must feel our connection. Emily is a doctor and really wonderful, but I don't sense any vibes between Emily and Peekaboo. Then again, perhaps they share that enduring bond of an old married couple, where passion simmers beneath the surface, occasionally flaring up like smoldering coals.

"More of this is needed. For sure," Peekaboo says with a wink, plucking my empty wine glass. Then, she navigates slowly, without any devices, to the kitchen.

Michelle notices and asks, "Why use a wheelchair if you can walk around like a regular person?"

I bite my lip. I might be new to this disabled status, but even I cringe. Michelle doesn't mean to sound rude, but the question is abrasive, ruining the light-hearted atmosphere.

Peekaboo frowns at her blunt question, leaning against the wall as she fills our glasses without answering.

Emily shakes her head and places a hand on Peekaboo's shoulder, saying, "I will handle Michelle." She shoos Peekaboo from entering the kitchen and gracefully tucks her short brown hair behind her ear while pivots to pick up the glasses and open wine from the kitchen counter.

Emily winks at both of us and places the wine bottle with two glasses on the coffee table for both of us to enjoy while she finishes the dinner with Michelle's help in the kitchen.

Peekaboo sits beside me with an unreadable, dark expression that doesn't match her happy-go-lucky disposition. I hope Michelle didn't ruin the night—I was enjoying myself, and Vlad hasn't even impaled anything yet.

In the confines of the small cabin, we overhear Emily's hushed conversation, explaining to Michelle, "So, you may not realize it, but when you use the words 'normal' and 'regular,' comparing a person with different abilities to someone else, it is offensive. What you said implies that a disabled person *isn't normal*, and that they should try harder to be a person they are not and can't go back to being."

"But they *should*. Why wouldn't a person with a defect choose a wheelchair when they can walk?" Michelle's comment cuts like the sharp knife slicing vegetables in the background.

Peekaboo instinctively put her hand over mine as we listened. She tries to reassure me with her nurturing presence due to my partner having the role of the verbal impaler.

I can hear Emily explaining the need for safety due to Peekaboo's reduced strength and that the wheelchair is a tool to help her do what she wants independently. As the stove top fan comes on, their voices blur into the background of cooking noises.

Peekaboo sighs, and I wrap my hand around hers, our palms hot and sticky against each other as we watch the fire crackle while we sip wine.

"I love being dissected and explained. How about you? Do you enjoy having people talk about you like you're not here?" Peekaboo asks, her gaze fixed on the dancing flames.

"It happens more than it used to," I agree, "But when your partner is a famous model, most of the focus is on her anyway," I add with a shrug. "I guess I'm used to it, even before my accident. I mean ... either being ignored or explained."

Peekaboo tilts her head, looking at me intently. "I see you, and you don't have to explain yourself."

Her words cut through the armor I have built around my heart, causing my eyes to tear up and my chest to tighten. I release her hand. This conversation is getting a little too heavy for casual dinner conversation.

Opening up to her, I say, "Before she'd tell everyone 'This is Caitlyn, my partner.' and most assumed she meant I was her partner for our social media stuff." I swallow and look at the fire, too. "Now it's, 'This is Caitlyn. She's been in an accident. She can't seem to tell people I'm her life partner, girlfriend, or lover. And somewhere along the way, we moved from lovers to sharing living space—shared, except the bedroom."

"You don't seem like the asexual type to me," Peekaboo raises a brow, trying to lighten my mood.

I shake my head. I've probably revealed too much and I feel guilty for sharing intimate details of my relationship.

"My sex drive is still here. I wasn't storing it in my lower leg." I say deadpan, then with sarcasm, I add "It's been so long that I am looking forward to my pap smear!"

We both burst into laughter, the tension easing.

I add, "Really, Michelle was so afraid of hurting me and seeing what I look like now, that she can't handle sharing a room, much less about anything else," I shrug, my words trailing off with my hand gesturing toward the kitchen.

She grabs my hand. "Hey, friends hold hands," she says innocently, widening her big brown eyes at me. She leans in and whispers in my ear, her warm breath tickling me and sending chills through my body, "Someone told me they kiss too."

Michelle appears, and Peekaboo moves her hand beside mine, so our hands accidentally touch. I feel her hands warm, and my fingers tingle.

"I'm really sorry, Caitlyn, Peekaboo. I didn't mean to upset either of you. It's just. . . seeing Caitlyn's accident and everything. . . It scared me. It made me realize how fragile life is, you know? And when I see you, Peekaboo, in the wheelchair, it's a reminder of that fear. I didn't handle it well, and that wasn't fair."

Peekaboo responds to fill the silence in the room. "It's okay, Michelle. I understand. It's a lot to process, especially when you care about someone."

I add, "I get it, and I know you didn't mean any harm."

Michelle smiles at us with tears and wipes her hands on her apron. "Aww, my heart is so full right now! Thank you both for your incredible understanding. I'm growing and learning. Caitlyn, babe, if there's anything I can do to make your journey smoother or what...tell me."

I nod, speechless at this woman that is now cooking and apologizing, she looks like my partner but is different. Emily is certainly a good influence on her.

I don't know if it's the fire or the kindness that radiates from her apology, but I can feel my body relax and the air is lighter. I feel more at home in this cabin than in my actual home with Michelle. I acknowledge her apology with a nod and a smile, that she returns before hurrying to the kitchen to continue with her dinner duties assisting Emily.

The fire crackles, casting its warm, flickering glow across the room, and we watch the kitties move positions, and the flames dance. The conversation in the kitchen sounds light and as the door opens to set the dinner table, I hear Emily asking Michelle how she got into modeling.

Michelle begins her story of being discovered by a filming crew when crabbing in Kodiak. The familiar story and the sound of our partners working together to set up the dinner table is a soft hum in the background as I sit next to Peekaboo in comfortable silence.

I break the silence, turning to Peekaboo and asking bluntly, "Why didn't you disclose your relationship status with Emily when we first met?"

Peekaboo's fingers absently stroke Geraldine Anne's fur, her gaze fixed on the dancing flames. A sigh escapes her lips before she answers, her voice soft, "I thought our connection was just a fleeting moment, you know? Adrenaline on the slopes. I didn't realize it would turn into something more. I never expected to feel this way about you."

I study her as she delivers those words.

She does have feelings for me.

Her words send a thrill through me, warming me from the inside out. "Fair enough," I murmur, my gaze lingering on the mesmerizing dance of the fire.

"It was unexpected for me, but I can't deny how awestruck I was the first time we met. Those beautiful blue eyes of yours just cut into me and there was something about you that just drew me in."

"Fair enough," I, again, responded, my gaze lost in the flames licking the logs. "I wasn't planning anything on the top of the mountain. It was a spontaneous moment but it felt really right." I look into her chocolatey, warm eyes, admitting, "But it's more than our chemistry and you being a hot howling woman." I add, "You make me feel understood and like you said, 'you see me.'"

I hold my breath and meet her gaze, the firelight reflecting in her eyes.

"I do," Peekaboo confesses, gazing into my eyes and biting her bottom lip. "I see you. You are beautiful, and stubborn."

I laugh. "The pot calling the kettle black, isn't it?" I add quietly, "And thank you for not pitying me."

Her gaze holds mine, filled with deep emotion that leaves me breathless. "I haven't felt this way about anyone before," she admits, her voice barely audible over the crackle of the flames. "Not even Emily, and we've been together for eight years and we have been friends long before that."

I bite the inside of my cheek. I know exactly what she means. "I love Michelle, and we've been together for two years. She's stuck by me," I say, patting my left leg.

Peekaboo nods, and her pinkie moves to stroke my hand. "Hey, I get it. It's complicated," she agrees, her voice tinged with sadness.

She continues to try and explain the complexity of her relationship. "But for me, Emily is more than just a partner. She's the reason I'm alive. I owe her my life."

I stay silent and listen, my heart heavy with the weight of her words.

Peekaboo continues, her eyes glistening with the start of tears. "When we were in high school, we were friends then dating. We dreamed of getting out of Girdwood and getting married. When I had the accident, she was the one who pulled me from the lake, did CPR, and kept me alive until the ambulance arrived. You see, she literally saved me. Then she cared for me. I owe her everything."

I reach out, squeezing her hand in silent solidarity. "That's heavy," I murmur, my gaze drifting back to the fire. "Emily truly is amazing."

Peekaboo chuckles softly, a bittersweet smile playing on her lips. "Yes, I guess you see why I would never leave her," she says.

My vision blurs with unshed tears, happiness for Peekaboo, and an unfilled longing tugs at my heartstrings. She's got a fantastic partner, and though I'm content with our friendship, everything in me screams for more. My lips feel parched, a physical manifestation of my discomfort, and I absentmindedly rub them.

Without a word, Peekaboo passes me her Carmex, noticing my discomfort. I smooth the warm balm over my lips, savoring the soothing sensation as I hand it back to her—our silent exchange speaking volumes as my heart beats faster.

Peekaboo speaks softly, her voice tinged with resignation. "The fiery lover's passion with Emily. . . it has faded and become more of a simmer. But I owe her everything. I guess I'm just the luckiest, unlucky person. I'm stuck living this dream life with a gorgeous doctor and our three furballs."

I smile and correct her, "Two kitties and a stray. You're not a crazy cat woman."

She shrugs, with a smile tugging at her lips. "Absolutely. How can I complain?"

"I understand," I murmur, my gaze fixed on the hypnotic flames. "I have Michelle. And she loves me and has stood by me. I guess she's a lot like Emily."

When I meet Peekaboo's caring eyes, my heart is heavier with unspoken emotions, looking at the fire in her eyes.

"But I do miss the old spark with Emily, and the new lover's magnetic passion and attraction," She admits.

I reassure her and say, "It wasn't too long ago that I had that with Michelle. The passion I have with Michelle is very different now. I guess because I'm so different than I was two years ago when we met. It's complicated, too."

Peekaboo listens, her expression empathetic, then her lips quirk. "Hey, I get it. Michelle isn't very pretty, and it's hard to love someone so hideously ugly, right?" She laughs and nudges me. "Seriously, she's the most gorgeous lesbian I've met. You shouldn't let her go. We'll make great friends. It's a bonus that our partners are already old friends. We can get together all the time on double dates."

I smile at her optimism, but I don't know how long I can fight the feelings and cravings I have for her, and we've only kissed once. The fire crackles and our shared secrets hang in the air.

A new furball joins us, and I stroke Vlad the Impaler with long strokes, rubbing my pinky along Peekaboo's leg with each pass.

"Did you hear anything I said?" she asks with a twinkle in her eyes.

"Friends can pet kitties together," I say, widening my big blue eyes.

She giggles and strokes him, rubbing my leg while he purrs between us.

I am really starting to like cats.

Our hands occasionally touch each other over the soft fur. In the silence of the cabin, we contemplate each other, ourselves and our partners. Our desires are laid bare in the warm glow, and the question lingers.

Can we just be friends?

Emily and Michelle emerge from the kitchen as if on cue, aprons on, glowing with shared laughter. "Dinner is served," they announce, as they place the silverware to complete setting the table with practiced ease as if cooking together for years.

We follow to the dining table, and the aroma of the food fills my nostrils. Emily is a wonderful partner to Peekaboo. Michelle is learning to be a better partner to me and I appreciate it. Also, it was nice to see the 'Em and M' reconnect by setting the table, cooking dinner, and joking around. I feel like the bad actors, playing along at becoming friends while Peekaboo and I concealing our genuine emotions beneath our laughter.

Michelle engages me in light conversation about our day on the slopes. "I heard you were a force to be reckoned with out there." She dazzles me with her hundred-watt smile. It's a compliment, but my cheeks redden in shame thinking about the day chasing Peekaboo.

Amid the clinking of cutlery and the soft crackle of the fire, Emily and Michelle maintain an upbeat conversation. They effortlessly fill the dining room with stories about university wet t-shirt contests and peeing in the men's urinals since there were never lines for the men's rooms. They fill our glasses and share inside jokes. We have a surprisingly good connection for our new friendship, despite the undercurrent of Peekaboo and my tension.

As if reading my thoughts, Michelle raises her glass, "To new friendships, Alaskan power lesbian couples, and a fabulous Caesar salad—I chopped the lettuce."

Before anyone can respond, the lights flicker out, plunging us into darkness and uncertainty.

Chapter 7

Peekaboo

The cabin's swift darkness is tempered by the warm glow from the fire's flickering shadows on the walls. Outside, snow falls steady and thick, transforming the surroundings into a white winter abyss. Our stunned silence prevails as we process the sudden darkness.

I open my mouth to reassure our guests that the power will return soon—occasional power outages are common in Girdwood. Before I can break the silence, I'm interrupted by the blaring of emergency alerts from our phones, making Cat squeal in surprise, and Michelle drops her phone. The distinct sound of her screen shattering makes me cringe, and she gasps.

"Emergency Alert: EXTREME WEATHER in Girdwood, Alaska. Power & roadways unavailable due to SNOWSTORM. Please shelter in place. Remain off the roads. Call 911 only for an emergency. Services will be restored as soon as possible."

We scramble to silence the loud devices, the messages' urgency sending a chill down my spine. Glancing out the window, the little moonlight illuminates a thick sheet of white in the air, making it impossible to see further than a few feet. The white snow creates an eerie feeling that there's nothing beyond the cabin. Trapped inside the cabin, I shiver.

Emily takes charge. "Cat, Michelle, you're staying the night. I'm calling the hospital, and Peekaboo will grab our candles and flashlights."

"Hey, at least we have wine," I say, attempting to lighten the mood by refilling glasses with the iPhone light, which illuminates the remains of our meal and wine.

With a tight smile, Cat mumbles, "Thanks. This is better than being trapped alone or in our car." She hands her phone to Michelle, who is visibly upset and now holds her broken phone. Then Cat locks eyes with me, and my gut knots thinking of her sleeping here tonight.

Will she wear only that T-shirt to bed?

Cat says, reading my thoughts, "Girls' night," and adds, after meowing interrupts her, "Gals and feline sleepover party."

"Okay, so hear me out, babes. We've got wine, we've got a cozy fire—total vibe, right? Who needs electricity?" Michelle chirps, giving me a smile that could melt even the iciest hearts.

I guess she really is nice underneath, and I'm begrudgingly starting to like her. I can see Emily and Cat nodding in agreement.

Michelle adds, "It's all good, girl! This is just turning into a super fun girls' sleepover, not a total crisis. Let's make the best of this situation and have a fab night together!" She pauses to take a selfie, holding her wine glass, pouting and handing the phone back to Cat. "The internet still works. This isn't a total disaster."

I see why Cat likes Michelle. If you can look past her *annoyingly* stunning appearance, she's lovely. Instead of being freaked out by an avalanche trapping her, she's an Alaska-girl chill. I guess she's not pretentious, and I might have to rethink my attitude towards her.

Did I get a bad first impression because I wanted the ice princess to be cold, then I had a reason to not feel guilty about befriending Caitlyn?

I shake my head to focus and move to the kitchen, opening a drawer to start lighting candles.

Despite the emergency and being plunged into darkness, the evening isn't ruined as we take it in stride. *We really are all tough Alaskan women*, I think.

I smile at the accumulating snow and I don't mind this unexpected situation. It *could be* fun and help us become closer friends. My stomach tightens as my mind wanders–Being trapped in the cabin makes it impossible to escape my growing feelings for Cat. Furthermore, it makes it difficult to hide them from Emily.

"Hey, let's move to the living room, and I'll throw more wood on the fire to keep us warm," I say, moving the party to the furry delight of the cats who enjoy the extra attention and warmth as I stoke the fire.

The cats, having assessed the situation, form a fuzzy pile in front of the cabin's sole heat source. We follow suit, relocating to the couch and chairs and draping blankets over us in the cozy living room. Michelle piles food, wine, and glasses on the coffee table as I take the spot on the couch with Cat again despite my gut telling me it's a bad idea.

Emily finishes talking with the hospital and comes in, reporting, "There are no injuries and they don't need me. But the main roads are blocked by downed trees, and the power substation is buried in snow. The weight of the snow brought down some of the lines that run out of it. It may be a while before we have lights." She takes a chair and glass of wine between me and the fire.

Emily's face, illuminated by the flickering firelight on this chilly evening, exudes an ethereal glow and strength that makes my gut churn with guilt. She refills our wine glasses and chats with Michelle about making snow ice cream as a child. And the flames cast a warm hue across her features, accentuating the delicate contours of her cheekbones and the soft curves of her lips. I'm really lucky to have such a wonderful partner. I can't believe I would even consider anyone else. My stomach churns with relief that she doesn't need to go out in the storm but disappointment that she's staying.

I edge away from Cat on the couch, the crackling fire casting a warm halo in our cozy cabin, nestled deep within the mountains of Alaska. Emily and Michelle settle beside us, the glow of the flames painting enhancing their beauty as we share stories of past winters beneath the beautiful northern lights and frosty snowscapes.

"OMG, have you ever stayed at Chena Hot Springs when it's snowing? It's seriously next-level, like something out of a dream! Soaking in the hot springs while fluffy snowflakes fall and the Northern lights paint the sky. It's the ultimate!" Michelle says, chatting.

"We have and it is," Emily replies, passing out more wine. "But we don't have near the astonishing pictures you have. I saw in the comments people thought your backdrop was fake, it looked absolutely heavenly."

Cat laughs next to me, the couch moving slightly, and her warmth nears as she leans forward to add, "I took those and I'm offended people think we'd fake pictures for our website. Alaska has beautiful backdrops, no filters are necessary. Chena Springs Resort ended up giving us a free stay because of all the business they got from Michelle's pictures."

Cat moves closer to me while I talk, and I start feeling more than the fire's heat radiating through me. Emily obviously follows Michelle on her socials, which makes me wonder why she's never really talked about her before. I should check out their website, and maybe there's even a picture of Cat in the hot springs. . . maybe in a bikini.

"Two cats, huh? You're a stereotypical lesbian, with three cats," Cat teases me, looking at the pile of fur that appears to be one multicolored cat as they are tangled together asleep.

"She has a section of her closet dedicated to flannel shirts that she wears too much," Emily adds with a laugh.

I shrug. "Hey, I'm a lesbian, and I will not let you guys gang up and lesbian-shame me," I say with a laugh.

Michelle adds with a wink to Emily, "Says the alpha, doctor lezzie with short hair wearing a man's watch!"

As we laugh together, the edge of tension disappears. Everyone leans into the unexpected situation of being trapped together for the night. I nervously clasp and unclasp my hands as I am aware of feeling Cat's leg pressing against mine on the couch. I pick up my wine glass to mindlessly swirl it.

The connection between Cat and me simmers, growing uncomfortably hot. I try refocusing. "Hey, do you want to play a board game?"

Emily, my social dinner party planner, lifts her brow. "Since it's turning into an old-school sleepover, let's *lean into it*. We can paint each other's nails, eat junk food, and play Truth or Dare."

"Yes!" Michelle shouts and claps with surprising delight in this idea.

She has either too much wine, or maybe I need more. Emily and I haven't played Truth or Dare as adults—the suggestion is random. I was expecting Scrabble. Maybe my wonderful partner, Emily, is more tipsy than I thought.

I smile at her shimmering eyes. *I hope so*. Emily is always *on*, being a doctor and taking care of everyone. She deserves to relax, drink too much wine, and have fun.

"I vote for Truth or Dare," Cat says, tapping her left leg, "I only have one foot for pedicures anyway."

I laughed at her joke: "Okay, guys, should we play the sleepover classic *Truth or Dare* or, *Spin the Bottle*? Unless you guys want Yahtzee?"

With the last comment, they all say no, and Michelle tosses a throw pillow at my head, making us erupt in laughter. I grab the wine at the same time as Cat to keep from spilling the bottle. We blush in unison, like a schoolgirl, when our hands touch. I'd rather not have to admit to kissing Cat in Truth or Dare, but Spin the Bottle makes my stomach tighten again. *What was I thinking, suggesting a game where I might kiss Cat again?*

To my surprise, Michelle chimes in, "Spin the Bottle. I've never played."

My eyes unwittingly move to Cat, who looks away quickly and shifts slightly on the couch. We've already kissed, and I wonder if her mind is replaying it, too. My heart thumps, and I don't know how I feel about the possibility of kissing her again. This time, we have an audience. My blood pounds with excitement and nervousness. Maybe her kiss wasn't as amazing as I thought. We are all adults, and a sweet kiss over a game isn't lewd. *Will Emily be able to tell we kissed already?*

"How is that possible that you've never played?" Emily asks, passing the massive bowl of sour cream cheddar chips.

"Remember I was the ugly duckling. Of course, being a lesbian in a small town didn't help me get invited to sleepover parties," Michelle thoughtfully says, looking away to the fire and stroking the pile of cats at her feet.

"I didn't come out until high school, but I always had Peekaboo. I never felt excluded," Emily says, smiling warmly at me. "Everyone deserves childhood sleepovers. I remember kissing Alex Curtis on a dare and that's when I knew. That kiss, right then and there, at a third grade sleepover—I like girls not boys." She looks at me with sparkling eyes and a goofy grin, reminiscing about her childhood discovery.

"Oofph. *Anyone but Alex Curtis.* She's a policewoman in Chugiak," I say, with Emily beaming at the memory.

"What can I say? I'm a sucker for a woman in uniform. And you always look good in your red ski uniform," Emily quips back.

Cat nods silently, and I mentally kick myself for even glancing at her when Emily's sitting right there, adoring me. I mentally chant, *No kissing Cat, no telling Emily about kissing Cat,* while my cheeks flush at the memory. Hastily changing the subject, I offer, "More wine?"

"Absolutely girlfriend! Finish that bottle, let's get wild!" Michelle chimes in, her enthusiasm infectious, sending us all into fits of laughter.

"Woah! We might need to get a restraining order for that one," Emily adds between giggles.

Placing the bottle on the rustic wooden coffee table, I notice how the alcohol is loosening my inhibitions, and I'm not sure what will happen if I spin and the bottle points to Cat. My mind races to conjure up a believable excuse to opt out of the game. Before I can voice any objections, Emily efficiently clears the table, creating ample space for the impending game of spin the bottle.

Just as I'm about to concoct a feeble excuse, Cat's whisper, brimming with emotion, catches me off guard, "This is my first dinner party this year. Thanks." Her simple, quiet gratitude speaks volumes about her sense of inclusion and newfound, easy grin.

"Alright, here are the rules: One spin per person, and the bottle must complete a full three-sixty. Wherever it lands, you've got to kiss that person. But, the recipient gets to choose where you kiss them," Emily declares, taking on the role of game master with a hint of formality despite her wine-reddened cheeks and jaunty glimmer in her brown eyes.

As the air crackles with anticipation, Cat inches nearer to me on the plush couch. With a swift motion, she drapes a wool blanket over us, concealing her hand unexpectedly resting tenderly on my thigh. A rush of adrenaline courses through me at her clandestine caress, causing my breath to hitch in my throat. My inner voice screams that the game is going to be trouble, but I'm frozen, unable to stop it.

With a mischievous giggle, Michelle grabs ahold of the bottle. "I'm the virgin. Me first," she announces with a wildly gorgeous flutter of her lashes.

What if Michelle lands on me and her kiss is more electric than Cat's? My heart pounds. This situation is getting out of control.

Emily laughs, "Always the star of the show and the first on the dance floor." Despite her casual demeanor, I catch glimpses of the carefree days at university when Emily was without worries. She's momentarily forgetting her professional guise as a doctor, and looks more happy than I have ever seen her.

A charged energy fills the room with eager anticipation and unspoken desires swirling in the air. I alone wear a mask of nervousness, feeling my stomach tighten into knots at the edge of imminent danger.

Michelle joyfully whips the bottle around and giggles as it spins, then stops, resting at Emily. Setting down her glass, Emily places her finger on her lips without hesitation.

I release a breath of relief, grateful the bottle didn't point my way.

Michelle hesitates momentarily, then strides over to Emily for her turn. Emily cups Michelle's cheeks tenderly, planting a soft kiss on her lips. As they part, Michelle nervously giggles, licking her lips and stepping back, nearly stumbling in the process.

Emily's obvious delight at the kiss tightens my muscles. While I want her to enjoy herself, seeing her lock lips with her gorgeous college friend replaces the previous relaxation with a knot of tension.

Sensing my tension, Cat redirects my focus by sliding her hand onto my thigh. The touch is distracting and enticing. Her fingers hover tantalizingly close to sensitive areas, sending a jolt of heat through me. Everything is coming to a head, and I giggle with nervousness.

Biting Llama, always seeking attention, notices the movement and hops onto my lap. I welcome her distraction, shifting my legs, but subconsciously, I've widened my legs, leaving more room for Cat's light touch. She takes advantage, tracing her fingers lightly up my inner thigh.

Sparks are in the air, and this room is nearly exploding. Michelle and Emily laugh at their innocent, sweet kiss. I laugh along from my nerves as Cat quietly moves her fingers further up my leg, lightly tracing figure-eight patterns that increase my bubbling giggle.

"My turn," Emily directs, spinning the bottle with a hard twist. The bottle sparkles in the firelight as we wait, watching to see where it lands. As the bottle slows, the air shifts when it points to me. Cat moves her hand away quickly, and coolness overtakes the hot trail along my inner thigh. She leans back on the couch giving Emily access to me.

"Ah, I won that spin, dear. My lovely partner." Emily coos and leans in for a kiss. I smile, kissing her familiar lips.

Emily plants a quick, dry kiss that is less enthusiastic than what she shared with Michelle. But then again, Michelle is a model, and the naughtiness of kissing different lips was probably what I saw.

After the millisecond kiss, the group looks at me.

"Spin!" Michelle shouts with rosy cheeks and a huge smile.

With determination, I give the bottle a spin, silently willing the electricity to come back on or a comet to collide into the house. As it twirls, a quiet anticipation settles over the room, and I hold my breath. Spinning forcefully, the bottle careens off the table, flying onto Cat's lap beside me.

Laughter erupts around me. "That's Peekaboo. Aggressive, playing to win, like her kissing style," Emily jokes with a wink.

While the others laugh, I'm biting my lip nervously. Releasing my bottom lip, I sigh. The bottle lands exactly where I hoped it wouldn't. The bottle stops, pointing to Cat. Glancing at her, I detect a flicker of vulnerability and amusement in her eyes.

Breaking the tension, Emily pipes up, "Where do you want her to kiss you, Cat?"

Cat looks at Michelle, who grins in delight and encourages her. "Oooo, trouble," Michelle teases. "Caitlyn plays to win. Watch out!" she dissolves into giggles.

Emily lifts her wine glass. "Kiss her already. You're stalling."

Cat meets my gaze with her hungry eyes, and she turns her body, making her warmth move farther away while the heat inside me intensifies. *It's just a kiss*, I tell myself, *don't react.* I wait, letting her take the lead, trying not to think about her lips and the taste of her while I blush to the ends of my dark hair.

She points to a spot below her ear on the sensitive part of her neck, tilting her head for me. Cat is forcing me to take the lead, while I had hoped to stay frozen while she planted a kiss on my unmoving lips.

Emily laughs as Cat licks her lips and cocks her brow, daring me with a tease.

"Snap! Troubles coming," Michelle teases and clinks the glass with Emily, who laughs with her.

I lean closer to Cat, our eyes locking in briefly, increasing the anticipation. My heart races and beats deafening. The scent of her bergamot and floral perfume envelops me, and knowing she tastes just as sweet makes me hesitate.

"Kiss her. Kiss her," Michelle and Emily playfully chant, their voices jolly, unaware of the precarious situation.

A hush falls when my lips hover near her neck. Cat's eyes widen in surprise, and goosebumps appear on her arm as my lips near her porcelain skin, and my breath warms her neck. The firelight casts a *too*-romantic glow on her face, heightening the fluttering of butterflies in my core and the suspense.

"Are you ready for your kiss?" I ask my voice barely a whisper, uncertainty mingling with the thundering of my heart and the bated breath of our audience.

She meets my gaze, her sweet honey eyes beckoning me. "I'm up for it, if you are," she replies, daring me.

My lips brush her soft neck as she holds her breath. The simple taste of her skin ignites a surge of electricity that overtakes us. Time stands still, the world outside disappearing, leaving only the warmth of my lips on her neck and the shared tender moment of tasting and smelling her sweetness with my heart exploding in heat, which makes me gasp.

She sighs softly, the sound echoing in the quiet room as my gentle kiss overwhelms her. My hand reaches to pull her closer and tangles into her blonde soft hair.

Her hand instinctively comes up to cup my face as she lifts her chin to give me more.

I remember where I am and what's happening, pulling back quickly with a nervous giggle that sounds oddly breathless and raspy.

The kiss is as brief as Emily's earlier kiss on my lips but completely different. As I pull away, her glistening, astonished eyes meet mine, and the atmosphere changes. I realize something has shifted. Like Emily's third-grade discovery with the budding policewoman, I've discovered something dangerous and life-altering.

With the kiss, our casual fun unravels, and Emily forces a laugh. She says too loud, "Only my partner can make a small kiss unexpectedly pornographic. Filling a room with lesbians and wine might not have been my best decision. Then again, this may be the best way to heat up a room with the power out."

Michelle giggles nervously. "Um, if this is the kind of fun had at sleepovers, then I definitely missed out!"

Cat meets my eyes and I can feel my heart drumming with the sudden surge of energy and passion remaining between us.

Cat looks away first and changes her position to move away from me. "You got the experience now, Babe," she responds and lifts her wine glass to Michelle.

Emily stands and knocks over her wine glass.

"Party foul." Michelle says while picking up the intact empty wine glass.

We all laugh and Emily looks embarrassed. She looks at our empty glasses and shakes her head. "It's late. I'll get blankets and show you the spare room."

Cat lifts her hand from my lap and adjusts her rumpled clothing. I can see her cheeks and neck are red, even in the glow of the firelight.

When I stand, I'm unsteady on my feet, not because of weakness but because of the kiss with Cat and the electricity between us. Emily notices, taking my arm to steady me. Her eyes flash with hurt and I glance at Cat who adverts eye contact with me.

The cabin's filled with underlying sexual tension and I wonder how we will all sleep under the same roof tonight.

Chapter 8

Cat

As the snow blankets everything outside and silence replaces the usual buzz of electricity indoors, a hush fills the cozy ski cabin, amplifying the tension brewing between Michelle and I after Peekaboo and Emily went to bed. Michelle stands in the dimly lit living room and stares at me betrayed and jealous of my obvious feelings towards Peekaboo that she witnessed when we kissed. I feel the precarious tension hanging between us that may become the fuel of an argument.

I pass her a set of blankets. "Here. Enjoy the couch," I say in a strained voice, offering her the couch for the night when she stormed out of the guest room. She hesitates, her gaze piercing mine with frustration and hurt reflecting in her eyes.

"You know the deal, babe. That bed is too small and I don't wanna hurt you," Michelle's words cut through the silence, echoing off the log walls.

My chest tightens and hands clench upon hearing the excuses. I want nothing more than to be close to her and how we used to be, but there are too many unsaid words between us.

Her eyes narrow, and she asks, "You're falling in love with Peekaboo, aren't you?" Michelle waits, tears lining her reddened eyes, and gestures toward the closed door of their bedroom.

My heart pounds, and I shake my head vehemently. "This isn't about Peekaboo. This is about us, and you were chanting '*Kiss! Kiss!*.'"

I shake my head in protest of her accusation of being in love, but doubt gnaws at the edges of my mind. My feelings for Peek-aboo have only grown after tonight, and there's no denying our strong connection.

My gaze falls on a poster of the Tundra Temptress hanging on the wall. "What about Emily?" I ask, my voice barely above a whisper. "Why haven't you mentioned her before?"

Mitchelle's expression shifts, a flicker of guilt crossing her features before she masks it with her resting bitch face and responds, "Emily was just my roommate. Nothing more," she replies, her voice in a slightly higher pitch than usual. She looks at the poster instead of meeting my eyes.

The flickering candlelight hides her face. Maybe she's right, and they didn't have an intimate relationship in college. However, it's obvious that Emily is in love with Michelle, and maybe she was in university, too. Perhaps it's not Michelle but Emily, who I don't trust.

Michelle meets my eyes, and I only see guilt, which burns me to the core. The sharp pain reminds me that I wasn't the only one who kissed someone else tonight.

Michelle's voice wavers as she continues, "Maybe we need a break. You know, like, time to figure things out and maybe see other people? It's not like I don't care about you, babe, but this just isn't working right now."

Her words hit me like a slap in the face, the finality of her statement echoing in the empty, cold space between us. Tears form at the corners of my eyes as I turn away, unable to bear the weight of her words, along with my swirling feelings of initiating this fight by being unable to hide my feelings for Peekaboo.

I do have a crush on her.

I stumble towards the bathroom, my steps heavy with heartache. Even before I met Peekaboo, Michelle and I were moving away from each other. Maybe the break-up during our lovers' ski vacation was inevitable, but I didn't even try to talk her out of it.

The sound of my sobs fills the small space as I rush into the bathroom and shut the door behind me. The cold tile floor and my crying echo off the tiles. All I can do is let my tears fall, mourning the love I thought would be my forever love. I abandon the idea of washing my face and decide to go back to the guest room.

Tears blur my vision as I turn on my phone's light to leave the bathroom, crawl into bed and hide.

"Oh!" I step back in surprise.

My light illuminates the fact that I am face to face with Peeka-boo, her eyes wide and hands deep in the pockets of her robe.

"Hey, I'm sorry, Cat," she murmurs softly, concern etched into her features. "Are you alright?"

As I open my mouth to respond, unexpected tears flow down my cheeks, betraying my usual composed demeanor. The tension of the evening and my surprise at seeing her have unraveled me. With guilt and confusion swirling inside me, I shrug in response, realizing that I'm happy to see her. The feeling is fleeting since it causes a rush of shame as it confirms what Michelle said.

Peekaboo steps closer and envelopes me in a comforting hug, offering solace in the midst of the storm raging inside of me and outside of the cabin walls. I return her hug, wrapping my arms around her and holding tight. Inside her arms, my tension dissolves, and my tears dry up.

"Hey, you aren't alone. I'll help however I can," Peekaboo whispers into my hair. I wish she could, but *she's* the problem.

I pull away slightly and look into her eyes, "Did you hear...everything?"

Her kind eyes meet mine, and she nods while chewing her lip. She brushes a piece of hair from my cheek with a feathery touch that further makes me melt into her. *How can I deny my feelings, especially as she holds me, making me feel safe?*

She leans down, and our faces draw close. I hesitate to cross the unspoken boundary again. Instead, I open my mouth to tell her how I feel—

The sudden flicker of lights jolts us back to reality, illuminating me with harsh clarity. I step back, and my blotch face, snot, and tears across it is illuminated. I look unhinged.

The moment of intimacy is shattered, and I step back to splash water on my face.

She stays silent and sets a hand towel next to me.

"I'll see if Michelle wants to drive back," I say, not meeting her caring eyes as I dry my face.

She opens the door, and I step out, looking out to the living room. Michelle is fast asleep on the couch, a contented smile playing on her lush lips as the cats are curled up around her. She looks so peaceful, so sweet, and another wave of guilt washes over me.

Peekaboo peers over to see the sleeping woman.

"I guess we're staying," I remark, opening the guest room door.

Her eyes are sad, but she doesn't say anything to stop me or acknowledge the tension between us. "Sleep well," Peekaboo finally says stiffly.

"Goodnight. I'll see you in the morning." It's an awkward goodnight, but my emotions are a mess. Despite Michelle suggesting a break-up, I know we'll likely remain together. Our lives are intertwined, and there's no chance with Peekaboo. She's in a committed relationship with Emily. Walking away from these confusing feelings is better than break-up two good partnerships.

With a heavy heart, I shut the door. The weight of my guilt and embarrassment makes me sigh. I almost told Peekaboo I loved her–*what a mistake that would've been!*

Chapter 9

Cat

"Hey. Good morning Cat. Coffee?" Peekaboo says, greeting me with a hint of a smile on her lush lips. I rub the eye gunk away and wonder why God created morning people and the rest of us to live with those morning people.

She's in the kitchen, her silhouette framed by the morning light streaming through the window. The new blanket of snow makes me grimace at the blindingly bright day. The aroma of freshly brewed coffee got me out of bed.

"Good morning," I mumble, looking around for Emily and Michelle. The previous night's events linger, and my headache says I drank too much wine.

"Where's everyone?" I ask, looking around and trying to sound less irritated than I feel.

"Emily had an early shift at the hospital," she replies, pouring me a cup of coffee and pushing the mug and creamer. "Michelle was, also, up and out before I made coffee."

I sit at the kitchen table, sipping the proffered coffee, the rich flavor perking me up a bit. "Nice," I state and sigh, taking a large gulp.

"Hey, you think you'll need a ride with your car gone and Michelle leaving?" Peekaboo asks, turning to make eye contact and leaning against the counter in a very sexy pose.

"Probably," I confess, realizing I need to talk to Michelle about last night and apologize before anything becomes permanent. "Actually, I should get going, too."

Peekaboo's eyes widened with surprise. "Don't you want breakfast? I mean, if you leave, then I'll be eating bacon, gravy rolls alone." She gives me a doe-eyed smile, making me grin back.

I nod, biting back a small smile. "Yeah, I guess I could stay. It'll give Michelle time to cool down anyway."

With our partners' early departures, we are alone in the cabin. The morning carries a taste of possibilities, and I chase that taste with another gulp of black coffee. Watching her leaning over to take eggs and meat from the refrigerator makes my mouth dry. I lick my lips, "About last night..."

I stop there and leave the statement hanging because I want to say something, but there's nothing for me *to say*.

"You had a fight with Michelle, and we all drank too much," Peekaboo summarizes for me and winks. "No worries!"

She makes breakfast while my body and mind wake up. I drink coffee and listen to her humming as she cooks. The smell of bacon and new snow can't keep me from smiling. "Do you have any students today?"

She sets the plates down at the bar for our breakfast. Her gaze lingers on me. "Not unless you want to hit the slopes," she says with a smile. "By the way, I'm glad you stayed for breakfast. I usually eat breakfast alone since Emily leaves for work early. Thanks," she says, pouring coffee into our mugs.

Silence hangs in the air after the mention of Emily, but it's not uncomfortable. I remind myself: our vibes and the spark between us don't matter. Despite how perfectly our lips fit together, ultimately we are choosing our partners–*as we should*.

"Are you hitting the slopes today?" she asks, her eyes warm and twinkling. I can't resist grinning back at her.

"I'm not sure. I need to talk to Michelle and we may head home," I shrug, hoping she'll try to change my mind.

"Umm," is all Peekaboo says in between bites. The air is thick with our unspoken thoughts, but neither of us attempts to verbalize them. It is as if by ignoring them the vibe and our feelings will go away.

The food is meaty and hearty the way an Alaskan breakfast should be. Eating with her is oddly intimate, and I realize I hadn't sat down to breakfast with my partner for a long time, too. Michelle goes to the gym in the morning, and I sleep in.

As I finish my last bite, my eyes lock with hers, and there's an underlying hunger that isn't satisfied with the delicious bacon gravy.

I collect the dishes as she starts the sink with soapy water. "I should get going, you know," I say as I put the dishes into the hot water.

She looks at me and nods. My hand brushes against her, sending a jolt of electricity coursing through me. The warmth of her touch lingers on my skin, igniting a fire that I thought I could deny.

For a moment, we freeze, our eyes locking in silent acknowledgment of our undeniable passion. Despite the rational part of my brain screaming for me to stop, my body moves on its own, an animalistic desire, drawing closer to Peekaboo.

The space between us closes in a heartbeat, and our lips meet in a hesitant kiss. Our bodies are guided by instinct that we can no longer ignore. The kiss begins gentle and tentative, as if we're both testing the waters to see how far the other is willing to go.

But then, something shifts. The kiss deepens, fueled by the raw passion simmering beneath the surface. My body presses against Peekaboo's solid feminine frame, and I push her against the counter to kiss her deeper. I yank at her apron strings, and I feel her hand in my hair and her slides into place squeezing my ass. We are a tangle of desire as we lose ourselves in each other.

"Is this position good," I grunt between breaths.

"Uh huh," she says, recapturing my lips. She meets me in a slow, burning, passionate kiss, holding all our intentions and unspoken words. The kiss is the opening, a build-up over our breakfast and last night, making us move faster and rougher to fulfill the need. We clutch and fumble, greedy, trying to kiss, touch, and embrace each other. There is so much more that I want as I kiss her our passion intensifies.

We lose ourselves in the kiss, ignoring all sounds except the noise of our heavy panting. The passion intensifies as our lips explore, and it's an intoxicating shared longing that binds us together.

Suddenly, Peekaboo breaks away, licking her swollen lips and pauses.

I gasp for a breath, my heart pounding. I meet Peekaboo's teary gaze, which is filled with passion and uncertainty.

"We can't," she whispers, the words catching. She looks at me with her honey eyes and frilly apron barely on one shoulder and says, "I'm sorry."

"Thank you for the kiss." It's the only response I can think of, with my heart still beating wildly and my body humming with energy.

My phone vibrates, and I pull it from my pocket, stepping back. The screen lights up with an unknown number. I hit the speaker-phone button, "Hello."

"This is Doctor Collins—*Emily*—at Girdwood Emergency Department," the familiar voice says in a clipped, professional manner.

My mouth goes dry, and I look at Peekaboo's wide eyes.

Does she know about us?

The guilt floods me as the gravity of the situation hits me. My life is in chaos, and I'm dragging Peekaboo into my mess. The pressing need to decide what to do with my feelings rushes over me, and my insides tighten.

I move a step further to get my jacket from the barstool. "Hi, Emily."

Peekaboo pulls her apron back on quickly as if Emily is physically walking in on us. I wonder about the shitstorm I created for her, hoping I haven't ruined anything for her.

"I couldn't reach you earlier," she explains with urgency. "You need to come to the hospital *immediately.* Do you know where it is? Do you have a way to get here?" she rapidly fires questions at me.

My mind is spinning, and my breath is knocked from my lungs. I open my mouth, but it's too dry to talk.

"I can take her," Peekaboo roars over the speaker, looking at me wide-eyed.

"Good. You're still at the cabin," Emily replies with the sounds of beeping machines and people talking in the background. "Yes, bring her to the Emergency Department. I'll tell the surgeon you're on your way."

"Surgeon ..." I whisper.

Emily's voice trembles as she delivers the news, shattering my fragile moment of joy. "There's been an accident. Michelle's here in the Emergency Room."

"We are on our way. See you in five," Peekaboo says, clicking off my phone and shoving me to the door now fully awake from my frozen confusion.

Chapter 10

Peekaboo

Driving towards the Girdwood Emergency Room, the Alaskan winter landscape surrounds me, cloaked in a stark beauty at odds with the crisis. The tires crunch on the snow, the abrasive sound only adding to the tension that tightens every muscle in my body. I look at Cat. She's tense, looking out the window.

My shoulders are tight, I lift and roll them back, loosening them as I drive my modified SUV. Cat shoveled enough snow away from the SUV to allow me to put down the ramp to get inside and drive us to get us to the plowed road. She wasn't surprised to see me driving in a wheelchair, with my hand controls, or at least she hid it well.

It's been ten minutes since Emily's call. I look at the untouched white landscape and marvel at the serene surroundings while our lives are in chaos.

"I can't believe this is happening," Cat mutters, her voice barely audible above the engine's hum and heater blowing on full blast.

I offer a reassuring smile, but the truth is, *I can't believe it either*. The past few days' events, the undeniable connection between us, and the unexpected twists—from losing her prosthetic skiing, falling in love, and a blizzard trapping us. And now, suddenly, Michelle got in an accident right after breaking up with Cat and leaving the house.

Of course, this all happened directly *after* our first makeout session.

Emily's call echoes in my mind. I recognized the underlying urgency in her voice, and there was no doubt that I needed to take Cat to the hospital immediately. "There's been an accident. Michelle's here." The words held a grimness that tainted our beautiful encounter and ruined our goodbye.

Five minutes later, I approach the hospital in my modified car, driving as fast as possible on the unplowed, buried roads. Cat would've never made it here without me—the white snow plains are barely identifiable as roads, and the hospital signs are covered in white.

I glance at Cat, who has unshed tears in her eyes. I'd like to hold her hand, but I need both hands to use the hand controls. I don't usually curse being disabled, but the simple act of driving with one hand and using the other to comfort Cat would have been nice.

The car is filled with an uneasy silence, broken only by the whir of the heater struggling against the chill. Cat hastily scraped the windows before we left, and ice blocked the edges. The car never warmed up enough to melt it. She sits beside me, frozen. Her gaze fixes on the passing scenery. The weight of her guilty conscience resonates inside the confined space. I want to discuss our morning and that it is *unrelated* to Michelle's accident.

But there's no time to waste.

I must get her to the hospital—to her life partner, who may be in serious condition. I'm not the right person to comfort her. I'm only making her feel more guilty. Our makeout session is already adding to her heavy emotions. Kissing her after their breakup probably wasn't my smoothest move.

I swallow hard, staring into the blinding white road that shows no lanes or lines, only a small plowed path. I should have only made her a nice breakfast and left it at that. We could have remained friends—even Emily and Michelle. We could've *all* remained friends. When it comes down to it, there isn't an excess of lesbian couples in Alaska and I enjoy spending time with them.

Am I driving fast to help Cat have a chance to make-up with Michelle, or because of my guilt? Why did I selfishly take advantage of her fragile emotional state after her breakup?

My heart thumps hard, and *I know why*. Cat is so damn awesome, and she deserves happiness. I'm projecting because ever since kissing her, I decided that I deserve passion and love too, and that we could find that with each other.

Our connection and passion are too big to ignore or deny. Even now, knowing she is rushing to her ex's bedside to hold her hand, kiss her cheek, and more than likely get back with her, I want to kiss her. She magnifies what is missing in my relationship with Emily—the burning passion and greedy need.

Maneuvering the SUV, I reassure her, "Emily is there. Michelle will get the best care." I try meeting her eyes, but she's withdrawn. Her face is blank, staring out the window at Girdwood's desolate streets.

As we pull into the hospital parking lot dotted with a few snow-covered vehicles, I pull up to the handicapped spot in front of the Emergency Department. Seeing the Emergency Room, our sighs of relief fill the air. The icy cold slaps me when I open the door, making me cringe.

Cat looks at me and swallows. "Thanks. This is a cool setup, by the way." She waves her hand over the wheelchair clamps, electric ramp, and steering joysticks.

"Can I unclamp your chair for you?" She gestures to the docking system, locking my wheelchair into place so I can operate the SUV comfortably while sitting. I can drive a standardized car in a pinch, but with my leg weakness and occasional spasms, this is the safer option. Having my wheelchair with me is also a benefit when I drive my SUV.

I meet her eyes, seeing her uncertain, scared eyes. I understand, she needs to do something for me to show her care since she can't say it. She wrings her hands and stares at me.

I nod. *The wheelchair clamps are a pain in the butt to reach, anyways.* "Thanks. Let's go see how Michelle is," I say with a tilt of my head at the Emergency Room doors.

She doesn't rush into the Emergency Room. She waits for me, even though I use my driver's side ramp and wheel inside taking more time. *Maybe she's afraid to see Michelle, or maybe it is bad memories of the hospital after her accident?.*

The winter air assaults us, biting our exposed skin as we approach the imposing, brightly lit building with the entrance beckoning.

Cat takes a shaky breath as she enters the Girdwood Emergency Room. The atmosphere is charged with fear and frenzied activity hidden behind the waiting room doors. I sense her anxious energy beside me, her fingers tapping rhythmically on her thigh. *Is she having a flashback to her last emergency visit?*

I smile and nod. "Ready?" I ask, trying to inject confidence and care into my voice.

She stares at the Emergency Room counter, her eyes reflecting a heartbreaking vulnerability. I wheel, with her trailing me, to the desk.

Inside, the sterile hospital smell fills my nose, and the low hum of activity surrounds us. The ride's tension and the hospital's reality fill Cat's eyes with tears. She stops at the reception counter. I reach over, placing a comforting hand on hers, offering a silent reassurance.

The receptionist glances up, her eyes scanning the room before landing on us. "Hi, Caitlyn and Peekaboo? For Michelle Harrison, right?" she inquires, her tone neutral, unaware of the emotional storm we're headed straight into.

"Yes," Cat confirms and grips my hand tightly with a slight tremor. She takes the clipboard of forms, agreeing to fill in the necessary information when the receptionist hands it to her.

"They'll update you as soon as they can," the receptionist says, pointing to the quiet waiting area. There are no clocks to watch, so minutes take hours to pass.

Cat sits in the uncomfortable plastic chairs, while I'm in my comfy wheelchair. I look at the flimsy, narrow chairs and wonder if they are designed to weed out people who aren't having a *real* emergencies. No one could tolerate the chairs for more than a few hours without excruciating pain to distract them.

Cat sits without complaints, in an uneasy silence, only getting up to return the forms. She's lost in her thoughts, waiting.

"I never imagined the day would turn out like this," Cat says, her eyes fixed on the patient area doors, willing them to open for any news.

I nod. The situation looms uncertain. Offering support, I say, "She'll be okay. You'll get through this." I move closer, holding her hand as she faces the unknown.

"I thought my luck changed," she says with a sigh, wrapping her hair into a loose knot, a messy bun without the hair tie with wisps falling out from the back.

I offer a sympathetic smile and pull a hairband from my wrist which she accepts for her wild blonde locks.

After an eternity, Emily rushes into the waiting room. She looks around and spots us. Then she strides over. "Michelle is undergoing surgery. Her car slid off the road and hit a tree. She hasn't woken up or responded appropriately to the neuro checks," she reports.

Cat shakes her head at me.

"In English Emily," I ask her.

Emily nods and starts again, "The neurologist is doing surgery since she's unconscious... still asleep."

"Why does she need surgery?" Cat asks, her eyes spilling the tears they've been holding.

Emily swallows and says, "The scans showed a brain bleed which might be why she's not waking. The neurosurgeon is going to relieve some pressure with surgical treatment. It's really not as bad as it sounds." She adds the last part in a soft voice, not her professional tone.

Emily looks at me, and then my hand holding Cat's. Her confident look falters, and her lips tighten, but she says nothing. "Thank you for bringing her here so quickly, Peekaboo."

I nod back and continue holding Cat's hand. Cat needs me, and Emily knows she was at our home all morning. Emily probably wants to know what's happening between us, but she's too much of a professional to ask. We *will* be *having words* tonight. But I can't think about that. *Cat needs me.*

The waiting game begins anew, with the cold room offering minimal comfort. Patients in pain enter and leave, and family members cry. We continue waiting, sitting in silence.

I glance at Cat. "Do you want me to get you a coffee or snack from the cafeteria?" I suggest, noting the worry lines on her pale face.

She looks at me, her eyes widening and her face a different shade of pale. "Please don't leave," she whispers. Her wet eyes and small voice break my heart.

My throat forms a lump and tightness at the thought of what Cat must be going through. Her partner, whom she left on bad terms, is getting emergency brain surgery. I can't even imagine what kind of stress and guilt she is putting herself through. Let alone what is going on with Michelle.

As we hurry up and wait, the uncertainty of Michelle's condition makes us tense and silent. Finally, a different doctor emerges from the depths of the emergency room, clad in scrubs denoting his role as the surgeon. He walks up to us and pauses to sit next to Cat. He levels eye to eye to talk with her, and this is precisely the position I would take if I had to tell someone their loved one passed.

Cat's breath catches, her eyes widening in shock. I squeeze her hand, ready.

Quite the opposite, the doctor explains the surgery was a success. He relieved the building pressure in Michelle's swollen brain and stopped the bleeding. He draws a crude picture of her head and the skull, showing the pressure build-up and how he relieved it with a small hole, saying it was a "simple procedure for a bruise." He continues, explaining, "the extent of Michelle's injuries won't be fully known until she wakes up."

"Do you mean she might have brain damage?" Cat asks with her hand trembling in mine.

"She *did have* brain damage, but I can't tell you the extent or her long-term outcome yet. We caught the bleed early and relieved the swelling. I'm hoping for no neurological deficits. Only time will tell," he explains in the way doctors do, which crushes our spirit with the cold, clinical manner of his explanation.

The weight of the news settles over us like last night's heavy snowfall but without the promise of warmth from coffee or the fire.

As the doctor leaves, Cat collapses into her chair, crying, and her emotions break free. I wrap my arms around her in a comforting embrace. The reality sinks in—Michelle could be a vegetable, never waking up.

"Do you think she could die?" Cat whispers.

I tighten my grip on her hand, not saying anything. The doctor left us in shock with more questions than answers.

In the quiet of the waiting room, Cat looks up at me, her red-rimmed eyes seeking something I can't give—*hope*. "Peekaboo, what do I do?"

Before I can answer, the nurse intercepts us. "Family and friends of Michelle Harrison?" she calls out, scanning the room. Cat rises, and I trail behind her.

"Michelle is in a room now. She's stable, but unconscious. She can have visitors." The nurse gestures for us to follow. We tag along behind her down the sterile corridors, and she directs us to Michelle's room.

As we walk down the corridor, Cat's hand brushes against mine. She glances at me, and I offer her a small smile and confident nod.

The door to Michelle's room looms ahead. She gently pushes it open, and we enter the private, dimly lit room. The sight of Michelle lying in the hospital bed, connected to various monitors, sends a pang of guilt through me. As I was eating breakfast with Cat, Michelle was here, undergoing brain surgery and fighting for her life.

Emily is at her bedside, leaning over, tenderly washing the blood from her hair with tears in her eyes. She's attentive, talking to her as she works.

I hear a whisper of something I recognize in Emily's tone, making my jaw clench and I chew my lip.

Is she in love with Michelle?

My mind flashes through our night. While I was focused on Cat, where were Michelle and Emily? What did they do in the kitchen last night or this morning before we woke up?

Cat's blind to the bedside scene and rushes to Michelle's side, her eyes filled with relief. She kisses her cheek and whispers, "Michelle, I'm here."

Emily steps back quickly to allow Cat to take her place at the head of the bed beside Emily.

I lock eyes with Emily as she moves to walk around me. She tenses and looks away from me, moving to the sink to wash her hands.

"I was staying with her until Cat could be here," Emily explains, putting her white jacket back on, and hanging the stethoscope around her neck.

"Thank you," Cat says, looking up from Michelle's side and crying.

Emily moves to hand her the tissue and puts her arm around her. "She'll wake up and be okay, I promise."

I'm in the doorway, feeling like a third wheel.

Cat sits down and holds Michelle's hand. She murmurs softly to Michelle, "You will be okay."

"I'll check in on her later. The surgeon will update you," Emily explains, still not looking directly into my eyes.

I know that Emily and the surgeon will give Cat updates. I back out of the room to give them their privacy. Michelle isn't alone anymore, and Cat doesn't need me here while she cries at her bedside.

Chapter 11

Cat

My heart almost exploded, when I stepped into Michelle's hospital room. Doctor Collins, Emily, was already seated next to her, and she immediately moved for me. I took her spot, holding Michelle's hand and praying for my unsettling still partner, so unlike the vibrant, wilderness woman I know.

How is she so pale and fragile? This can't be my Michelle— the social butterfly with charisma and exotic beauty.

Doctor Emily, who was so welcoming last night and a professional over the phone, has worry etched on her face. Her usually composed demeanor is shaken, hinting at the situation's stress.

I'm frozen. The antiseptic scent hangs in the air, mingling with the tension in the room. The sounds and smells transport me to last year when I woke, confused in the hospital, with pain stabbing throughout my body. Terrified, I didn't know where I was or why. A doctor told me I was losing my leg.

The only comfort I had was Michelle's hand holding mine. She was at my bedside, grounding me and taking care of me. Without her as my lifeline, I'd have been lost in a sea of misery.

I clutch her hand tightly. Her vulnerability draws me to her, and I wish I could transfer some of my energy and health into her. *She doesn't deserve to be here.* Throwing my arms around her, I kiss her warm cheek, holding back tears. *This is my Michelle.* This is my adventure partner—trapped and fighting for her life in a hospital from a car accident. She needs me.

My hand brushes against the intravenous needle sticking in her hand, and the red bruise forming on it. Seeing it sends a bolt of guilt through me—I'm the reason she rushed away from the cabin, speeding on the unsafe roads early this morning. I caused her distress, and she was running away from me.

Emily looks up from her charting and says, "Cat, I'm so sorry."

I turn to respond, but the words stick in my throat.

Her swollen, tired eyes fill with sympathy and care as she nods in response.

I nod, my throat tight. "How is she?"

"She's stable now. The surgeon did a great job. I've been at her bedside," she explains, her voice tinged with the emotional exhaustion from the last few hours.

The air in the hospital room is heavy, but I'm relieved her friend, Emily, was here. I'm glad she was at her bedside, but shame and guilt make my eyes water because I should have been with her.

I should've been with her, not kissing someone else. What would've happened if she wasn't rushed to the hospital? Or if Emily wasn't here and she was alone and scared? Will she wake up?

My heart races, and I let the tears fall freely. The cold white walls close in on us. Michelle's unmoving figure adds to my already suffocating guilt—seeing the monitors hooked up to her, the tubes snaking into her body, and the bandages binding her head make her look frail.

"Did the surgeon say when she'll wake up?" I ask, my voice shaking with worry.

Emily licks her lips and presses them together. Her gaze shifts to Michelle, and she says with a tremble, "We have to wait for the neurosurgeon to give the full update. At least she's alive."

I nod, my attention turning back to Michelle. I sit beside her and hold her hand, careful not to disturb the tubes snaking into it.

Despite having other duties, Emily sets down the charting and pats my hand. She takes Michelle's other hand and sits beside her, showing support as we wait. Today is a continuous waiting game—waiting for news, waiting for the doctor to announce she's okay, waiting for her to wake up, and waiting to apologize for *not apologizing* last night.

My stomach is so tight that I can taste acid as I watch Michelle, looking for any movements or changes. I engage Doctor Emily in strained small talk to pass the time, attempting to distract myself. I tell Emily about Michelle's resilience, determination, and strength, from our adventures to her modeling job. She's done photoshoots happily swimming in glacial water in a tiny red bikini to do over a hundred takes of a humorous commercial, needing to wait for the perfect shot of the beaver popping out of the water in the background.

Emily smiles at the stories and shares their funny university anecdotes of late-night escapades and epic mishaps. She regales me about a time that Michelle leveraged her charisma to prank the dorm, convincing them that they had to wear their underwear on the outside of their pants for a "spirit week" tradition. I chuckle, almost distracted from my worry, thinking of her as a freshman and wondering why she hasn't told me any of these stories. As we swap stories, the morning wait is replaced by the shared joy of old memories that are new to me.

The shrill of my ringtone pierces the hospital room, jolting me from my thoughts. I glance at the screen, my heart skipping a beat at the sight of the snapshot of Peekaboo and me, smiling atop Alyeska's slopes.. A rush of bittersweet longing washes over me, a reminder of my undeniable connection with her. My undeclared love for her is out of reach as I sit by Michelle's bedside.

"Yes?" I answer.

"Hi, is this Caitlyn?" The voice on the other end is bright and professional, a stark contrast to the heaviness in the room.

"Yes, it is."

"This is Arctic Edge Talent. We've been trying to get in touch with Michelle. Is she available? We have a really big opportunity and need her for the shoot," her modeling agency explains with urgency.

"Um, actually," I begin, faltering slightly, "Michelle's phone broke last night." I pause, swallowing the lump in my throat before continuing. "She's not available for gigs."

"We understand she's not taking jobs until you're fully recovered. But can you tell her this one is really big, like career-changing?" she asks.

Her response catches me off guard. *Michelle hasn't been accepting jobs for the past year because of me?*

"She's been taking a break..." I say, struggling to comprehend how I didn't notice her and the sacrifice she's made for me. As the weight of understanding sinks in, I feel a new surge of guilt. *How could I have been so blind to Michelle's selflessness, so wrapped up in my own struggles that I failed to see her sacrifices for me?*

I didn't realize she consciously chose to stay home with me, to not work and travel. The news adds a layer of complexity to our relationship. She loves modeling and traveling worldwide for her career. Honestly, I've been so wrapped up in my grumpy self that I overlooked her life. I feel silly now that I thought she didn't care for me or I didn't matter to her. Feeling like she was rushing me to "be normal," was her trying to help my independence so she could return to work.

The voice, on the other end, explains some national fitness chain campaign. I stop them, "She's still unavailable. Thanks," and hang up abruptly.

Emotions swirl within me as I come to terms with this revelation. I consider Michelle's unwavering support during my darkest moments. And I'm grateful she's my life partner. I gaze at her sleeping form, overwhelmed by love and admiration for the woman who has stood by my side, my adventurous wilderness woman partner.

"Michelle, why didn't you tell me," I whisper, more to myself than to her. I owe her the loyalty she gave me, and I grasp onto her hand, vowing to hold it until she wakes up.

Chapter 12

Cat

The distinguished neurosurgeon Dr. Lawrence strides into the room, his presence a beacon of hope in the bleak hospital room. My fleeting encounter with him in the chaotic Emergency Department flashes through my mind as I gaze up at him with eager anticipation, a silent plea for positive news etched on my face.

As he approaches Michelle's bedside, his polished shoes click against the cold floor, breaking the suffocating silence. With a calm yet compassionate tone, he states, "I'm Dr. Lawrence, the neurosurgeon overseeing Michelle's case." His voice is steady with a hint of compassion as he continues, "The surgery helped to stabilize her. I am monitoring her, and I have run some tests. She has a traumatic brain injury, and the nurses are watching her closely. Right now, we are waiting to see how she responds to the treatments, and if she'll regain consciousness with meaningful activity."

The weight of his words hang heavy in the air as he reveals the grim reality of her condition, *a traumatic brain injury*, leaving her fate uncertain.

Emily steps into the room behind him, listening. She pats my arm then instinctively rubs her hand on Michelle's arm. "I'm here for her *and you*. I'll let you know the second anything changes," she assures me.

I nod, surrounded by people who want to help, but Michelle remains unconscious without any change since I arrived.

Dr. Lawrence finishes updating us and checks Michelle's tubes and dressings. Then I am left alone with Emily and Michelle. But now, the uncertainty of Michelle's recovery looming is confirmed, and I'm stunned.

When the surgeon leaves, Emily steps beside me, looking like a supportive friend with tenderness in her eyes framed by her springy short curls. She translates what the neurosurgeon said into understandable information. She provides a clinical rundown of the situation—Michelle's not in danger of dying. Still, the extent of her injury is 'unknown.' We are at the "wait and see" stage. Michelle's physical body is functioning well without a life-threatening emergency. We won't know about her brain function until she wakes up.

Emily's update provides me with some reassurance amidst the uncertainty. Having a caring doctor at her bedside gives me confidence. As she checks Michelle, her hand gently pushes a strand of black hair from Michelle's face, and she tucks it behind her ear.

This is the first time I am seeing Emily in her professional role as a caring doctor and I can tell that she is dedicated to Michelle's recovery. I sense she doesn't want to leave the room, but she is hesitant to stay. Her strong connection and caring for Michelle is apparent.

I look at Michelle and promise her, "I'm here and we're going to pull through this together."

Emily checks and reviews the doctor's scribbles on the chart as I talk. When I declare my intentions, her forehead creases, but she says nothing. My chest tightens at her reaction. *Does she think Michelle's not going to make it?*

I hold onto Michelle's hand tighter, with a mix of emotions—love, regret, hope, and desperation. The hospital room is quiet except for the soft beeping of machines.

Emily gestures towards the door, her eyes encouraging. "You should go get some coffee too. I'll stay with Michelle. She needs rest, and I know she'd want you to take care of yourself," she says. "I'll stay with her."

She moves by Michelle's side, forcing me to step away to make room for her.

"Erm...okay," I agree. I hesitate momentarily, torn between staying by Michelle's side and trusting Emily's to not leave Michelle's side.

No, I'm not leaving her this time! She stood by me during my recovery, and I promised to stay here.

"I'm staying here until she wakes up. She'll want to see me. I'm not giving up on her," I say firmly and squeeze around Emily to be positioned, again, at Michelle's bedside.

Then, with a flicker of hope, Michelle stirs. Her eyes flutter open, and she looks at us, confusion slowly fading into recognition. "Emily," she mumbles, her voice weak but clear.

"Where's Emily?" Michelle groans, her eyes still shut. The question hanging in the air.

Emily doesn't hesitate, touching Michelle's leg in a strangely familiar, intimate gesture. Her concern is evident as she bends, rubbing Michelle's delicate leg. Michelle's eyes flutter open at Emily's touch. Her gaze roves over me, confusion knitting her brows, and then she looks beyond me to Emily.

When Michelle's foggy eyes lock onto Emily's, her face lights up with recognition. "There *you* are," she says, her voice filled with relief and an odd closeness. With a faint smile, Michelle grasps for Emily and I move to allow Emily to take my spot and hold Michelle's hand. Michelle closes her eyes and visibly relaxes.

The room focuses on a point around Michelle and Emily, with an unexpected tension growing. I'm not at Michelle's bedside and I don't seem needed or wanted. I shake my head, confused at what's happening.

I look at Emily, who doesn't move from Michelle's bedside for me. My chest tightens and burns as I watch Emily holding Michelle's hand with a slight smile on her lips.

"That's a good sign, that she can talk and recognize people," Emily murmurs with glistening eyes locked onto Michelle, and not stepping away from her bedside.

I nod, but my mind questions: *What is the extent of Michelle and Emily's relationship?*

"Great news, right?" I say to no one, as no one is listening. I exhale, still agitated. I need to talk to someone. And Peekaboo flashes into my mind. *Where is Peekaboo? When did she leave?*

Here I am, wrapped up in myself again. I didn't even notice when Peekaboo left. I should find her, and update her. I'm torn between my promise to stay by Michelle's side, and the feeling that I'm not wanted here.

My feelings don't matter—Michelle is awake, talking, and recognizing people. *This is what I was praying for, right?*

I study Michelle, her color is improving and she moved her hand to intertwine her fingers with Emily's. I should be relieved that Michelle woke up and everything, but. . .

What the actual fuck?

Chapter 13

Peekaboo

In the hospital cafeteria, I ponder my next move: *Should I stay close in case Cat needs support and to talk to me?*

I was so focused on rushing Cat here after Emily's call, in supporting her, and worried about Michelle that I didn't consider what I'd do after getting here—e*specially once it appeared that both Cat and Emily picked Michelle over me.*

I understand Cat's choice. I am a vacation crush, there's a strong physical attraction between us, but Michelle is her life partner. They've been together for years. Michelle helped her recover from her accident and is a *hot* model.

My mind is brewing with thoughts about Michelle and Emily–the way Emily looked at Michelle and where exactly I fit into the equation. I consider the strange familiarity between Emily and Michelle. They *were* roommates, but jealousy creeps in. I replay the image of Emily at Michelle's side when we arrived.

As I contemplate what comes next, I overhear a conversation at a nearby table. Two nurses are chatting in hushed tones about their work loads. "...I mean, I've taken care of famous people, but I never expected to see the woman plastered on my beer come in," a nurse says, shaking her head, adding, "I don't think she's going to make it."

My heart pounds in my ears, and I strain to overhear more of the conversation over the cafeteria sounds humming in the background. *I better stay.*

Lost in contemplation, I slowly sip my coffee. I don't notice Cat entering the cafeteria until she's standing before me. Her tired eyes are red-rimmed, but her smile confirms positive news about Michelle.

"How is she?" I ask.

"Good. She woke up, and she's talked a little," Cat reports.

Thank God!

She takes my coffee mug, brushing her hands against mine, sending a jolt of electricity through me. Then she sips my coffee, like sharing a mug with me is an everyday occurrence. My heart rate increases.

Cat says, "In the hallway, the neurologist says everything is better than expected. They're keeping her for observation, but he says she's fine."

"That's fantastic news," I offer, genuinely relieved for Michelle.

"I appreciate everything," she begins, "but I don't want you to feel obligated to stay. You've already helped so much."

I nod, understanding her unspoken message: *Please don't make this awkward. Leave.*

But Cat leans over, takes my hand, and looks into my eyes with sincerity. "Hey, can I be honest?" she asks.

"Of course," I reply, bracing for her dreadful news: *She doesn't want to be friends or ever see me again.*

"There's something off with Emily and Michelle. Michelle woke up calling *Emily's* name," Cat says, exhaling a deep breath with a pained expression.

I lifted my brows, unsure what to say but relieved at her unexpected statement. Rocking back and wetting my lips, I say, "I did sort of get a vibe between them. And it's weird that I never heard of Michelle until now, especially when we have her picture hanging in our cabin."

"Right!" Cat punctuates her statement by hitting the table and leaning forward to say, "There's something there."

I'm relieved that I'm not crazy and that she's seeing the same thing as I see. Thoughtfully, I add, "I think we need to wait to talk to Emily and Michelle, until Michelle is better. We deserve to know the extent of their relationship, but we shouldn't stress her now."

"I'm relieved that she's okay. I can wait," she says, shrugging and leaning back in her chair, swiping my coffee again to finish it.

"Hey, we're both pretty tired. Let's just be supportive, and we'll see what Michelle thinks when she's awake enough to tell us," I respond with an open mind.

Cat looks at me with the same spark of determination she had when towering over the mountains after gaining confidence. She levels her eyes at me, saying, "I care about you, Peekaboo. And not just because of our kiss and the skiing. You know?"

I meet her eyes and take her other hand, warmly whispering, "I do. And I want to explore *us,* when we get this sorted out–whether it be as friends or something more."

Cat looks at me, her eyes locking with mine, and a slight smile. "Peekaboo. I never expected this, but I'm *not sorry*. I'm drawn to you, and I want to explore us—*you*, more."

My heart swells, and I tear up a bit. With her confirming her feelings for me and the vibe between our partners, there's no chance I'm letting her go. I want Cat. I want to spend more time with her and get to know her.

This determination gives me the strength to face what I should've done years ago. I need to be honest with Emily and tell her how I feel. I love Emily, and we have a long history and deep friendship, but I'm not *in love* with her. I deserve the passionate sparks of love that I feel for Cat. Just as Emily deserves to be free and explore love with someone else. Maybe it was fate that her old college crush came back into her life to give her the opportunity to find that burning desire that we have been lacking.

Cat nods in agreement, grasping my hands harder with a dangerous twinkle in her eyes.

Emily suddenly appears at our table. She seems to have developed a knack for interrupting my attempts at romance with Cat, like with our morning kiss and at the lodge. Emily's appearance startles me, and reflexively I drop Cat's hand.

Can a girlfriend clam jam or run clitorference? Or is it just called being a girlfriend?

"Hello, Peekaboo and Cat. I was hoping to find you here," Emily says without commenting on the very imitated position she found us in. She adds, "I wanted to update you. Michelle. She is doing a lot better. She's groggy but ready to have visitors."

Chapter 14

Peekaboo

"Peekaboo, *we* need to talk."

With Emily's ominous words and her jaw set, the cafeteria's air gets thick, and I take a deep breath to get oxygen. Her serious expression, with conflicting emotions raging in her eyes, informs me that she's got bad news for me.

I swallow. Cat takes my hand under the table, holding it and providing me with reassuring warmth as Emily begins.

"Peekaboo, we need to have an honest conversation about our relationship. I think you will agree that it's long overdue."

I brace myself for what's to come. I feel Cat's comforting grip squeezing my hand, a silent gesture of support, giving me strength.

My eyes flip between Cat's confusion and Emily's grim expression. I nod. *Emily's right. The sooner we get this out of the way, the better.*

Cat glances at me, her hand solidly intertwined in mine, ready for the impending drama. She asks, "Should I leave?" But her firm grip indicates that she doesn't plan on leaving.

Emily glances at her. "No, please stay. This involves all of us, and I want to be honest. I want to get *everything* out in the open. I think it'll be better if we work this out before we join Michelle."

I lean back in my chair, preparing for whatever comes next. *I'm ready.* "Sure, Emily. Lay it on me...us."

Emily hesitates, her gaze distant, searching for the right words. "Peekaboo, we've been through a lot. From childhood friends to high school sweethearts—becoming lovers—the whole gambit. Adding to our relationship was the weight, or maybe a better word is the *dynamic,* of what happened at the lake—how it changed our relationship. Even without your neck injury, long-term relationships are complex, and they evolve. *Our relationship has evolved,* but not how I expected."

I nod and reach for her hand to show my support for her honesty as she acknowledges what's missing in our relationship.

"Hey, life has thrown us some curveballs, hasn't it?" I murmur and smile for her to continue.

"Yes, it has done that, and we've faced and overcome them together," Emily adds wistfully. Her eyes soften, and she says, "I love you. Our connection is real, but it's transformed into a friendship, or more like family tie, rather than a *romantic* partnership. The fiery passion we had, discovering our sexuality and each other, is more of a comfortable relationship. I'm not denying my love for you."

I blush at the memories her words invoke and squeeze her hand. "Hey, I totally understand. I feel the same. I love you, too. But I kind of just realized I'm not *in love* with you."

Cat raises her brows and says nothing as we sit in amicable silence.

I absorb her words. The conversation isn't unexpected, but admitting our feelings is more straightforward than I thought. We feel the same way and are stating facts. This is not a teary-eyed break-up, which surprises me.

"Changing our relationship to a friendship doesn't change the care we have for each other or erase our past. I consider you my best friend," Emily says in a steady voice.

I nod. "Me, too."

"Last night, when I was talking with Michelle, sharing our stories ... I found an instant connection, like we had in college. I wasn't looking for her or love. And I didn't *need* it ... but *there it was*. Do you understand what I mean?"

I smile and look at Cat. "I *understand*, completely."

"I don't want to lose you, because I care about you too much for that. But when I kissed Michelle, it ignited something I didn't anticipate. I think she's my soulmate—*not to be over dramatic*—it's like it's *meant to be,* like we were brought together again for a reason."

My eyebrows shoot up in surprise. *Soulmates?* Emily is sensible, so hearing her talk about soulmates is unusual.

How did I not notice Emily and Michelle's strong affection?

I guess hiding my attraction to Cat and trying not to hurt Emily meant I wasn't seeing the whole picture, the romance blooming between them.

I glance at Cat, whose expression is unreadable. She's gripping my hand tightly, and I wonder if her admission is as much of a surprise to her as it is to me.

Cat starts, "So, Michelle and you ..."

Emily nods. "Yes. It was not planned. I'm really sorry. We weren't trying to cheat or hurt either of you. After you both went to bed, last night, we hung out on the couch, reminiscing and this bond between us became obvious."

"I want to be honest with you too, Emily." I look at Cat as I say this.

She squeezes my hands and nods her consent for me to continue.

"I also have a pretty strong attraction to Cat. When I met her on the slopes, I knew there was something there. I've been dancing around the feelings, not wanting to hurt you or break up their relationship. I guess I didn't think about you or Michelle," I shrug, admitting my truth to her. "That game of Spin the Bottle really opened up a can of worms," I say, biting my bottom lip and waiting to see her reaction to our secret.

"Dear, I am a doctor. Not much gets past me," Emily says with a quirk of her lips. "Plus, you both were out of breath this morning and I called several times before you answered."

I laugh, relieved she's not mad. And Cat shakes her head. I breathe easier, and my stomach releases its tight knots. I'm embarrassed that I thought I could hide our obvious attraction from my lifelong partner and childhood friend. *Of course, she knew.* She knows everything about me.

Cat lets go of my hand to pull her hair into a tighter bun and says, "Michelle got into the car accident because of our fight."

Emily shakes her head and lays her hand on her arm, creating a circle between us. "Not at all. Michelle was rushing to see me. We were going to discuss our future and how to talk to both of you guys about all of this," she explains.

I shake my head, surprised by this unexpected twist. "But, why didn't you tell us all this when we got here?"

Emily's eyes meet mine, and there's a tenderness and vulnerability there. "I didn't want to mention it until she was stable. I feel terrible about not saying anything, but I thought it was best to withhold it, especially with her condition."

Emily turns to Cat, pleading, "I hope you understand. She didn't want to risk her relationship with you. And I don't want to lose the friendship that we all just found. Michelle feels the same way, which is what we talked about when you left the room, Cat."

I laugh. "This is the most elaborate and mature break-up plan I've ever heard of," I tease, breaking the tension.

Emily slowly blinks at my joke, and Cat chuckles with encouragement.

I ask, "Cat, how do you feel about all this?"

"I agree with staying friends. I mean we're all lesbians and in Alaska, that's a pretty exclusive group. We *have to be* friends," she says with a shrug and squeeze of my hand.

Emily sighs and smiles. "Good!"

I take both of their hands, saying, "Emily and Cat, that's all I want. I want both of you to be happy." I smile and add, "And Michelle, too."

"Ah, you guys get a room," Cat jokes, and we erupt in giggles, defusing any tension remaining.

Cat meets Emily's eyes and says, "Thanks for your honesty and being there for Michelle. We have a history similar to yours, and I can't imagine a future without her."

"Hey, this has got to be the sappiest break-up in history," I say.

Cat nods and smiles, saying, "Thanks guys. Should we move this party back into Michelle's room?"

Emily nods, "But will you grab Michelle some coffee on your way back? She's rather cranky without it."

Cat nods.

"Well, I said my piece, and I need to get back to check on her before Doctor Lawerence decides if he's going to discharge her tomorrow," Emily says, standing up abruptly.

I take her hand, not letting her escape so quickly. "Thanks for initiating this talk, and for being a wonderful partner."

She smiles at me and hugs me, kissing both of my cheeks. "Right back at you, dear!"

As Emily leaves, I feel sad despite the perfect break-up situation. The evolution of our relationship was inevitable, but it didn't make the conversation or my feelings any less sad at our breakup.

Cat and I sit silently, processing the conversation and our future. She breaks the silence by asking, "Does this mean we need to have another sleepover, and paint our toenails next?"

I giggle. "Definitely." I grin. "But first let's get Michelle better."

She rubs her hand over her tired eyes. "I should get her coffee and go back to sit with her, especially if Emily's working."

I nod. "I agree."

She smiles. The electricity between us is charged with our new beginning.

"Hey, when Michelle is recovered, you're getting back on the slopes to ski with me," I warn with a wink.

Cat laughs. "I'm still sore from our last ski date. Can't we have a dinner date like normal people that are dating?"

"We aren't a normal couple of people," I tease her. "Besides, you cheated on our last race down the mountain. I deserve a rematch."

"Deal," she says. "How about I grab us all a round of coffees, and I'll meet you in Michelle's room?"

"That sounds like I plan," I say, reaching for her hand and offering one last comforting squeeze before I wheel to her room.

She adds, "Emily *is* pretty great, you know."

I smile. "I know."

Chapter 15

Cat

Laughter dances around the room, the sound swirling with relief and joy. Emily and Michelle's voices blend in a happy stream of giggles, making me grin as I stride into Michelle's hospital room. Their laughter is infectious, and even Peekaboo laughs along, holding the tray of coffees.

My heart skips a beat as I catch the tail end of their conversation, a groan escaping my lips in a futile attempt to hide my embarrassment. *But it's too late.* They've already spotted me, all their eyes turning and waiting for me to explain.

Michelle's mischievous glint meets mine, and I can't help but chuckle at the playful twinkle in her eyes. Despite her worries and condition a mere hours ago, her mood shines as vibrant as ever, reassuring me that she's on the mend.

With my silly grin plastered on my face, I step closer to her bedside, eager to enjoy the warmth of our friendship. "You don't have to look so happy to be free of me," I quip, trying to change the subject away from the thread they were talking about—*me*. "Looks like someone's back to her old, happy self."

Emily chimes in, her voice laced with amusement. "Oh, we were just talking about you," she says, her words accompanied by a mischievous glint that can only be blamed on Michelle's bad influence.

Peekaboo smiles and says, "Michelle's was just telling us about your fabulous career. What does Cat do exactly?" She turns to ask Michelle, joining in on the joke.

"OMG, Cat didn't spill the tea? You're going to love this. It's priceless ..." Michelle's words trail off, and a mischievous glint in her eyes meets mine.

I shake my head. Stepping to her bedside, I grin at her playfulness, confirming Michelle is doing fine. Quickly, I interrupt, my cheeks burning. I chuckle, saying, "We should save potentially embarrassing stories until we know each other better, like—I don't know—many, many, *many* years from now." I shoot a side eye at Michelle, but there's no stopping her when she starts *the story.*

Michelle looks up at me from her lashes, blinking innocently.

I sit, shooting her a grumpy glare and then a grin. "You think I'm going to let you off easy just because you're in the hospital? You know what's worse than your longtime partner breaking up with you?" I say, scowling at her with amusement in my eyes.

"What?" Michelle asks.

"You're partner's *new girlfriend* breaking up for her! You bum," I say, pressing my lips together to not laugh.

Emily chuckles, a warmth in her eyes as she looks at me and shrugs. "Don't shoot the messenger. I have the most experience breaking bad news, being a doctor. I volunteered," she explains, patting Michelle's arm as Michelle nods.

"She volun-an-told you. Don't let Michelle's gorgeous smile fool you, too," I smirk at Emily and wink at Michelle.

"We talked last night and basically broke up," Michelle remarks. "Emily was just the deal closer."

I tilt my head toward the tray of coffees on Peekaboo's lap. "Peekaboo got both you, bums, coffee," I say, passing them out. And secretly hoping this diversion has halted the personal story.

Instead, Emily turns to Michelle. "What *does* Cat do for work? Zamboni Driver?" she inquires, then looks at me with angelic eyes.

Emily is just as much of a troublemaker as Michelle—*they were made for each other.*

I bite my bottom lip and shake my head. I should've known I couldn't escape this discussion.

Peekaboo furrows her brow, thinking for a moment before shaking her head. "Hey, we don't do a lot of talking when we're together," she says with a wink and lifts her chin at me.

Leaving Em & M cackling, I laugh along with the duo, and the warmth of our friendship is evident.

"Okay, the suspense is killing me. What do you do for work?" Emily prompts once the laughter dies down, her curiosity piqued, and Peekaboo leans in to hear.

"I'm nowhere near as accomplished as all of you: a famous model, a ER doctor, or a ski instructor," I start before launching into my well-rehearsed, long-winded explanation.

"Growing up, my dad was a patent lawyer so throughout my childhood I pestered him with ideas for the next, best-selling invention. He patented some of my odd ideas, and one of them took off," I said with a shrug. I ended my explanation there. "I've been living off the royalties ever since."

I take a sip of coffee, hoping that'll be the end of the explanation.

Peekaboo tilts her head and asks the dreaded follow-up question, despite my attempts to hide the pertinent details.

"Now, I'm intrigued—what, in the world, did you invent?" Peekaboo asks.

Michelle bursts into hysterics, taking a tissue to wipe her eyes. Her shoulders shake with laughter. Before I respond, she says, "You guys are gonna love this," between her giggles.

I put my hand over my face, already mortified. "*Please,* promise not to tell anyone," I say, my cheeks flushing deeper with embarrassment.

"Cross my heart," Emily promises, with a glint in her eyes betraying her words.

Peekaboo nods seriously.

"Okay. I invented underwear called *Wee Wear*," I admit, bracing myself for more laughter.

Emily and Peekaboo exchange glances while Michelle's giggling increases.

Emily furrows her brows and says, "I've never heard of it."

Peekaboo asks, "What's *Wee Wear*?"

Michelle's unable to contain herself and jumps in, explaining, "It's quite popular in Europe and Asia. Wee Wear is a type of underwear for women that helps them pee standing up so there's no mess," she explains. Her eyes danced with amusement.

Peekaboo looks at me quizzically.

I say, "When I was little and camping, I hated peeing outside. Mostly, I hated it because I wanted to pee standing up, like my dad. So, I invented underwear that moves things out of the way to direct your pee. You don't pee on yourself and you can pee standing up."

"That's genius!" Peekaboo exclaims with a smile.

I nod. "Yeah. I thought so when I was eight, too. *Until* I found out that Wee Wear isn't being used for camping. It's popular in Germany for fetish gear. You know *golden showers* and all," I admit, my cheeks flaming.

"But they're still adorbs!" Michelle interjects with a grin. "They come in rabbits and kitties. You squat and pull up on their ears to spread your lady parts and pee without any obstacles."

The giggle attack starts again, and I sip coffee. I should be used to this, but *the story* results in hysterics every time I explain why I don't have a career. My invention is bizarre and obscure, but it's enough of a trickling income that I don't have to worry about money.

"Hey, I know a famous inventor," Peekaboo grins and lifts her cup.

"You're *dating* a famous inventor," Michelle corrects.

"We don't move as fast as you two, bunnies," I say. "We're only slumber party friends for now."

"Ski competitors, really," Peekaboo chimes in.

"Does this mean that we're all getting cute Wee Wear for Christmas this year," Emily says, her eyes glowing with amusement.

I groan at the thought of ordering everyone matching Wee Wear. I haven't even mentioned the holiday line. I guess I could surprise them with a pair of *Jingle Cheeks* or *Santa's Secret*.

Luckily, the neurologist enters the room to end the conversation. With a smile, he announces, "I've got news. Michelle's scans are all clear. It looks like the swelling has gone down and there's no permanent damage...Except for the scalp incision and hair we shaved off. That'll grow out."

We cheer at his news as he signs off on the tests and chart. The weight of the day is gone.

The doctor adds, "I'm signing her out of my care. I'll let the hospital discharge you when you're ready."

"Are you guys up for another sleepover?" Emily suggests.

Peekaboo adds, "Hey, it sounds like a doctor's order, as a safety precaution, you know."

Michelle laughs and says, "No more Spin the Bottle, though."

I nod, and we smile at the prospect of spending more time with our friends. The room buzzes with laughter and chatter. I'm grateful for the unexpected twists and miracles. We toast our coffees to new beginnings and friendships.

"To Wee Wear," Michelle giggles, raising her coffee, and with laughter, we toast to underwear.

Chapter 16

Peekaboo

The frigid Alaskan nips my rosy cheeks as Cat and I race down the slopes of Alyeska Ski Resort.

The weeks since Michelle's hospital stay feel like only yesterday. Cat and Michelle stayed to let Emily watch over Michelle's progress, although she is doing okay. Cat and Michelle have remained in Girdwood to enjoy our new friendship.

Today, we're carving through the powdery snow as the sun casts a dazzling glow on the pristine slopes. The mountain is a winter wonderland. I marvel at the beauty of Alyeska and the confidence Cat's gained since her first one-legged ski crisis weeks ago.

Cat zooms ahead, her laughter carried by the wind. I follow. The thrill of the downhill skiing is exhilarating. As we reach the flattened area between slopes, we slow, catching our breath and stealing a moment to take in the breathtaking view.

"Isn't this amazing?" Cat says breathlessly, her eyes sparkling with delight, outshining the glittery mountain.

I nod with a wide grin. "Absolutely. Awooooo!" I howl into the wind with a giggle after.

Cat leans in and, after a laugh, presses a quick kiss to my cheek. "I was thinking of quitting skiing before I met you. Thanks, Peekaboo."

I playfully nudged her, "Hey, it's my job. And, I know you—you don't give up. You would've figured it out, even without me."

"Nope. I would've never survived my first day, without you," she says thoughtfully as we gaze out at the peaks before us. She points to the Sleeping Lady mountain. "She's still waiting."

"Like me, at the bottom of the run, waiting for you," I tease, and Cat barks out another laugh. I can hardly remember the grumpy skier I met weeks ago.

Our close friendship grows stronger daily, and our relationship is rocketing faster than our ski runs. I'm considering asking Cat to move in with me now that Emily has decided to move out of our cabin.

I even caught Emily looking at hospital job openings in Seward, closer to Michelle. I suspect she'll be moving in with Michelle soon, *and that's okay*. They are perfect for each other: high-energy, driven, gorgeous women.

Plus, Seward's only a two-latte drive away. That is close enough to enjoy plenty of sleepovers and visits together.

True to her word, Emily's relationship with me hasn't changed, except for the sleeping arrangements, of course, and the sleeping partner's too.

As I gaze at Cat, admiring the mountain slopes below us, the wind tousles her blonde, unruly hair. With the sun and the snow-covered peaks, I suggest, "Let's take a pic."

She skis beside me and takes out her phone. Bending down and pulling up our ski goggles, we pose for a selfie with the glittering Alaskan landscape as our backdrop.

"Smile, Snow Siren!" she says, teasing me from the shout during our first ski together.

The resulting picture shows our genuine happiness: red cheeks, glowing eyes, windswept hair, and arms around each other. Cat looks at the photo and grins, declaring, "This one's a keeper. I'm posting it!"

Happiness looks good on Cat. I smile, "Agreed. We are stunning. Make that one your new wallpaper pic. And send it to me, okay?"

She laughs, clicking away on her phone before tucking it securely into her pocket. "Done!"

I take advantage of her distraction and pull on my goggles to start down the hill first. The snow crunches beneath my ski sled, and Cat follows, yelling, "You're a Cheater!"

"Geronimo! Awoooooo!" I howl, echoing as I rocket down the mountain.

The world is a blur of whites and blues. The wind whistles past, and for a moment, I'm in the zone, just me and the mountain.

We reach the bottom of the slope at the same time.

"Hot Chocolate, ASAP!" Cat gasps as I laugh at how out of breath she got trying to beat me.

Heading into the ski lodge, I find a table and let Cat go to the counter. The ski resort is bustling with activity and welcomes us with warm soup and hot chocolate.

"There's a certain magic here, isn't there," Cat says, setting down the overflowing mugs of chocolate and whipped cream goodness.

I laugh. "Hey, are you going to turn into a ski bum like me?"

She grins, her eyes crinkling at the corners. "Maybe. It's a pretty sweet life."

"You better get used to cooking, though. I lost my cook recently to a hot model in Seward," I say with a laugh.

"That happens," she says with a knowing nod. "We can live off chili and hot chocolate, right?" she says, lifting her mug.

I nod and laugh with her. Cat and my relationship is natural and easy, and it's hard to imagine we only just met. Taking a break at a rustic mountain lodge, the scent of hot cocoa wafts through the air with the fireplace crackling. I smile and enjoy the cozy moment, the heat seeping through my cold body as we relax after our morning ski.

Cat goes to the counter and picks up our chili. I lick the whipped cream off my hot chocolate and catch Cat staring at me. I shrug, and she laughs.

Today isn't just about skiing. It is about us finding joy on the slopes and in each other's company.

I swallow the sip of the cocoa, and lick more whipped cream from my lips, and a feeling of contentment settles over me. Cat returns with the cheesy chili bread bowls. "So, Cat," I begin, with a playful smile, "what's the plan now? You've mastered all the runs on Alyeska."

She smiles and thoughtfully responds, "I'm going to master my relationship-building skills."

"Will that involve any travel?"

Lucky jumps in her lap, and Cat laughs. She looks at me. "Maybe it's time I settle down and enjoy Alaska. A little cabin with two or three cats sounds like a pretty good plan. Girdwood isn't too bad." She lifts her mug and winks at me.

I laugh, responding, "Hey, I might know a cabin like that. I think there's an extra room, if you don't mind becoming a crazy cat lady."

Cat leans in, her lips brushing against my ear. "I'm not the crazy one."

"Kettle calling the pot—"

Cat stops me with a kiss. She whispers, "I was thinking we should start my plan tonight. What do you think?"

I chuckle, a delightful warmth spreading. "Why am I always so attracted to fast-moving women? Did I forget to ask you to move in?"

"I saved you time by already saying yes," she grins.

"I have lessons! You go back to the cabin and buy some wine on your way home," I tell Cat.

She chuckles and nods in agreement. As she leans in to kiss me, a fluffy tail hits her nose, and she gets a mouthful of fur. "Lucky!"

Lucky looks at her with large eyes, circles, and she lies in her lap.

"See, he is lucky," I smile, pet Lucky, and lean in to kiss her frown, which dissolves into a smile under my soft lips. Pulling back slightly, I suggest, "Sounds like a splendid plan to me. We don't even have to cook tonight. Emily is making pasta."

Cat's face lights up again, and she pulls me into her lips again, kissing me to seal the deal.

I can't help but feel that my life has ended up even *more* perfect than I had ever expected. With Emily, Michelle, and Cat in the cozy cabin and my furballs, I can't imagine a better night.

I'm the lucky one.

EPILOGUE: Cat

ONE YEAR LATER

Gliding down the slopes, with the slick run beneath my skis and the wind whispering tales of countless adventures, I shout, "I'm going to catch you!" to the gleeful student in front of me. Somehow, I've managed to become a ski instructor, like Peekaboo. She's turned into a positive influence for me. Plus, I love my students and enjoy skiing even more.

Jake laughs and tries to ski even faster down *Money Two* to *Chump Change* on the mountain's North Face. He graduated from Peekaboo's intermediate skiing class to my advanced class. Today, we are working on speed. More to the point, I'm chasing him as he zips confidently down the hillside.

This is our last run for the day, and he's ready to attack the mountain solo tomorrow. Although I'm sure I'll see him again, probably rushing past me as I teach another student.

At the bottom of the slope, I congratulate him on his progress and remind him to commit to the slope and trust his skis. I hope he doesn't get into too much trouble without me around.

As I clip off my skis and head to the cabin, I marvel at life's twists and turns. I stomp off my boots and enter the cozy cabin perched on the edge of Alyeska. Despite the late hour, the scent of freshly brewed coffee wafts through the air, a comforting aroma that lingers in the cozy corners of our home.

Tonight, Peekaboo and I are entertaining. We'll need a caffeine boost after a long day of skiing since Emily and Michelle are *always* high-energy. The evening's agenda is staying up all night, talking and laughing over wine.

"Cat, you're home," Peekaboo calls from the kitchen. "Our guests arrived early and are busy cooking up a storm," she says, wiping her hands on her apron and bringing me a mug of coffee.

True to form, Michelle and Emily, peek out of the kitchen and wave. Em & M are too busy cooking to stop and greet me properly, but a delicious dinner is almost ready by the smell of things.

"Emily still doesn't trust me to cook," Peekaboo whispers with a smile.

"She knows you too well," I tease, finishing hanging up my skiing gear.

I catch movement out of the corner of my eye. "Whoa, what is *that*?" I almost jump on the couch to avoid the large rodent in front of Geraldine Anne, who's licking it instead of eating it.

Laughter bubbles from Peekaboo. Emily and Michelle emerge from the kitchen to see the fuss.

"OMG, Cat, seriously," Michelle says, scolding me for looking like I'm ready to kill the intruder with my ski pole. "You're freaking her out!"

Michelle approaches the pink blob of wrinkles and pets it, making its head emerge. The hairless cat licks her hand.

"Okay, Babe, brace yourself. It's your belated housewarming gift—*Naked Pussy*."

I glance at Peekaboo to see if it's a joke, but she's no help. Her hands cover her face as she laughs into them. She looks between her fingers at me and shakes her head.

Emily excitedly explains, "We stumbled upon her on our recent Brazil trip spelunking. She was half-starved, spunky, and so adorable. Michelle thought that she's *just like you*. We knew you'd love her."

The cat's gaze meets my eyes. She turns with aloofness to lick her weird paws. Her uniquely prickly attitude and hairless body make me wonder precisely what Michelle saw that made her think of me—*I thought we were friends?*

"Ummm, a hairless cat in Alaska is definitely a unique housewarming gift," I mutter, unwilling to set the ski pole down.

"Hey, take a look at her collar," Peekaboo says, stealing the pole from me and pushing me toward the freakish animal.

As I approach Naked Pussy—I'll be changing that name because there's no way I'm sitting in the veterinarian's office with them calling out *Naked Pussy* at me—the creature burrows deeper into Geraldine's furry side. She looks up at me with fiery eyes, like she'll take a chunk out of me if I attempt to touch her.

"She'll grow on you," Michelle adds with a giggle.

Taking a closer look, the feline is not anymore attractive, but I spot the pink collar with a frog charm hanging from it, which only makes the cat look even more pale and hideous.

"*Charming*, is the word you're looking for," Michelle pipes up with a sparkle in her eyes.

Before I reply, I remember the early wedding present I brought for Michelle. Digging into my bag, I pull out a small box wrapped in colorful paper.

"Speaking of gifts, I couldn't resist giving you something early," I say, handing her the box.

Michelle's eyes light up as she unwraps the package, revealing a pair of lucky frog socks identical to the ones I always wear.

"OMG, looks like our gifting theme is frogs this year," Michelle laughs.

"Great minds think alike," Peekaboo says, adding, "We are getting you a *real* wedding gift too."

Michelle slips the socks onto her feet. "Thanks, Cat. They're absolute perfection." She hugs me.

I grin, feeling a warmth spread through me. "Consider them your something borrowed and blue," I say, leaning in to give her a quick kiss on the cheek. "For under your wedding dress, of course."

"I thought I was supposed to be naked under it," she teases, and we laugh together.

"Let's open that wine and get this party started," Emily announces. She hugs me quickly, smiling at the newest furry addition. Then, they head back to the kitchen to finish making dinner.

"I need to buy them Miss Manner's book. They need to review the list of appropriate housewarming gifts," I grumble, looking at the growing pile of felines in front of the fireplace.

"Hey, at least she won't shed," Peekaboo laughs. She motions me to relax on the couch with her.

Curled on the couch, I watch our new houseguest take ownership of the coveted spot in front of the fire.

Emily and Michelle chuckle at the scene and my horrified gaze. They hand out plates to eat by the warmth of the fire.

"Speaking of gifts, we finished our wedding registry. Now we get to move on the guest seating chart this week," Emily says, pulling out her oversized wedding planner. "It would be a shame not to include your whole family in the wedding. Maybe there's a way to get the cats to be ring bearers and flower girls with matching outfits?"

Peekaboo laughs. "Emily, do you think you can get these guys to follow instructions? I don't think there's enough catnip in the world."

I whisper to Peekaboo, "Maybe we can regift *Angry Pussy* to them."

She laughs. "Do you mean, *Bald Rage*?"

"You can't rename her. She's used to *Naked Pussy*! It's already inscribed on her collar," Michelle says firmly.

Even as she's saying it, Naked Pussy gets up and circles our legs, then jumps onto the couch to lay in my lap.

"Oooooh. She *is* cute," Peekaboo says and pats her hairless, pink back.

"You like the most prickly creatures," I grumble, hesitantly giving the puss a pat.

Emily laughs, and Michelle nods, looking at me, "Ain't that the truth! No cap."

Michelle and Emily dissolve into laughter. After their giggles die down, they brief us on their upcoming wedding plans. It will be a small ceremony on a yacht performed by the boat captain during the summer on Seward's Resurrection Bay. Later in the year they planned an elaborate trip to Fuji for their honeymoon, as summers are too short in Alaska to waste taking vacations.

Michelle excitedly shows us her scattered sketches of the dress. Her eyes sparkling with enthusiasm, she explains, "I got inspired to design it myself. Picture this, it's a combo of a ball gown and a parka. Think fairytale princess meets Arctic explorer chic. The bodice will be lined with faux fur for that cozy Alaskan touch, and the skirt will cascade like snow drifts around my feet. OMG, our Tundra Trendsetter followers will love it!"

I can't help but burst into laughter at the idea and her enthusiasm. "You're going to be the most stylish ice queen Seward has ever seen," I tease, wiping tears from my eyes.

Michelle grins, undeterred by my jest. "Exactly! And just wait until you see the matching fur-lined snow boots and veil. It's going to be a winter wonderland extravaganza!"

"Emily, fill their glasses. I have another announcement to make," Michelle says with a mischievous twinkle in her eye. She turns to me, her expression brimming with anticipation. "Cat, brace yourself for this one," she begins dramatically.

I drink the wine and straighten up, intrigued and nervous. "Alright, lay it on me," I respond, trying to match her enthusiasm.

Taking a climatic pause, Michelle dramatically says, "I want *you* to be my Maid of Honor."

I gasp dramatically, clutching my chest for effect. "Oh, the honor! The prestige! The pressure!"

Peekaboo takes my wine glass. "I'm cutting you off."

Michelle giggles at my theatrics before continuing. "But wait, there's more," she adds, her grin widening.

I grit my teeth, anticipating what could be next. "What could possibly top being your Maid of Honor?"

With a flourish, Michelle drops the bombshell. "I'm designing your gown too!" she declares, her eyes sparkling with excitement, and she claps bouncing in her chair.

My eyes widen in alarm and I feel cold sweat on my forehead. "Wait, what?" I sputter, my mind racing with visions of neon-sequined bikinis.

But Michelle is undeterred by my panic. "Trust me, Cat. I've got some killer ideas that'll make you the talk of the town," she reassures me, her confidence unwavering.

"But we live in a small-town. The talk of the town doesn't sound like a good thing," I say nervously, looking for my wine. Peekaboo takes pity on me and hands me the glass.

I gulp nervously, mentally preparing myself for whatever fashion monstrosity Michelle has concocted in her mind. "I guess I will survive," I mutter, trying to be brave.

"She looks great in pinks and yellows," Peekaboo says with glee.

Michelle grins, clearly relishing the prospect of transforming me into her fashion muse. "Oh, don't worry, Cat. I promise to keep the sequins to a minimum," she teases, her laughter filling the room. "Our followers want to see you too. They love your skiing pics."

As we share a laugh over Michelle's outrageous idea, I can't help but feel a twinge of excitement mixed with apprehension. Whatever dress she designs for me, one thing's for sure—it will be a wedding to remember.

We continue brainstorming and giggling over the wedding plans, with warmth and happiness settling into my heart. Despite the chaos of life and challenges, moments like these remind me of the joy found in friendship and love. And if anyone can pull off a fashion-forward parka wedding dress, it's Michelle.

If you loved Peekaboo & Cat's sapphic adventure, then you'll love Bree & Serena's thrilling Kodiak Island romance in *Wilderness Rescue: Tides of Love.*
CHECK IT OUT HERE.

Discover the books in the *Wilderness Rescue* series.
CHECK IT OUT HERE.

Keep reading to enjoy the next book.

Wilderness Rescue: Tides of Love
Chapter 1: Serena – Chasing the Wave

Gulf of Alaska in the Pacific Ocean, Kodiak Island

The Pacific Ocean's swell comes barreling toward me, a liquid freight train tearing through the inlet with raw, untamed power that fuels surfers' wet dreams. My arms slice through the icy foaming water as I chase the monster—except in this version, the monster is totally tubular. I paddle hard, bracing myself for the magical climax when the wave catches me. When it does, I'm flying on the ocean with my board.

This is *it*. This is the kind of wave I love and chase around the world, starting as a kid in Hawaii and then as a teenager doing sloppy pop-ups in Oregon's frigid waters. Alaska's stormy waves make those waves look like kiddie pool ripples. The board lifts, the icy water propelling me forward, and I stand, every muscle twitching with adrenaline.

Carving through the wave, I hoot, surfing the universe's best-kept secret—a beach off the remote island of Kodiak. The air bites at my cheeks, and the water beneath me sparkles like diamonds. It's colder than I expected—like Arctic penguin cold—but my wetsuit is doing its thing. And I didn't come here to swim. I came here to crush the storm's surf.

Kodiak's rugged shoreline looms in the distance, jagged, windswept cliffs, pines, and rocks plotting my demise. Storm clouds lurk on the horizon, but for now, the sky's a crisp, blinding, unreal blue that is better than my daydreams of this Alaskan surfing adventure.

Riding the wave, I catch myself laughing—like an *actual* lunatic. Who laughs while precariously slicing over deathly cold water?

This girl, apparently. I'm living the dream. Conquering the wild ocean storm is the holy grail of Arctic surfing. Followers told me I was nuts for coming here. They were right, and I don't care.

In the morning sunlight, my board hums with the raw power of the wave. The surfing high surges through me, so potent the liquid courage makes me shimmy on the board, then reach out my hand, scraping and spraying the wave's edge until my hand is numb.

"This is it, Siren," I mutter, then whoop louder, the sound echoing over the water.

The surge lifts me higher, making me shift to carve a path down its gleaming face. My wetsuit clings like a second skin, somewhat shielding me from the freezing water. I'd snap a pic of the ride if I weren't focused on being awesome. My toes grip the board with practiced ease, and I glimpse the shoreline as I near.

Something catches my eye.

There, on the shoreline—a figure.

I almost miss it, tucked between driftwood and rocks. A woman. Definitely not the grizzled old fisherman I hitched a ride with. She's bent over, picking through beach debris. Her long braid swings like a pendulum, and her oversized jacket hangs bulky on her petite frame like it's survived more storms than I have.

The fisherman who dropped me off this morning swore that this coastline stretch was "so remote" that I'd only see bears and eagles. The only other person who comes here is, according to him, "a Kodiak hermit."

It's not a bear—definitely not a bear—unless bears have started wearing faded flannel shirts and braided hair.

The beachcomber isn't a little old hermit either. I guess she's a mystery. A smile tugs at the corners of my mouth.

Whoever she is, she's cute.

I squint, trying to make out more detail. *What's she doing here?* Admiring me—obviously. Why else would she be on a nowhere beach during the early morning surf?

Word about me must have spread across the little island, a daring, young, good-looking surfer. I heard the whispers when I arrived by plane with my board in tow. The braver and friendlier Alaskans greeted me as I strolled through their quaint, one-street town. They didn't see many surfers here, and most were delighted to strike up a conversation with me.

Ambling along in the early hours, a fisherman hollered, "Need a lift?"

Only here a few hours, I'm the talk of the town, and people are offering me rides. A raven stealing fries from a toddler was the most watched video from Kodiak yesterday—*I did my research. Kodiak* needs a little excitement, and I'm just the girl to bring it!

I grin wider, my chest swelling with confidence as I arch back on my board like it's my throne. *Play it cool, Serena. You're the surfing queen here!*

"Siren, slay!" I cheer myself on with another jubilant whoop, the thrill surging through me. I straighten and shift my balance with practiced ease. Shooting my fan a dazzling smile while flashing the classic hang-loose gesture, there's no way she could miss me.

She doesn't even look up or pause on the beach. I shake my head, the irresistible itch to get her attention increasing. She's pretending not to notice because she's a shy, small-town girl.

Swerving off the crest, I'll catch another, *bigger* wave for a more impressive show.

The next wave rises like a skyscraper, its glassy curve gleaming. It's perfect—wild, unrelenting, and *mine.*

I paddle hard, my arms burning in a satisfying way, and position myself.

"Showtime." Flashing a grin at the roaring beast beneath me, I tip my board forward, slicing into the wave. I'm invincible, a warrior queen commanding the ocean, destined to conquer the Arctic's untamed waters.

Then—*disaster.*

My board wobbles, and my weight shifts wrong.

The nose of my board dips at the worst possible angle. My stomach plummets as I'm suspended, weightless.

"Oh shi—"

I'm not riding the wave—I'm eating it. Water slams into me, cold enough to punch the air from my lungs. I tumble, my limbs tangle. The ocean tosses me like a rag doll. Cold water slams into me, filling my ears with roaring chaos. Salt stings my nose as I tumble in the icy current.

Up! I need up. My arms flail, grasping at nothing, and panic claws its way into my chest. Finally, I break the surface, sputtering and gasping, only for another wave to smash me back under. The cold sinks its teeth into my skin, along with a few rocks the wave throws me against as a rip tide claims me. When I resurface again, the beach looks impossibly far. My heart thuds in my ears, louder than the crashing waves and stronger than the tide dragging me away from the beach.

Is this it? Am I really going to make the evening news as a crazy surfer lost at sea?

Through my blurred vision, I catch a silhouette against the jagged shoreline, waving. A small, sharp inner voice rallies, *Swim, Serena!* Swim like your life depends on it *because it does.*

My body aches, my ears are ringing, and the current's dragging me past the rocky shore, closer to her—*I have her full attention now*—but away from the sandy beach. My strength fades fast—it must be the freezing water.

"Swim to the islet!" she shouts through the tumultuous roar of the crashing waves.

The islet? I squint against the spray, my eyes narrowing as I see a rugged outcrop to my right. It's a pile of rocks, minor in the churning ocean, jutting from the frothy surf. It's nestled perilously far from the familiar safety of the sandy shore I started from. I falter for a heartbeat, torn between instinct to fight the current back to the beach and swimming towards the islet. Every muscle in my body screams for me to fight and unleash my strength, swimming against the current to the closer beach.

"Not that way!" she shouts again, her voice sharp as a knife. "The current's stronger there!"

Her warning slices through the fog of doubt, clouding my mind and igniting a flicker of clarity amidst the swirling confusion. I must listen and surrender to the current, swimming for the rocks.

I grit my teeth. My frozen muscles ache from the cold, but my gut is working, telling me to trust her.

With a surge of effort, I pivot toward the islet. The figure grows larger as I claw through the freezing water. My limbs scream in protest, but I don't stop until I collapse on the sharp barnacled rocks, choking and shivering. I rest my head against a rock, and I think about kissing it for a second.

"What were you thinking?"

The icy voice above me penetrates like the wind cutting through my wetsuit. I blink the saltwater from my eyes and look at her.

Wearing brown knee-high, rubber boots, and she's wrapped in an oversized plaid jacket overwhelming her petite frame, stands a woman with sharp cheekbones and blue-grey eyes as stormy as the waves I escaped. Her long, dark hair is trying to escape her messy braids, and her expression is more wary—*annoyed* than the friendly small-town welcome I received from everyone else I've met here.

"Excuse me?" I croak.

"You're lucky you didn't drown." Her tone is clipped as she hauls me upright. "What's wrong with you, trying to surf here without knowing what you're doing?"

"First of all," I say between gasps, "I totally knew what I was doing." My legs wobble beneath me, and she catches me before I faceplant. "Second of all... what are *you* doing out here? Who are you? A lifeguard?"

She snorts—a soft, incredulous sound making me almost forget my lungs are on fire. "Lifeguard? Hardly. More like the poor sucker forced to save your sorry butt."

I shrug off her steadying arm. "I've got this!"

"Clearly," she mutters, peeling off her jacket to remove her second layer—a flannel jacket—and she drops it over my shoulders.

My first impression of her being cute wasn't wrong and heat rises to my cheeks, as my heart skips. Her expression is exasperation, with a gruff vibe, but with her jacket off, she's a curvy, petite one—*just my type.*

"I'm serious!" I insist. "I can handle it!" But I make no move to return the jacket because the heat and smell lingering on it are impossible to give up.

She raises an eyebrow. "Sure, hotshot. Let's get moving before you freeze to death."

I'm too cold to argue. She grabs my arm with a grip that says she's not here to negotiate.

"Hey. I have a jacket and boots in my bag," I say lamely, shrugging the wet bag hump, covered by her bulky jacket as I follow her. My wetsuit squelches, and I start coughing up what feels like half the inlet.

She stops to let me catch my breath. "What are you doing here? Tourists are only out here on fishing charters."

"Not a tourist," I explain, puffing up a little. "I'm a surfer. And that wave? It's on my bucket list to crush."

Her expression slightly softens. "Yeah, well, maybe the Gulf of Alaska isn't the place to learn to surf."

"Thanks," I say with a grin. "Well, bossy, it's been a pleasure crashing into you. Erm...I mean in front of you. Are you done with the lecture, *brah*?"

She rolls her eyes but doesn't say no.

"It's Bree and you're an idiot," she says in a flat but not unkind voice.

"That's...a little harsh. I'm actually a genius international surfer who had...a minor mishap."

"Minor? You were two seconds away from being a human pancake or being dragged out to the Pacific Ocean, never to be seen again."

I wince, taking a step and feeling a bruise forming across my back. "Dramatic, much? I *wasn't*, and thanks for your lifeguarding."

Bree watches, unimpressed, her arms crossed over her chest as if deciding whether I'm worth the effort it took to fish me out of the ocean.

"Don't let me keep you from collecting your rocks," I say, nodding toward her bucket. "I'm fine."

"Sea glass, not rocks." Bree doesn't budge. "You're not fine. You're blue."

I glance down at my hands. Sure enough, they're more smurf-like than human. Staggering with my shrug, she grabs my arm again to steady me. Her grip is firm but not rough. "Seriously, though," she says, her voice low. "These waters don't mess around. People don't always make it back."

Her words settle in my chest like a stone, heavy and sobering. I glance at the waves still crashing behind us and shiver—not from the cold. "Have you..." I trail off, unsure if I want the answer.

She stiffens, her hand dropping from my arm like I've burned her. "Lost anyone?" she finishes for me. Her jaw tightens, and she looks at the horizon, where the gray sky melts into the darker ocean. "Yeah. Every Alaskan has. Let's leave it at that."

Her words are clipped and final, but they carry a weight that pulls at me. There's a story there—one she doesn't want to tell. I should let it go, but something about her makes me curious, like there's more to her than the tough, no-nonsense act.

I clear my throat and try to lighten the mood. "Well, Bree, you make an excellent rescuer. Do you save reckless surfers often, or am I extra special?"

She snorts again, but it's closer to a laugh this time. "*Extra*, sure. Let's go with that." She gestures toward the rocky path leading to more rocks with no beach in sight. "Come on, you'll freeze out here. There's a cave nearby to get out of this wind and warm up."

"A cave? *Wow*! You really know how to show a girl a good time," I tease with a wink, but she doesn't turn or laugh.

There's something about her—this guarded energy, like she's built a wall around herself so high my jokes can't touch her. What's behind her icy exterior? The challenge of finding out makes me chuckle.

"Hey," I say, stumbling but catching myself. "Thanks for, you know... not letting me die out there."

She glances back, and for a second, her expression softens. "We watch out for each other here. And you're welcome," she says quietly. Then the wall snaps back into place, and she's all business. "Watch your step. These rocks are slippery."

Whatever this rocky place she's leading us to—wild, freezing, and unpredictable—I want to see more of it with her.

I chuckle and scamper over the slippery, sharp rocks, following the hot stranger.

Chapter 2: Breezy, Bree – Rough Waters, Rough Start

Five minutes before...

A bone-chilling shriek pierces the air as I stand on the windswept shores of my peaceful Alaskan beach. The unnatural sound sends a jolt through me, making every hair on my arms stand on end. It's violent and raw, clashing with the soothing symphony of waves rolling in and out. My heart races, thumping wildly in my chest as my instincts kick in, alert and ready for whatever wild surprises the Arctic wilderness is throwing my way.

The salty air smells different, underscored by a metallic tang warning of an incoming storm. My boots sink slightly into the sand as I stand in the tangle of driftwood, placing the rare treasure—a frosted piece of sea glass–in my bucket. Pale blue, teardrop-shaped, perfectly smooth, I was admiring the beautiful gift from the ocean—my mom would have loved it. It's the perfect shape for a necklace.

The shriek comes again, scattering a few nearby gulls. I scan the beach, my heart hammering harder. My isolated stretch of shoreline is my haven and very private.

"Yeah, baby!"

It's not an emergency plea. A human shout of triumph. I lift my gaze to search the water, squinting against the low morning sun. At first, there's nothing but the rolling surge of the tide, icy and relentless. Then I spot her.

A figure on a surfboard, cutting through the waves with careless grace. Her wetsuit glistens like seal skin, and her hair—*blonde*, I think—trails behind her. She moves like the ocean's hers, claiming it with every yell and slice of her board.

I blink hard. *She doesn't belong here.*

"Tourists," I mutter under my breath, irritation flaring. *Who comes here to surf?* This isn't California or Maui. Kodiak's waves are unforgiving—freezing cold, treacherous undercurrents, jagged rocks hidden beneath the foam.

She catches a wave, arms outstretched in victory, carving a flashy arc through the water. The ocean surges beneath her, mighty and unpredictable. Show-offs and big egos are no match against Alaska's brutal coastline. My stomach turns and tightens as I debate. Should *I yell at her to come to shore before the storm hits or ignore her?*

Right on cue, the wave turns. The nose of her board dips, pitching her forward. Her arms flail before she vanishes beneath the churning water. A second later, the board resurfaces, riderless.

"Idiot," I mumble, already moving. My boots hit the beach's edge tide in seconds, the icy water soaking the soles. She's in trouble, no doubt about it. The beach is far from town and outside of cell phone range, with no other person in sight. This makes it perfect but forces me to help. *I'm her only chance if she's injured.*

Her head pops up—*thank God*—but she's coughing, spluttering, kicking weakly against the drag of the waves. The current's already pulling her sideways, away from the shore and toward open water. She will freeze or drown if she doesn't get to the rocks.

"Swim to the rocks!" I shout, cupping my hands around my mouth to project my voice over the crashing surf.

She doesn't hear me. Or she's too panicked to listen.

"Go left!" I yell again, louder.

This time, her head swivels. Blue eyes lock on mine for the briefest second—startled, desperate. A wave smacks her face, and she vanishes again. When she surfaces, she angles her body toward the rocky islet just yards away from where the ocean carried her.

I jog along the beach, boots sinking into the wet sand as the rising tide erases my footprints. I rush to the last outcropping of rocks before the Pacific.

Heart pounding minutes later, I reach her with relief and exasperation. She's clawing at the jagged rocks, coughing and trembling, her wetsuit slick with seawater.

"Nice day for a swim," I call, wading into the freezing water. My insulated boots keep my feet dry, but the cold still bites.

She rolls onto her back, blinking up at me. "Nicer day for a rescue, brah," she says, grinning.

Unbelievable.

I sigh and grab her arm, hauling her to her feet. I scold her and try not to allow my annoyance to keep me from assisting her. She's heavier than she looks, and her slight frame is dense with muscle. My hand slips on the slick fabric of her wetsuit. I'm used to gripping slipper things while pulling the slippery salmon from my dad's fishing nets, so I keep my grip and steady her.

When she's steady, she grins, and I bite back a grimace. I turn for her to follow me back to the beach.

Does she even realize how dangerous it is to surf out here? These waves aren't forgiving, and neither is the weather this late in the season. Does she know how to survive out here? The first lesson to teach her: stop being cocky, thinking you're tougher than Alaska. I walk, and she follows after she attempts friendly conversation–there's no time for chitchat.

She pulls a phone from a waterproof case, turns on the camera, and loudly starts monologuing. "Not only did I conquer that gnarly wave, I'm meeting a real-life tough Alaskan wilderness woman! Yasss, Siren Surfing fans!"

"There's no coverage here." I roll my eyes. The tide is rising fast, and the clouds overhead are darkening. There's no time for her to record her reckless bravado.

"No prob. I'll post it later," she says, pushing her phone back in her dry bag.

"This isn't a tourist beach."

She's shivering hard now but still manages to puff up a little. "I'm not a tourist. I'm a surfer, remember."

"Next time, bring a buddy," I say over my shoulder as the first raindrop hits my cheek, and I glance back from the rocky outcrop to the sandy shore. As I'm assessing our situation, she's clueless about the danger, continuing her idle conversation.

The tide is rising too fast for comfort. "Come on. We'll be stuck out here on these rocks until low tide if we don't move fast."

She laughs, though it's strained. "Noted. So, what's your deal?"

Thankfully, she continues walking as she talks. I remain silent, hoping she'll get the hint.

"I'm Siren," she says.

I snort. Of course, her name sounds Californian and smug. She pauses, so I turn to see if she's fallen, but she's just smiling and waiting.

I give her the shortest responses I can as I try moving faster, but by her wincing and groans, she's hurt. I stop to ask her about her injuries, but she interrupts me before I check.

"Bree. Is that short for something? Sabrina? Brianna?" Her grin turns sly.

"Nope. Short for *Not Interested.* Keep moving."

She laughs, bright and unapologetic. "Well, Bree, you've officially earned a spot in my extreme surfing memoir. *Chapter One: The Alaska Wave*, When a Hot Beachcomber Saved My Life."

I roll my eyes, but there's a flicker of something beneath my irritation. Amusement, maybe. She's reckless, but her annoying positivity is hard to ignore. I motion for her to hurry up. "Do you always wipe out this hard, and try to kill yourself, or is it a special occasion?"

"Only when someone's distracting me," she says, flashing a charming grin.

I roll my eyes. *Tourists!* Raindrops thump heavier on my back, and I look back. Her grip is firm, helping her as her feet slip on the slick rocks. Her hand is calloused but warm even through the cold.

As I steady her, our eyes meet for the briefest second. Hers are sharp blue, the sea glass color—fitting for someone surfing. "Is Siren short for anything?" I ask to distract from the warmth blossoming in my chest, almost forgetting about the oncoming tide and my disdain for tourists, especially flirty, egotistical outsiders.

Almost.

"It's really Serena. But everyone calls me Siren. I'm going to change it for real, when I have time," she explains, pausing to wipe her hair from her face, which gives me time to reassess our situation.

"Hey, thanks again," she says casually as if she's not in danger.

"Don't thank me yet," I reply. "You owe me for interrupting my beachcombing, and if we don't warm you up, you'll freeze your butt off and be a popsicle."

"Hey. Lots of people like popsicles," she flirts.

The tide covers my feet, covering the dry rocks. The raindrops hitting me are increasing. I pull her toward the rocks, abandoning my plan of returning to the sandy shore as it rapidly disappears.

Trudging through the water and onto the rocky beach, I shiver with her as the wind whips around me and pierces my warm layers.

"So, Bree," she says, "what's a beachcomber like you doing on a beach like this?"

I roll my eyes. "You're lucky I'm not leaving you to freeze for your bad flirting skills."

"Harsh," she teases. "You're a tough nut to crack, Bree."

"And you're too chatty for someone who nearly drowned and might freeze to death."

"I love testing the limits. Pushing boundaries. You know," she explains, "living!"

"Losing your board in the Pacific and almost dying, you mean," I correct her.

"That too." She grins, and for the first time, I smile back.

"You know you aren't exactly safe," I warn. "I really don't have time for your pickup lines while I'm trying to save you."

"Ouch. You're really leaning into the whole mysterious local girl vibe, huh?" Siren's tone is teasing, but her smile falters when I don't respond.

The word *mysterious* digs under my skin. I'm not mysterious. I'm careful. Out here, careful means staying alive. Outsiders that don't get that don't last long in Alaska or with me.

"Let's focus on getting you out before the tide traps us," I say, brushing past her and climbing onto a higher rock.

She gasps, clutching her chest like I'd stabbed her. "You're not much of a welcoming person, are you?"

"Nope," I deadpan, scanning the horizon. The storm clouds are closing in, darker and closer than I'd hoped. My boots slip slightly on the wet rock, my body lurches, and Siren reaches out, steadying me before I can react.

Her grip is not casual and flirty, it is solid and confident. The strong wind dies down momentarily as her blue eyes lock onto mine. I don't flinch, but my defenses rise like a tide. People who play it fast and loose with danger have a way of wrecking everything they touch.

"Thanks," I mutter, pulling my hand back from her grip.

She doesn't let go immediately. "You know, you're kind of hard to get to know," she says softly.

"That's the point," I reply, stepping away.

The wind picks up, carrying the scent of rain and salt—the storm. I glance at the disappearing shoreline. I swallow and halt, changing direction to the dry rocks on our left. "We're stuck here until the low tide and the water drops. A few hours, maybe longer."

Serena groans, flopping onto a tall rock that could easily be a recliner. "Awesome. Guess we're hanging out. Admit it—my pickup lines worked, didn't they?"

"Don't get comfortable," I warn, sitting a safe distance away. "We'll need to move if the storm gets worse."

She grins despite the cold, her teeth chattering slightly. "You're like a survival manual come to life. Do you ever relax?"

"I relax just fine," I shoot back, but my tone is sharper than I intended. "Usually, my beach walks don't require survival skills and conversation."

Her smile softens, curiosity flickering in her eyes. She doesn't push, though. Instead, she leans back, looking up at the clouds. "Well, Bree the Alaskan Beachcomber, looks like we're here for a while. Got any good stories?"

She opens her bag to pull out a pair of gloves with shaking hands, and I almost laugh. *Stories?* I have plenty—none I'd ever tell her. But I must warm her up as the rain and wind increase.

"Not today," I say, leaning back against the rock. "You're chatty enough for both of us."

Her laughter echoes against the rising tide, and I shake my head. I explain, "We're stuck here and with this storm surge the tide may be higher than usual."

Her brow furrows. "Wait, what?"

I gesture to the rising water covering the rocks and beach I crossed seconds ago. "The islet's surrounded at high tide. We are trapped out here until the tide drops. Fifteen feet of water will cover the walkway and the shoreline. There's no way back until low tide when we can cross the rocks that are now underwater.."

Her face falls, and she looks like she might argue. Then her eyes narrow, and she tilts her head, studying me, "I could swim."

"With the current and the temperature, you'd be better off waiting a few hours," I patiently explain.

Her grin falters, and for a split second, her confidence disappears as she takes her situation seriously. But then she laughs, running a hand through her wavy, wet hair.

"You're funny," she says. "Grumpy, but funny."

I roll my eyes. "And you're reckless and cocky."

"Adventurous," she corrects.

"Reckless," I repeat, turning away. "Let's move and get into the cave."

"You're the boss, Breezy," she answers with chattering teeth. "With your carefree, easy vibe, that's your new nickname."

I frown and shake my head at the nickname, refusing to acknowledge her, which might only encourage her to continue to flirt with me. No one has ever given me a nickname before.

She follows me quietly for a blessed minute this time. I climb onto a higher patch of rock, scanning the dark clouds on the horizon.

"So, how long are we trapped on these rocks?" she asks, her voice fading into the increasing wind.

"Four, maybe six hours. Depends." I don't want to tell her the tides are hitting record levels these last few days, which is why I was out beachcombing. Stormy weather brings unusual treasures.

Her eyes dance, and she chirps, "Wait, this is just like the *Lost* series, brah?"

I rub my temples. "It's not a movie. It's real life, and you're lucky I was here."

"Hey, I was just sayin'. No need to bite my head off."

I take a deep breath, letting the cold air cool my irritation. "Look," I say, forcing my voice to stay level, "if you want to survive, we need to focus. The temperature's dropping, the tide's still rising, and we're miles from help."

She bites her lip, and for a second, she might actually take this seriously. Then she shrugs, the easy smile sliding back into place. "Got it. You're the boss, Breezy."

"You're cold," I say. It's not a question.

"I'll survive."

I dig through my little backpack, shake out the emergency blanket, and hand it to her.

Her eyes widen, and she crinkles the silver blanket. "Seriously?"

"Just wrap it around yourself. It'll insulate you and keep you warmer."

She hesitates, then pulls it over herself. Grinning, she says, "Thanks, Breezy."

"Don't push it," I mutter, smiling instead of frowning at her.

I glance at her and wonder if she will ever stop talking. She's a mess—her hair tangled, her wet wetsuit half off with her bikini top, and only my old flannel dry over her top. She must be freezing.

She takes this pause to pull a thermal top from her dry bag and pulls off the flannel to reveal an impressive octopus tattoo across her chest. I try to look away as she puts her shirt and my flannel over that, and she crams her wetsuit into the bag. Siren slips on her shoes and flashes an annoying surfer sign indicating she's ready.

Something is endearing about her, too. She's like the stray puppy who wandered to my door during a snowstorm years ago. I couldn't help but bring the lost, cold puppy inside. When no one claimed her, I named her, and she became my best friend.

"Let's go." She charges in front of me across the slippery rocks while wrapped in the shiny blanket.

Looking at Siren, I shake my head but follow her–there's only one direction to go–up to the higher part of the rocky islet. Her blonde hair sticks to her long neck, and I notice the curve of the tattoo, making my fingers itch to move her hair and trace the tattoo.

I vow *I will not fall in love with this stray!*

Continue reading Bree's heartwarming story in *Wilderness Rescue: Tides of Love*.
CHECK IT OUT HERE.

Join us to discover your next favorite story at HarmonyNoble .com &
Sign up to receive the e-newsletter for exclusive news and giveaways.
CHECK IT OUT HERE.

COMING NEXT
WILDERNESS RESCUE:
TIDES OF LOVE

HARMONY NOBLE

Trapped in the Alaskan wilderness?! Seriously, what experienced outdoorsy woman lets this happen to her?

When Serena is surfing a once-in-a-lifetime bore tide and injures herself, she encounters a cute stranger.

Self-proclaimed Alaskan Hippy, Bree, is clamming nearby and wants nothing to do with the surfing adrenaline junkie.

However, the independent Alaskan Wilderness Women discover they'll need each other's help to escape being trapped by Kodiak's deadly bore tide in the frigid waters of a remote island named after the fearsome Kodiak brown bear.

The excitement of the Alaska rescue takes a backseat to the surfer vs hippy's heartwarming opposites-attract lesbian love story in "Tides of Love."

Author's Note: Yearning for more heart-pounding rescues and heart-warming love? Explore each of the standalone stories in the Wilderness Rescue Series.

Experience an Alaskan surfing adventure when Serena and Bree embrace love while rescuing each other in this thrilling sapphic romance, *Wilderness Rescue: Tides of Love.*
CHECK IT OUT HERE.

Discover your next favorite story at HarmonyNoble.com.

OTHER TITLES BY HARMONY NOBLE
For the most up-to-date list visit Harmony's website at
www.HarmonyNoble.com.

<u>Aurora's Wilderness Love:</u>

Hot Girl Summer Love

<u>Wilderness Rescue Sapphic Romance Series:</u>

Crashing Into Love
Unthaw My Heart
Winning Love
Stormy Hearts
Scoring Love
Flooded Hearts
Healing Hearts
Tides of Love
Iditarod Love

<u>Coffeehouse Romance Series:</u>

Love, Joy & Lattes (Joy's Story)
Test Driving a Millionaire (Tara's Story)
Shattering Crystal a Bully Romance (Crystal's Story)
Choosing Love, Namaste (Meaghan's Story)
The Wrong Bride for Christmas (Monica's Story)

Coffeehouse Romance Short Stories:

Joy's 4th of July Holidate

Tara's Valentine Holidate

Crystal's Easter Holidate

Meaghan's New Year Holidate

Monica's Halloween Holidate

My Accidental Christmas Fiancé

Joy's Coffeehouse Romance

UNLOCK YOUR GIFT

Happy Reading & EMBRACE TRUE LOVE!

Snag the latest swoon-worthy reads and stay tuned for upcoming stories at <u>www.HarmonyNoble.com</u>.

About Author — Harmony Noble

Meet the unstoppable twins from the rugged wilds of Alaska—Harmony & Melody, the duo of "Author Harmony Noble." Fueled by endless lattes, their character-driven stories brim with authenticity, humor, and heart—featuring Alaskan grit, journeys of self-discovery, and swoon-worthy happily-ever-afters.

When they're not crafting adventure romances, the twins can be found hiking trails with breathtaking views, enjoying charming coffee shops, or exploring new cultures and destinations worldwide.

Join the e-newsletter for exclusive content and giveaways at
website: https://harmonynoble.com
Email: TrueLoveWriters@gmail.com
Instagram/Facebook/TikTok: @truelovewriters

Stormy Hearts

Harmony Noble

SCAN FOR GIFT

TrueLoveWriters

**Thank you for choosing this book
by Harmony Noble. We hope the story
brought you as much joy reading it
as we had in creating it!**

We'd love to hear from you! Feel free to reach out via email at True LoveWriters@gmail.com, and don't forget to follow us on <u>Instagram</u>, <u>Facebook</u>, <u>TikTok</u> at @truelovewriters for the latest updates and be-hind-the-scenes fun.

Get access to exclusive offers, bonus content, new release updates, and recommendations for more great reads. Sign up for our e-newsletter at HarmonyNoble.com.

Dedicated to the true hero of this book—**COFFEE!**

You, my caffeinated confidant, are the MVP,
turning 'I can't even' into 'Watch me go!'
Thanks a latte!

Stormy Hearts

Harmony Noble

SCAN FOR GIFT

TrueLoveWriters

Chapter 1

Maria

"COLE!"

I shout into the gusting wind, and just as I open my mouth, a wave crashes against the boat, filling my mouth with saltwater. Spitting and wiping my lips on my cold, bare arm, I can't get rid of the bitter taste from the violent sea and toxic fear crashing over me.

No! This cannot be happening! How can a few hours transform the happiest day of my life to the worst day?

I was on a leisurely boating trip in Kachemak Bay, just outside my new hometown of Homer, Alaska. We were celebrating six months of marriage and a new chapter of our lives.

Cole was teaching me about boating, his passion, and business on the calm ocean while I enjoyed his enthusiasm in showing me how to steer. I watched the harbor disappear as the minutes turned to hours on our Alaskan adventure.

Cole's so busy with the family ferry business, the Homer Harbor Hopper, that this boating lesson is one of our few intimate moments. Although I'm excited to learn about operating a boat, I'm more excited to share the news with him that we are starting our own family soon. I waited on the swaying boat for the perfect opportunity to tell him.

I lost my family at a young age, and Cole is an only child. His parents had him at an older age, and they died years ago, which is something we share: missing family. Hence, being pregnant is a pretty big deal for both of us. Our dream!

We want a big family and children running around, learning to sail on the ocean, and taking over the family business. Then we can happily retire in our big house overlooking the beautiful bay and wait for our grandchildren.

Of course, Cole's boating lesson and the good news on the tip of my tongue was my carefree life *before the murderous storm and a rogue wave knocked Cole overboard.* One moment, he was checking the sputtering engine to motor us out of the grey clouds rolling in. The next, he was no longer leaning over the railing. The waves swallowed his bright life jacket before I realized what was happening.

I stood there, frozen and helpless.

I shake my head. *I should have done something, then!*

The rain and wind hit my cheeks, wet and numb with tears, the ocean and the foul weather. My hands tremble as I clutch the side of our large boat. It seamlessly glided over the smooth waters when Cole was at the wheel, but the boat is tossed relentlessly in the dark, unforgiving bay without him. The waves batter it, leaving me wet. My cute summer dress is heavier than the weighty gold and diamond jewelry on my neck and wrists. The jaunty boating lesson transformed into a raging crisis.

I wrap my arms around my growing belly and grab the side of the boat, bracing for the next crashing wave threatening to flip it. My feet are numb with the water rising and sloshing on the deck over my sandals. Instead of enjoying my first outing to celebrate our marriage and the start of our family–*I'm left alone, stranded!*

"Cole!" I yell into the gray night. The deafening wind snatches my words and responds by throwing icy water at me. I continue clinging to the side of the boat. My voice is lost in the howling, furious storm.

"Cole! Cole! Where are you?" I cry out. The boat shudders with the relentless assault, and panic claws at my chest while I struggle to keep my footing on the slippery deck.

The Alaskan afternoon is turning dark and ominous with the storm closing in.

Terror surges through my veins. Never in my worst nightmares would I imagine myself in this situation. I stop yelling to rest my raw throat and shield my eyes from the ocean spray to search the dark water for any sign of Cole–*anything*!

There's only the miles of ocean with no land or boats in sight.

I try pushing away the suffocating panic. My jaw tightens with fear, and despite the water dripping off my face, I cough, swallowing the dry lump in my throat. I fumble blindly for the radio in the dusky light as my slippery fingers search.

My numb fingers touch the hard edge of the radio. My cold fingers can't grip or make sense of the buttons in the cold, with my fear overshadowing my mind.

I can't keep searching and yelling into the storm. I need help!

With the device firmly in my grasp, I twist the knobs with frantic desperation, hoping it'll do something and send a signal to find someone—*anyone to help find Cole.*

"Help, HELP! Anyone? I need help!" I shout into the receiver with my wavering voice, but the storm's furies louder than my pleas, and there's no sound coming through the radio.

In frustration, I toss it aside.

It's just another thing I don't know how to operate. I can't start the motor. I can't call for help. It's hopeless!

Cole is gone. Even if I spot him, he'll be frozen after being in the water this long. And the only way he couldn't swim back to the boat were if he was knocked unconscious.

Will I be able to pull him over the rail and back into the boat? Has it been minutes or hours since he fell overboard?

Time stopped. I look at the swirling, angry ocean and try to determine where the current would have pulled him.

I can't drive the boat. I don't know how to get to shore. Honestly, I don't even know which direction the harbor is. *I'm useless!*

I'm frozen, clutching the rail, overwhelmed as the darkness and chaos erupt around me. I peer over the rail, looking at white-capped waves, but they offer no clue of Cole's whereabouts. My tears are the only warmth as I shout his name over and over, my voice edged with desperation.

"Cole-COLE-Cole Cole Cooooole!"

I grip the rocking boat, my voice cracking—the relentless wind and rain punch me, blurring my vision, and saltwater is all I taste and smell. The futility suffocates me.

I lost everything and everyone when he vanished. No one is left to save me—Cole is my only family.

I'm finished!

The boat bucks and lurches on the raging sea.

"Where are you? How could you leave me here?!" I whisper with a whimper into the abyss.

Each wave crashing over the boat threatens to wash me into the ocean with him.

Maybe I should let go and let the ocean take me?

Sudden lightning shooting through the dark sky flashes against my colossal diamond wedding ring, costing more than everything I owned in the Philippines before I met Cole, alongside the simple gold band with the ancient Baybayin script, *Pamilya,* on it. The Filipino word is for *family,* which reminds me of the family the ocean stole from me in the tragic hurricane. My grip tightens, and I stand taller.

The ocean is not taking anything else today! I am going to survive!

I grip the boat for dear life. My fingers white-knuckled with terror but holding.

This time it's different. I'm not a helpless child, and I have something to fight for. I bite my lip and widen my stance, using my elbows to protect my belly from hitting the boat with the pounding waves.

Minutes stretch into a never-ending night as I search the turbulent waters for any sign of Cole and keep my hands gripping the boat. The boat's erratic jostling and the relentless storm are making me nauseous.

The boat is like a toy thrown around in the waves, bobbing and staying afloat despite the storm. Every scream of the wind and crash of the waves erodes my hope of finding Cole and escaping the storm.

"Cole! Where are you?" I sob with rain-soaked words and a scratchy sound.

Clinging to the boat, isolated and scared, my imagination smashes me harder than the waves. With each lurching movement of the boat, I fear it'll be the last, and it'll flip or crash into something and sink.

Each second is a battle to stay afloat, to hold on, and to stay alive. The darkness of night mingles with the unrelenting storm shrouding me in black despair.

The man who promised me a family, a future, and a dream life is nowhere–*gone*! And I'm left alone, barely able to hang on in this horrible Alaskan ocean without the faintest idea of what to do.

Cole's gone, and I'm going to die, too.

I grip my only lifeline, the radio.

"Please! Someone! Help me! Please," I sob into the radio.

Chapter 2

Jackie

The storm changes the rolling ocean waves into walls of unpredictable breakers, pounding into my boat, *The Sea Otter's Pride.* Hours earlier than expected, the storm hit, but that's how the weather is at the end of summer in Alaska, *unpredictable.*

I *should* head back to the shore, but my clients are waiting for a boat taxi across the bay, and I'm already halfway there. My heart hammers as I contemplate my options: complete the trip for my waiting clients or be realistic, turning back to the safety of Homer as the violent storm front grows more hazardous each minute.

"Stupid weatherman," I grumble, the rain drops hitting my ball cap and the wind pulling my blonde hair from the messy bun stuffed under it as I drive directly into the gray storm.

I genuinely hate to lose the business–*really the money*– as I own and operate my one-woman water taxi service. The boating business is profitable in the touristy summer. Still, in the fall and winter, I can barely keep the business afloat while competing with the larger, established taxi service, the *Homer Harbor Hopper.*

There's enough ferrying business in Kachemak Bay for all of us if they weren't so damn competitive. I grind my teeth, thinking about their slogans, *Ride with the Best or Float with the Rest, leaving our competition in our wake for over 40 years.*

I tuck a strand of hair behind my ear and shake my head. My trustworthy boat is over forty, but I've only started ferrying people in the last few years. Since the *Hopper* only hires men and my boat is my only source of income, doing my small ferry runs is a more reliable income than fishing with its unpredictable, dwindling annual salmon numbers.

Homer's leading economy is fishing, but tourism is booming, and I pivoted despite learning a new business model. As long as I'm alone, on my boat, on the water, I'm living my dream.

Growing up in this tight-knit community, people trust my boating skills to ferry them and their cargo across the bay. Although the Hopper has larger vessels with many scheduled trips across the bay, I can make my own hours and accommodate last-minute, unscheduled cargo and passengers. I do my best to help others, even referring passengers to the Hopper's boats when I'm overbooked, but they've never sent me a client—*not a single one.*

Thus, I work solo without business partners or support from the Hopper ferry captains. I overhear them radioing they are *too full to take all the passengers.* In spite of knowing I can move their extra people, they avoid radioing me and instead make their passengers wait hours for their next trip across the bay.

Consequently, each of *my* clients appreciates my immediate ferry service and the personalized service I provide. I appreciate their reviews and return business. I might not have a fancy boat or ten sailings a day, but I get the job done, and I'm a *damn good sailor!*

The rain increases and I pull out my yellow rain jacket from the locker under my bench. If I can't complete this trip to drop off cargo and pick up passengers across the bay, the clients may switch to using the Hopper's evening ferry. I should've turned back when I saw the winds start kicking up two hours ago. Now, even if I make it across the choppy waters, I'm stuck over there since we can't return until the storm passes.

"Dammit!" I slam my hand on the wheel and sigh, relenting to the storm and turning my boat around to go to Homer. I pinch my nose and push my hair back in defeat as the wind starts howling and the sky darkens.

It's just my luck! I'm losing the fare, time, and the gas to get this far. Plus, I might lose the clients if I can't make it across later tonight.

Since visibility sucks, I mess with the buttons to set my navigation system for Homer when my radio crackles.

"Someone. . . HELP. .—one!"

A desperate female's voice pierces through the radio's intermittent static with garbled pleas for help in the soupy gray evening. There's no location attached to the distress call.

I turn the knob to increase the volume, and the voice stops, eerily silent.

Scanning the dark waters with the brewing storm already causing choppy waves, I look. Without a doubt, someone is in danger out here, and I am the any other vessels on the water, I may be their only chance.

Surely, I can't be the only one who heard their call, I think, my heart in my throat. I nervously lick my salty lips as I continue searching the rough water. My hands tighten, gripping the wheel, my eyes narrow at the horizon beyond the frothy crests for any sign of another vessel.

The first rule of boating is that rescuing is a priority, *no matter what.* And the closest vessel is required by maritime law to give aid.

Without hesitation, I slow The Sea Otter Pride's engine to help locate the distressed vessel. My boat is solid as it plows through the fierce waves. I steer it into the oncoming waves and toward Homer, hoping to see the caller in distress.

Surely, they'd be en route to Homer, not navigating the storm in the middle of the bay.

However, no other vessels are in sight, and I certainly haven't seen any Coast Guard vessels out here. If the mayday caller is here, I must find them before the storm traps them, giving them no chance of rescue until it passes.

I crack my knuckles and grip the steering wheel. *A mayday from a boat in this kinda weather doesn't end well.*

Suddenly, a red ship bobbing inside the storm's chaos catches my eye. The boat is battered and adrift, taking relentless blows from the ocean's fury.

My pulse quickens. *This must be the Mayday call!*

I see the boat taking the full force of the crashing waves into its port side, jostling the vessel and causing it to tilt brutally, unbalanced in the violent waters. The wounded vessel must be water-logged with its engine off and unable to bow into the waves for protection. My jaw tightens at the boat's situation, barely staying above the foaming sea.

I pilot the Sea Otter's Pride with the singular purpose of reaching the boat to provide assistance and rescue if needed. My reliable skiff responds readily to steering through the waves despite being pushed and pulled by the storm.

As I approach, my eyes lock onto a lone, odd, pink-clad figure without a jacket or life vest on the foredeck, starboard side.

A woman!

Her petite frame is hunched from the cold, fear, or an injury. Either way, she needs to get out of this desperate situation.

She sees me and begins frantically waving both arms in the universal distress sign, with her shouts swallowed up by the storm.

Dammit! If she doesn't hold on to the boat, I'm going to be rescuing her from the water!

"Hold on. I'm coming. Just keep holding tight," I say uselessly, as one of my hands grips my steering wheel and my other signals high above my head in a nonverbal response that I am coming. The fragile woman won't be able to hear me over the roaring of the storm.

I guide my boat as close as I dare in a position alongside the tilted drunken vessel.

Quickly, I move to the side and extend my hand for her to take. "Grab my hand!"

My boat lurches as her larger vessel slams against the side of my smaller but sturdy boat. I don't hear the boats crashing with the storm's howling winds, but I feel the jarring with each wave.

Motioning frantically for her to grab my hand before the next wave hits us, my urgency thrusts the sopping-wet woman into action.

For a moment, she hesitates, looking back into the Bay behind her. Then, her brown eyes locking onto my eyes, she lets go of the rail and reaches for me.

I'm close enough now to see her red lips trembling with her dark, wet hair in her eyes and mouth.

And then, with a quick surge of determination, she lunges toward me, her fingers grasping mine.

I lock her hand in mine, the cold ocean dripping down our intertwined fingers. With all my strength, I pull her from the unstable deck of her boat onto the relative safety of mine. The boats collide in the turbulent waves, adding a chaotic dance to her rescue.

"I'm Captain Jackie. You're going to be fine," I reassure her, my voice firm despite the situation's urgency. The wide red eyes that meet mine hold fear and gratitude. I want to wrap her in a warm blanket, shield her from the biting cold, and cocoon her in safety. But time is of the essence, and I have to move quickly. "You're safe now. I've seen worse weather." I manage a tight smile, attempting to convey confidence, but her stunning, albeit wet, appearance steals my breath, and my heart flutters unexpectedly.

Why is she alone out here? Who is this exotic beauty?

I furrow my brows and wipe the hand not holding hers over my face. I'm momentarily caught off-guard by the delicate touch of her hand and the intensity in her big eyes. I'm drawn to her, like a salmon swimming upstream, drawn to its innate spawning grounds. I find myself irresistibly pulled towards her amidst the Alaskan storm.

She's dressed in a way that screams *I'm a tourist* in the harsh Alaskan weather—bedazzled flip-flops, expensive jewelry, a summer dress now clinging to her tan skin. The tropical flower pinned in her drenched black hair adds a touch of unexpected beauty to the grim surroundings. As she stands there, her tiny frame accentuated by the soft curves visible through the soaked fabric, I can't help but imagine her fitting perfectly on my lap.

I shake that enticing image from my head. *Stay focused! This is an emergency*, I scold my wayward thoughts.

"Are there any other people?" I shout over the roaring wind, pulling her closer to me to hear me and to shield her from being swept away by the rough waters. The urgency intensifies, but in the midst of the storm, a different kind of intensity simmers—a magnetic pull that goes beyond the immediate danger.

Her voice whispers with a plea, "Cole. . .He's gone, he's gone..." Her unfocused eyes look into the ocean, and she continues to whisper.

Colton Sanders? I was so focused on her that I didn't recognize the Homer Harbor Hopper's logo on the yacht.

Amid the raging Alaskan storm, I find myself grappling with the irony of rescuing none other than my business rival, Colton. *Figures.*

"Where is he?" I holler, pulling her closer to decipher her mumbled words over the wind. Her slender form melds into my solid frame, her pale face inches from my mouth. Despite my urgent inquiries, her wide eyes, fixated on the storm outside, show no comprehension.

"Did he fall overboard?" I ask louder, giving her a gentle jostle. She nods numbly, her legs giving way, and I instinctively catch her, cradling her cold, delicate frame in my arms.

I guide her to sitting on the deck, securing her safety with an extra life jacket and tethering her to the boat's lifeline, a safety rope around the boat to keep her from falling overboard. Ensuring she won't be tossed overboard in the storm's chaos becomes my priority.

"How long has he been in the water? Is he wearing a life jacket?" I demand, desperate for information. She nods, eyes shutting.

"No! Stay awake with me! Tell me! What happened to Cole?" I lift her, slightly shaking her until her brown eyes flutter open.

"Where is he?" I shout, pulling her closer so she can hear my voice and I can try to decipher her mumbling.

"How long has he been in the water? Is he wearing a life jacket?" She nods her head, and her eyes shut.

"No! You need to stay awake with me! Tell me! What happened to Cole?" I lift her and lightly shake her until her eyes open.

Cole won't survive in this Arctic water long. I have to find him NOW!

"I don't...maybe...two hours...he has a life jacket," she whispers with a cracked voice through her chattering teeth, her eyes brimming with tears.

I clench my jaw, my eyes softening. Maria isn't whispering in shock. She's exhausted, her voice lost from hours of yelling and searching for Cole.

"I'm Maria," she whispers, closing her tired eyes.

A pang of guilt hits me for shouting and shaking her. She's tiny, fragile, and exhausted. I can only enclose her in my arms, hug her into my warm body, and bury her against my chest. I want to comfort her and assure her that she's safe.

Cole's life is seriously in danger if he's been in the icy water for so long. Prolonged exposure to Alaskan waters, even in the summer, can lead to hypothermia. Despite his life jacket, the longer he remains in the water, the slimmer his chances of survival become. The ticking clock amplifies the urgency, leaving us on the edge of hope and despair.

I snatch the radio to call in the mayday report and toss my life ring in the water to mark the spot for the Coast Guard to search. As I convey the information, I wrap Maria in a rain jacket and put a dry winter hat on her head while keeping her propped up next to me.

"Location? Over," the Coast Guard radios back.

I look at the coordinates and relay them back while scanning the waters once again for any sign of Cole.

"Captain, come into Homer. We've marked the location. The storm front is increasing, and the winds will be up to forty knots within the hour. Over."

I glance at Maria, wondering if she understands the significance of what the Coasties relayed to me. The storm is worse, and they want us out of it, but to leave means Cole loses any chance at rescue.

A cold wave crashes and washes us with icy water.

Not that I think he's alive. . . but leaving will decrease his chances of survival. I swallow. We can't stay out here any longer and risk our lives in the storm.

"We are going back. The Coast Guard will take over searching for him," I tell her.

The boats are still beside each other, rocking and slamming together in unison.

"Maria, what's wrong with the boat?" I ask. I look at the expensive Bayliner; it seems fine, just waterlogged.

She shrugs, her eyes still shut, and replies, "Nothing. I don't know."

I'm close enough to easily tie my towline to Cole's boat and drag it along.

I secure the larger vessel to mine because if she were my boat, I'd want someone to bring her in and not leave her to be destroyed by the weather. With the quick tow secure, I turn my attention to navigating back to the harbor, and Maria clings to me, her body trembling.

Gazing upon the stunning, delicate woman I've rescued, her eyes gently closed as she slumps against the deck, every instinct urges me to gather her into my arms, to shield her in warmth and safety. Yet, the pressing need is to remain steadfast at the helm, guiding us swiftly to the safety of the shore. The internal struggle between desire and duty intensifies, creating a yearning to cradle her fragile form despite knowing my duty to get us to shore.

With the quick tow secure, I turn my attention to navigating back to the harbor. Maria continues to cling to me, her body trembling.

"We can't leave him. He's my family. He's all I have," she whispers, her voice heavy.

I hold her closer and look down at her, my lips tight, unable to give her false hope. I tighten her hug against me, watching the water, looking for him in the waves, and navigating silently to the harbor. Then, I set her down, increasing the throttle to get us back to safety.

Amidst my driving, a muffled sob reaches my ears. Her warm, honey-brown eyes lock onto mine. The tension is heavy, yet we share a quiet understanding. I give her a small smile of hope, and her uncertain eyes lock onto mine with raw emotion.

She stands and wraps her arms around me, her warm breath grazing my neck. The storm rages around us, pushing and pulling at us. Our connection is the only solid, warm place to grasp. Our bodies are pressing together, and my heart races with a determination to survive and to save her.

Instinctively, I move my face closer to hers, leaning in, my mouth pressing tenderly against her salty forehead. As I pull back, her head tilts up, and her lips, soft and parted, draw me in. Her warm breath tickles my cold lips, making my stomach clench. A raw desire explodes in me.

Before I can taste her and wrap her into my arms to give her more, the boat lurches with a bang, throwing us hard into the steering wheel. I let go of her to yank the wheel back on course to Homer.

Something is off! The boat isn't powering into the waves but dragging backward. I look back, and the back of the Sea Otter's Pride is gone—*Destroyed*!

The ocean quakes underneath us, making the boat tip, and the gray sea swallows us whole.

The cold water jolts me into action, and I grab her life vest, un-clipping the lifeline, before she is dragged underwater with my sinking boat.

"Swim," I shout towards her wide, dazed eyes, dragging her along as we swim a few feet to the larger vessel we were towing.

My arms and legs are already numb by the time we reach the side of the boat. I grab the taut tow line coming off the boat and roll myself aboard, then reach down and hook her life vest to throw her on deck with me.

Miraculously, we made it aboard Cole's boat. Maria's dazed and barefoot but appears unharmed.

I crawl over, immediately unhooking the tow rope that was attaching it to the Sea Otter's Pride. My boat is almost invisible, sinking beneath the waves from the ripped-out tow shaft.

Damn! My boat! I shake my head, *my insurance premium is going up, for sure.*

There's no time to worry or do anything about that—we need to get ashore before we are killed by the storm or freeze to death.

I turn the key of the Harbor Hopper's boat, and the motor sputters, roaring to life. *Thank God!*

Increasing to full throttle, we bump over the waves to shore, leaving my sinking boat and Cole behind in the bay.

Chapter 3

Maria

Confident Captain Jackie effortlessly navigates us through the turbulent waters toward Homer. I let the fear and tension drain from my body, trusting that we're almost there—she'll keep me safe. *After all, she's rescued me twice already.*

I silently assure myself that I'm going to make it and the Coast Guard *will* rescue Cole.

Jackie's grip on the wheel is steady, her eyes fixed on the path ahead as if daring the storm to challenge her. The boat rocks, but Jackie moves with the confidence of someone intimately connected to the ocean. Her movements fluid and deliberate as she expertly guides us through the waves.

The dampness clings to my clothes like a second skin, but Jackie appears unfazed, her yellow jacket a beacon of resilience against the storm.

A surge of gratitude washes over me for Jackie's presence. Without her, we'd be facing certain death. Relief floods my mind with the memory of her appearance during the perilous moments after losing Cole and trying to find the will to survive. Jackie saved me and enveloped me in her protective embrace.

The next thought is the *other moment–* when her gentle lips touched my forehead. My lips tingle as I contemplate what *almost happened* after that. . . Swiftly, I push aside that random, impulsive, and oh-so-wonderful thought.

I'm married, building a life with Cole, I remind myself. My flash of desire was just a response, the gratitude and relief of being rescued.

With determination, I focus on the current task—*to get back to Homer, bring Cole home, and ensure our dreams carry on.*

A bright light engulfs us, and I blink.

"Here they are. We have them, Lieutenant Johnson," an Asian man announces, and the Coast Guard ship emerges before us, shining a spotlight and interrupting our freezing trip and my spiraling thoughts.

Jackie's voice cuts through my confusion, "We made it, Maria!"

I shield my eyes. "Is that the Coast Guard?"

Jackie grins, her yellow jacket glowing in the light. "Yep, they're our ticket home."

As we approach the Coast Guard ship, I shiver. Jackie lays her hand on my shoulder. "You did great out there."

"Thanks," I manage to mumble, feeling exhaustion and relief.

I see the familiar backdrop of the Homer Boat Harbor behind the ship. Astonishingly, I survived two boating emergencies and arrived back home to Homer.

I look down at my bare feet. I must've lost my sandals in the panicked swim to the boat. Tears form as my mind wanders to the memory of frolicking on these docks in my golden sandals to enjoy a carefree day on the water with my new husband, Cole.

My missing sandals are the least of my problems.

I wipe my wet, numb cheeks on the jacket Jackie found and draped around me as the large Coast Guard Rescue ship approaches.

As they come within reach, Jackie's hand finds mine, a silent reassurance that we're in this together. She helps me to the men waiting to wrap us in blankets and take over the boat to let us ride with them into Homer.

I breathe with shaky laughter, sinking into the seat. I'm visibly shaken with exhaustion and fear. However, we've survived the storm. I slump into the arms of a Coast Guard man helping me onto the larger vessel.

Sergeant Wong, his name displayed on his uniform tag, reassures me, "You are going to be fine." He comforts me and wraps another woolen blanket around my trembling form as we reach the docks.

My numbness begins to wear off, allowing the emotional turmoil of my ordeal to finally sink in. Tears stream down my cheeks, and a lump lodges itself stubbornly in my throat.

The salty scent of the sea lingers in the air, clinging to the damp clothes drying to my body. I inhale deeply, absorbing the reassuring sounds of the men organizing themselves to assist.

Despite the cold, Jackie snaps into action, securing the boat to the dock before the Coast Guard crew can tie it up. She's holding out a hand and helping them to step off the ship. I watch in awe of her skill and confidence.

Following her example, I throw my legs unsteadily over the side of the boat and reach out my trembling hand to the wooden railing on the dock. Jackie takes my arm to help me. Her gaze meets mine in silent acknowledgment of what we've survived.

I nod mutely, unable to find the words to express my gratitude and the anguish in the uncertainty of not knowing if Cole is out of the storm yet.

I turn my attention to the Coast Guard personnel as they approach me with authority.

Jackie stands beside me as the handful of uniformed men advance, their clean appearance starkly contrasting the gloomy weather. A sigh of relief escapes me, marking the transition from turmoil to relative calm. I'm ready to unburden myself of the weight of Cole's desperate situation to the professionals who assist in such emergencies.

An older, stern-faced officer steps forward, his authoritative tone cutting through the howling wind. "I'm Lieutenant Johnson," he declares, eyes scanning us to assess our condition. "I understand you've been through quite an ordeal. Where's the man, the Captain, in charge?"

Jackie steps forward confidently, "I'm the one in charge. I called for the rescue."

He frowns looking from her to me, then looking past us. "Can you tell me what happened?" His eyes settle on Jackie since there's no man, and she's less shaken than me.

Her expression tightens, and her robust and assertive demeanor pronounced as she explains, "Cole, Maria's husband, fell overboard and is missing. Maria originally called for a rescue, and I was the only one out there, so I responded. Perhaps you should talk to Maria first?"

He looks at me, his brow furrowing even further, then back to Jackie, deciding to ignore me. "You said you saw someone swept overboard?" His lips pinch tightly together as he rubs the back of his neck.

I wipe my eyes on my sleeve, wondering if I appear hysterical or unhinged. I can't blame him for ignoring me—Jackie is the local boater, and she's confident and collected. In comparison, I'm barefoot, crying, wrapped in a blanket, and mute.

"I'm the captain of The Sea Otter's Pride," Jackie interjects, with her unwavering voice, "which responded and rescued Maria. My boat became disabled and sank. We came back on Cole's boat. He's the one missing, and I called in his coordinates for a rescue."

As she speaks, the Coast Guard ties up our Hopper boat behind the large rescue ship.

"When did he disappear?" Sergeant Wong asks me.

I start to answer, but Lieutenant Johnson interrupts, "Let's talk to the girl who speaks English first."

Jackie's eyes narrow at him as he ignores me. I shrink behind Jackie. I don't mind being invisible. I'm used to it, being a foreigner in this nondiverse town. But I need to know if they've found Cole y et.

She protests, "No. You'll want to ask Maria those questions."

"Do...You...Work," he pauses after each word, "...for Cole?" He asks me slowly and deliberately as if I can't understand basic English.

My voice barely makes a whispering whoosh as I try to respond. *I've completely lost my voice.* My heart speeds up, and I look at Jackie.

She sees my wide eyes and takes my hand, stepping forward to address Lt. Johnson.

"Maria isn't an immigrant fishery worker. She was boating, and her husband fell overboard."

"Where...is...the boat...you were fishing...on?" The older man continues in the same slow rhythm and louder volume.

"Do you have your work visa with you?" he presses, while Jackie tightens her grip on my hand, and I shake my head.

"Do you speak English, ma'am?" Sergeant Wong asks, his eyes showing apology.

I nod, wondering if they even sent out a search for Cole or if their assumptions about me are causing a delay in his rescue. My eyes start watering again and I wipe them on my sleeve.

Jackie stands next to me, fingers wrapped around mine in support.

At least I have someone willing to help and listen.

Johnson speaks louder and slower as if expecting me to confirm everything he's already decided, "You think around four in the afternoon he fell in while you were illegally fishing? Did he have a work permit?"

My husband is in danger, and he's not listening to me! A frustrated sign escapes my lips, and I want to fight back, yelling and punching. My breathing increases, and I start shaking.

"You have to find Cole. What are you doing to find Cole?" I finally croak, swallowing the lump in my throat, ignoring his useless questions.

Jackie says firmly and commandingly, "Maria isn't a deckhand. She's Colton Sander's wife. He went overboard during the storm. You need to get your thumb outta your ass and find him."

Johnson's eyes fix on Jackie in a cold grey stare. As tension mounts, I look at the storm, realizing this delay in conveying the information to the US Coast Guard is costing Cole time that he might not have.

Sergeant Wong steps closer. "Cole? Homer Harbor Hopper, Captain Cole?"

I nod. My voice is shaky, but I'm determined to get Cole home. "Yes, sir. We were caught in the storm," I begin, my gaze shifting between Jackie and the man. "My husband, he fell overboard. He was there, and then. . . he disappeared. I couldn't find him, and he was wearing a life jacket. That's when Jackie came. She searched but didn't see him either. Her boat was ripped apart by my boat pulling out the back of hers. Her boat went under. . . Everything was getting lost in the storm. Cole. He's out there. We couldn't find him. He's still out there."

My words are urgent, running over each other. I know I'm repeating myself, but I need them to listen to me and find Cole.

"Was he ferrying people?" Johnson directs the question to me, realizing the potential scale of this search and rescue operation.

"No. Today is his day off, and we were alone on the water taxi, just enjoying the water," I reply, wiping snot and tears with the blanket.

Jackie adds, "You did everything right. You called for help and searched for him until I got there."

The more likable guy, Seargent Wong, adds, "I'm afraid it's not uncommon for storms like this to get the best of even the most experienced boat captains."

"We'll initiate a search and rescue operation immediately. But I must prepare you for the possibility that the odds of survival in these conditions are slim," Johnson says with a more sympathetic tone, now addressing me as Colton Sander's wife.

The weight of his words settles on me, a reminder of the sea's unforgiving nature. My heart aches, and my eyes water at the thought of Cole lost in this storm and the hurricane that took my family. Jackie's hand offers comfort, and she puts her arm around me as I sob.

"You think around four in the afternoon he fell in?" Johnson asks Jackie, confirming my story.

"That's what she said," Jackie responds. "The storm was sudden, and I almost didn't see her or Cole's boat until it was directly in front of me. Then my tow bar got ripped out from the stern, and the entire aft was totaled, so we got on the Hopper Boat to get back here."

"Cole's boat wasn't damaged?" Johnson scowls and drills Jackie, "Captain, you never saw her husband fall overboard?"

"It's like I said, I heard the call and found her."

"So, anything could've happened to your husband?" Johnson states, then pauses, "do you want to amend your story?" He studies me with steely eyes, and I open my mouth without words.

I cross my arms in the bulky blanket to hug myself, my numb legs buckle, and I start to fall.

Jackie raises her arms to support me, growling to him, "You have the coordinates and all the information you need. We are getting a drink at the Salty Dawg. Find us there and update us on the search ASAP."

"Got it," Wong says, opening a map and trying to redirect Johnson's attention away from scowling at me.

Chapter 4

Jackie

I push open the creaky wooden door to the Salty Dawg with Maria on my heels as we enter Homer's notorious local pub on the end of the Homer's Spit, the sandbar jutting into the sea, just big enough to have a lane stacked with a row of tourist shops.

"Let's warm up and wait for news," I tell the shivering Maria.

The lively conversation, raucous laughter, and the clinking of glasses swallow her quiet response.

Is the crowd of grizzled fishermen, curious tourists, and local shop owners really the relaxed ambiance she needs?

Probably not—but the Salty Dawg is a welcome distraction and my usual after-work hangout. We need a warm, dry place to wait, and we can get drinks here, after all.

I confidently step forward and flip my wet hat around so it doesn't drip onto my face. A hot toddy will warm her up and buoy her spirit. But at the same time, she's a petite gal, and the alcohol might hit her hard, fueling an emotional breakdown.

I pause, standing in the crowded bar with her, uncertain if I should get a table, grab her a drink, or offer to take her to a local diner instead.

Boris, the burly Russian bartender with an almost psychic knowledge of all the local happenings and gossip, sees us standing in the doorway and lifts his chin in a welcome gesture. His usual smile turns into a subtle frown, signaling he's already caught wind of the day's events. In this tight-knit community, news travels faster than a salmon swimming downstream. Everyone knows that the Salty Dawg is the place for breaking news and Homer's juiciest gossip.

The room silences, even the music is between songs, as all eyes turn to Maria. No one says a word. *Boris isn't the only one who heard the news about Cole's accident.*

I glance at Maria, staring blankly at a wall pinned with crumbled dollar bills, messages, and pictures with writing scribbled on them. Even from the doorway, I can read the more prominent scribblings: "CALIFORNIA here!" Another with an arrow pointing to that one, "Who do we hate!" A hot pink bra hangs from the ceiling with dollars stuck on it—"For a good time, call Susan 907-267-2512." "Susan's married!" "Steve, have one on me. JT."

The walls have more money pinned to them than what's stuffed in Boris' cash register. A tourist writes his name and the date on a dollar bill to take a selfie as he stuffs it into a taxidermy squirrel's mouth.

Maria cuts through the silence. "I need to use the restroom." She uncurls her delicate hand from my arm, and I immediately notice the absence of her warmth.

I point my finger towards the back corner, behind the crowded bar. "I'll grab seats over there." I point while I give her distracted, unfocused eyes a confident nod and a slight smile.

I watch as she weaves through the crowd of people standing at wood plank tables on her path to the bathroom behind the double saloon-style swinging doors.

As she disappears into the dimly lit hallway, I scan the room. Aside from the dim, nautical Alaskan fishing and hunting decor, with the dollars tacked onto every surface, I don't see anyone I need to avoid for being too annoying or too drunk. The salty scent of the sea mingles with the inviting aroma of chips and bitter IPAs.

I relax as the crowd's noise returns, and I push through to grab us drinks and buy warm hoodies.

Boris waves me away. "Just take 'em. I'll drop drinks at your table." He throws me two Salty Dawg hoodies, small and extra-large.

Poor Maria needs something warm to wear and a warm drink!

I slide on the dry sweatshirt and navigate to the worn corner barstool, *my spot*. I sit away from the young guys peacocking at the pool table and the locals gabbing at the bar.

My hobby is sitting on my corner barstool, people-watching, and hearing the latest gossip as a quiet observer. I'm not antisocial, but I don't enjoy socializing, making small talk, or small-town politics. Drinking a beer and saying *hello* to Boris is the extent of my evening entertainment.

A group of fishermen at the far end of the bar engages in a lively discussion about the day's catch, their voices carrying over the sounds of clinking glasses and laughter. Under the glass top bar are faded photographs of boats brimming with King Salmon and pictures of Alaska Halibut larger than the men holding them taken years ago before the size of the fishing and their numbers dwindled. Now, the catch limit barely lets you survive, and the fish are half the size of the former monsters displayed.

"There. You'll need it." Boris drops off my beer, a shot of fireball, and a steaming cup of peppermint tea with a honey stick.

Tea? WTF.

I look up. "I was going to get her a hot toddy–something with plenty of alcohol and sugar," I say, poking the tea with my finger and scrunching my nose.

"Maria doesn't drink." He responds with his thick accent.

Boris knows everyone, so I should've expected he'd know what to bring her.

He's been serving the locals, which includes me, drinks for years. He leans in, his grizzled face softened by genuine concern. "Jackie, I'm sorry about your boat. How's Maria holding up?"

"She'll make it. It's gonna be a tough time for her. She thinks the Coasties are bringing Cole back tonight." I shake my head and raise my eyebrows at Boris.

He whistles, sucking in air, and shakes his head. "In this storm?!"

I glance back to the bathrooms. I'm guessing she's probably washing her face and drying her hair under the hand dryers. "She's *somethin'*. Cole's a workaholic and rough-looking. How'd a dog like Cole end up with a hot woman like that?"

Boris cocks his head. "Ah, you don't listen to enough of the local gossip. She's from the Philippines, been here for a few months now." He nods to a bearded local calling for a pitcher of beer and wipes his hands on the bar apron.

Before he walks away, I ask, "You keepin an ear on the radio?"

He nods. "I'll let you know when I hear something. There's nothing yet and they called for helicopters but the weather's too rough right now." He presses his lips together, and his eyes darken. "The guys we lose in the bay, it's never the ones you expect, right?"

"The weather snuck up on me, too. Cole shoulda known better. . . But, still, it's a damn shame," I agree.

Cole's an asshat sailor, and his bad karma with the other boating businesses caught up with him. I do feel bad for poor Maria. She's a sweet woman and didn't deserve this traumatic introduction to Alaska.

Despite the locals' whispers, no one approaches me to ask about the search for Cole or my rescue of Maria. Although Homer, Alaska, is my home, I'm a loner, spending my days on the water. I'm not surprised by the cool welcome since I keep to myself, and I'm not the kind of woman to waste words with mindless chatting.

When people talk to me, it's to hire me to move a boat, ship their cargo, or pick up passengers. I'm an excellent sailor, and I charge reasonable prices, so the locals use my service.

My jaw tightens, and my grip around the shot glass is firm as the last sight of The Sea Otter's Pride flashes in my mind, her bow sinking into the angry waves. My life, my business, my future was *that* boat. I quickly tip the shot, and the cinnamon burns as the liquor warms me.

Maria returns, her eyes dry and the rain jacket covering her wet clothes. The eyes of the entire bar follow her. I'm slamming down the empty shot glass, wiping my mouth on my inner plaid shirt when she appears.

She slides onto the wooden barstool beside me, and I hand her the hoodie that she shrugs on immediately. Her shoulders drop slightly, snuggling into it with her hands instinctively going into the pocket, hugging her belly to keep warm.

I sense her ominous mood in the silence as she wordlessly moves a hand to cradle the hot mug of tea and stares into the cloudy mug.

Before I can say anything, a Hopper Boat Captain, Ben, walks up, giving me a brief nod. His blonde hair and blue eyes are striking, the same as his cousin Cole's, but he looks less rugged and more like a salesman than a sailor. He places his hand on Maria's shoulder with his eyes momentarily lingering on her wet legs and looks into her eyes with a sly smile.

"I heard, and I'm sorry. You know, I'm here for you." He looks to the bar and yells to Boris, "I'll buy her next drink." He leans down, rubbing her shoulders, and she stiffens.

I cringe, not because of his interruption or his relation to Cole. My jaw tightens at his blatant hitting on the wife of his missing cousin. Cole's only been missing a few hours, and sweet Maria is already getting guys ready to fill in his spot.

This town is small but *not that small.*

She frowns, remaining silent, with the tears of anguish starting to flood from her eyes. Rather than comfort her, his words have caused her another cascade of tears.

"Ben, I've got his." I stand and box him out, making him step back and remove his hand from her shoulders.

"*Whatever*, Jackie. Why don't you go back home and spend more time with *your boyfriend*, Sammy. Also, tell Sammy to stop scaring away all the salmon from the harbor. He's a real menace," he says.

I don't respond to his taunts and stay standing, staring him down. I lift my chin slightly, not wanting to talk and give him any reason to continue the conversation.

He's bigger than me but not stronger or smarter–*by a long shot*.

"Boris, put both their drinks on my tab," he says, pointing to our drinks as he slinks away to the end of the bar joining a group of local guys.

Maria uses her sleeve to wipe her eyes and hesitates, unsure. Her gaze scans the room as if searching for something, and her eyes settle on the tea in front of her. She circles both hands around it and slowly sips the peppermint honey tea.

Is she going through shock?

"I wanted to order you a stiff drink but Boris said you'd prefer this," I explained, trying not to sound like my usual crusty self.

She bites her lip and nods. "Captain Jackie," she begins, her voice soft, and she takes my hand in her soft, smaller one. "I wanted to thank you for saving me and everything you did. I can't say I'd be here without you." Her eyes water, and she grabs my other hand, enhancing her words of gratitude.

My heart kicks into high gear, and I hope she can't tell her touch is turning me on. I offer her a warm smile. *I should be comforting her, not her thanking me.*

"I'm just glad you're safe. I'm sure we'll hear from the Coast Guard soon," I respond, "And, call me Jackie."

"Jackie," she repeats softly.

My name on her lips warms me quicker than the fireball shot and causes a spreading heat in my belly. I nod and want to drink my beer, but her hands over mine are the best thing that's happened to me since I met Sammy, my unique partner in crime.

"I can't thank you enough, and I'm terribly sorry about your boat being destroyed."

I turn my hands over to cover her fingers with my larger, rougher hands. The alcohol hasn't deadened the wound of losing my boat, but obviously, the loss of her husband is worse–*for her*.

I meet her curved almond eyes and savor the golden flecks floating in warm brown. *How in the hell did Cole find her? She's a goddess!* I lean in and tell her, "Anyone would've done the same. No boat compares to a man's life."

Her eyes fill, and she releases my hands, wiping them with her sleeve.

I add, "You did everything right. That was just a freak accident."

Her eyes widen and leak more from the wet, thick eyelashes edge, making me want to pat her cheeks with my napkin. I leave my hands on the table, hoping she will encase them in her delicate hands again.

"I should've known how to operate the boat. I could have circled and found him." She wads the bar napkins to wipe her face and discreetly blow her nose. The sheen of tears and her reddened cheeks make her glow even more.

How in the hell can I find a crying woman so hot? There's something wrong with me.

"You did a mayday call and stayed, searching. There's nothin' else you could've done," I say, standing and pulling her in for a hug to help calm her tears.

She leans into me, as she did on the boat, and fits perfectly at my collarbone, inside my solid arms.

Amidst the hubbub of the bar, I notice the conversations around us quieting, then increasing.

Ben complains loudly, "You could wait a few days at least, Jackie!" He shouts from across the room.

A group of regulars exchanges disapproving glances as if I'd try my luck on a grieving woman. They've noticed the attractive woman and the circumstances of her day are public knowledge to anyone listening. For a small, tight-knit community, the Homer locals, or at least the Salty Dawg crowd, brutally spread their opinions and gossip as facts.

I catch snippets of their hushed gossip as Maria and I sit back down to finish our drinks, awaiting Lieutenant Johnson's update.

Another local joins the group at the bar. And I overhear snippets of their conversation. "Did you hear about the rescue today?". . . "Seems like she did more than rescue. She's taking Cole's wife for a test drive.". . . "Wait, is *that* the wife? I thought she'd be Asian."

I shake my head and drink the last gulp of beer. "Do you wanna get out of here?" I ask Maria, knowing the gossip increases as the beer drinking increases. The gossip is probably only going to get louder and worse, not better.

She shrugs and sips the last of her tea.

"I'll tell Boris to have them call your cell with any news. He'll call me too," I explain, heading to the bar to update Boris that I'm taking Maria home—*to her home!*

As I pass, Ben whispers, "Don't get any ideas. If Cole's not found, I'll be handling everything, including Maria. She'll be taken care of."

I ignore the whiskey-fueled comment, not wanting to start a fight. "Boris, I'm taking Maria home. Tell the Coasties to call her cell or find her there, okay?"

Boris nods and waves me off when I pull out my credit card.

"He picked her out and paid shipping, like a new Sears dishwasher," Ben says to the guy on the stool beside him.

"Huh. Filipino gal, I guess that's the same as a getting a new dishwasher, and she probably cooks." The guy responds, clinking his glass, and they look over to Maria, who is standing by the door, ready to leave.

Their cold assessment and gossip are rude and disrespectful to the woman who just survived an ocean emergency and is worried about her husband. I can't get her out of here quickly enough.

I should've taken her to a diner!

I shoot a daggering stare in their direction, unwilling to let the gossip stop me from comforting this poor, beautiful woman who doesn't have anyone to defend her.

I turn my attention back to Maria and walk to the doorway. She stares out the little window, tears on her cheeks with a contemplative look, her fingers gently pulling the rain jacket down over her sweatshirt and body.

In her eyes, I see the weight of the day's events, the unknown future, and her sorrow.

I put my arm around her–I can't help it. She's so vulnerable and sad. I want to tell her everything will be okay, but I won't lie. More than likely, her husband is dead.

"Bye Jackie. Good luck," Ben yells across the bar, lifts his drink, and winks at me.

Damn him! I'm not him–preying on a hot woman who's nearly a widow. I release my arm from her quickly, but I'll hear about this tomorrow when the rumors are spun about me trying to steal Cole's wife.

How I feel about Cole and his business, the Homer Harbor Hopper, is no secret.

"Thanks," a whisp of a voice comes out of her quivering lips.

I look down at her. I was so worried about the rumors that I nearly forgot the reason I was worrying. I extend a comforting hand to her shoulder. "You don't have to figure out anything right now."

We walk out the door into the dying storm, away from the prying eyes. "Do you want me to take you to a friend or family member's home tonight?"

"The only family I have is Cole," she says.

My heart opens, breaking at the pain in her voice and knowing she will be alone and worrying all night.

"Maria," I say gently, leaning down to meet her eyes. "You're not alone."

"I am alone," she says hollowly, looking out over the blackened ocean beyond the Homer Spit.

I pull her against my chest to embrace her. Her body shutters as the grief and tears that she was holding back flood to the surface. I ignore the stares from the pub behind us and wish I had taken her somewhere more private.

My houseboat with Sammy?

Chapter 5

Maria

Where am I? What am I doing here?

I wake to the fragrance of unfamiliar blooms dancing, wrapping around my senses with each sweet, intoxicating note–the fragrance opposite of the earthy smell I grew up with. Keeping my eyes closed briefly, I allow the unknown flowers' perfume to permeate me before the sun's brightness wakes me.

As I open my eyes, I'm in a soft, massive bed in the heart of a white expanse with the blue ocean reflecting from the floor-to-wall windows onto the crystal chandelier, creating rainbows. The size of the room is disorienting, especially for someone raised in the cozy, dirt-floored corners of a small home. These walls stretch endlessly—the room is larger than my entire childhood home in the Philippines.

The pink and white bouquet is the source of the sweet aroma and stands out in the pristine room. They're a reminder of Cole, doting on me with floral arrangements throughout our house. Being surrounded by flowers and their scent throughout our home is a luxury I'd never dreamed of as a child.

My mind clears—*I'm in the extravagant house Cole and I share.*

Our home overlooks the murderous Kachemak Bay with the last bouquet he bought me. The morning sun paints the room in golden hues, and I pull the goose-down duvet—soft as ripe peach fuzz—over my head, hiding from reality.

My hand reaches to the empty space beside me, and it's cold. Tears form in my eyes as I fully wake, remembering Cole's missing. This home always felt welcoming, like *my* home with him next to me. Now, I feel out of place, a stranger in this big house without Cole.

Yesterday's events replay in my mind relentlessly, with the swirling storm and Cole checking on the engine when a colossal wave rocked the boat. I fell onto the cold deck, my hands and knees getting wet, and I clutched my belly, worried. When the ship was back at an even keel, I stood, and Cole was no longer there.

I worried about myself and should have noticed him falling overboard.

From crying all night, I'd think my tears would've been depleted, my tear ducts broken from overuse. But already, they've started to fall down my cheeks again. Maybe crying is like using a muscle: the more you use it, the stronger it becomes. Every day, I'll sob more and more until I drown in my tears.

The phone rings, shattering the silence and my pity party. I scramble, sitting up and finding it on the bedside table to answer it—my heart pounds in my chest.

Cole?!

My hand trembles as I lift the phone to my ear.

"Maria?" The voice on the other end asks with a cold, official tone.

"Yes," I say hesitantly. *This isn't Cole's familiar voice.*

"This is Lieutenant Johnson. I'm calling to update you on the status of the search for Colton Sanders," he says.

My mouth dries, and blood rushes from my hammering heart so fast in my ears that I can't talk above the noise. I can hardly hear his next words.

"We have *not* located Colton. At this point in the search, we're transitioning from *a rescue operation to a recovery mission. . .*"

Every word echoes, ringing in my head, and I can't comprehend what he's saying. I can barely hold the phone steady as the Coast

Guard officer continues. The words are a distant murmur, lost in the pounding of my heart.

". . .still looking for him. . . we will update the coroner's office. . ."

Then the line is dead.

The reality of what he was saying hits me like a tidal wave.

Cole is gone—lost and alone in the frigid ocean. They've given up and are pronouncing him dead.

New tears spring in my eyes, blurring my vision. My husband, who promised me a family, *our little Alaska family*, is still missing in the unforgiving ocean. The tears puddle on the blanket, and I don't move to wipe them.

I pull it back over my head with the phone, unmoved, heavy against my ear. I pull it away with great effort, setting it back on my nightstand.

Bang, bang!

A soft knock on the bedroom door makes me gasp.

Cole!

Before I can respond, the door swings open.

Jackie stands in the doorway, holding a tray with a steaming cup of tea and a plate with a delicious-smelling, fluffy omelet.

I wince and sag more into the bed. My eyes meet her soft blue eyes, unlike the hard, confident stare when she saved me and steered us through the storm.

Her kindness makes me start uncontrollably, ugly sobbing. Tears, snot, and saliva leak out as I try telling her about the Coast Guard phone call.

I'm a mess–*I don't care. My husband is dead!*

She comes over, sits beside me in the bed, and sets the tray on the table. She hands me the tissue box. Her presence is strangely reassuring and familiar despite only meeting her yesterday. Perhaps our crazy life and death event created a unique bond between us.

Whatever it is, I don't want to be alone right now, and she's easing my pain.

"Maria," she says softly, "I thought you could use tea and breakfast."

I nod, responding with a shaky voice, "I'm sorry. I thought you were. . . *Thank you*, Jackie."

She moves the tray, placing it in front of me, and stays beside me. Her gaze is deep, and she bites her lip as she carefully stirs honey in the tea, handing it to me. Then, she silently watches me drink and nibble on the eggs.

I note the dark circles around her eyes. She must've had a sleepless night after bringing me home from the pub. She stayed over last night, periodically checking in with the Coast Guard and getting me tea and water.

I'm ashamed to think of how I despondently stared out the window for hours without talking to her. I didn't ask her, but she knew I needed her to stay.

I want to ask her if she stayed in one of the guest rooms or on the couch, but I'm embarrassed. The house is so large I don't even know where my guest slept last night. The big home won't be too big when I have children running around.

I realize my stupid dream and shake my head. My eyes tear up more, and I take an offered tissue to wipe them. Now, the house is ridiculously large for me.

She stays silent, and we look out the window at the now-calm bay as I sip my tea. I glance at her, and she's stoic, looking outside without emotion. She's an Alaskan sea captain. She's probably seen everything.

I'm glad she stayed. Being alone would've broken me, and her presence is comforting even without words. It must be her commanding attitude, the clear blue eyes, the blonde hair pushed into a ball cap as if she doesn't recognize how amazingly thick and wavy it is. She's nothing like me, but she makes me feel connected and *here*.

I sip the tea. Its warmth soothes my scratchy throat. The omelet sits almost untouched on the plate. The overwhelming worry churning in my stomach ruins my appetite.

Jackie's hand finds mine, her touch gentle and reassuring. "I heard the phone ring. Did they tell you anything?"

I open my mouth to tell her, but an overwhelming nausea hits me, and I jump from the bed, sprinting to the bathroom before I vomit.

She stands and waits at the bathroom doorway as I embarrassingly dry heave into the cream-colored toilet in front of her.

Thank god for the flowers to cover the smell! I wish I could stop my body's reaction to the news and the entire situation.

"Are you okay?" she asks as I stand and move to the sink to rinse my mouth. I grab the toothbrush and do a quick brushing of my teeth.

"Sorry. It's. . . they think he's dead," I say, looking at my own red, puffy eyes in the mirror and not her caring reflection. I'm afraid her eyes will show her agreement with the Coast Guard's assessment, and I can't bear to see it in her eyes.

"I'm sorry, Maria. I'm here for you," she says gently. I'm glad she doesn't tell me false platitudes, like *not to worry* or that *everything will be fine.*

"Have you lived here for a long time?" I change the subject, drying my hands.

"My whole life and I've always lived on the bay, fishing and doing the water taxi, now."

She probably knows Cole better than me, or at least longer than the short months I've known him.

I turn off the water and look into her eyes. "It's probably uncomfortable for you, losing a friend and now meeting me like this. We planned to have a big celebration so I could meet everyone when the tourist and fishing season were done."

She nods, looking away.

She is grieving Cole! I should have considered how it affects everyone here, as Cole grew up here and is a big part of the community.

"I should probably get back home."

"Please don't leave," I whisper, my voice shaking.

Her eyes are clear and steady, watching me and telling me she understands without words.

I turn to her and explain, "It's just that I moved here only six months ago, and Cole is the only person I know. I've been keeping to myself so I haven't really left the house or met anyone."

"What about your family? Can they fly here to be with you?"

I shake my head. "I lost them five years ago, my parents and brother to Typhoon Yolanda. Meeting Cole online and moving here was my chance to have a family–*my chance to start a new family*," I explain. Most folks in town knew the situation and whispered about Cole's *mail-order bride,* a term I despise and one of the main reasons I have been hesitant to venture out alone in the town while Cole was working.

She leans in closer. "I understand. I don't have a family, either. I have Sammy, and Boris at Salty Dawg. Although, I know everyone so I have this wacky community, too."

I move to the doorway and hug her, which turns into her embracing me. She wraps her stronger, long arms around me, holding me tightly. I appreciate her words, but I appreciate her solid arms around me more. I melt into the needed affection.

The last person to hug me was Cole, and I couldn't remember if we hugged on the boat. We were lucky to be matched by the dating agency, and we have a strong connection with the same goals and zest for life.

After matching, meeting online, and talking for months in a long-distance relationship, he came to the Philippines and popped the question to me after the meeting. There weren't Hollywood sparks when we kissed, but we were building a physical connection over time to match the emotional connection we created from our FaceTime conversations.

Cole was an attractive, social, hardworking man. And I'm shy and delicate, but I felt completely protected and taken care of by him. He wanted an at-home wife to start his family, and I wanted a family and stability. Our international match was a success, and we were falling in love each day together.

The intangible spark missing from my marriage relationship—the immediate electric passion is instant with Jackie. My body yearns, and bubbles with warmth that fills me with her touch.

This spark scares me!

I'm Cole's wife, even without him here. *I made a promise and a commitment to having a family with him.* I'm not ready to give up our dream, which means that Jackie and our flame must be ignored.

"Jackie," I begin, leaning away from the cozy hug. "There's something I need to tell you."

I want you to be more than a friend, but my life's complicated.

I can't say this. I can't let my frivolous feelings and fear of being alone ruin the life I'm building with Cole.

At the same time, it pains me more to think of telling her to leave or that we can only be friends. I *want her* here and to stay snuggled in her arms. And even more than that—I want to explore the feelings she's stirring inside me, wherever they take us.

I shake my head. *I can't let this go any further than a hug. I can't betray Cole.*

Cole!

Thinking of him lost at sea burns my eyes, and my heart rips into pieces. Even though we were strangers a year ago, we've been married for five months, and I love him. He showed me kindness and understanding. Most people don't understand that an arranged partnership doesn't mean a loveless one.

I fit the criteria he was looking for on the international dating website. We talked for months about our pasts, hopes, and dreams. Not knowing or seeing the other made us more honest and vulnerable than in a standard dating relationship, bringing us closer than traditional dating would have. I understood and respected him. We shared the same family values and work ethic.

I didn't know the first thing about the Alaska boat business. Still, I graduated with a Bachelor of Business degree and planned to assist him with his accounting, scheduling, and, eventually, business operations. We were excited to share everything in our lives with each other.

I was just getting over the prolonged sickness we thought was from traveling and then from getting new viruses in a new country. It turns out it was prolonged morning sickness—we must have hit the baby jackpot on our first try.

My eyes fill, and I hesitate, wanting to bury my face into Jackie's gentle embrace.

She leans closer, her eyes fixed on mine. She runs her pink tongue over her lips, sensing my desires and being ready. "Maria?"

There are many things I could say, but I have my dreams, and she has Sammy. I won't lead her on.

I take a deep breath, my heart pounding in my chest. I struggle with what to tell her, and I settle on the truth. The thing I didn't have a chance to tell Cole.

I exhale and meet her creased, soft eyes. "I'm pregnant."

Her eyes widen, and she drops her arms and steps away. Her reaction makes it abundantly clear her thoughts on being with a pregnant woman.

The words are heavy between us driving a wedge in the warm, comforting embrace. I watch as Jackie's expression changes, with surprise and confusion flickering in her eyes. Then her face calms and returns to look of the confident captain who pulled me from the storm. Her mouth tightens in a line of determination with her jaw set.

"Pregnant?" she repeats, her head tilted.

I nod, tears welling up in my eyes once again. "I found out a few days ago. Cole and I were so happy, planning for our future. He didn't know. . . but wanted become a father. And now . . . now, I don't even k now *if* he's coming back. . . or if the Coast Guard is right. . ."

Her hand reaches for mine and tightens around it, her grip firm and unwavering. "Maria, whatever you need, I'm here. You and your baby aren't alone."

She doesn't step closer but doesn't run away from me, knowing the truth.

As her eyes soften to look at me, my tears slow, and I nod. Seeing her towering confidence, even with my surprise, makes me warm. Her presence and support mean more than I can express. She's already done so much for me, and I can't imagine asking for more, but I also can't imagine being totally alone.

I lean into her, pressing my head against her solid shoulder, and my tears flow with relief at telling someone the truth. It's not just my husband who's missing, but the father of my child. And she's the only person I've told.

I should've told Cole. I worried—what if I was wrong— then what if I lost it? I was waiting for the perfect time to share the news when he wasn't so busy with the summer rush of tourists. *Now it's too late!*

Jackie holds me, offering me silence in her steady arms as I cry. We stand embraced for enough time that the tears abate, and I can breathe again.

But as the minutes pass, an uneasy thought gnaws at me. The warmth she is creating grows, especially with her arms wrapped around me, and I want more of her. I want our bodies pressed together, to smell her hair, and run my fingers along her muscular back.

I can't keep entertaining my feelings for Jackie and allowing them to grow. I can't let this connection between us become anything but a much-needed friendship. I'm still married, and I made a promise to

Cole. He's out there, lost in the vast expanse of the ocean outside my window.

I pull away from her embrace, my eyes meeting hers. She licks her top lip and bites her bottom as if she, too, feels the magnetic attraction to me. Despite knowing my situation, she can't stop herself, either.

I'll have to be the one to stop it then, *for Cole's sake.*

"Jackie, thank you. I appreciate your support, but I can't. . . I'm still married, and even if the Coast Guard is right, I can't betray him."

Her expression darkens, and her eyes blink rapidly as hurt crosses her face. "Yep, understood. I never meant to make you uncomfortable."

She doesn't deny her feelings for me, confirming that she feels the same dangerous attraction.

I see the conflict in her eyes, and she stays silent. She's waiting for my lead.

First, I asked her to stay, and then I pushed her away. I'm giving her mixed signals, and it's not fair to her. Hurting the woman who rescued me is the last thing I want to do, but I won't let our feelings jeopardize my commitment to Cole and the family we're building.

"Maybe you should leave. I need some time, Jackie," I say, turning away so I can't see how much my words hurt her and she can't see my lip trembling. "I need to figure things out, and I can't do that with you here. Please."

"Of course. Take all the time you need, Maria. If you need me just call or you can drop by the Salty Dawg," she says, then walks out the door with me, staring out the window.

My heart is thundering, and I don't know how much more emotional turmoil it can handle. Jackie's an amazing, kind woman, and I can't deny my attraction. But right now, I must focus on finding Cole and protecting my family.

The room is cold and empty, with Jackie gone. I hear the front door shut as she leaves the house. I'm left alone with my thoughts and regrets. I can only hope that, somehow, Cole will return, and we'll continue our life together soon.

I'm not ready to give up on him and the life we planned.

I pick up the mug of tea and sink back into my too-big bed.

Chapter 6

Maria

I stand in the heart of my messy kitchen, my turbulent emotions transformed into casserole dishes, trays, and plates of food. The aroma of my Filipino comfort food, meat, and vegetable lumpia bubbling in the deep fryer, Chicken Adobo in the oven, Leche flan started on the stovetop, and my favorite, Arroz Caldo, a slow-cooked rice porridge on another burner.

I moped and stayed in bed for the first few days at home, but I am moving to the kitchen this week. The growing baby and my boredom fueled my newfound love of cooking food from my homeland. The smells of my culture swirl around me.

I open the frig for more milk and frown, seeing the door lined with caffeine energy drinks and beer. The unfamiliar American labels, remnants of Cole's favorite drinks, remind me of the void he left behind. I can't stand to see them untouched. Nonetheless I can't bear to toss them into the bin.

The kitchen, once a place of shared laughter and culinary experimentation, as I tried adding new American spices and salmon to my dishes to Cole's delight, is quiet with my solitude. I attempt to navigate my emotions and ingredients, to create a dish that connects me to my roots and my new home in Alaska–Salmon Sinigang, a sour and savory stew, but I can't get the taste correct. The sizzle of the pan and hiss of the lumpia cooking harmonize with no one to hear but me.

I rub my slight belly–*and baby.*

The phone rings and my heart jumps into my throat as I rush to pick it up as I do every time it rings. Breathlessly, I answer, "Hello."

"You gotta pay the guys or they're gonna stop workin'," Ben says without a greeting or context.

I exhale. *It's not a call to give me news about Cole.*

"Isn't payday normally next week?" I haven't started going through the business account, but I have the office calendar, and nothing was written to be paid or done this week.

"Yeah, but the guys don't trust you not to clean out the accounts and go back to your motherland. They want to make sure you pay them," he barks back.

I sigh and look at the photographs scattered across the walls. Images of Cole and his cousin Ben, captains of the Homer Harbor Hopper boats, capture moments frozen in time of them laughing on the boat and fishing together. The camaraderie between them is evident in the easy smiles and shared responsibilities, and I know that Ben is grieving in his own way. He's just choosing to complain and be more angry than usual, instead of cook like I am doing to deal with my emotions.

"Okay, I'll take care of it. Tell them please," I respond as I walk to Cole's home office.

"Good."

He hangs up before I can add anything else.

In the office, the hum of the answering machine pulls me from her thoughts, a reminder of responsibilities that extend beyond sorrow. Vendors and employees leave messages, and the urgency in their voices persuade me that it's time for me to get out of the house and start working at the Harbor Hopper office on the dock.

Tears cascade down my cheeks, thinking about spending all day next to the ocean and in a busy office with all his friends. I fight against the overwhelming tide of anxiety, overwhelmed with having to take over the business and pretend that my life isn't a dumpster fire. Standing in Cole's office, surrounded by the artifacts of his life's work–folders, bills, boat registrations, licenses, overdue notices, and the stack of mail–the weight of the Homer Harbor Hopper legacy presses down on my tired shoulders.

I can't let the business fold in his absence. He's the third generation of his family to run it and the last child in the family. I rub my belly–our baby was supposed to be the next generation to give the thriving family business to.

The doorbell rings, a sound cutting through the oppressive silence. I hesitate. A mixture of hope and trepidation courses through my veins as my heart speeds up. I quickly walk to the door and fling the heavy wooden door open to reveal a burst of vibrant flowers on the doorstep.

Sticking my head outside—this is the most I've been outside of the house for the last ten days—there's no sign of a person or delivery truck, an unexpected gift from an unexpected source.

Intrigued, I cradle the bouquet in my arms. The riot of colors contrasts the muted tones of my grief, which match the end of summer gloom. Someone stuck a card among the blooms.

"In every bloom, find a reminder that you're not alone. Call anytime. Jackie."

A smile stretches my lips, and my mouth aches from the unfamiliar movement. The weight on my chest eases for the first time in days, and the isolation threatening to engulf me begins to recede. The lovely gesture, a lifeline from Jackie, rekindles the spark of our connection, and it's nice to have someone think enough of me to send flowers.

I take the flowers to my room and toss the wilting pink flowers that need replacing. I place the vase on the table by the big window and in front of my bed, a symbol of hope and friendship.

With a newfound sense of purpose, I dry my tears and prepare to face the challenge of managing the Homer Harbor Hopper. The flower delivery got me a step out of the house. Tomorrow, I'm running errands and going to the harbor to meet everyone at the office. I will ensure the business flourishes for Cole, me, and the next generation.

I pull out Jackie's card, re-reading her thoughtful words once more. I move the card to my bedside table, my isolation shatters, and my resilience awakens. I'm armed with my business degree and the memory of Cole's dreams to motivate me.

Chapter 7

Jackie

The Salty Dawg reeks of stale beer and lingering regrets. Nursing my umpteenth drink, my mood is as dark as the clouds forming above these log walls. Boris wipes a glass with a towel, his bushy black beard giving him the appearance of a wise old sea captain, which his Russian accent only enhances.

"Jackie, you look like you lost a battle with a bear. You're always a grump, but you're downright rabid today."

I grunt, taking a swig from my glass. "Just life. And I'm stuck here, drowning my sorrows when I should be raking in the big bucks. The Harbor Hopper has been operating at half force all week. I need my boat."

"Is it *really* just yer boat troubles?" He raises an eyebrow and starts stacking the glasses.

I scoff. "You have *no idea*. The damn insurance is jerking me around. That's the thanks I get for trying to save that asshat captain, Cole."

Boris hands me a shot, a sympathetic glint in his eye. "You did save Maria."

"Yeah, I expected to be thanked or at least acknowledged that I lost my boat to save her. Instead, she's ghosted me—not that I expected her to become my best friend. I mean, with the bad blood between her husband and me."

I pick up the shot and lift it, saying, "Cheers, a delicious depressant for my depression." I down the shot, the vodka burning, making me feel alive for a moment. I rise with the burning motivation swirling in my belly.

He eyes me, his gruff voice cutting through the smoky air. "No, friend, that's inspiration's fuel. It's all in the dose." He puts down the towel and orders me, "Go to the bank and get a boat loan while waiting for the insurance payoff. If the taxi business is that good, you'll pay off the loan before your insurance money comes in and be rolling in it."

I grunt, still standing. "Speaking of dough, have you seen Cole's mansion? Inside his fridge is more cheese than in a grocery store. The place could house the entire town."

Without commenting on my griping, he pours himself a shot of vodka, tips it to me, and drinks it.

I push my shot glass back to him for another. Glaring at him, I say, "Like I have a choice anyway. Waiting on the insurance money, competing in a business against a millionaire, and I'm here stuck with my thumb up my—"

Boris interrupts, "Enough with the pity party. What's stopping you? You're a damn good captain. Figure something out."

I scowl at him. *I don't need tough love. I need another shot.*

"What about Sammy? She's your inspiration to get a boat. You got to get back on the water for her. She loves you and needs you. Come on," Boris says.

I pull out my phone and begrudgingly flip through pictures to show him the clip of Sammy in the ocean yesterday. The clip plays with Sammy triumphantly on my houseboat deck and a pile of her shellfish on my deck as she grins, showing off her harvest. Her brown eyes glow, and the happiness radiates from her, even through a picture.

Boris grins. "She's quite the oyster hunter. And I see you're less grumpy now, huh? I knew talking about Sammy would help."

"I'd be better if you'd give me another shot."

He shakes his head. "You got work to do, friend. I have a box of Maria's special tea, and one of the ladies at the church gave me pumpkin bread for her. Go deliver it, and then go get your bank loan." He places a bag on the bar before me and points to the door.

I scowl. "I'm not your errand boy."

Boris leans in. "You're not doing anything else, are you? Either deliver the gifts or stay and wash dishes to work off your bar tab."

I grumble but take the bag as he pushes me out the door, kicking me out of the Salty Dawg.

"And don't forget to stop by the bank. I don't like you *enough* to see you in here every morning and every night."

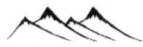

I find myself at the Homer Credit Union Bank, which I usually avoid like the plague. I might own a business, but I spend most of my time working, not banking.

As I walk inside, the bell above the door jingles, drawing curious glances from customers who are locals and know me. No one says *hello*. There's no animosity, but I'm sure the current rumors about Cole going overboard with me unable to find him and then, being with Maria, aren't helping my popularity any.

I'm seeing the bank manager, asking for a loan, and getting out of here ASAP! Being surrounded by men in suits and chatty people is uncomfortable. I'm not in my element here. I can feel their judging eyes watching my every move.

I stop before the line, when I see the back of Maria at the bank teller's counter. She's the only customer who didn't turn–*and frown*–when I walked in.

I haven't seen her in over two weeks, and now, Maria and I are in the same place at the same time–*what rotten luck.*

No wonder I was greeted with silence. *The attention is fixed on watching Maria, and with me here, they get double the pleasure. The eyes move from her to me, hoping to confirm the rumors of our shameful relationship.*

Maria's shoulders slump, and she appears tiny and fragile next to the tall counter, with the young bank teller ignoring her and waving her away. Despite the clerk's glossy lips and meticulously lacquered nails, the tightness of her pursed lips, and the cold atmosphere is unmistakably hostile. Another catty young clerk peeks over the divider, offering an unfriendly smirk in Maria's direction.

Debating the merits of sneaking out of the bank before Maria spots me, I decide to stay. Since I ran into her, I could give her the bag from Boris without having to go to her outrageous mansion again.

Before approaching the line, I see her reflection in the divider's glass with tears streaming down her cheeks.

The blonde teller, a smug grin plastered on her face, announces loud enough for everyone to hear, "Sorry, *madame*, but you're not the primary account holder."

The next teller smirks as if she's got a beef with Maria, and she waves *bye-bye* to her.

I stomp up to the counter around the line of four people. I won't let this horrible behavior slide. Everyone *knows* who Maria is, and her husband is missing and *presumed dead.*

How can they treat her like a second-class citizen? Why? Are they simply jealous of her good looks, marrying into wealth, or generally racist against her cocoa-colored skin?

If nothing else, the clerks are rude, and they need to stop badgering a grieving woman who needs community support, not *their snobbishness toward outsiders.*

I step forward, towering over the clerk's counter, my mood darker than ever.

"Excuse me," I growl, my voice cutting through the bank's tension. "What's going on here?"

The teller turns and opens her eyes wide, batting them, and sweetly says, "Just a misunderstanding. This woman is trying to access funds that aren't hers. She isn't even an account holder. It's difficult to deal with these foreigners, *you know.*"

The girl beside her bites her lip to stop giggling and nods along with the other clerk's disparaging remark.

I glance at Maria's downcast eyes and wet cheeks, silently apologizing for what I'm about to do.

"I don't care what the computer says. *She's a customer.* Treat her with the same respect you'd treat her husband or *any local businessman.* Your uppity attitude doesn't belong here," I growl at her, practically frothing at the mouth.

"And you," I point to the clerk next to her, "You weren't even born here. Didn't you immigrate a few years back? *You* should know better!"

Boris is right—I am rabid today!

The bank manager rushes over, hearing the raised voices and sensing trouble. "I apologize for any confusion. How can I help you?" he asks me and then looks at Maria.

She stammers, "It's just I don't have the checks to pay Cole's employees and they are calling and stopping by the house needing their paychecks. I know there are funds in the business account."

She pauses to catch her breath and continues in a rush of words, "I need to have checks printed, or I can write them. But I'd like to get them their paychecks today."

The bank manager nods and hands her a nearby tissue box. "Let me check the records," he says, clicking through the screens. The teller

moves to the side, whispering with the other girl. The other customers continued watching the drama without commenting.

The teller and her sidekick whisper loud enough for us to hear,
"Life insurance scams and mail-order wives. Small-town drama,
huh?"

Maria takes another tissue and wipes her red eyes. She looks up at
me with a small, forced smile. "Thank you, Jackie."

I nod and face the tellers, my patience running thin. "Enough
with the gossip! Your job is customer service."

The manager looks at the teller with a frown, and his eyebrows
raise, then to Maria. Finally, he locks eyes with me. He exhales and
says to Maria, "Your name is on the account. Let me check your ID,
and I can get you cash, check, or money orders. I'm happy to help
you, Mrs. Sanders."

The room is silent as Maria nods, and the hostile conversation
turns into a regular bank transaction.

With a pinched expression and tight jaw, I glance from the rude
teller, then to the customers, and my eyes land on the manager. I raise
my eyebrows, and before I say anything, he swallows and nods to me.

"Monica, lock your cash drawer, bring me your vault keys. You
can get your purse and jacket, and go to my office. I'll be there in a
minute to discuss this."

Maria hands the bank manager her list with names and amounts,
and the line of customers finally moves when the clerk calls for the
next person, breaking the bank's hushed atmosphere.

Maria breathes a long sigh of relief and gives me a grateful smile.
Her eyes clear, and she raises her chin up. "Let me buy you a coffee
or tea, Jackie."

I nod, realizing I've inserted myself into her life once again, and
defended her with a crowd of witnesses. It was bound to happen,
though. We live in a small town, and there's no avoiding each other.

"Actually, I have some tea as a gift for you in my truck."

The other bank teller raises her eyebrows and licks her lips as she helps the other customer but overhears this newest gossip.

I ignore her, and Maria looks at me with a question but turns to take the stack of cashier checks from the bank manager.

He again murmurs an apology to her and thanks her for her business. Then he nods to me, "Jackie, always a pleasure."

I nod back my thanks and turn with Maria to the door.

Leaving the bank together, I open the heavy glass door for her. She walks through, pausing in the crisp, damp Alaska air. The short rain shower is dissipating, and the sun is trying to escape from the clouds.

Suddenly, Maria pauses, the color drains from her face, leaving her complexion paler than the snow-capped mountains on the horizon. In an instant, she staggers, her movements unsteady, and then, without warning, she faints.

Reacting instinctually, I move swiftly, closing the distance between us. With a firm grip, I catch her falling, pulling her into my arms and supporting her delicate frame. Her weight is heavier than I expected as if the days of worrying and the banking tension added weight to her small frame.

"Whoa. Are you okay?" I ask, helping set her on the ground as I shrug off my jacket to place it under her so she doesn't get wet.

Her eyes flutter open, and she shakes her head but says, "Yes."

Sitting on the ground with uneven breathing, she wrings her hands and looks up at me with wide eyes and trembling lips. Instinctively, I want to wrap my arms around her.

The banking incident must have been more stressful. The situation dawns on me as I realize the seriousness of her condition: she's pregnant and alone, trying to run her husband's business with no help. Plus, she has to deal with unfriendly, intolerant people.

She's been thrust into a difficult situation, coping with losing Cole and grappling with the reality of living in a new community in addition to taking on his business responsibilities. It's no wonder she's unsteady!

She's brave for getting out of the house and caring about getting the Hopper's employees their paychecks.

I help her find a more comfortable position on the pavement, ensuring she's not hurt as I squat next to her, my eyes at her eye level.

"Take deep breaths," I say gently, my voice soothing. "In . . . and out. You're going to be okay."

As she breathes, I can't help but feel a surge of concern for her. The unexpectedness of running into her, then rescuing her from those bank bitches, and catching her as she falls leaves me shaken, too. I take a deep cleansing breath.

I glance around, grateful for the relative privacy of the bank's exterior, shielding us from the prying eyes of curious onlookers.

"When was your last meal?" I ask, trying to help her.

She hesitates and swallows before replying. "I was cooking yesterday," she says with a small smile.

"Maria, you gotta eat!" I frown. She has no one to check on her and ensure she's doing okay. She likely needs a meal, a sweet cup of tea, and a friend to help her through this difficult time.

Even if she resists my friendship, I can be here for her now. I'll just ensure she's alright until she gets back on her feet.

"Come on," I command, offering her my arm as support. "I can't leave you on the pavement, ready to blow away with the next gust of wind. Let's get you somewhere more comfortable."

She rises from the ground with my arm under her, still looking a bit unsteady. However, she's stopped crying, and her eyes are focused as I guide her to my truck.

Getting her food and letting her relax, away from all the prying eyes, is essential! *It's the least I can do for her.*

As we approach my vehicle, I try to cover my worry about her with a smile and light conversation, which is difficult as I don't have much practice with friendly banter.

"Weather's good. I'm grabbing a Big White Starvin' Marvin's pizza," I say, not waiting for her response. "We'll have lunch at my place. *And* I have someone special to introduce you to."

She gives me a weak smile, gratitude evident in her eyes, and her cheeks color with a light blush as I help her into my truck. The sun has escaped and peaks over the mountains, making the bay glittery as I drive her to my cozy houseboat.

I hope I remembered to clear the table and take out the trash before I left. And I hope she likes Sammy.

Chapter 8

Maria

The air inside Jackie's houseboat smells of warm pizza and the sea. Sitting at her cozy wooden table, I relax, the dim light casting a soft glow on the teak-paneled walls. A stack of boxes from Starvin' Marvin's, our impromptu lunch, occupies the center of the table.

Jackie hands me a slice of dripping white pizza, and I smile, my mouth watering.

"Thank you for this. It's been a while since I've sat down to eat a proper meal." My stomach rumbles in agreement, and I blush.

She chuckles. "No worries. Starvin' Marvin's is awesome. I figured I'd introduce you to Homer's best pizzeria." She takes a big bite.

I follow her lead, folding my pizza and devouring it. The cheesy goodness fills my mouth, a distraction from the last few days' stress of waiting by the phone for news and keeping the Hopper operating. With the soft, honeyed crust and the savory sharp cheese, a moan escapes from within me.

Jackie laughs. "Good, right?"

She nudges a bag towards me. "I have your tea delivery from Boris and some sweet bread."

I raise an eyebrow. *Tea?* She mentioned this at the bank, and I don't have a clue what tea she's talking about. "He must have confused me with someone else. I didn't order any tea."

She cocks her head, then rubs her eyes and flips her ball cap backward. Looking at me, she shakes her head, saying, "No mistake. Boris fancies himself a matchmaker, and we're his latest victims." She chuckles, then takes another bite.

I glance at the bag, "Are you sure? It's probably for someone else."

"No one would mistake you for anyone but you," she says firmly. "No. Boris likes to meddle which is why he's a bartender. I'm surprised he didn't have me deliver flowers," she adds with a laugh.

I bite my lip and blush. "Ummm. . actually." I look at her and say, "I was going to thank you for the lovely flowers."

"Boris!" She throws another slice of pizza on my plate. "I did want to stop by and I would've brought flowers. I just wanted to give you space and time."

I shake my head, uncertain. *I guess I was wrong about the flowers and her feelings for me. She's not single, so the idea of us getting together is ludicrous.*

"He should have sent you a pizza from me. Flowers are not creative or unique." Jackie shakes her head in disapproval. "This is adding fuel to the gossip from people that we're dating," Jackie adds.

"Let's check inside the bag," I say, changing the subject and wiping my cheesy mouth on a napkin.

She shakes out the bag, and there's my usual pub order: peppermint tea and honey sticks, with a loaf of bread wrapped in tin foil. Then, a small gold book, *Special Edition: Alaska Kama Sutra,* falls out.

I frown and pick up the small, gold-etched book. I open the book to a picture of a moose and polar bear in a cowgirl position.

Jackie laughs hard, and I join in. "Whoa! This is definitely Boris!"

"He certainly has an odd sense of humor," I say, giggling at the ridiculous picture.

"I'm sure he's getting a good laugh at having me deliver this to you!"

"It *is* a funny distraction. How should I repay him for the weird gift?"

"My specialty is sailing or beer drinking. I don't have any ideas about funny gift-giving." Jack says with a smile. "What are you thinking, Maria?"

"Something equally funny and, maybe, unique," I say, tucking my hair behind my ears, thinking.

Well, I never thought a joke sex book would be the highlight of my day. *I'm having fun, though.*

"A fake break-up for our fake relationship?" she suggests.

"No, more creative. Could we reverse the matchmaking and set him up with the bank teller?" I ask, brainstorming.

"That's cruel!" she says with a laugh.

"Let's give him a candy gram with vegetables instead of candy."

"Weird, but I like it! I bet Sally over at Glacier Cafe will make us a vegetable bouquet. She makes carrot and radish roses for their salad bar."

"Yes!" I high-five Jackie, and we grin at our quirky plan.

She grins, her eyes crinkling at the corners. "Maybe he's not a terrible matchmaker." She winks at me, and I look down, unsure if she's being friendly or flirty—and *if I want her to be friendly or flirty.*

We finish eating, the atmosphere is more relaxed, and I'm less shaky and stressed from this morning. I'm glad I left the house and went to the bank.

I take a moment to study the soft waves in Jackie's blonde hair, which are haphazardly tuck in an old ball cap. She looks beautiful in the basic white t-shirt, jeans, warm flannel, and heavy combat boots that complete her Alaskan Boat Captain look.

She's proving to be a good friend, helping me despite my efforts to push her away.

I ask, "Before you saved me, again, why were you at the bank?"

She sighs, putting down her slice. "Business trouble. My boat was fully insured, but the insurance payout is taking forever. I need to get a loan to get back to work ferrying people."

With my worrying about Cole and the business, I forgot she lost her boat, too. I feel bad because she lost it, saving me, and it means she's unable to work.

"I'm sorry about your boat and the whole situation."

She nods with a tight smile. "Thanks. My business is a mess, but I'll figure it out."

An idea percolates, forming in my mind: a plan to help Jackie and, in turn, help myself with all my business stress. *Jackie knows the business, and I have boats.*

"You know," I begin tentatively, "The Hopper is struggling with Cole gone. The employees are *not showing up for shifts* and we're losing clients. What if... what if I help get you a new boat, and you help me manage the business—just while you sort things out with your insurance, of course?"

Her eyes widen, and she takes a sharp inhale. "You'd do that? Let me manage the Hopper?"

I smile, my confidence returning with the decision. *I want to get the business in order, and Jackie is precisely the person to help.*

"I would. And it's a bigger favor to me since I don't know the first thing about the water taxi business or boating. In fact, you can have the boat we brought back from the storm. It's not in the fleet and hasn't moved from the dock."

"That Bayliner is worth ten times what mine was. Are you sure about this?"

I nod, covering her hand with mine, and look into her eyes. "It's the least I can do. Do we have a deal?" I put my hand out.

She smiles and shakes my hand. And as we finish the delicious pizza, we discuss the logistics. Jackie agrees to work from the docks, and I can work from the home office, with her managing the boats and crew and me managing the bills and vendors.

"This is perfect. I didn't know how I'd fulfill our ferry contracts, when I don't know the bay or the guys," I say, with the tension in my chest finally lifting. *I might actually pull off saving the business.*

Her eyes dance with determination, and she looks as if she's been waiting for a challenge like this.

I smile at her. *I'm doing the right thing for her, me, and Cole.*

Had I known she needed to work, I would've given her any boat she wanted anyway. This solves the issue of what to do with the boat that I lost Cole on, as I already know that I don't ever want to get on that Bayliner again. In fact, I don't want to get on any of the boats.

The conversation transitions to lighter topics and a comfortable silence. Jackie cleans up the pizza box and plates.

"I forgot, I was going to let you meet Sammy." Her eyes light up mentioning her partner, Sammy.

I look around, not seeing anyone else or any pictures indicating if Sammy is her male or female partner.

Before I can ask, she pulls me with her, saying, "Everyone loves Sammy!"

She leads me outside to the houseboat's deck overlooking the calm bay. The crisp Alaska air hits us as Jackie whistles, and I see Jackie toss a red ball that bounces across the water. A cute, fluffy sea otter with mischievous eyes emerges from the water.

"Here's Sammy, the most adorable sea otter in Alaska," she says with a grin, "This is why my boat was named The Sea Otter's Pride."

"He's adorable!" I exclaim, watching Sammy splash and roll the ball to us.

Jackie says proudly, "He's a *she*, according to a visiting marine biologist. We all had been calling her a *him* for a long time so the name Sammy stuck." Jackie takes my hand and leads me to the edge. "She's a handful, but she keeps me company. Wanna to meet her?"

"Yes!"

As I crouch down to pet Sammy, a fluttering sensation inside me distracts me and makes me stand and hold my abdomen.

"What is it?" Jackie says, putting her arm around my back for support, worried I'm feeling faint.

The tiny life growing inside me comes to life, reminding me *I'm making a family.* The baby is moving, and I feel it for the first time. The slight whooshing sends waves of excitement and fear through me.

There's really a baby–Cole's baby–growing inside of me!

Jackie looks at me with her jaw tight, ready to help me to a deck chair. "Dizzy?"

"No, Jackie," I whisper, my hand on my stomach. "The baby just moved."

Her eyes widen, and her hand covers mine. "Really?" She looks at me and then looks at my little belly bulge.

I wish I were further along than four-ish months. Then, my pregnant belly would be obvious to everyone. I want to show off that I'm carrying Cole's legacy and that we are starting a family.

I nod, emotions filling me. "It's the first time I've felt it. I'm scared, but kind of excited."

She places her hand tentatively on my stomach, and I put my hand over hers to show her it's okay. We wait for more movement from my baby, but it rests after the flurry of activity.

Instead, my heart pounds, and a wave of heat surges in me the longer Jackie's hand stays on my lower abdomen.

She shakes her head and shrugs, not feeling anything.

When I look up, meeting her eyes, she reddens and licks her lips. *She feels something, too.*

Silently, she takes my hand, and we leave Sammy playing in the bay to return inside, holding hands.

I look at her and hold her hand tighter, wondering how she'll react if I ask her for more, especially since I've given her mixed messages. I tentatively ask, "Can we snuggle on the couch?"

She nods, saying nothing, leading me there. We kick off our shoes, climb onto the couch, pull a fuzzy blanket over us, and I melt into her arms, the houseboat rocking under us.

The unspoken possibilities and our strong connection rekindle the heat between us. I tingle with hope filling me, the heavy burden that I have been holding on to these weeks is lifting.

Everything is falling into place. I find myself content after feeling the baby's moving, finding a business solution, discovering that Sammy isn't her girlfriend, and being in Jackie's arms. I lick my lips and think I must be dreaming–*a delightful, wonderful dream*–as I snuggle deeper into Jackie's warm embrace.

Then I bite my lip hard, tasting salty blood.

How can I be happy when Cole is gone?

Chapter 9

Jackie

The sea stretches before me, the surface reflecting the incredible, steel-gray morning sky above. I'm at peace on the water, the gentle rocking of my houseboat beneath me as familiar as my heartbeat.

Except, I'm not solo enjoying the solitude–Sammy pops her head out of the water. She floats on her back and bites at her flipper, not wanting to play but joining me for the lazy sunrise.

She keeps me company, a welcome presence in this quiet harbor. I rescued the sea otter, untangling her from fishing nets years ago, and she's been my companion since. She stays nearby and visits me throughout her day, dancing and twirling in the water as I sit on the deck relaxing, watching the glassy mountains reflected in Kachemak Bay and tides stealing the shoreline.

Setting my coffee down, I dangle my legs over the houseboat's edge to talk to my energetic, goofy furball. She's a good friend, listening and never judging me.

"Sammy, you won't believe it–*your grumpy captain is falling in love,*" I say, my voice as soft as her velvety ears. I lean forward, and she meets my eyes as I whisper, "And with an off-limits woman. Not only is she pregnant–*not mine, obviously, Sammy!*–she's the wife of Cole, the guy I'm always griping about. He's dead, so she's his *widow,* which makes it *so much worse* for me to be dreaming about her." I put my head in my hands, then look at Sammy who's waiting.

The sea otter gazes at me with dark, expressive eyes as if listening intently. Her silent understanding is reassuring.

"When I met her during that storm–*I knew that she was the one I'd been waiting for,*" I say, thinking back to her shivering, alone in the raging sea, beautiful and strong, even being terrified in the storm. My gut clenches with what could've happened to her if I hadn't been in that precise spot at that exact time when she called for help over the radio.

Fate keeps pushing me toward her.

My mind wanders to yesterday, with the rude, snobby bank tellers tormenting her. I imagine she feels very much like an outsider in her new home and in this town so far from the country she grew up in.

"Seeing her helpless and her eyes filling with tears, then later, how her eyes lit up with her baby moving–I want to wrap my arms around her when she's desperate and elated. I want to share with her how special Homer is and that she fits into our small community."

I'm already fiercely protective of this woman I've known for only a few weeks. Maria deserves all the snuggles and happiness the world can give her, and I'm happy to provide her with some of mine.

On top of that, with her and Sammy's influence, I'm becoming less of a grump and actually looking forward to doing something besides being on the water all day.

Sammy floats on her back in the water, her webbed paws paddling idly. Her eyes still watch me, urging me to go on and tell her more—my faithful companion paddles in the water, offering her approval. The sea otter may not understand the intricacies of human emotions, but she knows the importance of her companionship to me.

Embracing the peaceful vibe of the harbor's tranquility and her silent support, I'm ready to talk with Maria about more than business. I'm happy to help with the Hopper, but our connection and feelings are more significant than my need to replace a boat.

After deciding that I was coming into the Homer Harbor Hopper office this week to be the *acting manager*, we snuggled as if we always ended the day cozy in each other's arms. She didn't talk, and I didn't want to ruin the fleeting, tentative embrace with questions, but her phone rang, calling her away.

She might not be prepared for a relationship, but she could use a friend. And I'm willing to be whoever, whatever she needs.

As I gaze out at the vast expanse of the sea, I know that I play it safe with my emotions and gravitate towards a solitary life. Still, my connections with Boris, Sammy, and Maria make me happy and part of the larger community. Maria, especially, leaves me wanting to share my future with more than the ocean. The connection makes the coming day sparkle, more vibrant with possibility.

A strange warmth fills me, and a smile plays on my lips, ruining my trademark grumpy Alaska Captain demeanor. I sip my coffee, grinning, and Sammy squeaks, somersaulting under the smooth surface.

"Sammy, I'm falling in love—"

Our one-sided conversation is cut off abruptly with the ringing phone.

"Ugh! What is it now?" I mutter, reaching for the intrusive device.

"This is Jackie," I say gruffly.

"Hi, Jackie. I'm a reporter from the Homer Newspaper. I wanted to ask you a few questions about last week's ocean rescue. Are you good for a quick interview?" the male voice on the other end asks.

Interview? The word ruins the morning's softness, making my blood bubble and jaw clench. But the town has been discussing it for weeks, and having Maria's story in the news will pressure the Coast Guard to continue searching.

Maria needs answers and closure. The fastest way for me to help her find that is for the Coasties to find Cole's body.

"Yeah, sure," I reluctantly agree, despite the dark mood settling on me.

The reporter doesn't miss a beat to introduce himself. He cuts right to his questions.

"Tell me about Colton Sander's *alleged accident*?" he starts, his tone loaded with skepticism.

What?! I narrow my eyes and take a quick breath, ready to defend Maria.

"It wasn't *allege*. He fell overboard after losing his footing during the storm. The storm was unexpected and winds were up to thirty knots. Cole was lost at sea in the tragic *accident*. No one could've predicted or prevented it."

Without pausing, he asks, "What's your personal relationship with Colton?"

The question is quick and sharp, like a slap.

"He's a fellow boat captain. We both ran our harbor taxi services out of the harbor," I reply, my voice firm.

"And did you have beef with him? He was trying to drive you out of business, right?" The unsaid accusation hangs in the air.

A scoff escapes me. "Colton is a businessman. We had our disagreements, but that's normal between competing businesses."

"So would you call Colton and Harbor Hopper a business rival?" The reporter pushes, searching for a sensational angle.

"No. Not a rival. We were both making a living in Homer, and we are both boat captains," I say, my patience waning.

"What about his new wife, Maria? What's your relationship to her?" he asks, shifting his questions to focus on Maria.

"She's not a boat captain. And she's the woman I rescued during the storm. That's it," I respond, my tone leaving no room for further inquiry.

"Was it *just* you and her who witnessed Cole's tragic *accident*?" The reporter digs.

"We were in the middle of Kachemak Bay, so there may have been others out there. I happened to be the closest boat when her distress call came over the radio requesting help," I say calmly, refusing to let him twist the narrative.

"How well did you know Cole's wife prior to the accident?"

"I didn't know her."

"Really? Homer's a small town to not have met her before then?"

"Our paths may've crossed, but I don't recall meeting her. I don't go out. The storm was the first time I met her," I say, a hint of frustration in my voice.

"Seems like she's getting a pretty good deal after this *tragic accident*–inheriting all her husband's wealth after only a few months of a *questionably-legal* marriage," the reporter says, trying to provoke a reaction from me.

My jaw tightens, and I say nothing for a beat. "Her marriage and the circumstances around it are none of your business, and I can't comment on that. What I can tell you is that Maria's dealing with enough, with the aftermath of this tragedy, without your *baseless questions and spreading more false rumors.*"

"And she has you to run Cole's business now, right?"

My jaw aches as it's unintentionally clenching tighter and tighter with each question. He's tipping his hand that someone is feeding him information since I have not told anyone of Maria's offer, and today, she's announcing it to the employees.

Plus, I know Maria doesn't have anyone close she's talking to.

"Yes, I'm helping her manage the Hopper. This is a community, and we don't want to lose the biggest ferry service in the harbor. Also, in this tragedy, her employees need work and not to lose their jobs. Maria is dealing with personal matters, and I'm familiar with the business. It's called being a decent human being." I retort, my words laced with irritation.

"To sum it up, you met for the first time when Cole died. She's a wealthy widow, and you are now running the biggest ocean taxi company in town now. Is that right?" The reporter attempts to angle this scenario to sound sinister and add more fuel to the current rumors.

I run my hand over my face and lean forward, my voice steady. "Her financial situation and mine are not up for public scrutiny. The focus should be on finding Cole, not encouraging gossip. Maria should have the community's support during this challenging time, don't you think? What is the Homer News doing to help Cole's family? As I recall, he runs the largest daily advertisement in your newspaper. Are you helping find him or are you trying to incite a lynch mob to go after a widow?" I fire the last statement in a growl at him.

With that, I end the conversation, slamming down the phone with a resounding thud. The reporter may have sought to stoke the fires of the current rumors, but I won't let him tarnish Maria's name or our relationship with his innuendos.

Homer is a friendly community, and despite my dislike of Cole, I know he was well-liked and an upstanding member of this community. I don't understand why these negative rumors are swirling.

And why is no one visiting or supporting Maria? *I don't know what's going on, but something is, and I need to figure it out before she gets forced out of Homer with vicious rumors.*

The thought hits me like a frigid Alaskan storm. Anger builds, a storm waiting to unleash its fury, and I have nothing to lash out at. *Who started these rumors? How dare they pry into my life and Maria's?* The rumors were bad enough, but having a reporter call to confirm them is *too much.*

Slamming my fist into the deck, I seethe with frustration. The nerve of some people, treating Maria like an outsider and spinning my rescue and help into a rotten scheme.

The reporter strengthened my resolve to help Maria. *She needs a friend!* I won't judge or be rude to her based on the town's gossip. Quickly pulling on my jacket and boots, I head to the Harbor Hopper's office further down the Homer Spit for the scheduled morning meeting with all the employees.

The brisk, icy wind stings my face as I stride toward the Hopper's office, my mind sharpened by anger and determination. I must set the record straight and stop these rumors for Maria and me.

Chapter 10

Maria

"Why should I take orders from someone who doesn't even know port from starboard? You're a pretty figurehead for the Hopper. I'm not wasting my time!" Ben growls with his eyes narrow, his arms crossing, and stepping forward to face me, the other employees behind him all glaring.

The employee meeting could be going better–it definitely can't get any worse!

I hug my arms to my stomach and step back, my mind spinning about how to diffuse the situation and get these guys happy and working again. Getting the Hopper operating is vital to the local companies that have called to remind me they need the ferry business for their resorts across the bay–and for me. I might be a millionaire with Cole's assets, but it's not money in the bank–it's our home and this business.

If I lose this business, then I lose our home. *I won't have anything!*

I must get these guys working and the business up and running again–*or I don't know what I'll do!*

Cole loved being a boat Captain and was passionate about the water taxi business. Plus, he knew every person, was a friend to all his employees, and community members appreciated the Hopper.

It's up to me to keep his legacy from imploding without him, and *I'm failing!*

If only I were half as connected and knowledgeable as him! I can't afford an employee revolt, and these men hate me without even giving me a chance to save their jobs and the business.

My heart races, and I'm dizzy with sweat forming on my temples as I stand on the dock in front of the employees for what I hoped would be a successful meeting with everyone pitching in to help save the business. The salty air stings my skin on the cold, gray morning, and the clouds above multiply.

The men, led by Cole's cousin, Ben, are gathered around me, with faces hard and lined by anger and resentment. They're all itching to tell me what to do with the business–*give it to Ben*–and refuse to listen or discuss a plan with me.

They lost their boss and friend. However, they forget that I lost my husband and future!

I focus on the frosty line of men in front of me. Clearing my throat and taking a deep breath, I say, "Listen, I understand that you are getting paid late, and the business is crazy-disorganized with Cole gone. But your jobs haven't changed, and we have water taxi contracts to fulfill. We have a schedule to honor and we need to get back on the water, working."

The response is immediate and cutting.

"I'm not taking orders from a mail-order bride," one of them spits out, his eyes flashing with disdain. Ben looks at him and nods. The others glower at me with defiance.

The anger builds, and my unsteadiness turns to frustration. These guys were Cole's friends, and we should be working side-by-side for his business during this time. The employees were friendly when Cole introduced me. I painstakingly memorized each of their names, so the disrespect in their attitudes blindsided me.

My body shakes, and I keep the tears behind my eyes. I want to yell at them. *What would Cole think? You refuse to work and are disrespecting his wife?!*

If they gave me a chance, they'd see I want to save their jobs and the Homer Harbor Hopper. I'm more than a homemaker. I studied business and international economics at my home university. Cole trusted that I could help in the business alongside of him, which is why he added me to all the contracts. I might not know how to drive a boat, but I care about this business. I can do the scheduling and accounting if they would do *their part* and work.

Why won't they give me a chance?

Ben is leading this pack of schoolyard bullies. And their grumbling is escalating to angry words.

"That's enough!" Jackie appears, booming with authority and stepping beside me.

Thank God!

Her stern voice cuts through their overlapping chatter, and the men look at her.

"Maria owns the business, and she's trying to keep your jobs–Damn ungrateful Brats! She signs your paychecks, so start listening to her. I'm helping her manage the Hopper, and if you want to get paid, you better start working." Her eyes are fierce, her stance unyielding.

I'm stunned by her confidence, frank words, and standing up to the men. My heart floods with relief, and slowly, my heart rate moves from thundering to steady.

"Of course, your *girlfriend* is here to bail you out—predictable," Ben mutters.

The men grumble and exchange glances, but they don't say anything. They are listening to her.

"Didn't know you talked, Captain," a guy says looking at Jackie.

She stares down at the men, takes a step to Ben, and says, "I'll be in the office. See me if you need to discuss your schedule or give your notice. If not, I expect you to be working."

I stand beside her as she directs them, and they disperse to their boats. Her ability to handle the situation allows me to take a breath, and I tell her, "Thank you, Jackie."

She turns with her body blocking their view as she leans her face down, and her warm lips are close to my temple. "Don't back down or show weakness. They'll stay." She gives me a wink, and her eyes convey a shared resolve to get them working and the Hopper operating.

With her, I'm not alone on the dock. I tilt my head, giving her a slight nod and tight smile, keeping my serious demeanor intact for the remaining men.

"Okay, does anyone else have questions?" I ask.

Their quiet movement around the dock, walking to their assigned boats and untying ropes, signals agreement. *Hopefully, not too many will choose to resign!*

"If there's anything else, talk to me," Jackie says, making eye contact with each of the men gathered. Most look away or nod instead of meeting her steely eyes.

They grumble quietly but no longer are openly defiant. The Hopper is operating for the community, the employees, and me. Now, I need to start working on the tedious office work, including opening all the bills and collecting mail in the office and my home.

The guys' back to work is a small victory, a step toward proving that I belong here and can run the business. I look at Jackie with her set jaw.

I won't back down. I can do this! I'll keep the Homer Harbor Hopper alive, and the tragedy won't destroy Cole's dream, his family business.

Ben rushes past me, his disregard evident as he bumps me, leaving me stumbling backward.

My feet slip on the damp wooden dock. I desperately try to regain my balance, but it's too late as I fall hard, impacting the solid wooden planks.

"Ohh!" The pain shoots through my butt, and panic surges in me. Instinctively, I wrap my arms around my belly, terrified of hurting the baby growing inside.

"Maria!" Jackie's voice cuts through my racing thoughts. I focus on staying calm and deep breathing.

She swiftly moves to my side, anger flashing at Ben and his callousness before her eyes soften, moving to look into mine as she stoops over. She quickly helps me up and gently wipes the dirt from my jacket and pants.

"I'm okay," I assure her, and the guys who had paused their movement to make sure I was okay fell back into their familiar work routines.

The tightening of her jaw and her narrow eyes tell me she isn't going to let Ben get away with making me fall. The tension that she dissipated getting the guys working is back, twofold.

She wraps a friendly arm around me, glaring at Ben stomping away. She's itching to chase and confront him but chooses to stay with me.

I offer her a grateful smile, trying to downplay the pain radiating from my butt. However, she must see the pain in my eyes as she pulls me into her warm side to steady me, her arms shielding me from the cold and calming me.

"I'm glad to help," she says. She's gentle, and the unspoken undercurrent of caring is there. She doesn't care who sees her holding me.

Despite the ache in my body and stormy emotions, I smile at her confidence. After the emotional roller coaster of the employee meeting and now the uncertainty for my baby, my heart is thumping in overdrive.

"I always seem to need rescuing whenever you're around," I say, leaning my head into the warm spot between her neck and chest. "I promise I'm not usually so accident-prone." My voice is light, and I joke, dispelling the remaining edginess from Ben.

She chuckles, her response matching mine. On the dock, Ben is moving out of sight, and the guys are back to work. "I'm happy to rescue you, Boss. Let's get you to the hospital and check the baby," she says, her tone commanding yet soft when directed at me.

I nod, releasing the breath I didn't realize I was holding. *I'll feel better knowing the baby is fine.*

But a sudden eruption of angry words cuts through the atmosphere like lightning. "You're pregnant!" Ben roars, his eyes ablaze with fury.

I forget how sound carries across water, and my heart pounds from his reaction. I wasn't sure how he'd feel knowing I was pregnant. Now, I know–*furious!*

I wrap my arms around my belly. Jackie moves protectively in front of me, her arms on her hips. She's coiled and ready to fight him.

I'm exposed, vulnerable, with my secret out, and a rush of anxiety courses through me.

Ben's anger is palpable, and I brace myself for whatever verbal onslaught is about to follow.

Jackie speaks with a steely edge, "Watch your tone, Ben. Maria's well-being is our priority. She's more invested in this business than you. You should apologize for shoving your pregnant cousin-in-law and hope she lets you keep your job." Her eyes narrow at him, and she squares off, waiting for his response.

His expression tightens with anger and disbelief. "You stole the family business, and you're having a baby?" Ben sneers, his words dripping with disdain.

I swallow and glance at Jackie, who wraps her hand in mine and squeezes, waiting for Ben to say more. The revelation makes him stride back onto the dock.

Jackie maintains her protective shield against Ben's hostility as he seethes, stopping before reaching us.

"Cole chose her to run the business, not you, Ben! I'm taking Maria to the hospital. Step aside," she says, her tone unwavering.

He scoffs, resentment evident in every line of his face. "This foreigner took the business, is taking the house, and now she's weaseled her way into staying here by having a baby. You don't belong here, Maria," he spits out, his eyes drilling into mine.

Jackie steps forward, placing herself firmly between us. "She belongs here as much as anyone. *Step back. NOW!*" Her gaze is ice, and a nearby employee moves to stand, not next to Ben, but by Jackie.

The standoff continues, the tension thick. And I notice the other guys stepping away from their boats and away from Ben. They are choosing to side with Jackie.

Ben looked around and, seething with anger, relents, turning around with a final glare. As he storms off, his parting words cut through the air. "You're taking everything from me, and I wouldn't be surprised when they find out that you pushed Cole overboard. This isn't over!"

Jackie watches him leave, her expression unwavering. She turns back to me once he's really out of earshot. Her features softening, she says, "Let's go to the hospital, Maria. We'll check that everything's okay." Her voice is calm as if she didn't just face off and win against a six-foot-three two-hundred sixty-pound angry Grizzly.

I nod and keep holding her hand as we walk off the dock. Together, we head toward her truck, leaving the echoes of Ben's anger behind us.

"Do you think he'll cool off?" I ask.

She helps me step into her truck. Then she leans over and clicks the seatbelt across me, her hair tickling my cheek and making me flush.

She defends me and is taking care of me. *I couldn't have asked for a better friend or new business partner!*

"He better, or we'll fire him. I don't care if he's family or about his seniority. If he's not going to respect you, he's gone."

Her eyes flash. I want to disagree since he was Cole's only family and our primary ferry operator. *But* Ben is being an asshole, and he did cause my fall, then yelled at me in front of our employees.

Shouldn't family be supportive and caring at a time like this? Does he really think that I pushed Cole into the bay?

Chapter 11

Jackie

The roar of my engine mimics the thunder from the summer rain. Maria is visibly nervous beside me, clutching her small tummy, and reassuringly hugs the tiny life growing within. Usually serene, the bay is stirring up with white-capped waves as we rush above it to the Homer Hospital Emergency Room.

Like the trees in the wind outside, my emotions sway between helping Maria with the morning employee meeting–more of a *confrontation than a meeting*–and her fall. Luckily, I was there to support her. *I didn't realize Ben was such an ass!*

I steal a glance at Maria. Her furrowed brows and the delicate tension around her kind eyes reveal the quiet worry she's containing. Her plump bottom lip, usually soft and full, is wedged between her teeth. There's a vulnerability in her lips, a silent plea for reassurance. Despite her anxiety, her eyes glimmer with her strength and resilience.

"Jackie, do you think everything will be okay?" She looks at me, her eyes searching.

"It'll be fine," I reply, my gruff response belying the softness beneath. I steer the truck with a steady hand, my focus alternating between the rainy roadway and her.

She's running her hands over her belly and frowning.

I distract her with a question, "Are you making friends in Homer?"

"Only Boris and you," she confesses. "I know people think it's crazy to move here and marry a man I never met. But Cole and I got matched by a renowned agency and we talked online for months."

"People meet online all the time," I say. *Who am I to judge? I haven't dated in years!*

"Cole and I wanted a big family. He told me so many stories about Alaska and growing up here. He explained his family business, about each employee, and the ocean. His life was an exciting adventure. I studied business and the life he described was a dream, to be a partner in his business and start a family in Homer. I fell in love with Homer, and I fell in love with him. Everything seemed perfect for us." She shrugs and looks out the dripping window.

I nod. *I can understand how easy it is to fall in love with her. She's stunning, caring, and very devoted to Cole.*

"I can imagine it's not easy to move to a small Alaska town. Most people that live and work here, were born here," I reply. "I'm a loner by choice, but I know everyone. I promise this little town will feel like family. It just takes time to adjust and for people to get to know you."

She lowers her gaze, and I instinctively move my hand to rest on her thigh, offering a comforting squeeze as I navigate. The simmering warmth beneath my touch, the soft curves of her thigh in denim, create an immediate mutual affection. The warm connection compels me to share more and be vulnerable.

"Maria," I begin, hesitating, "before you finalize me as your business manager–*and close friend*. I need to be honest with you."

Her gaze flickers and settles on me, waiting and warmly expressing her acceptance. "Go ahead."

I know I only just met you, but I love you.

Before admitting my feelings, I should tell her my actual relationship with Cole, the man she still loves, before the reporter prints it in the paper. It is close to what the reporter insinuated this morning:

rivals. We *are* in the same business, and tensions brewed beneath the surface of our amicable relationship on the water.

"Jackie," Maria's voice breaks through my thoughts, drawing me back to the present. She looks at me with a mix of curiosity and concern. "You can talk to me. Is something bothering you?"

Usually, I prefer silence, but now is as good a time to tell her. "Maria, there is something I need to tell." I take a deep breath and tighten my grip on the wheel. "Cole and I weren't friends like he is with most everyone in Homer. We were competitors, rivals in the boat ferrying business. We weren't friendly to each other *at all*. In fact, he wouldn't have hired me even if every captain in his fleet quit."

Maria's eyes widened in surprise. "Competitors? But you've been helping save the business, and you tried to rescue him. You saved his boat and me. That sounds like friends."

I look at her and shrug.

"Why didn't you say something before?"

"It's complicated," I admit, my gaze locked with hers. "Cole and I had our disagreements. He's competitive and takes pride in being the best ferry business in the harbor. He wasn't excited when I started ferrying. Then, when I responded to your distress call. . . I didn't know who I was assisting."

A weighted silence hangs as my revelation sinks in. Maria processes the information, her eyes searching mine for sincerity. Unexpectedly, a small smile tugs at the corners of her lips.

"Jackie, you saved me *and* Cole's baby. You *are* saving his business," she says, her voice resonating with a heartfelt warmth that conveys the depth of her feelings. "And you're helping me now. I appreciate that, Jackie."

She adds, "I thought that Cole's friends or neighbors would check on me. . ." She rubs her new baby bump. "But I'm totally alone without Cole, and you're the only one who's been with me during all of this."

"When other people get to know you, I promise you won't need me anymore," I joke with a smile.

She looks at me. "No. I'll still need you, and if Cole got to know you, he'd have liked you, too."

I nod, relieved to unburden myself of the guilt related to holding back my relationship with Cole.

"Also, Cole would've thanked you and approved of me giving you this job *and the boat* for what you've done for me– *for us,*" she says, looking at me with a radiant smile. Her anxiety long forgotten.

The storm outside relents as if the universe is granting us respite from its fury. I take Maria's hand with an unspoken understanding, our intimacy deepening. So far, telling her the truth hasn't scared her away. *I might as well let everything out in the open.*

I continue talking and move my hands to grip the wheel, "This morning, a reporter called and made the same accusations that Ben was making on the dock. I think Ben is creating the rumors, and there may be a story printed that alleges Cole was pushed over and that there was no accident. Also, the reporter was asking me if we're in a romantic relationship."

She blinks and looks at me. She moves her hand to *my* thigh. I take that as a sign to continue telling her what I've been holding back.

"Maria, the relationship rumor isn't completely untrue because ever since I saw you. . .I've fallen for you," I confess, my voice low, al-most lost in the rain pelting the windshield. "I didn't agree to manage the Harbor Hopper to save Cole's business. I. . . I care about you. . . more than a friend. I want to see you happy."

Her eyes meet mine, and I see a flicker of realization. The honesty between us electrifies the cab. The truth is out, laid bare like the turbulent sea outside, and I wait to see how she'll answer.

"How could you want a relationship with me? I'm a mess, preg-nant, a widow, and always crying. Also, I'm the most un-Alaskan person in the world. And you are the epitome of an Alaska Wilderness

Woman—a boat captain, strong, outdoorsy, independent. . .You even have a sea otter as a pet! Look at me. . . I wear designer sandals to go boating. Seriously, I thought Cole was an airline pilot when he first told me he was a Captain!"

I gaze at Maria, her eyes softening with sincerity. A genuine smile on my lips as I say, "Maria, you're not a mess. You're a survivor. You've been through a lot. That doesn't make you weak; it gives you grit. Alaskans are full of grit! Yeah, you're pregnant, but that's not a flaw. It's a miracle. And you are more than Cole's wife, you're a business owner."

I stop, the silent tears fill her eyes, and she bites her lip and smiles. I continue, "But it's not the whole story. As for the tears, they're not a sign of weakness, either. They're proof of the love you had, that you aren't afraid to embrace your emotions and the strength it takes to keep going."

I reach over and gently wipe away a tear from her soft cheek.

She smiles and laughs a little at that. "Really?"

"Yes. And about being the most *un-Alaskan* person in the world? Alaska is more than just wearing Xtratuf boots and being able to drive a boat. It's about facing challenges head-on, embracing the unexpected, and finding beauty in the wild and in eachother. You don't need to be an Alaskan Wilderness Woman to belong here. You need grit and you've already got that in spades–moving to an isolated foreign place, taking a chance on Cole, and surviving. Maria, your heart is wild, beautiful, and full of grit. You're more Alaskan than me!"

She grins, a hint of mischief in her eyes, and the tears dry.

"Maria, I love you and I want to be a part of your life in whatever way you are ready for. I knew from the first time I saw and held you in the storm that you're my person," I admit. "I've never felt this way about anyone, and I think fate brought us together for a reason."

She looks at me with shining eyes and out the window. The warmth of her hand on my thigh provides a comforting anchor, grounding me.

"I think I've known for a while," Maria says, her voice soft and smiling. "I care about you, too."

The admission diffuses the anticipation between us in the truck, and we settle into a comfortable silence with the storm outside. I place my fingers over hers, and our fingers tighten, stitched together. This is more than a spark or casual love. Fate is pushing us together because we are right for each other.

The glare of the hospital's sign interrupts my thoughts. We turn into the driveway, the rain stopping as I park by the entrance and hop out to open the door for Maria. The hospital's bright lights welcome us from the gray day.

Walking inside, I find the hospital's calm and sterile ambiance contrasts with the wild rain and branches blowing outside. Still holding onto her tummy, Maria follows me through the maze of white hallways. The scent of antiseptic hangs in the air as we follow the arrows to the Emergency Room check-in.

The clerk looks at Maria, holding her stomach, and says, "Pregnant?"

Maria nods. "I fell, and I'm worried about the baby."

The clerk waves her toward the elevator. "Go up to the OB Unit, and they'll see you there."

I want to yell at the clerk to be nicer and offer her a wheelchair, but I hold my tongue. The clerk isn't being rude. *I'm being extra-sensitive* with the woman I love, so I guide her to the elevator.

Upstairs, I sit on the uncomfortable green chairs and grab a Woman's Day magazine from 1993 to read about how to bake a chocolate sour cream cake in the microwave oven, or "science oven," as the article calls it.

Maria peeks out at me from the doorway in a blue hospital gown. "Jackie, I'm good so far. They're going to do an ultrasound. Will you come with me?"

"Yes." *With her wide eyes and quivering lips, I'd agree to give her my kidney!* I stand, and the nurse walks us across the hall into the ultrasound exam room.

We enter the small room with an exam table, weird cushioned wedges, and the giant machine. The technician, a middle-aged woman with kind eyes, motions for Maria to lie on the examination table, and she dims the light as she explains the procedure. I stand by Maria's side with my hand intertwined in hers for support.

The ultrasound machine comes to life, emitting a soft glow and hum. The room is dark and quiet as she positions herself while the woman lifts her gown and squeezes goo onto her lower abdomen.

I squeeze Maria's hand and smooth her hair, tucking the stray dark strands behind her ear.

The doctor, entering the room, says in a soothing voice, honed from her years of practicing in Homer, "I'm Doctor Lou. I'll check on the baby and let you know how everything looks today."

She's kind and experienced as she moves the ultrasound wand over Maria's little belly. The image of the gray moving form begins to take shape on the monitor.

It's a tiny miracle!

I thank god it's moving, and the doctor is smiling confidently, clicking the mouse and noting odd locations in the image.

Maria's eyes are fixated on the swirling image on the screen. She exhales and smiles at me, her eyes bright.

I'm captivated by the tiny flickering image on the monitor, a slight movement that means so much. The baby is a beacon of hope in this storm for Maria, and I'm melting inside, watching Maria's happiness.

"There's the baby," the doctor says, pointing to the screen. "Strong and healthy, just like we want to see."

Relief floods Maria's face, and her tight shoulders drop with the news. I squeeze her hand, our connection strengthening with the joy of witnessing the new life.

"I am going to take some pictures and measurements while you're here. Is that okay?"

Maria nods.

"I didn't see your chart. Is this your first prenatal visit?" the doctor asks.

"Yes. I've been busy," she explains.

"Well, your little one won't slow you down, but I do want you to come in for check-ups every month until we get you a doctor, okay?"

Maria squeezes my hand and nods to the doctor. She looks at me, her eyes shining with love and excitement. "Thank you for being here with me," she whispers.

I smile, my heart full. "Always," I reply, leaning down to watch the screen with the jellybean bouncing.

Surprisingly, I blink back wetness as I feel my eyes filling with tears of joy at seeing the baby. I'm relieved for Maria and amazed at the image.

Maria smiles and squeals, with the doctor zooming in on the image and pointing out the blobby parts for us, providing us with tangible proof of the miracle inside her.

"The flickering there is the heart. Very strong! I'll turn up the volume so you can hear it."

She turns the volume on, and we listen to the fast rhythm of the baby's heart.

Maria's eyes spring with tears of happiness, and I squeeze her hand reassuringly.

The doctor prints two ultrasound pictures and hands them to Maria—*the baby's first pictures.*

"Excellent. The ultrasound is perfect. Everything is within a healthy range," she says, the sound of the little, beating heart dancing through the room.

"Would you and your partner like to know the baby's gender while you're here? I got a good look." She turns with her eyebrows raised.

She mistakenly thinks we're a couple—and I don't mind one bit. *I did just admit my love to her on the ride here.*

"Yes, we would," Maria says instead of correcting her. With a smile, she looks at me, her eyes still glistening.

I exchange glances with her, a silent acknowledgment of our shared feelings and this fantastic miracle we are witnessing.

"In sixteen weeks, you will be welcoming your daughter into the world," she announces with a smile and pats Maria's shoulder.

Maria's mouth opens without sound, and her eyes widen with wonder.

"Maria—"

A nurse interrupts, popping her head into the exam room, and we blink at the brightly lit intrusion.

"Did you hear? That boat captain missing in the storm has been found," she says.

With that atomic bomb, our newfound happiness shatters.

I fumble for my phone, seeing seven missed calls from Boris.

Maria looks stunned.

"I have to go," Maria says, quickly sitting up and rushing out of the room without saying anything to the doctor or me.

Chapter 12

Maria

Under the ominous sky, I step carefully over the slippery boards of the docks going to the Coast Guard dock. I clutch the edges of my jacket tighter, attempting to shield myself from the biting cold, but it chills me to the bone as I look over the bay, waiting for the Coast Guard boat's arrival.

With the reports of finding Cole over the marine radio, community members are crowded on the dock, waiting to see a miracle–Cole, back from the dead. People patted my shoulders and murmured well wishes, clearing a path and making room for me as I walked to the end of the dock.I stand in front, Jackie is behind me, and my employees—*Cole's employees*–and the community mingling around me.

The wooden planks on the dock creak with each person's arrival, and time moves slowly as we watch the boat coming in, but it's too far away to distinguish anyone on the deck. I glance around at the mass of people who've come out to the docks despite the terrible weather.

I spot Boris, who gives me an encouraging wink. I see an unfamiliar person with a camera and notepad in his hand, which I assume is the offending reporter Jackie told me about. *I'll avoid him.*

A figure pushes forward, emerging from the crowd, a silhouette against the gray backdrop–*Ben*. His smirk and hard eyes cut through the optimistic chatting of the people around me.

I tighten my grip on the edges of my jacket, bracing myself for whatever venom he will spew at me. Jackie's hand finds mine and holds tight.

"Well, well, if it isn't the grieving widow," Ben says, his words dripping with malice. "Looks like you'll have to cancel that funeral and hold off on selling the business or spending your big life insurance payout. Poor you."

His taunts slice through the air like icy knives, and I cringe. I bite my tongue, refusing to let his cruelty cause a rise out of me. I remain still and quiet. I've faced the worst storms, *literally,* and I won't let Ben's bitterness make me cry or steal my attention away from my husband's return.

Jackie growls, "Go away, Ben. We don't have time for your nonsense."

He glares at her. "Cole won't want to see *you* here–*the person sleeping with his wife, trying to be his replacement.*"

Boris grabs Ben and says, "Sorry folks, looks like my friend had more to drink than he can handle." Ben gives a forced laugh and nods to me that he has it under control.

Ben quiets with Boris now babysitting him. The big Russian hand is a vise grip on Ben's shoulder as he is led towards the back of the crowd.

I smile back at Boris and give him a slight nod to thank him for helping.

Ben's right, though. I don't want Cole's first sight to be me holding the hand of his business competitor. Despite the comfort Jackie's presence gives me, I release her hand and step away from her. She understands the hint and sensing my intention, she takes a step back.

Cutting through the drizzle and fog, the huge Coast Guard boat appears and approaches the dock from the stormy waters of Kachemak Bay.

"There it is!" Someone from the crowd shouts, and we all watch the arrival of the red and white Coast Guard boat in silent anticipation. It cuts through the waves, a beacon of promise in the enormous gray ocean. The Coasties jump off the boat, springing to action in their heavy weather-worn gear to secure the ship to the dock in front of us.

My heart races, and my stomach clenches; uncertainty and dread mixed with excitement and hope. I haven't seen Cole yet.

Lieutenant Johnson, with Sergeant Wong, steps from the deck and approach me with solemn expressions. I still don't see any sign of Cole, and everyone behind me is silent, waiting to hear the news.

Wong sets a heavy bag on the dock next to me and pulls it open to reveal a familiar object—a life jacket. *Cole's life jacket*!

My breath catches in my tight throat, and for a moment, time freezes. Johnson picks up the torn and battered orange life jacket and hands it to me to examine. He locks eyes with mine, and that is all the confirmation he needs to confirm his suspicions are correct. This is the life jacket that Cole was wearing when the storm took him from me 16 days ago.

I step forward and clutch it in both hands, holding it in silence with unanswered questions haunting my dry, trembling lips.

"That's all we found," Lieutenant Johnson says to answer the questions in my pleading eyes. The words slicing through the hanging silence on the dock. He clears his throat and continues, "I'm sorry for your loss."

Loss? The word reverberates through me. A tear rolls down my cheek. I stare at the life jacket I grasp, my knuckles white and fingers leaving indents on the sides of it.

What? "Where's Cole?" I whisper and divert my eyes around the men to look at their boat.

Lieutenant Johnson sighs. Sergeant Wong steps closer to me, removes his hat, and I shift my focus to his concerned eyes. "Ma'am, we found his life jacket adrift on the other side of the bay. I'm afraid that's all we found."

His words are kind but firm. The crowd's mood on the dock becomes solemn.

I shake my head. NO—*People said the Coasties found him*. "No... no, it can't be. He's... he's still out there somewhere. You have to keep l ooking!"

Lieutenant Johnson touches my hand to remove the life jacket from my grip. I look up from the life jacket and refuse to let my fingers release it. He shakes his head and leaves the life vest in my clutches. "We are lucky to find anything. He's already been declared dead. I'm sorry, but he's gone. We are not wasting any more manpower on this cas e."

I look, pleading inside for them to be wrong, as Jackie steps beside me and puts her arm around me to comfort me.

My eyes once again look to Sergeant Wong. He frowns at Johnson, who's already returning to the boat. "We did our best, but the ocean and the tides we have here can be unforgiving. There's no chance of his survival. I'm truly sorry. Cole is... lost at sea."

My fingers trace the lifejacket's fabric. Jackie squeezes my other hand as I look out into the bay.

"Lost at sea." I faintly hear my own voice repeat the phrase.

The people on the dock are silent. The only sound is my quiet sobs as the reality of Cole's fate sinks in.

I thought I'd come to terms with Cole being gone, but the radio announcement and waiting on the dock in anticipation with everyone's support rekindled the spark of hope hidden in my heart that was holding on to the belief that Cole was alive. *He was coming back, and everything would return to what it was before.*

I weep for Cole's irrevocable absence and the shattering of my dream of our family, now sinking to the ocean's depths with him. The grief at the realization of that loss came pouring out of me.

"Once again, I'm truly sorry for your loss," Sgt. Wong offers his condolences.

With Wong retreating to the ship, I stand alone on the dock, overcome by the heart-wrenching truth. Jackie, steadfast by my side, grips my hand, silent support as I navigate the emotional turmoil of grief. My body shakes with sobs as the grief relentlessly pounds me.

Others on the dock share in my sorrow, their sympathetic murmurs mingling with the heavy air of disappointment.

"Let's go, everyone," Boris declares. "First round's on me."

The crowd disperses, and their expectations of a dramatic rescue celebration quickly change to disappointment. Left alone, I hug the cold life jacket and stare at the unforgiving Alaskan water.

"I suppose the search has come to an end. It's over," I murmur, turning to Jackie. Her nod conveys understanding and compassion.

My tears, indistinguishable from the raindrops, blur my vision. The numb fog over the bay has somehow penetrated my mind.

Cole's absence echoes in the stillness of the harbor, a cruel reality sinking in—*I'll never again see the man I married. All the warm memories of our whirlwind online romance and late-night musings of our future together, the last memory of him is here—this cold life vest and this dark ocean.*

Jackie enfolds me in a tight hug, the life jacket slipping from my grasp to the cold dock. Her murmured promises offer little solace in my numb heart.

Ben, a vulture circling, snatches up the life jacket, his words dripping with suspicion. "This doesn't look fishy at all."

His toxicity washes over me, but I'm beyond feeling. His rudeness is futile–there's nothing left inside me for him to destroy.

Unfazed, he continues, "No need to stress. I'll take over the business. I will let you stay in my quaint little town. No need to go back to whatever third-world country you came from."

His words, like empty shells, aren't penetrating my grief-stricken armor. I lean into Jackie, seeking strength, scanning the desolate dock for an escape from his verbal assault.

Jackie, my anchor in this storm, shoots him an icy glare, her silent support louder than any words. She tightens her grip, offering quiet sanctuary against the onslaught.

Ben's red eyes falter momentarily. I see he's also disappointed and grieving. I wish he'd stop lashing out at me and allow himself to cry and let the grief out instead of bottling it up.

Nestled in Jackie's embrace, her jacket protects us from the biting cold surrounding us.

"He's all talk and no bite," Jackie whispers, reassuringly calming my shattered soul.

A voice from our Hopper crew cuts through the tension. "We're here for you, Maria. Get outta here, Ben. Cole would be ashamed of you!"

With a shove from his coworker, Ben stumbles away, his face cold, without sympathy for me or support from his friends. He storms off, the echo of his retreating footsteps lost in the cold.

"Come on, let's go and share a drink at The Salty Dawg in Cole's memory," a sympathetic voice offers, an invitation signaling support for me.

Jackie nods to him and takes my hand.

"Thank you," I manage in a shaky voice. I squeeze Jackie's hand as we move away from the desolate dock, leaving behind not just Ben but the hope I brought.

We march to The Salty Dawg along with the crowd of friendly community members. My employees and the town folks buzz around us, creating a migrating pack, moving together in the rainy Alaskan evening.

The wooden doors creak as I thrust them open, a warm heat rushing to greet us. Heads swivel, eyes meeting mine, nods of acknowledgment, and small waves welcome me as I enter. The bar is bathed in a dim, amber glow, and I notice a man swiftly vacating his cozy stool, offering it to me with a grin.

In this friendly pub, a haven from the stormy weather, community members are eager to celebrate Cole's return and have started an impromptu commemoration party for Cole. They turn around to acknowledge our arrival, and people holler *hello*, send drinks, and wave to me. No one is frowning or gossiping. Their faces contain a shared sorrow and a welcome to me.

As I settle onto the stool, a hushed ambiance descends. Glasses clink, but the sound is subdued, carrying a respectful cadence. The strangers who once ignored me now clink glasses with me, and Boris refreshes my tea. We gather united by grief and memories of Cole.

Jackie raises her glass first. "To Cole," she declares, her voice resonating over the subdued crowd. "May his spirit find peace on the open ocean he loved."

A cheer erupts, glasses raised in unison. I sip the honey-sweetened peppermint tea, its warmth coursing through me. In this dimly lit sanctuary, surrounded by these familiar faces, my spirit warms and awakens to the comfort of this place and this community.

The night swirls with shared memories and laughter. What once felt cold and unfriendly transforms into an embrace, the community enveloping me and with me in this vulnerable moment.

Jackie remains devoted by my side. As the night unfolds, she prompts friends to share tales of Cole, and I hear the kind and entertaining. Employees share jokes, and new stories of my late husband emerge as I learn more about him. This beer-fueled tribute at the local pub on the ocean he loved is a suitable memorial for Cole.

I imagine Cole's grin from above, approving of this unconventional celebration.

". . . And he storms into the office, bellowing, *There's a brown bear in the bay. . .,*" a friend recounts a tale of Cole encountering a grizzly bear swimming miles from shore. ". . . We thought he'd had one too many beers fishing, but sure enough, the picture on the front page the next day was a massive grizzly swimming across the bay!"

Amidst the flickering lights and shared laughter, I join in. My laughter is a remedy for the tears. Another tale begins, a narrative of Cole hitting a sandbar, and I find myself lost in other people's memories that make me love Cole even more.

Within the walls of the Salty Dawg, the storm may rage outside, but in the company of these people and these stories, there's a calmness. A nostalgic sense of belonging sweeps my mind back to the memories of anticipation of my marriage and arrival to Alaska. I'm glad I'm here. This was my dream.

In the crowded pub, Jackie emerges as an unexpected social planner, seamlessly joining the laughter of the guys and encouraging stories and camaraderie as if she's been their lifelong best friend.

As the night unravels and the last patrons disperse, Jackie guides me back to my little car. The rain has retreated, leaving a calm sea with the sweet, salty wind tousling her blonde hair, a playful dance around her head.

"Maria," Jackie murmurs gently. "You're not alone in this. Your employees, Boris, and the town care. And I'm here for you every step of the way, whenever and whatever you need."

I nod, tears welling in my eyes. The realization that Cole isn't the end of my dreams and our plans. Instead, I'm finding a new path, taking over Cole's business with the support of his employees and Jackie at my side to help me.

Who would have thought this grumpy boat captain would become my friend and help me to create a new dream?

With my community, I confront the unknowns of impending motherhood and business ownership, embracing my new Alaskan life with hope.

"Thank you, Jackie. I appreciate you and without you..." I stumble, words failing to capture the depth of my gratitude.

Jackie's gaze intensifies, reflecting emotions beyond words. The rain subsides, leaving a dampness in the air. She steps closer, her warmth enveloping me.

"Maria," she murmurs tenderly, "I never expected to find someone like you. But here you are. You are strong and courageous. I'm in awe of you."

I shake my head, disbelieving in her words, but she continues.

She takes my shoulders, locking my eyes. "It's true. Cole saw it in you, and I do, too. You'll be an amazing mother and a successful businesswoman, too!"

A nervous laugh escapes me, but her words draw me closer. The salty breeze carries potential, and I see our strong connection mirrored in her soft eyes.

Cupping my cheek, she whispers, "Maria, I care about you more than words can convey. The storm took something precious, but it brought something beautiful into our lives. I love you and want to stand by your side, not just as a friend or a business partner, but as someone who will be there for you always."

A profound silence envelops us, broken only by the gentle lapping of waves. Her sincerity, illuminated by dock lights, creates a cozy halo in the Alaskan night.

She leans in, her lips meeting mine in a tender, light kiss. It promises more but asks for nothing. Her strength and confidence in me quiet everything around us—the rain, the sea, the storm—this unexpected love is the comforting current that mutes all the noise around us.

"I knew you guys were perfect for each other!"

Boris stands outside the Salty Dawg, earning a playful rebuke from Jackie. We exchange a smile, and I rest my forehead against her, feeling her warm lips on my head and her breath against me.

"Boris, you are killing me!" Jackie shouts back at him with a laugh and looks down at me, a twinkle in her eye. "We've got to get back at him soon!"

I smile, rest my forehead against her, and feel her warm lips kiss the top of my head and her breath against me.

"You're not alone, Maria," she repeats to me. She links her fingers in mine and lightly squeezes, her warm signal of caring.

We stand next to my car, the harbor, my business, and the Salty Dawg behind us. We gaze beyond the pier lights to the vast expanse of Kachemak Bay. In the darkness, a warm connection envelops me. Acceptance in the small town, a family beginning with my baby, and Jackie's words make the ocean's reflection of the scattered stars above even more beautiful.

Cole's dreams are still alive in me, our little baby, and Homer.

Despite the darkness, I feel a warm connection here. I found love here. Putting my hand over my tummy, I smile.

Chapter 13

Maria

The phone's shrill ring cuts through the air, jolting me from my thoughts. I glance at the caller ID—*Homer Newspaper*. I take a deep breath and answer, not knowing what to expect after the disappointment on the docks a week ago.

"Hello?" I say tentatively.

The voice on the other end is apologetic. "Maria, this is Elaine from the Homer Newspaper. I want to sincerely apologize for the confusion caused by our earlier article."

"Okay," I say, unsure if this is a fishing expedition to get more dirt to print.

She continues, "We were misled, and we want to set the record straight. Cole's accident is officially reported as just that—an accident. We're retracting the suspicious death story. Again, I am so sorry for the pain this may have caused you."

Relief floods me, and the tension gripping my chest slowly releases its hold. "Thank you," I manage to say, my voice tight with emotion.

The newspaper representative continues, "Ben called us and asked us to kill the story. He admitted he was wrong when giving us the previous information. We are correcting our mistake immediately. Again, I'm truly sorry for any distress this has caused."

I nod, even though she can't see it. "I appreciate this. Thank you for calling."

As the call ends, I hear the familiar chime of my doorbell. *Jackie!*

I rush to open the door. "Here already? I haven't finished getting ready," I say, opening the door to a smiling, friendly face. We have been meeting at the Salty Dawg for drinks and to discuss the Hopper after our workday—*it's an unofficial, scheduled date that leads to dinner and sometimes more.*

"You look drop-dead gorgeous as always! You don't need to change," she says. She gives me a warm smile, handing me a framed picture.

I flip it over and gasp. It is my ultrasound picture, capturing the delicate outline of the not-so-tiny-anymore life growing inside me. I rub my round, growing belly.

"It's beautiful!" I say with tears gathering in my eyes.

She notices my emotions and pulls me into a comforting hug. "Come on. Let's talk shop and grab a pizza on the way."

Wiping away a tear, I manage a grateful smile. "Thank you, Jackie. You have a knack for being perfect and unexpected at the same time!"

She chuckles, pulling away. "Well, I've got something else that you'll love." Jackie reaches into a bag and reveals the most peculiar bouquet I've ever seen.

"What on earth is that?" I ask, examining the concoction of shredded pickles, bleeding beets, and alien-like poking out made with root vegetables.

She laughs heartily. "Sally at Glacier Cafe made this for Boris. Remember, a little payback bouquet for his antics. Isn't it hilarious?"

I can't help but join in her laughter. "Yes! He's going to be surprised."

"Sally has a weird talent for revenge bouquets, right?"

"She does. Let's stay on her good side." We exchange amused glances, contemplating the bizarre creation.

After a moment, Jackie nudges me playfully. "Come on, let's go deliver this monstrosity to Boris at the Salty Dawg. It's sure to be the talk of the town and I need to feed you."

"Good plan. And I just got an odd call. I'll tell you all about it," I say, skipping out the door with her.

Arm in arm, we leave my house, ready for our evening date in our small town.

Chapter 14

Jackie

"Aren't we going to the Salty Dawg?" Maria asks me as I drive over the frosty road to the much-anticipated baby shower.

Boris offered to host it weeks ago after the funeral because he thought it would give Maria a much-needed distraction. But with Maria's busy schedule: winterizing the boats, making the Fall schedule, prenatal appointments, and the funeral last month, we are *finally* going to celebrate this new life she's creating. And Boris planned the *perfect* party. After all, Maria deserves cake and fun after her crazy-stressful summer.

He consulted me about the party plans, and *I can't wait to see how much she loves her party!*

"Nope. You'll see," I tease as I drive past the Salty Dawg and towards Mariner Park on the end of the wintery Homer Spit.

The fires and brightly dressed festival-goers illuminate the Homer Spit, creating a mystical atmosphere. This is Boris' surprise, throwing Maria's baby shower during Homer's big community art event, the Burning Basket Festival. This is Homer's fall time, collaborative art celebration to connect with our change of the beautiful Alaskan seasons.

Maria's eyes light up with curiosity. "What's going on?"

I smile at her excitement and explain, "Every year, we create a massive, natural woven basket. This takes days of working together and creates a visual artwork with everyone's positive intentions. It's a big deal around here."

I hope the event will help her feel a genuine connection to the community and, more importantly, help her find closure and accept the changes in her life. Boris, myself, and the community have meticulously planned a unique baby shower during the festival. The excitement is palpable as everyone eagerly anticipates her and the baby into our community.

As I open the truck door for her, a chorus of cheers erupts from the beach, "She's here!" But there's another surprise waiting.

Ben, her cousin-in-law, steps forward, a solemn expression on his face. He looks down, puts his hands in his pockets, and then looks at her. "Maria, I... I need to apologize. I know things have been tough, and I haven't been the most supportive. I'm truly sorry for any pain I may have caused."

His sincere apology hangs in the air, and Maria, touched by his unexpected gesture, nods appreciatively.

"I was angry with grief. I don't have any brothers and I've never lost anyone before. I looked up to Cole and it didn't make sense how the best sailor I know could be lost at sea. I took it out on you, and I was stupid. I'm sorry."

"Thank you, Ben," she says, touching his arm. "You know you're still my family, and I want you in our lives."

I see a tear start to leak out of the corner of Ben's eye. He quickly looks down and nods. "I'd like that a lot."

"Of course," she smiles at him, and I love her ability to forgive and accept him so quickly.

She adds, "Someone has to teach this kiddo how to hunt and fish. That'll be your job, Cousin Ben."

I smile at the family reunion, but I still regret not beating him to one inch of his life on the dock when he knocked her down. *I'm keeping my eye on him, just in case.*

Boris interrupts, rushing to greet Maria and escort her to her special party on the blustery beach.

"I have a cup of tea for you and a cake–a *whole cake, just for you*," he gushes.

Inside, the heated tent is jubilant, filled with Alaskan wildflowers, fairy lights, and the smells of Filipino dishes everyone learned to make to surprise her at her baby shower. The community is gathered, each face reflecting support and joy for Maria.

Stepping inside, a wave of emotions crashes over her and she smiles so broadly I think her face will crack. The unexpected shower of love with the potluck foods everyone proudly share with her makes both of our eye's water. I'm as surprised as Maria with what Boris planned. My heart swells at seeing her so happy.

Boris takes the small stage in the tent, his presence commanding. "Ladies and gentlemen, tonight is not just about celebrating new life. It's about embracing family, community, and cake–the ingredients of a happy life!"

Applause ripples through the tent, and I exchange a glance with Maria, her eyes reflecting the same astonishment.

"Before the main festival events, I'm hosting this small–" the crowd in the enormous circus-sized tent laughs, "baby shower for our lovely new Homer-ite, Maria!"

The crowd cheers, the baby shower begins with tea and scones circulate, and laughter dancing in the air. Soon, the tent fills with the sweet aroma of happiness, a mélange of foreign spices, Earl Grey, chocolate, and coconut cake.

As Maria basks in the celebration, the gifts she opens are thoughtful and heartwarming. She opens hand-knitted wool socks to provide warmth for the upcoming winter and a tiny snowsuit for the baby's first winter.

Boris gives me a wink and hands her an elaborate box of chocolates.

"Do not eat that!" I cry, and everyone laughs, looking into the delicious-looking box that is *not* hand-dipped chocolates. Boris gave her a box of intricately decorated moose droppings.

"Payback! Pickled radish tulips, that was horrible!"

Amid the joyous atmosphere, Cole's elementary teacher steps forward with a set of books for the baby. The carefully selected titles are a sweet reminder of Cole.

Maria's eyes glisten with gratitude as the local bakery contributes a big basket of cookware and recipes. Included is Cole's favorite recipe–blueberry sourdough pancakes–with a sourdough starter.

"Jackie, you're going to make this for me, right?" she teases me as I'm becoming our breakfast cook, letting her sleep in.

"You're the boss!" I reply with a wink.

Ben steps forward, holding a small box. "I thought I'd give you a gift from Cole," he says. He presents the sentimental gift—a pair of Cole's baby shoes and a baby book, including Maria and Cole's wedding picture on the first page.

I guess I will take back wanting to beat him up.

She hugs the tiny shoes to her big belly and then hugs Ben for the poignant gifts.

Maria opens the last gift with a squeal and a heartfelt thank you, displaying and gushing over the unique treasure, a Baby Hopper Captain's outfit handmade by an older neighbor. She holds it up and smiles radiantly as she runs her fingers gently across the gold embroidered anchors.

"For your future Captain," she says with a twinkle in her eye.

There's a shout outside, and Boris announces, "It's time to walk the contemplation labyrinth to start the Burning Basket festival, everyone."

I help Maria up from the chair, her round belly throwing off her balance. She waddles through the tent to the beach outside. Before she can start winding through the labyrinth to view the massive basket, people stop congratulating her, hugging her and thrusting more gifts into her arms.

I graciously hold the gifts, my arms quickly filling as we approach the massive basket sculpture.

"This is amazing," she breathes, her eyes shining and radiantly smiling.

A man wearing a hotdog on his head offers her a hotdog, and she accepts it while studying the twenty-foot-high, colorful woven basket structure surrounded by fur-covered fire dancers performing to an orchestra of kazoo-blowing unicorns. Children and dogs run around the basket while we watch and soak in the positive vibes.

Her eyes get even wider. She says nothing, glowing and looking more stunning than I've ever seen her.

I understand the feeling. *Homer is a pretty special community.*

When I first visited the Burning Basket Festival, I thought it'd be a hippy-fest. But it's a crazy infectious vibe of fun, family, and community that's indescribably enchanting.

She looks at me and laughs, taking a big bite of her hot dog as another person sprays bacon cheese whiz on it for her. Her laugh turns to a gleeful giggle, licking the cheese whiz and swaying to the party music.

She points to the tables of paper cranes and pens, her eyes full of questions.

I say, "You're supposed to write a message of remembrance, a secret that you'd like to let free of allowing more positive intentions into your being. You place the message in the basket."

"What happens after?"

"At midnight, we watch the basket set ablaze, and the community gathers to celebrate," I explain.

Boris appears and adds, "Jackie's simplifying it. It's a symbol of letting go of the past and embracing the present. The natural beauty of the art, along with watching it disappear, reminds us to cherish the moments we have, the impermanence of life, and the strong bond of community."

I hit his shoulder, "Thanks for the man-splaining. I have a fancy chocolate you should try. . ." I lift my eyebrow at him, and he laughs with us.

She releases her grip on my hand to walk to the table. And I leave her to write her message and enjoy the festival. I turn, looking at the late fall, snowy beach with driftwood sculptures sparkling with frost overlooking the bay.

Raven, the local artist behind the festival's conception, climbs part of the basket to stand tall above the crowd in her brightly knitted hat. The crowd gathers to hear her.

"This year's Basket Burn is called Create, and it's a Basket of Remembrance and Unburdening that, as a community, we brought into being. Our inaugural basket took form in 2004, and every year, with the collective love, support, and hands of All, we *Create* and become creators in this community festival." Raven's voice conveys the importance and community connection of this event.

As the basket towers above, people crafted it from the gathered materials—alders, spruce, fireweed, and grasses–all intricately woven together. Raven continues, her words weaving seamlessly with the essence of the festival.

"We are on a journey, as individuals, as creators and destroyers of the tangible and intangible parts of our lives. We come together to *create!* This year's basket, *Create*, means to conceive, design, and construct," she declares with passion.

Maria rejoins me, her hand finding mine. She whispers, "It's truly a magical experience. I've never been a part of something like this. It's *perfect!*"

As Raven concludes her speech, her words resonate, carrying the festival's spirit. The crowd cheers, and the festival takes over with music, dancing, and people's joyful noises.

Maria says, "That was a beautiful speech. Thank you for bringing me here and for helping organize all of this. This really is amazing and I'm happy to be a part of it."

I bask in the joy radiating from Maria as she admires the celebration Boris and the town organized for her. "Boris and everyone helped me plan to make this perfect for you. Homer is special, and you are a special addition to our town." I wrap my arms around her, her happy tears tickling my neck.

"Thank you, Jackie," she says, stepping back and rubbing her lower back, a hint of fatigue showing.

With a nod toward the beach, I suggest, "I have a good spot to sit and watch from. I'll get you more cake, too."

Walking to the beach, I spread a blanket and cushions over the light layer of snow. Maria lies down on her side, watching the festivities, and I settle beside her, putting a wool blanket over us. She snuggles into me, and we revel in the festivities while awaiting the big basket burn.

As the countdown begins, a fire is lit, gradually transforming into a beautiful, flickering dance reminiscent of the earlier fire dancers' graceful movements.

I turn my gaze to Maria. Her eyes reflect the dancing flames. "I'm glad to share this with you."

She looks up into my eyes, her happiness evident. "I'm so happy here and with you."

My message, etched into the paper engulfed by the fire, was a promise to care for Maria, her baby, and Cole's legacy. I wrote down the words containing the resentment I've carried for too long for Cole and over our business rivalry. I'm determined to let go of bitterness, making room for love and new beginnings.

I'm not sure what Maria wrote in her message, but her eyes shimmer with tears as the basket and our messages burn, released into the night. I hope she's filled with as much joy and love as I feel. Squeezing her hand, I hold her close as we witness the transformation.

She turns away from the fire, her body facing mine, the glow illuminating her face in the evening's starry darkness.

Leaning down, I softly kiss the nape of her neck.

Maria looks up at me with tenderness, and we share a slow, deep kiss in front of the fire. A sense of contentment washes over us as our messages turn to ash, drifting into the night sky. The past no longer constrains us, and the future holds boundless possibilities. The warmth of the fire fans, the passionate heat between us.

Suddenly, Maria winces, her hand gripping mine with unexpected strength. The warmth of the fire is momentarily overshadowed by the warmth spreading between her legs.

"Jackie," she gasps with a mix of surprise and urgency. "I think... I think my water just broke."

Epilogue: Maria
ONE YEAR LATER

My life is in a comfortable rhythm, the ocean's rocking. The crisp Alaskan air carries the scent of saltwater and the promise of a beautiful night on the water of Homer, Alaska. I stand on the deck of our houseboat, gazing at the picturesque evening view.

Collette Stormy nestles in her baby carrier against my chest, her curious eyes absorbing the world. Beside me, Jackie adjusts her boating gear and then playfully pulls a soft brown beanie with the Carhartt patch over little Leti's head.

"Look at her, Maria. Our little boater," Jackie says, a smile playing on her lips as she clips a life jacket over me and the carrier. My hands are filled with essential baby gear, a thermos of tea, and a container of lumpia.

Leti giggles, excited by the prospect of being on the water and her favorite people doting on her.

The harbor bustles with activity—Sammy swimming, fishermen returning, seagulls in chaotic flight, and the Salty Dawg standing tall against Kachemak Bay.

"You're not coming with us, Sammy," Jackie hollers. "She scares off my fish and steals the spotlight. Tonight is about our family," she grumbles to me.

I kiss her grumpy lips and respond, "You can get more fish, and Sammy is family."

Leti giggles in agreement, a spit bubble causing a gleeful squeak. Jackie salutes me, wiping Leti's chin. "You're right, Captain Maria."

I laugh, the sound blending with the waves against our boat, *Miss Maria*. "I'm always right, Captain Jackie. Our little first mate here seems eager to enjoy the bay, too."

I turn the key, letting Jackie untangle the lines as she steps onto the boat. Guiding us into the bay, I'm confident in navigating my boat after getting my boating license shortly after Leti's birth.

Known as *Captain Safety* to our employees, I continuously check radios, emergency beacons, and life jackets. I even ferry people across the bay occasionally. With enhanced safety measures, I'm confident on the water, ensuring Homer Harbor Hopper is the safest operation.

As we set out into the bay, I tease my grumpy partner, "Are you ready for another perfect night in your sunshine-filled life?"

Jackie looks at me and the giggling baby at the helm. She winks back, her grumpy facade crumbling into a grin.

Reflecting on the past year's events, we head to the Burning Basket Festival, celebrating the transformative power of community. Enjoying the festival on my new boat with our baby is the perfect way to commemorate the past year and our community.

Approaching Mariner Park, the grand woven basket stands out on the beach. The scent of burning wood mingles with laughter and joy.

"Here we are, Leti," I whisper to our daughter, gently rocking her in the carrier. "Our first Burning Basket Festival as a family."

Jackie reaches over, holding my hand. Collette coos in response, sensing the significance. The night sky shines clear, stars illuminating the fire's soft glow over friends, neighbors, and fellow Homer-ites on the beach.

Cozy on the bench in the covered cockpit, we snuggle together, enjoying the symphony of light and sound—a celebration of letting go and embracing life.

"This is nice, but next year, we need to be on the beach dancing with little Leti around the fire," Jackie whispers, careful not to wake the now-sleeping baby.

"Okay," I laugh. "But she's a little young to be next to a fire inferno, don't you think?"

"She'll be ready next year." Jackie nuzzles my ear. I lay my head on my favorite spot as she tucks her chin over me, wrapping me in her arms.

Her hand finds mine as the last embers rise. Her hand speaks volumes, squeezing mine, and she wraps her body warmly around me and our sleeping baby.

Sploosh! The ocean next to us bubbles and crashes. Sammy appears, splashing beside the boat, a familiar silhouette against the moonlit bay. And I laugh in delight.

"Don't encourage her," Jackie grumbles.

"Ah, Sammy wants to join the party, too. Now the whole family is here."

I feel Jackie's smile behind me. Snuggling into her arms, I listen to the tiny breaths at my chest and the playful splashes in the water as the night ends under the crisp Alaskan sky. The echoes of laughter and the scent of the sea surround us—*an Alaskan family*. We float on the waves, love encompassing us, with our sea otter splashing around the boat to scare off the fish.

Smiling at the sky, I imagine Cole looking down, happy with his daughter, his wife, and his legacy in Homer.

This is the dream I chased when I ventured across the world to a little town in Alaska. The sweet sound of music floating across the water, flickering light and shadows of dancers around the fire, my family in my arms, gently rocking on the ocean.

I am an Alaskan.

If you loved Maria and Jackie's sapphic adventure, then you'll love Chloe and Sterling in *Wilderness Rescue: Scoring Love.*
CHECK IT OUT HERE.

Discover the books in the *Wilderness Rescue* series.
CHECK IT OUT HERE.
Keep reading to enjoy the next book.

Wilderness Rescue: Scoring Love
Chapter 1: Chloe

Is this what kills me? My chunky calf.

My whole body shivers, and my brain goes into overdrive, figuring out how to get out of the embarrassing, life-threatening situation. I gasp, bending over the ice, trying not to fall.

Sugar Flakes! My leg is not budging!

My brown leather boot is wedged solidly inside the slushy hole on Chena Lake's walking path. Freezing water seeps over the top of my boot, soaking my wool sock, which undoubtedly accelerates my dangerous predicament.

Stupid, ice fishing hole!

The city of Fairbanks doesn't stock trout in this lake, so only an idiot would ice fish here. The *idiot* drilled his fishing hole in the cleared walking path.

I shift my position, squatting to take the weight off my left leg, and using my arms, I try pulling my stuck leg out.

My unstuck, dry boot slips as I cry out, and crash, falling hard on my butt. Unfortunately, my leg is still imprisoned in the perfectly calf-sized round opening.

Panic grips me like icy hands squeezing as I fumble in the morning darkness of the remote, lonely lake. The stark realization hits—I'm alone, *trapped,* and my leg will frostbite soon in the freezing lake, and worse—*if I don't get out, I could freeze to death!*

A shaky breath escapes me, the frigid air clouding it, blinding me, and intensifying my trembling and squirming. Desperation sets in. *At least*, I console myself, *there are no broken bones.* Yet, the biting cold could mask a numb, hidden injury beneath the thick ice.

"UGH! Oomph!" I wrestle, attempting to free my leg from the lake's death grip on my soft calf. Desperation fuels my efforts as I struggle to remove my boot, but the zipper is below the ice, and my hand can't fit into the narrow hole to unzip the boot.

The cute, furry leather boots are one-of-a-kind, made by my university Professor of Native Arts friend as a go-out-and-enjoy-single-life divorce gift last winter. I've never found sexy boots that'd fit over my calves. These hug my small ankles and curves to make my legs look stunning, and they're Alaska-warm. They *were* my lucky boots!

My butt is freezing to the ice as I yank my leg in vain. An unsettling thought creeps in—I wonder if I'll be able to pry my frozen backside off the ice once my leg is finally freed.

My anxiety increases with the white breath cloud growing around me, urging me to hurry. Leaning back, I rock and push against the unyielding ice with trembling arms. Adrenaline courses through me, lending extra strength, but the frozen trap holds firm.

Either my leg is swelling, or the hole is freezing tighter around it because my calf is even more unmovable than seconds ago.

I reach into my pocket to call for help, and I don't feel my phone.

Of course, I don't.

My phone was dead, so I left it charging in my car while I meandered around the lake, hoping to catch a morning display of the northern lights. The temperature and sky are perfect for the aurora borealis to appear. I need the inspiring color palette for the art design I'm painting this afternoon in my university pottery studio.

Ugh! So much for a refreshing hike, inspiring view, and enjoying my morning before going to the cafe.

"Help! Anyone?" I shout across the quiet lake, holding my breath, waiting for a response.

Don't freak out, Chloe! I pep-talk myself. If only I told Kate when I was coming into the cafe, she'd have noticed I was missing. But since I help out before classes with no schedule, no one knows I'm missing.

Is this the reason married people live longer? They have someone to miss them and send out a search party.

I shake my head and exhale a heavy cloud around my face. If I were still married, my husband would be at the rink or an out-of-town game and not notice me missing anyway.

Okay, I'll just have to MacGyver the crap out of this situation, Man vs. Wild style. What can I improvise to save myself?

I wriggle uncomfortably on the frigid lake, trying to ignore the biting cold as I reach inside my deep pockets to take stock of my potentially life-saving tools. I empty them onto the ice in front of me.

The quick inventory reveals a mishmash of items – some practical, some utterly ridiculous.

My fingers close around a half-eaten granola bar. The crumbly, pungent salmon blueberry bar triggers amusement and disgust. I didn't finish Kate's new unique cafe breakfast bar because of its challenging flavors of fish and sweet berries this early in the morning.

I love my friend Kate, and kudos to her avant-garde culinary creativity, but even if my survival depended on it, I'm not eating the gross breakfast bar. My cat wouldn't touch it, and she eats kale chips.

With a half-hearted shrug, I fumble for the next item to surely save me: a crumpled, forgotten to-do list. I unfold it, revealing the comedy of my daily tasks.

Buy catnip for Mr. Whiskers, learn to juggle, & find lost sock's soulmate, milk, gluten-free double-stuffed Oreos.

I crumple the list. I should learn to juggle–it'd help me relieve stress, and then I'd have a hobby aside from pottery, drinking coffee, and university classes.

Really, Chloe?

I giggle at the absurdity of my priorities in the face of potential frostbite or dying because my phone was dead. Why wasn't that on the list—*charge phone*?

Next up, a paperclip. There's no help there. I move on, desperate to find the ice auger in my pocket, *which I've surely stashed and forgotten about and will totally save me.*

I chew my lower lip, and my chest heaves with fear.

I often carry my pottery tool, a fettling knife. It's for smoothing edges and is pretty dull but stainless steel. I could chip away the ice with it.

No such luck!

I pull out a small bag of rubber ducks. I shake my head at the cute army of rubber ducks the size of my pinky nail.

Why do I have these? Maybe I had grand plans for a rubber ducky project. My famous ex got all our friends in the break-up, so Kate is my only friend, and she's not having a baby shower. She's not even hetero or bi-like me. She's Fairbanks Team Lesbian–the captain. Thus, there is no chance of a pregnancy!

I can't help laughing, imagining using the duckies to free my leg.

Then, a two-inch disco ball keychain falls onto the ice. *Because, you know, every Alaskan adventurer must carry a disco ball in the wilds.* I ponder the sheer randomness of my pocket contents, forgetting my icy predicament.

My brain distracts me from the dire situation, thinking *I'd learn a lot about a person based solely on what's in her pockets.* Maybe I should suggest to Kate that we ask our dates' to empty their pockets. No ice auger, no second date!

I giggle. There's no way I'm suggesting that to Kate, though. She'd take it as an open invitation that I want to date again—which *I don't.* She believes she's a cafe connoisseur of relationships, and I'd be scheduled for a date every night for the year.

Focus, Chloe! How am I going to get out?

I need something to break the ice around my boot.

Channeling my inner Alaskan and pushing my fear into survival-rage mode, I clutch the disco ball keychain in my fist and punch its glittery awesomeness into the ice surrounding my leg. With surprisingly effective whacking, the disco ball makes ice chips fly, sending sparkles across the lake.

The ridiculous disco ball-cracking rhythm compels me to sing.

"Stayin' Alive. Stayin Alive, aye aye aye aye, Staying Allllllliiiiiiiiiiiiii-iiveeee."

If I'm stuck in a frozen lake with a disco ball to save myself, this is the most appropriate disco-style ice-chipping song.

The ice around my boot remains solid, and I'm not making headway. And surprisingly, even my loud singing isn't cracking the ice. The situation is hilariously dire.

I continue my disco punching and disco chorus.

As fear threatens to ruin my melody, a figure glides up on the lake's cleared skating rink.

The woman soars, a graceful figure skater but wearing chunky men's hockey skates.

She's more surreal than the rubber duckies spread around me. She has blond hair, crystal-blue eyes, long legs, and a radiant smile—*my hallucination of what an angel looks like*—but wears winter hockey gear instead of a beautiful robe.

I clear my throat, hesitating.

Her eyes, a vivid blue, lock onto mine with intensity, and her lips quirk into a smile.

"Your chorus stopped. I thought I'd come over to make sure disco doesn't die, eh?"

Chapter 2: Sterling

In the frigid air of the ice-covered lake, the hot university student gazes back, her expression deadpan. "Disco will never die," she declares with a broad smile, the cold not diminishing the warm tone of her voice.

I saw an old car with a university parking pass in the deserted lake parking lot and wondered who would share my early morning lake workout. I didn't expect a disco-singing walker.

Our eyes lock, and time freezes. In that instant, a spark ignites, and my smile falters at the magnetic pull of her striking hazel eyes. Her brown curls, a chaotic nest beneath the University of Fairbanks blue beanie, add to her quirky cuteness. She captivates me with her irresistible smile and undefinable something.

My gaze makes it past her bright eyes, with smile lines creasing the edges–she's older than me when I look closer. I scan down from her puffy jacket to her feet—foot! I correct myself. I see the problem.

The disco dream girl's leg is jammed into the rock-solid frozen lake.

"I stepped into an ice fishing hole," she says, following my eyes.

My shoulders drop slightly. After seeing the hottie, I hoped she was another super-fan, puck bunny, stalking me during my morning skating practice. Kissing her would be reasonably easy if she was here to flirt.

It's not a puck bunny–it's simply a singing hottie stuck in the lake. But a damsel in distress might be an easy victory, too.

"You're in luck. I'm definitely the strong hero type." I wink and skate next to her to check out the damage.

She casually sits by the ice fishing hole, with her leg disappearing into the lake. An odd assortment of items is scattered around her like she's choosing this exact moment to organize her junk drawer.

Bizarrely, her strangeness makes her more enticing. My lips part, and my eyes fixate on the lovely curve of her thigh.

Who is this unexpected, gorgeous creature? And thank you, God, for delivering me this goddess!

Instead of freaking out, she's calm, witty, and throwing off enough pheromones to redirect a hockey team. I better save her before someone else swoops in. I tear my gaze off her legs to inspect the lake. No one else is here.

"Is that granola bar for real? A Salmon Blueberry Breakfast bar ... or is it like ... a joke item?"

Her easy laugh rings out across the empty lake.

"I wish it was a joke! I'll tell my friend–maybe she can sell them to lower 48'rs as tourist items."

I recognize the term. Alaskans don't consider themselves part of the larger USA. They are an independent, wildly adventurous breed and, as Harry Potter uses the word Muggles, Alaskans call their lesser counterparts, Lower 48'rs.

She continues, "I was emptying my pockets to free myself, but I haven't figured out how. The bar is from the cafe I was going to after this walk, but ..." She shrugs and points to her leg.

I throw off my heavy gloves and bend down to pull on her leg. "Sorry, may I?"

"Oh, you can have the bar, it's horrible! Taste it, you'll see!"

I close my eyes, press my lips together, and try not to let her distract me from being the hero.

Although, I did enjoy the smoked salmon-flavored shots from last night's playoff party.

"I'm Chloe, by the way," she says seriously, ignoring the emergency of her leg in the frozen lake. She tucks an errant curl into her winter hat with her stubby, paint-smattered finger.

Oh, she's an art student. I love artsy-girls! They're creative and get wild at parties. I've dated at least ten art majors. I'd say that's my type, but I'm an equal-opportunity dater—there's enough of me to go around.

I flash a broader smile, laying on my heroic charm. "Hey, Chloe! I'm Sterling, obviously." I lift my chin and tilt my head at the name on my hockey jersey as if she doesn't know exactly who I am.

Since being recruited and moving here, my face has been on every UAF Nanook Hockey team's social media post and news article. My face is on the "Go Nanook's" posters throughout the university dorms for our playoff games. Also, I was on the paper's front page with, "Sterling to take UAF to the Championship Victory this year!" Then there's the fans–students around campus wear my jersey number, and, of course, being a female right-wing hockey star makes me legendary.

"Goooooo, Nanooks!" she exclaims, mimicking cheerleaders' shaking pompoms with playful enthusiasm.

I smile wider. Chloe's already cheering for me without a hat trick!

But then again, I can't walk through campus without having ten people jump me to say hello and invite me to parties. My only peace is my early morning skating practice before the team's official morning workout at the Cartman Arena, Home of the Nanooks, a crowded indoor rink.

William Cartman, the coach who recruited me and the rink's namesake for his contributions as UAF's best player in history, is my coach and mentor. He is the youngest retired NHL player with the most goals and–currently–an unbeatable coaching record. Of course, I admire him. He achieved everything I dream of becoming—being recruited by the NHL, dominating the hockey world, and, most of all, being famous.

Coach Cartman called, and I didn't hesitate to move from Canada to Alaska. I had to look up where Fairbanks was—it's inland, hidden between mountains—and the mascot, a Nanook, which is the fancy Alaska name for a polar bear. A fitting team mascot, as the eight-foot-high, 800 kilogram, or 1700 pounds as Americans say, polar bear is ruthless. They are the largest land predator, using stealth to sneak up and savagely attack their prey.

I look at Chloe, and right now, this hottie is my prey, and I don't even need to sneak up. I pull my sweaty, blonde ponytail tight and lean back on my hips to flex my substantial arms and show off my curves, pulling out all the stops to impress her.

I don't just have hockey skills. I'm a spicy, well-formed athlete with the curves and charm to date anyone I'd like, male or female. Licking my salty lips, I'm sure I'm especially tasty looking after working out.

She reaches up to me. "You planning on watching me freeze to death? Or are you going to help me get out of this hole, Player?"

I laugh and shake my head. "Sorry. I wanted to ask how you managed to get stuck, but let's leave some mystery for you to tell me over breakfast," I say, flirting with a grin.

Her mouth opens and closes like a guppy, and I fill in the dead air, saying. "Hold on a sec."

I clap my hands to warm them and pivot around her, then get on my knees to get a good grip.

She stuffs most of the scattered trinkets into her pocket and nods at me.

Squatting behind her, I gently place my arms under her armpits, avoiding being too forward with an accidental touch, which I am dying to do.

"Thanks," she breathes and holds my shoulders with an unusually strong grip for a girl. Her fingers press into my solid muscles.

I guess I'll give her the freebie, but the next time her hands touch me, I'm going to devour her.

"No prob," I reply.

"Should I countdown?"

"Nah, just enjoy the ride," I say, giving her a wink.

She's cute and sweet—just my type.

With a swift movement, I use my strength and leverage, hoisting her into a better position to lift her straight out of the ice. Her dry boot slides on the slick ground, unable to get a grip on the icy lake with the baby duckies underfoot.

I hold her tighter against me. Our bodies press together to help her catch her balance, and I enjoy the soft curve of her butt before I squeeze her against myself and away from the ice. Giving a quick, healthy yank, I dislodge her.

She squeals, and I can't help but chuckle.

We're dancing on the ice for a moment, and I'm struck by how light she is in my arms. The contrast of her dainty softness against my solid weight sends a shiver down my spine.

Her leg comes free, straight off, with a wet, squelching sound. And her boot disappears into the abyss, leaving a colorful wool sock. I keep her safe in my arms and skate, carrying her to the bench by the parking lot.

"Gimme a sec, princess," I say, kicking off my skates and putting on my boots.

I easily pick her up again, with her sock dripping, and she directs me to her car.

The morning sun plays hide-and-seek behind the snowy peaks, casting a golden glow on the frozen landscape. It's a picturesque scene, and I steal a glance at Chloe, who's looking at her little red Subaru.

Reaching her car, I open the door. Her keys are left in the ignition, and her phone is plugged in.

"Wait, open the back. I have a pair of shoes."

I carry her over the snow to let her rummage through her very messy trunk, producing a pair of rainbow Crocs that have witnessed better days. I transfer her to the driver's seat, setting her down gently. She tugs off her sock to check her toes—all there and wiggling—then pulls on her crocs.

The radio blares static, and she shrugs. "You know Alaska beaters, as long as the heater works, it's a good car." A mischievous twinkle sparkled in her eyes.

How have I never met Chloe before? She's completely unlike the average, dramatic university girl I date. Last night, a sorority girl playing beer pong with me broke a nail and freaked out crying, reacting worse than Chloe, who was stuck and could've died in the frozen lake.

"Thanks!" Chloe says casually. "So, Sterling, what's your deal? Do you usually go around saving women in distress? Or perhaps you planned this whole accident?" she quips, flashing me a playful smile.

"You caught me! I like to play the hero when I'm really a scumbag," I reply, playing along. "But I only target women who carry salmon-flavored granola bars and sing disco."

She giggles and pushes the bar into my jeans pocket. "Your payment then!"

Her hot hand spreads its heat from my pocket, zinging through me. Damn!

Her laugh resonates in the arctic crisp air, like the soft jingle of wind chimes.

I can't help but laugh along and enjoy the easy flow of our vibe. There's an unexpected comfort in talking to Chloe as if we're already friends or more-than-friends.

With her shoes on and the heater on high, Chloe smiles at me, and the air crackles with our strange energy and a mix of lingering heat from our unspoken connection.

I clear my throat, breaking the brief but potent silence. "Alright, Chloe, consider yourself saved. Let's get breakfast before I have to save my next damsel." I wink. "Are you good to drive, eh?"

She nods. "Follow me to my friend's cafe, Player. I'll buy."

Chapter 3: Chloe

The cafe door swings open with a jingle as Sterling holds it for me. I step inside, escaping the biting cold of the Alaskan morning. My leg is wet but warm and wet from the car ride. The aroma of freshly ground coffee beans shrouds us with caffeinated love, a comforting, familiar smell to forget the neverending winter cold outside.

"Hey, Chloe!" My best friend waves from behind the counter and then gives me the up and down. Her eyes stopped at my croc and wet pant leg. She raises an eyebrow.

I shrug and smile in response. Kate's used to seeing me covered in dust and paint from my hours at the pottery studio.

Her attention moves to Sterling, and she opens her mouth, taken aback. Then, she shuts it and gives me a ridiculous salute and a little wave to her as I lead her to my cozy corner table.

Pulling off my hat and shaking my head to set my curls free, I toss my jacket behind my chair. Usually, I work here with Kate during the morning rush and then head to my university classes.

I look around and only a handful of people are here. She doesn't need my help right now.

This is the coziest cafe in town. And better yet, all my drinks and treats are free—a perk of being Kate's friend and helping out at the

FrostyBean. Honestly, I'd never see her if I didn't help. Between her busy cafe schedule and my pottery studio sessions, we need the caffeine and friendly gabbing, or we'd have no social life.

Sterling slides into the other chair, and despite her bold exterior, she ducks her chin and gives me a nervous smile. She takes in the quiet cafe and burrows her head a little further in her oversized faux-fur denim jacket. Her demeanor is no longer the cocky, flirty hockey player. She's smaller and more hesitant than the girl I met on the ice.

I break the silence. "Thanks for rescuing my leg, Sterling. I would have missed lefty, it came as a matching set, you know."

She grins and cracks a smile, her eyes lighting up. "Well, finding a match is hard when you break up a stunning set. It's the least I can do as an everyday, regular hero, eh."

"A real Disco Hero!" I say enthusiastically, pulling out the mini disco ball to shake it, the reflective dots peppering us.

"Is this a party?" Kate asks with a twinkle in her eyes, delivering vanilla lattes in heavy clay mugs that I made and frosted donuts.

"Apple cinnamon donuts with salted caramel sauce and vanilla lattes," she says, setting the tray down.

"Thanks. Sounds delish," Sterling says.

Kate nods at her, and when Sterling looks down to palm the mug in her big mitt, Kate sneaks a wink and a sly smile at me as she drifts away back to the counter.

"Kate bakes all the sweets. She made the salmon bar, too. I'll have to break it to her that it's not her best recipe."

Sterling responds with a mouth full of donut, "These donuts are the best. Soooo good!"

I giggle and have a bite. She's right. They're divine, soft, and sweet, topped with a hardened caramel sprinkled with salted crunchiness.

"Ummmm." I close my eyes and savor the donut melting on my tongue and the sugar rush sweeping through me, giving me happy sugar shivers.

Sterling laughs at my tiny shimmy, the tension in the air replaced with a playful spark. "I'm glad I could be your hero. And thanks for showing me this cafe. I haven't been out much, and I think I've found my new studying spot."

"We're open until ten, so it's a great place to load up on caffeine, and study," I agree.

"Sorry, think you can steal me another donut?" She looks at me with wide, unblinking, sky-blue eyes, biting her bottom lip.

I laugh at the cute Canadian-way she begins her sentences with sorry. Also, I'm falling for her coy, innocent look. I sneak behind the counter to get her another donut. I'm too old to fall for a sexy, wild university student. But, at the same time, it's only a coffee, and she did save my life.

Just as I'm handing her the gooey donut, her phone buzzes. She juggles the donut and settles on stuffing the entire thing in her mouth and answering the phone with a weird grunt.

Her expression changes from joy to a stern frown and then a scowl. The playful glint in her eyes dissipates.

"Sorry. Yes, Coach," she mutters and swallows.

I can only catch snippets of the conversation, but it's clear that Coach Cartman is telling Sterling to skip practice because her grades are less-than-stellar. He sternly orders her to hit the books, or she won't be playing.

Orders and ultimatums from William Cartman are things Sterling and I have in common. I was married to him for five years before realizing that, even after he left the NHL and returned home to coach, I would never be his priority. Like in high school, when he missed our prom, it was always about winning, scoring, and being the best. His priorities were the team, the boosters, the fans, the media, and—if there wasn't anything else hockey-related left to choose from—me.

I should have known the relationship was doomed when we start-ed couple's counseling six months into the marriage, and I was going alone because of his hockey travel schedule. Then there's his win-at-all-costs attitude, forcing me to end our marriage since he wouldn't admit defeat in our relationship. He certainly couldn't fathom that I'd want to leave him—the local hero, the famous William Cartman.

After Sterling hangs up, a palpable tension lingers, fueled by the Coach's loudly shouted directives resonating through the phone like a chilly wind in the cafe. The weight of his words hangs in the air, casting a shadow over the playful atmosphere.

Adding to this tense mix is my dark mood from the complicated history with her coach, a past filled with unresolved emotions and tensions. The mood is downright dreary. The low hum of conversation in the cafe quiets more with the unspoken thoughts. Sterling wears her frustration and inner conflict with a furrowed brow and downcast eyes.

Feeling the heaviness, I opt to retreat to the counter, allowing space for her swirling emotions to settle.

I hate hockey and anything related to it, after being married to William Cartman. And when he retired, instead of spending time with me, he moved his focus to coaching the NCAA Nanooks division team, and winning the NCAA Tournament title every year.

It's just my luck that I befriended a hockey player, the very thing I'm trying to avoid!

Sterling cradles the mug, savoring the sweet latte, her eyes narrowing in delight. A grin plays on her lips as she calls across the cafe, "You picked a damn good cafe, Chloe."

I blush, basking in the warmth of her compliment. "The next coffee I'll make you is my specialty, a Cinnabon latte. I've work with Kate for years and perfected the art of lattes." I raise my brow and cock my hip.

Kate slides in next to me, her eyebrow raised as she remarks, "I'm guessing Sterling doesn't know who you are?"

"I met Sterling five minutes ago. She doesn't need to hear my sob story. She's a helpful stranger," I retort.

Wait—she said Sterling's name. Before I can ask, we're interrupted.

A blonde sorority girl struts into the cafe, wearing a pink hat with a hole for her messy ponytail and a ski jacket adorned with an impractical number of buckles and zippers. Her eyes light up at the sight of Sterling, and after a giggle, wave, and a fish-face pout directed at Sterling, she turns to saunter to the counter.

Posing like she's on a runway, she flips her ponytail and places her order without sparing me a glance. "Medium, sugar-free hazelnut skim cappuccino." She then leans seductively on the counter, waiting for her fussy drink and pretending not to stare at Sterling.

Uck! Of course, it's my luck that April, who's as fussy as her drink order, appears when I am behind the counter. Fussy drink orders are not the only thing she's known for–her university major is in dating, and it's obvious that she's familiar with Sterling. She applies cherry lip gloss with exaggerated slowness in Sterling's direction.

"Hey, Sterling!" she chirps, flipping her hair. "I saw on socials you're skipping practice this week. You're not injured, are you? I could take care of you to help you recover quicker?" April pouts her shiny lips and bats her eyelashes.

Sterling forces a tight smile at April. "When did you read that?"

"Twenty minutes ago, on the hockey page."

Sterling looks like she could murder someone with the coffee spoon in her fist. Obviously, the team and followers knew about Sterling's situation before the coach called her.

"Sorry, yeah. I get more time for studying, apparently," Sterling replies with a forced casualness.

April pouts. "I'll miss seeing you practicing. Do you want a study buddy?"

I hand her the coffee in a to-go cup and bring a donut and latte for Sterling, taking the opportunity to sit between Sterling and April.

ALASKA HEARTS BOOKS COMPLETE COLLECTION

I glare at April, who looks doe-eyed and confused.

"Who's this?"

"Oh, sorry. This is Chloe. Chloe, meet April," Sterling introduces, and I offer a polite smile.

April should know my name, as I serve her coffee a few times a week. She's always on her phone and with a group of tittering sorority sisters.

Sterling's phone interrupts, buzzing again, and she looks down to text whoever it is back.

April leans in, speaking in a not-so-hushed whisper. "Sterling doesn't usually do non-hockey girls or older women. Just so you know, you know."

Before I reply, Kate calls out, "April, I have a gluten-free protein bar for you to try."

April gives me a cold stare and flips her hair. "Fat-free, right?" she asks Kate as she takes the offered snack.

Sorority girls are the worst!

Kate nods, walking April to the door and shoving her out with a smile.

As I observe Sterling, her mood darkens even further while she reads the text. When she looks up and catches me studying her, she explains, "Sorry, I have to get a tutor, like yesterday, for my Art Influencers 201 class, or I'm screwed. My easy elective requires an essay on the relevance of Romeo and Juliet. Sadly, that's not one of my talents."

Kate interjects, "Chloe will tutor you. Art is her passion. She's an expert." She smiles wide, her eyes seemingly innocent, but I can sense the matchmaking scheme behind them.

She cocks her head at me. "Coach says it has to be a certified tutor, not a distracting puck bunny, or someone writing it for me."

"Chloe's certified to tutor and she isn't fazed by hockey players," Kate chimes in before I can say anything.

"That's perfect! Besides, you owe me for this morning, anyway." Sterling beams at me and sips the latte.

I laugh, scrunching my nose. "That's what this coffee is—your thank you!"

"Okay. I'll see you at ..." Sterling pauses.

Knowing my schedule, Kate calls out, "Tomorrow at two." Her eyes shine, and a grin splits her face at playing cupid.

"Great. I'll see you here, then, eh?"

"I'm not—" I start, but Sterling is already up and halfway out the door.

Kate walks over to watch me watch Sterling get into her truck and race out of the snowy parking lot, going faster than necessary.

"You know who Sterling is, right?"

I turn to my friend. "A failing student?"

"No, dummy. Sterling is the Canadian hotshot right-wing that your ex recruited to take the team to the championships this year. Do you never open up social media or read the paper?"

Why would I when Coach Cartman and his team are always in the headlines?

I whine, "Then why did you volunteer me to tutor her? It's bound to piss William off, and I don't date hockey players anymore."

"You don't date narcissistic hockey players. Didn't Sterling save your life?"

I shrug with frustration, but a flicker of something—I can't quite put my finger on—makes me grin.

Continue reading Sterling & Chloe's heartwarming story in
Wilderness Rescue: Scoring Love.
CHECK IT OUT HERE.

Join us to discover your next favorite story at <u>HarmonyNoble.</u>
<u>com</u> & sign up to receive the e-newsletter for exclusive news and

giveaways.
CHECK IT OUT HERE.

Coming Next

Wilderness Rescue: Scoring Love

Hockey was her game plan until love changed the rules.

In the heart of Fairbanks, where temperatures drop to -66°F, a hockey star's perfectly planned life is about to get checked by love. When hockey hotshot Sterling saves local artist Chloe from falling through the ice into the freezing waters of Chena Lake, neither expects the heat that ignites between them.

Sterling's a star on the ice, but her life outside the rink is crashing. With her hockey scholarship hanging by a thread due to plummeting grades and a "player" reputation that's become infamous in this small Alaskan town, she's running out of chances to turn her game around.

Chloe isn't interested in becoming another score on someone's board or dating. But as the Northern Lights dance in the night skies of this small college town, these opposites find themselves drawn together in an unexpected second chance at love.

When hidden truths threaten to shatter their growing connection, Sterling must prove she is ready to trade her player status for something real, while Chloe must reveal her age and that the hockey coach is her ex-husband.

Can Sterling trade in her player status to win Chloe's heart?

Can Chloe open up to love and reveal her hidden truths?

Ready to score more wilderness romance? Explore each stand-alone story in the series and witness how fiercely independent Alaskan women ignite passion in the untamed beauty of Alaska.

Author's Note: Explore these thrilling LGBTQ+ adventures intertwined with sweet sapphic romances in the <u>Wilderness Rescue Series</u>.

Experience a Hockey romance filled with angst and witty banter as Player Sterling and Chloe find love in the second chance romance in <u>*Wilderness Rescue: Scoring Love.*</u>

<u>CHECK IT OUT HERE.</u>

Discover your next favorite story at <u>HarmonyNoble.com.</u>

Coffeehouse Romance Short Stories:

Joy's 4th of July Holidate
Tara's Valentine Holidate
Crystal's Easter Holidate
Meaghan's New Year Holidate
Monica's Halloween Holidate
My Accidental Christmas Fiancé
Joy's Coffeehouse Romance

UNLOCK YOUR GIFT

Happy Reading & EMBRACE TRUE LOVE!

Snag the latest swoon-worthy reads and stay tuned for upcoming stories at www.HarmonyNoble.com.

About Author – Harmony Noble

Meet the unstoppable twins from the rugged wilds of Alaska—Harmony & Melody, the duo of "Author Harmony Noble." Fueled by endless lattes, their character-driven stories brim with authenticity, humor, and heart—featuring Alaskan grit, journeys of self-discovery, and swoon-worthy happily-ever-afters.

When they're not crafting adventure romances, the twins can be found hiking trails with breathtaking views, enjoying charming coffee shops, or exploring new cultures and destinations worldwide.

Join the e-newsletter for exclusive content and giveaways at website: https://harmonynoble.com

Email: TrueLoveWriters@gmail.com

Instagram/Facebook/TikTok: @truelovewriters

www.ingramcontent.com/pod-product-compliance
Lightning Source LLC
Chambersburg PA
CBHW072008020726
47501CB00006B/1728